The Ghost at His Back

Cameron Lowe

For Ryan, Mom, and Dad,
Please skip past the dirty parts. And the violent stuff. And the scary bits. In fact,
after you've finished with this page, just pretend you've read it. Cool? Cool.

Table of Contents

Chapter 1

"Ghosts are assholes."

The bartender stopped running a greasy rag through an equally greasy glass and gawked at the shabbily dressed man sitting on one of his well-worn stools. The guy was the only one in the bar. The cold was hellish outside, and he really should have closed up early. But the thought of going out into that mess was as equally unappealing as staying inside and watching shitty movies on the television, so he opted for warmth and liquor. "What?"

"Ghosts." The man tipped the neck of his mostly unfinished beer towards the crummy made-for-TV movie blaring on the screen. "That guy right there? Someone that decent, they'd never stick around in the afterlife. Not if they had to."

"Look, mister—" the bartender started to say.

"Nope. Guys like that, they'd be up there, doing shots off an angel's boobs." He considered that for a minute. "If angels have boobs. Wonder if they have Pyramid beer in heaven? I mean, they gotta, right?"

"I think I'm gonna have to—"

The customer held up a calloused hand as if to shush the bartender. He glared at the rack of booze under a stuffed mountain lion carcass, its skin ratty and threadbare from age. The bartender couldn't figure out what had drawn his gaze. "We good to go?" the stranger asked. His eyes tracked upwards, as though he were staring at something on the bar. Within a few moments, his glare broke into a laugh he tried to cover up with a cough.

Wondering what the heck the guy was looking at, the bartender said, "As soon as you pay, yeah, we're good."

The nutjob glanced over at the bartender. "Wasn't talking to you." He dug in his wallet and tossed a bill on the bar. As he threw on his coat, he said, "Word of advice, guy? Clean your dishrags. Your glasses are filthy. And get a safe. If not for the cash box you've got under the counter, then maybe for the weed you've got baggied up and ready to sell in the back office." His face lost any good humor and he pointed at the bartender, his eyes cold. "And keep it to weed. Anything stronger than that, and I come back here. You won't like what happens then."

The bartender's mouth dropped. He fought to say something, anything, but before he could fight through the shock, the stranger was out the door, a blast of frigid February air and a swirl of snow the only reminder he was there. That, and the twenty he'd left on the bar. All for one solitary beer he'd hardly touched in three hours.

* * *

"Murphy, you dick." If Garrett could have punched the intangible man, he would have. Not hard. He was laughing too much.

"You didn't like my dance?" The squat man jumped on the trunk of a long-rotting Cutlass, missing all its tires and almost buried in drifts of snow. He kicked a leg out, his hands on his hips, and did a forty-five degree turn and clapped, a gross pirouette of a square dance. Phantasmal streamers of pale gray and a bright sky blue drifted behind him in excited spirals, mimicking his movements. He hopped off and grinned. "Western bars. Ugh. That place looked like it had seen a hootenanny or two."

"Who the hell says hootenanny?"

"Shindig?" Murphy asked, running a hand very literally through his short curly black hair. His clothes shifted unconsciously to a red and blue checkered shirt, jeans, and long black cowboy boots. Before Garrett could point out the humongous belt buckle on Murphy's waist, his clothes had already changed back to his usual stylish sport coat, white shirt, and black slacks.

"Shindig's a little better."

"Good old incestuous ass play going on there, at the very least."

Garrett laughed, and started coughing almost immediately from the icy stabs at his throat and lungs. "Too damn cold." A half minute later, they stopped at the Santa Fe and he opened up the trunk. Garrett unzipped a hefty gym bag, full of shorts and sweats, ostensibly for working out. He rooted around underneath them and dug out a slim leather tool belt, most decidedly not full of the usual sorts of things one would expect. After slipping that around his waist, he pulled on a ski mask, leaving it rolled up and his face exposed. This late at night, people would probably shoot him on sight for wearing a ski mask on the street thinking he was a burglar, but rolling it up made it look like a thick wool cap, which suited the weather just perfect. He slung a nearly empty cheap backpack across his shoulders. Last was a baggie of rubber gloves. These too would have looked suspicious on him that late at night, so those stayed in the pockets of his hoodie.

"You're forgetting your wand, Harry Potter."

"Harry Potter? Really?" The "wand" was actually a telescoping baton, meant for self-defense. Garrett dug it and its holster out, and clipped it to the tool belt.

"What', you'd rather I have said Gandalf?"

Garrett shut the trunk and shoved his hands into his pockets, the cold stinging them already in the brief minutes they'd been exposed. Februaries in Montana could be venomous, and that night was proof. "Who the hell is Gandalf?"

"What? Gimli? Legolas? Big ass eagles? None of this rings a bell?

Overhead, a streetlamp fizzled and burned out. Both men ignored it as they walked. They were used to this oddity. "No. Should it?"

"Man, Garrett, you need to read a damn book."

* * *

The barbershop wasn't exactly in the kindest, gentlest part of Rankin Flats, but at least most of the surrounding buildings were empty or closed, leaving the street lifeless. The front door was barricaded behind a security gate, impossible to open this late at night without waking up the owner in his apartment above the shop. Instead, they walked down the alley beside the building, heading for the side door. Garrett pulled down the ski mask and dug out the gloves. He would be silent from that moment forward, something Murphy cared little about since no one in the world could possibly hear him. From a pouch on his tool belt, Garrett produced a tension wrench and a pick. At the door, he knelt down and winced as his knee sank into crystalline snow. Mentally, he reminded himself to buy a pair of long underwear for the next job. Murphy walked through the wall next to the door. He would keep an eye on things inside and upstairs, just in case the proprietor woke at just the wrong moment and decided to investigate.

He felt out each pin's position with grace and speed born of practice until the plug finally rotated and the door was unlocked. The first steps inside were always the tensest for him—Murphy could spy out a place, but it just wasn't possible for them to figure out all the old bones of a building. A creaky floor could mean the end of a good plan as fast as anything. He slipped inside, his breath baited, but there wasn't so much as a squeak from the black and white tiles. The keypad for the alarm blinked but did not beep until he punched in the six-digit code. He winced at every chirpy button press, ready to run if there was any hint of footsteps upstairs. The light on the alarm flashed at him twice and turned green. He let out a pensive whoosh of air and put his tools away. He swept a pencil thin beam from a flashlight across the hallway, charting it mentally. Murphy's verbal pictures were always accurate, but it was smart to get an idea for himself before moving forward. A row of lockers, a trashcan, and a rug were all the ornamentation in the hallway, just as Murph had described. The door on his left led to the barbershop, the door on the right an office, and a turn at the end of the hallway led up to the apartment.

Murphy poked his head through the floor. "You're good up here. Richter's still sound asleep. And mostly naked, by the way. You should see the size of these tighty whiteys. Well, at some point I think they used to be white."

Garrett gave him a thumbs-up. The office was locked, but he didn't need his picks. Every night, Richter locked up the office with a key he kept atop the row of employee lockers. While it should have saved him time, Garrett lost almost a minute searching for the key with the tips of his fingers.

"Damn, man, I told you, first one," Murphy said cheerfully as he watched Garrett almost fumble the key off the edge. "Guess I should have clarified. First locker... on the left. My bad." He snickered at Garrett's annoyed glare.

Inside, the office door was flanked by a row of short, dusty filing cabinets and a sagging leather love seat. Two mismatched chairs faced a surprisingly beautiful wood desk. Etched into the legs were figures with the bodies of men and the heads of lions. They seemed to keep watch over the room and were quite striking. Garrett regretted that he couldn't take the desk with him. Atop it was an ancient computer complete with a CRT monitor the likes of which Garrett hadn't seen in over three or four years, as well as a hodgepodge of office detritus.

Overlooking the room was an enormous painting of a stern old woman. Her face was puggish, both round and severely wrinkled. Garrett gave the woman a mocking half salute. It was her he was after— or rather, the treasure she held behind her thickset midriff. He ran his finger around the edge of her frame, seeking out the catch with his penlight in his mouth. Once he found her secret button (and fought down the urge to snicker at all the nasty jokes his mind made about it), the painting swung away from the wall. The size and modern touches of the wall safe might have surprised anyone who thought Richter was just a barber.

"You won't remember the combination," Murphy crowed. It was probably true. Shorter key combinations weren't a problem for Garrett, but he sometimes—often—had trouble remembering longer ones without writing them down or getting Murphy's help. It became a running bet with them on jobs like this—if Garrett remembered the code, the split went fifty-five-forty-five in his favor, and if not, it went to Murphy.

Garrett punched in the nine-digit security code very carefully, the cadence of the numbers passing his lips inaudibly as he pressed the buttons. The safe popped open without a hitch, nearly sending him into an impromptu jig. He grinned up at Murphy and pantomimed shoving a head towards his dick.

"Yeah, yeah, asshole," Murphy grumbled. His head disappeared back upstairs.

First to come out of the safe were stacks of bills, held together with rubber bands. Garrett unzipped the backpack and dropped them in unceremoniously. There would be time to count the cash later, but that was only half of why they were there. He flipped through a pair of ledgers. One was full of legitimate business figures for the barbershop and of absolutely no consequence, so he put it back inside. The other was full of coded names and figures. That was definitely Richter's bookie business. There was no cipher he could see, but he shoved the book into the backpack anyways. It might have some information he or the Ball Chomper could use.

Last to come out was a cigar box full of bits of Richter's life. A pair of rings from the local Polecats baseball team. Some stubby joints wrapped in a baggie (those went into the backpack too). A thick stack of photographs. He flipped through those slowly, running the penlight across them. One was a picture of Richter in his younger years, standing next to the same woman in the painting, her face less severe. Another was of a man sitting on the hood of a car, a cigar hanging out of the corner of his mouth. The next picture seemed innocent enough. A pretty young woman, her eyes unfocused and a dopey smile on her face, sat beside one of Richter's two employees at a bar or a club somewhere. With a sinking feeling, Garrett realized he knew what the rest of the pictures held.

The next one was of the same young woman, laying nude on her stomach on an unmade bed. She looked back at the camera, but there was no recognition there. She was doped to the gills. Someone off-camera had a hand on her ass. The third in the series was focused more on her lower back and what had been done while she'd—hopefully—been too out of it to know what was going on. Someone had branded her with the Legion's signature, the backwards-and-forwards pair of L's. Not with ink, but with hot metal, the skin cooked to a blistering pink and black. The rest of the pictures showed other women with Richter and his two companions in the same predicaments. Garrett wanted to look away and couldn't. Richter wasn't just a bookie—he was a Legion recruiter, and this was one of their initiation rites. When new members joined, they branded an innocent person's flesh.

"Murphy," he said, not caring anymore if Richter heard him.

"Keep it down, man, he's—"

"Look."

He spread three of the photos on the desk and flashed his penlight across each of them slowly. Murphy shook his head. "Motherfucker. Plan Z?"

"Yeah. Plan Z."

"Right." Murphy lost all his joviality and became strictly professional. "Three guns that I know about here. Pump action shotgun and a rifle upstairs. Probably nothing you can do about those. Pistol in the desk. Top left drawer."

Garrett pulled the 9mm out of the drawer, checked the safety, and slipped it gently into the backpack along with most of the pictures of the women. He left two of them with Richter in the shot on the desk.

"Be careful, Garrett," Murphy warned.

"Mmm," Garrett murmured noncommittally. He set his backpack by the lockers near the back door, concealed but ready for him when he needed it. He re-entered the office, leaving the door cracked just wide enough that Richter would know someone was in there, and unsheathed his baton. With a flick of his wrist, it was fully extended. He yanked out the cord of a small ceramic desk lamp, hefted it with one hand, and pitched it hard at the wall. The smash wasn't terribly loud, but in the silence of the office, it might as well have been a gunshot.

From upstairs, bed springs creaked and a pair of feet thumped against the floor. Richter's footfalls were unsteady but swift Murphy leaned down through the floor. "Shotgun, he's got the shotgun, got maybe fifteen seconds…"

Garrett situated himself as tightly against the loveseat as he could get. The door would give him enough cover to gain the advantage, and that was all he needed. The feet hit the stairwell and plodded down quickly.

"Five. Four. Three." Murphy dropped from the ceiling and leaned casually against the desk.

"Whoever you are, you fucked with—"

The door swung wide and Garrett charged right back into it. The shotgun roared in the darkness, deafening Garrett and Richter both. The fat man slammed into the short cabinets, careening off them badly and aiming the gun at the ground. Garrett smashed the baton across the back of his skull, dropping Richter to his knees, the gun clattering as it fell away from him. Richter fell towards it, his hands scrabbling across the tiles for the butt of the shotgun until Garrett drove the heel of his sneaker down onto the man's hand. Bones snapped as he ground his foot. Richter screeched, but had the presence of mind to try to grab Garrett's leg with his other hand. Surprised at the barber's quick reflexes, Garrett almost went down, but a decade and change of hard training and fights hadn't left him without reflexes of his own. He caught his balance and drove the baton down across the arm. It wasn't much of a blow, but it caused Richter to involuntarily release him.

Richter pushed himself shakily up on his knees. Without missing a beat, Garrett snapped the baton down again and again, a cavalcade of blows against Richter's soft, doughy flesh. The barber made the mistake of trying to anticipate the blows and reach for the baton, leaving his side exposed. With a grunt, Garrett hammered the baton into Richter's kidney. Richter's eyes bulged and he fell back onto his ass, scooting away from Garrett back towards the cabinets. He held up his hands, his fingers bent awkwardly. "Whoever you are—ah shit, that hurts—you're one dead motherfucker."

There was still fight in the man. Good. Garrett grinned and said nothing as he came at the recruiter a second time. He had to be fast in the fight. Cops might take a while to respond to reports of a gunshot in this shithole part of town, but they'd come eventually.

Richter reached behind him for the cabinets and rose shakily to his feet. He raised his hands up, trying to make fists. Murphy snorted. "He looks ridiculous. Take this son of a bitch out and let's get out of here."

Garrett launched forward. Richter's eyes followed the baton, not realizing the real threat of his wide open stance. Garrett feinted another strike, and Richter went for it, his arms coming up in a defensive maneuver that was meant to catch the swing of the baton. At the last minute, Garrett turned the feint into a football punt, right into the bookie's exposed crotch.

Richter screamed.

As he pitched forward, Garrett grabbed the back of Richter's head and smashed it into the ground. Again. He felt the snap of cartilage in Richter's nose. He thought about those women—not much more than girls, really. About what they'd woken to after Richter, his men, and his recruits had done. What they'd be called, what they'd be subjected to. His baton came down, finding all the weak points, all the pain centers he knew about—and Garrett knew many of them. He was beyond rage, in that calm, cool point of no return, when he stepped beyond emotion and thought only about causing as much destruction as efficiently as he could. As the barber tried to weakly ward him away, he took the man's good hand and broke every finger, yanking them until they cracked in all the wrong ways. The baton found its mark across his belly and back, and finally his head. Up and down, up and down. It was like chopping firewood one handed.

"-stop, man, stop, the guy is done, fuck, Gar, you gotta go—"

Murphy's voice might not have brought him out of it, but the ghost fell over Richter, trying to come between Garrett and the mark as ineffectually as fog. He looked up at Garrett, his eyes pleading. Garrett stopped his arm in mid-swing.

Murphy pleaded with him one last time. "It's over, man. Over."

The wet wheeze of Richter's fight for air. The hand spasmed against the ground, trying to form itself into newly impossible shapes. The stench of urine and the puddle under the man. The fight was done.

Garrett sheathed the baton. "Watch him for me. And the cops. Sixty forty, your way, no argument."

"I'll keep an eye out. But those pictures, man, I ain't even worried about the money."

"Thanks. I…" Garrett watched Richter fight for air for a minute and shook his head. "Just… thanks."

* * *

Blocks away, he stripped out of the hoodie and the gloves. They went into a dumpster. His jeans had flecks of blood on them. He pushed back the driver's seat as far as it would go and stripped out of those too, changing into a pair of sweats. As he tossed the jeans into the dumpster, sirens in the distance wailed. He sat in the Santa Fe for a long minute, his hands shaking as he tried pointedly not to look at the scarred, burning thing watching him in the rear view mirror.

When his hands were steady enough, he punched in a number on his cell phone. Groggily, the Ball Chomper snapped, "Garrett, it's late, what the hell—"

"Your tip. It panned out. I'm coming by."

Silence for a minute, then a sigh. "I'll get the Keurig ready."

* * *

Garrett had a sneaking suspicion that if Monica knew his and Murphy's nickname for her, she'd be amused rather than pissed. Ball Chomper wasn't metaphorical. Shortly after they'd first come to their uneasy agreement to work together, they met up at a restaurant in town that served up Rocky Mountain oysters. He ran late due to traffic, and when he got there, Monica was sitting at a booth, fork in hand, working her way through a trio of bull testicles as though they were the most delicious thing she'd ever eaten. Horrified and wildly amused, Murphy had taken to calling her the Ball Chomper and the name stuck between them.

She lived in a duplex on the southwestern side of the city. At one point, her neck of the woods had been called Ryegate until it had been absorbed by the all-consuming mass that was Rankin Flats. It was popular Hollywood bullshit that all single cops were destined to live in shitty studio apartments, but Rankin Flats cops were in high demand and paid well above the piss-poor city median. The Ball Chomper was careful with her money, too, and she'd jumped at an opportunity to buy up a place up for auction after a murder. If Garrett hadn't known her better, he might have assumed from her nature that she might have committed it just to drop the selling price. He still wasn't entirely sure that wasn't what happened.

He pulled up to her place and regretfully killed the engine. The blast of hot air in the Hyundai had just started to cut away at the chill in his bones. The temperatures outside had continued to drop to the point where it was flat-out painful to be outside, and the wind was getting even angrier. He jumped out of the SUV, backpack in hand, and made for the door as fast as he could. Somewhere back out on the street, a streetlight fizzled out. He didn't notice.

As he stomped through the fresh drifts of snow, the outdoor light popped on and the Ball Chomper opened her door, her bathrobe done up tightly. Her hair was a mess of tangles and she had on no makeup, but neither of those was out of the ordinary for her even during the middle of the day. "You own a coat?" she asked.

"Thought I had a spare in the car," he said through gritted teeth as he pushed past her through the door, stomping his feet on her welcome mat. "Got coffee?"

"Mm. K-cups are sitting out." She followed him into the kitchen and didn't speak as he fixed himself a mug and warmed his hands around it. "Dry creamer's up above there, or…"

"Black's fine," he grunted.

"Suit yourself." She poured herself a cup. "I'll get a fire going while you talk."

In front of the fireplace, he sat on the edge of her couch, still keyed up from the fight. He sipped coffee and cleared his throat. "So the barber was Legion. You were right about that."

"Yeah? What'd you find?"

"Pictures. The branding rite. And not just him. His men, a few others. He was a recruiter."

She dropped a piece of kindling in the fireplace and looked back at him. "Fuck."

"Yeah." He set the coffee down and unzipped the backpack. Her eyes widened as one of the bundles of cash fell out. He ignored it. Monica knew what he did, if not necessarily what he saw. Not entirely, anyways. He tossed the pictures on the coffee table. She finished arranging the kindling in a loose tepee, lit some crumpled newspaper under it, and watched the fire take off. She plodded over to the table on her knees and flipped through the pictures. "Monsters."

"Mm hm."

"Did you do what you do?" Monica was not a weak person—far from it. Her hesitancy to ask about his methodology wasn't about any sort of squeamishness, but out of a need to protect herself at work.

"Mm hm. The paramedics and cops will find him with two more of these stapled on his back."

She thumbed through the photos again. "Good." She threw them into the fire. As evidence, they were useless, and if they were found in her place or Garrett's, there would be a world of hurt for them both. She glanced at him, calculating something internally. "You want to fuck?"

He looked her over, at her bulbous nose, the squat thick frame, the pillowy, slightly sagging breasts. He thought about her spearing the bull testicles with her fork and nearly gagged. But she was a warm body on a grim night and he didn't have anywhere else to be. His cock surged in approval. He sighed and swallowed the last of his coffee before he stood up. "Yeah."

Chapter 2

Hospitals drove Murphy crazy. They were stark reminders of how he and Garrett had started out, that dark period of time when Garrett thought he'd gone crazy and Murphy, out of sheer astonishment, didn't know the damage he was doing to a boy and his family. Only an unempathetic fool lived by a credo of no regrets, and Murphy was no fool.

But his history with them wasn't the only reason. For a place where people came to rest and recover, they were inexplicably, spuriously loud, even that early in the morning. Doctors and nurses whooshed by, nursing assistants chatted with the housekeepers, and everywhere, the sound of medical machinations beeped, sucked, and gurgled the life right back into people. How people were supposed to rest, he had no idea.

And the ghosts! Hospitals were lousy with them. Rankin Flats General was a sprawling complex of departments, not the least of which were a nursing home, skilled care, and a cancer ward, all of which saw bodies drop on a pretty regular basis. Not many stuck around, but a few had friends or family in the hospital and made the place their wandering grounds. Even more came through to look after sick family and friends. His conversations with them usually amounted to him trying to be friendly and them either pointedly ignoring him or telling him where he could stick a certain part of his anatomy.

Settled into a plastic chair, his legs sprawled out, Murphy tried to meditate. With focus, he could bring himself to a state of near-sleep, where his mind drifted and he could feel the edges of his ethereal existence like a membrane. Hours would slip by, feeling only like minutes, but it required a deep, uninterrupted concentration he couldn't get in that room with Richter's machinery beeping at him every few minutes. He thought about heading down to the nearest vacant ICU waiting room, but he was earning his keep watching over the Legion bastard and didn't want to get too far away in case he had visitors. But, as his focus was shattered by a series of wet coughs from Richter, he decided a walk couldn't hurt. Just a short one.

Strolling down to the end of the hallway only took a minute, especially since he could walk right through medical carts and the odd person or two. A window overlooked the parking lot and the medical complex. He stopped for a few to gaze out over the city he'd come to think of as home. The sun wasn't even at a false dawn yet, but Rankin Flats was already coming alive. The truckers would be on the highways and interstate, getting ready to head west to Great Falls or south to Billings. Some of the early risers were coming there to the hospital—the parking lot below buzzed with workers arriving or leaving. He watched them brace against the bitter winds and the subzero temperatures. He didn't envy them the walk. Although he couldn't feel cold or heat or anything else physical, he could remember the sensations as clear as a bell. Something about being dead did wonders for the memory—it wasn't picture perfect, but he could soak up and keep knowledge as easily as a child, and his memories seemed far more in focus. Sensations, tastes, and smells were all as clear as day, though he could not take in new ones. Why it was he should be allowed sight, hearing, and speech but denied his other sense, he had no idea.

As he walked back to Richter's room, two men he recognized got off the elevator. "Finally," Murphy grumbled to himself, and sprinted down the hallway to Richter's men. One, a short Mexican with bedhead and a face full of acne scars left over from his teenage years, argued with the other, his hands pointing down the hall and gesturing animatedly as he talked. The other one, a mullet-sporting bodybuilder type straight out of a Jean-Claude Van Damme movie, listened to the other man without betraying a hint of emotion. In fact, his face was the very definition of wooden. If he'd been carved out of an oak, Murphy wouldn't have been surprised.

"...hit the road right now. I've got a cousin in Arizona, he's got connections there, we could get into business for ourselves," Freckles said.

Mullet turned a slow gaze upon the smaller man. "We run, we look guilty." His voice sounded like a dump truck shifting into low gear.

"The cops won't—"

"Not the cops. Finson."

Freckles' eyes widened in fear. "Oh. Ohhh."

They stopped outside of Richter's room. A plump middle aged nurse sidled up to them, eyeballing Mullet's frame appreciatively. She informed them they couldn't go in, and they told her that was fine, that they were just checking on him. Once they introduced themselves as his employees and slipped her a couple of bills, she broke any number of HIPAA laws and told them Richter's condition and that he'd probably need to see a neurosurgeon out of Missoula after he stabilized. That could be days or even weeks. Murphy was satisfied with that, though he was still troubled by his friend's brutality. Garrett had nearly lost it. Not that he could blame him, but still, the man's temper seemed to be getting worse and worse these days.

Once the nurse left, Mullet dialed a number. Murphy stepped into him, his head tilted upwards to hear the conversation, his frame half in and out of the man.

"How is he?" The voice on the other end was old, gravelly, and not at all perturbed by the hour at which the call came in. He'd been waiting for the phone to ring, Murphy realized.

Mullet spoke slowly and carefully, making an effort to relay every bit of information as told to him by the nurse. He moved on to the cops questioning him and Freckles earlier, explaining that they'd both been at home sleeping and that they had no clue what had happened until the cops pounded on their doors. "The cops weren't our guys."

"No," old man Gravelthroat said simply. "We weren't expecting this. There was no time for control. Who did this?"

Mullet frowned. "Don't know. Mexicans, maybe. They've been around the shop lately, sniffing us out."

Gravelthroat sighed. "Maybe. This seems a bit too precise for them. You're in charge of the games now. Forget your boss's other duties."

"You sure?" Mullet asked, looking pleased with himself.

"Yes. Whoever did this was sending a message. They know who you are and what you do, presumably. We'll shut down the shop for a while and evaluate things. They remain calm, we'll keep you in the barbershop. If not, well, we cross that bridge if and when it comes to that. In the meantime, stick to Richter. See him off to Missoula. We'll make arrangements here and bring you back when it's time."

"Thanks, boss. For the Legion "

"For the Legion, soldier." Gravelthroat hung up.

As they walked to the nearest waiting room, Mullet filled Freckles in. Pleased their star was on the rise, Freckles seemed to forget all about running. Murphy listened to them for a little while, at ease now that he knew Garrett hadn't left a trace of who he was. Blaming it on the Mexicans could lead to trouble if hostilities between the two gangs erupted again, but that was tossing a match onto an already blazing dumpster fire. All that mattered to him was that his friend was free and clear.

* * *

Perched on the edge of Monica's worn couch, Garrett leaned over the ledger on the coffee table, mumbling almost silently to himself as he tried to work the code out in his head. It was utterly pointless. He'd never learned a thing about cryptography as a kid, and even if the cipher was obvious, he'd never guess it. Still, he felt compelled to try. He was still too wired up.

"Did you get any sleep last night?" she asked as she came out of the bedroom, doing up the buttons on her blouse.

"Couple of hours," Garrett grunted.

"Hm." She leaned over the couch to look at the book. "What's that?"

"Ledger from Richter's. His bookie business, I guess. Can't figure it out." He glanced over his shoulder. "You any good with codes, that sort of thing?"

She made a gimme motion and he passed her the ledger. She thumbed through it and shook her head. "It's all Greek to me."

He took the book back. "I think I got a friend who can figure it out. I'll run it by him."

"You really expect to find anything?" she asked as she slipped back into her bedroom for her holster and badge. "Seemed like he was small potatoes."

"He was. I don't know. Worth a shot."

"I guess." There was a pause and then she said cautiously, "So, uh, about last night. I'm gonna be blunt so I don't give you the wrong idea. It was fun, but…"

"…but that's all it was."

She came out of the bedroom, adjusting her holster on her belt. She patted him awkwardly on the shoulder. "Thanks. And if you need to blow off some steam again sometime, hey, stop by, but relationships and me… ugh."

He grunted his agreement and shut the ledger. "I know how hard it'll be for you to resist giving me the puppy eyes, but I'm with you."

"Good. Thanks for not making this awkward." She slipped on her shoes. "I've gotta get going to work. You want a coffee to go or something? You look worn out."

15

"No, I should get going too." He shoved the ledger back into the backpack. "You want any of this cash?" He took out a stack and rifled through the bills with his fingertip.

"Maybe a couple of twenties. Donuts and coffee for the crew." He tossed her the stack and she peeled off a couple of bills. After thinking about it some more, she took a few more. "For a steak dinner and a couple of bottles of wine." After another pause, she said, "Ah screw it, a lot of wine," and took four or five more bills, and tossed him back what was left.

Once he was ready, she walked him to the Santa Fe, clipping her badge to her belt as they walked. As he got in, he said, "If there's any blowback, lemme know."

"I'll keep you posted, but for a Legion recruiter, they'll do the bare-ass minimum to sniff you out." She paused, looking a bit pained. "Unless one of theirs lands it."

"Fingers crossed that doesn't happen."

"Yeah," she said, laughing bitterly. "Fingers crossed."

* * *

The quiet morning's drive brought him down faster and harder than his morning antics with Monica. There was something soothing about the vibration of tires on the road, even if it was dangerously icy. No music. No distractions. Just a good loose grip on the Santa Fe's wheel, the comforting soft blast of the heater, and the slow, easygoing residential traffic to focus on. It was a little piece of bliss.

With nothing rushing him and the tension of the previous night finally draining out of him, he decided to not jump on the Interstate and instead meandered towards the downtown district. His stomach grumbled unintelligible foul threats of mutiny at him if he didn't stop to get a bite soon, so he punched up his accountant and best living friend on his phone. "Ed, you at the office?" he asked without preamble.

"Hi. That's how normal people talk on phones, Garrett. We say hello first." Ed couldn't hide his good cheer behind the faked exasperation, especially with the pop beat blaring in the background.

"Hi." Garrett held the phone away from his ear for a second. "Are you... is that Britney Spears?"

"Don't judge. Hit me bay-bay one more time. C'mon, you know the words."

Garrett didn't, and was damned proud of it. "So I take it you're not there yet?"

Ed lowered the music. "Nope. Headed in that general direction though. What's up?"

"Had another win last night," Garrett said. "Another win" was code for Garrett's jobs. His paranoia about getting caught amused Ed to no end.

"No kidding? Come on by."

"Better plan. Meet me at the Jackpot Corral."

"Oh hell yes. And Garrett?"

"Yeah?"

Ed cranked back up the music. "I must confess, I still believe—still believe!" His wild laughter left Garrett shaking his head.

The snow had mercifully abated, but the wind still kicked around plumes of white crystals. There was something astounding about Rankin Flats in the midst of winter. The fat low-hanging comforter of storm clouds gave a merciful reprieve to the city's nearly corporeal smog. The creeping infection of the city's inner blight could be masked if just for a short three or four months. The sheer number of businesses with soaped windows and closed signs on the door somehow seemed lessened in the drifts. Crumbling and badly cracked pavements were hidden under all the packed snow and ice too, and for just a little while, the residents could pretend that the city council actually cared about the beautification of the inner city rather than just the big box commercial districts in the suburbs. So too could the common man pretend that the bumps they drove over in the road were caused by ice heaves and weren't the result of years and years of neglect by overpaid underworked road crews who perennially failed to give one shit about their job. It was all make-believe, of course—Rankin Flats was forever doomed to fight a losing battle for its few patches of beauty and winter could only delay the inevitable onslaught for a little while. Once the snow melted, so too did the illusion of the city's good fortune, fading back to its normal drudgery.

But every winter came the idea that this might be the spring Rankin Flats woke up, that the city's hungry and angry out-of-work lower class would finally see the return of industries and better jobs, that roses would bloom among the shit-heaped middens. Every spring was a disappointment. Even as the city grew and widened by uncomfortable leaps and bounds and the tax dollars rolled in, the lower class fought decreasing prospects of finding a well-paying job they could hold their head up about. Too few potential employers saw them as anything other than someone who could potentially serve them a coffee at a fast food place. There was no shame in serving others, Garrett thought, but everyone should have the potential to move into something they enjoyed. That eternal cycle of hope and disappointment defined the city as a whole, but its people grew tired and slowly but surely they were resorting to whatever they could do to make ends meet and live out the lives they thought they deserved. Even as he railed against their desperation and tried to bring about a little change, his own profession was being fed by destitute men doing what they could to get ahead. The irony was not lost on him.

Garrett took comfort in the familiarity of the urban sprawl. As old as the railroads, Rankin Flats took every threat to its well-being squarely on its chin and kept bouncing back for more. Ranchers and the city's most elite residents claimed their stake early in the city's development on the western edge, presumably so that they could see the faintest outline of the mountains in that direction. As one progressed further east from there, closer and closer to the city's heart the income largely dropped. There were exceptions, as with any city. Small pockets of rich and trendy urban renewal projects had taken shaky root in some of the more popular downtown areas. Skyscrapers towered above it all, gleaming steel and glass cocks garishly contradictory to the gloomy rat's nest of the "real" city below. It might have been an ugly place, decayed and scarred from a century and a half of feverish growth and massive shifts of fortune, but he loved the scrappiness of it all, that there were still pockets of people who fought back and kept hope for better days. It was why he did what he did.

He made one stop on the way to the diner, at a high-security storage unit. They charged outrageous prices up front but their staff was paid well enough to never poke around or ask questions. He had several such places across the city, bug-out spots where he kept cash, clothes, and all the paperwork he'd need to make a good run for it if need be. His unit there was full of boxes of books, a couple of pieces of decent furniture (with seams that could be quickly torn away to get to the cash wrapped in plastic inside), and random upscale detritus that masked what the unit was really there for. He slipped the 9mm from Richter into one of the boxes of books. Come spring, he'd make a point of coming back to grab it and dump it in a river. From the backpack, he tossed the joints under his seat.

Ed's Touareg was already in the Jackpot Corral's lot when he pulled in. It was some sort of unspoken rule that every other restaurant in

Montana had to be named after farming, ranching, or mining. Business owners in the area weren't exactly the creative types, so a passerby might have been forgiven for assuming the Jackpot was just like a hundred other generically Western-named diners in the area. They would've been dead wrong, though. Better breakfasts could be found on the eastern side of Rankin Flats, but none in such quantities as the Jackpot with such friendly, regular staff. It was one of those rare restaurants in Montana where the employees acted like they were happy to be there, and treated their customers like family. When Garrett entered, his backpack slung over one shoulder, he was hit with the homey waft of fried meats and potatoes. It might have been a second home, given how often he showed up there after a job.

"Ed's in back, hon," one of the waitresses said to him, smiling widely.

He fished for her name and caught it at the last possible second. "Thanks, Emily."

Past a line of bleary-eyed long-haulers and early risers, he found Ed squashed into a booth, his overcoat folded neatly beside him. His thick, giant fingers encapsulated the mug he sipped from. Ed might have been pushing fat when they first met years ago, but with both Garrett and his wife's goading, Ed had become a terrifying mass of muscles after discovering a fondness for weightlifting. He still packed a few extra pounds, but by and large, he'd make a professional wrestler jealous in the gym.

Garrett crashed onto the plush bench across the table, nodding his thanks when Emily padded over and poured him a cup of black coffee without bothering to ask. She knew him and his habits well. The bruises and raw skin on his knuckles caused her to raise her eyebrows, but she said nothing. When she'd gone, he handed the backpack over the table. "Seventy thirty split, favoring California." California was his nickname for Murphy's son Eggar. Since Murphy had no use for the money himself, he had Garrett send his only kid the money he earned. At first, the money had been sent via carefully sealed UPS packages, but once Garrett brought Ed into the fold, that had changed to a discreet trust fund.

"Seriously? Again with the whole barking at me thing? Try saying it—hi."

Garrett made a sour face. "Hi."

"Atta boy. Any special instructions with your thirty percent?"

Garrett sipped at his coffee. "Nah. Spread it around. I think—"

"-so if that's what you want me to do with the paperwork," Ed interrupted, slightly louder than normal. Emily sidled up just a moment later, pad and pen in hand. "I can get the taxes sent in by this afternoon." Once they'd ordered and Emily had moved back to the other customers, Ed leaned in conspiratorially. "Sorry. Didn't spot her until she was almost here. Oh hey, though, your taxes really are just about done. You're pretty flush at the moment and the market's good. We need to go over the possibility of opening a new business or two. I got some ideas in mind if you want."

Garrett shrugged. "Sure, do whatever you think is best. I trust you." He sure hadn't, once upon a time, but the big man had long since won him over. Apart from Monica, he and his wife were the only living people aware of his less-than-legal activities. Without Ed, the whole thing fell apart.

"Good. There's an investment company out of Sioux Falls looking to make inroads here. I've been checking into their background, and it looks like they've got some legitimately well-grounded ideas. I'm really curious about their idea about bringing in a quality day spa…"

A woman in a long red dress walked through the walls not five feet from their booth and Garrett lost focus on Ed's words momentarily. Her colors trailed her like adoring paparazzi, flashing and fading in a swirl of purple and white. For a moment, Garrett thought she might be there to talk to him, but she kept walking through the diner, her head held high and her attention fixed elsewhere. Ghosts were a bit like spotty AM/FM radio. Some came in perfectly in tune with his perception, like that woman or Murphy. Others weren't always so attuned to his bandwidth. Sometimes he'd have the vaguest hint of a ghost, just beyond his sight but there regardless, like the slightest change of static for a station that a person couldn't quite hear. He glanced back at Ed as the accountant finished talking about… well, whatever.

Irritably, Ed asked, "You okay? You zoned for a minute."

Garrett nodded. "Yeah, sorry. Just tired. A day spa sounds interesting. See what they want, and keep checking their background. But if we have the capital, take the risk if they check out."

"Will do," Ed said, somewhat placated. He tapped the backpack. "So, cash? Anything else?"

"There's a ledger in there too. Coded. I didn't find a cipher… key… thing, but maybe you can figure it out. Or maybe you know someone?"

Ed brightened immensely. "Cryptography! Heck yes, I love that stuff. I'll be happy to give it a look. When do you need it done?"

"Whenever. I don't know if it even has anything I can use in there, but I guess we'll find out."

"I'll take a look at it tonight. Rose is gone for a couple of days so it'll give me something to do."

"Oh yeah? Where's she?"

"A teamwork thing up at the Showdown ski resort."

Garrett laughed. "Poor her." Rose made a healthy living by organizing events for a local food product corporation. A month or two back, she'd been in Tokyo, eating sushi with upper middle management and touring some of their overseas distribution centers. Sometime before that, it was three days in Seattle for a training conference that sounded suspiciously like a thinly disguised excuse for salted caramels at Molly Moon's and fresh crab cakes.

"No kidding, right? With all that fresh snow last night, I'm sure she'll be miserable up there. Three days of skiing, hot cocoa, and snowshoeing."

Garrett tapped his breast. "My heart goes out to her. Well and truly."

"Oh, she wants you to come by Saturday. Dinner. She wants to make baked ziti." Ed's face grew stormy. "Don't screw this up for me and say no. I never get ziti. Never."

"I wouldn't miss it for the world, Ed. You know that."

"Good."

Their food came. Garrett didn't so much eat as shovel down his spicy chicken biscuits smeared in spicy peppery gravy and the roughly half a pig's worth of bacon he'd ordered on the side. Ed, showing remarkable restraint, kept himself to a breakfast burrito and roughly his weight in thick cut fried potatoes, covered in a blend of salsa, melted cheese, onion, and mushrooms. When both men pushed away their plates, there wasn't a scrap left, and at the Jackpot, that was mighty impressive.

After Emily brought them their check, Garrett sighed. "Gym tonight for me. You want to come?"

"For a bit, sure." He grinned slyly. "Danny's daughter Brianna is back in town. Guess she's gonna help run the Hammerdown."

"Why are you grinning like that?"

"You know I'm not a betting man, right?"

"Right."

Ed leaned forward, his elbows on the table. "Well, I'm gonna break that rule and make you a bet right now. Twenty bucks says you wind up following her around like a lost little puppy dog."

"Brianna?" The last time Garrett saw her, she'd been a wiry beanpole fresh out of high school, scrappy and full of piss and vinegar like her dad. That had been almost six years, though. "Really?"

"Uh huh."

"Huh."

"Uh huh."

* * *

Exhaustion finally caught up with Garrett by the time he reached his condo. He lived on the third floor of a pleasantly nondescript modern steel and glass building with "upper middle class" written all over it. Garrett liked it for its security and quiet tenants—not to mention the indoor heated swimming pool and Jacuzzis on the first floor, relative rarities in Montana. In the building, he checked his mailbox and gave the elevator a forlorn loving look, but opted for the stairs. When it came to exercise in the winter, every bit counted.

Three other sets of tenants lived on his floor. A nice Chinese-American couple, surprisingly young, ran a popular local chain of buffets that prepared their food by hand rather than via the usual pre-cooked Chinese garbage found in the generic buffets around the state. The Hardisons were a pair of aloof retirees, gone to Arizona for the winter. The third, Claire and Phil Gable, had seemed like such a normal couple when they moved in. When they'd first came to Garrett's apartment looking to meet their new neighbors, he found them charming and dull, perfect in his books. But Murphy, being Murphy, shook his head and muttered that Phil had smiled too much and too widely. Garrett thought Murph was just being paranoid.

As he trudged past their door, gym bag in hand, he could hear shouting inside. The walls in the building were pretty thick, almost soundproof, so for him to hear the yelling, he figured things must be really bad. Something banged off the door. He stopped for a moment and thought he heard Claire crying. "Not your business," he muttered under his breath, trying hard to believe it. He'd heard them arguing more and more over the last few weeks. Phil had gone from mild-mannered to an ugly, screaming verbally abusive douchebag. Murphy had looked into it, and the two of them hadn't liked what they'd found, though domestic disputes and marital problems were, both agreed, out of their particular wheelhouse.

When he finally got into his place, his eyes half-lidded from need of real sleep, he slung his gym bag into his exercise room—really a converted bedroom with a rowing machine, exercise bike, and a few dumbbells. The allure of just crashing on his overstuffed leather couch or the plush recliners was massively appealing, but he made his way through the largely spotless living room for the comfort of his master bedroom. He didn't bother shedding his clothes, content to fall on his stiff bed and bury his head into the pillows. He lay there for a long minute, trying to forget the dull impotent bellows across the way. But he was who he was, and it wasn't long before he flopped over onto his back and got up with a regretful sigh. His head thumped, his body was leaden and nearly ready to drop whether he wanted to or not, but he stood up anyways and readied himself for yet another asshole.

He didn't so much knock on the Gable's door as pound on it. Whatever was going on quit immediately. He thumped the door again and kept pounding right up until the point when Phil opened the door, that too-wide snake oil smile stretched across his face, eyes gibbous and his crooked nose flaring.

"Well, howdy, neighbor—"

"Cut the shit, Phil. I'm too tired." Garrett pushed the door wide open, catching Phil completely by surprise as he brushed past him. "Claire? I heard shouting and a thump. You okay?"

From the kitchen came a snuffle. "Garrett? It's not really the best time—"

"So I heard. Just here to make sure you're okay."

Phil laid a hand on Garrett's shoulder. "You're gonna want to get out of here right now, Garrett."

Garrett turned and unleashed an ugly smile of his own, making sure Phil saw just enough tooth. "Phil. Take that hand off me. Right the fuck now." Phil's hand tightened and something within Garrett roared in anticipation of what was coming. "I warned you."

Faster than Phil could even register it, Garrett snatched two of his fingers and twisted. Phil yelped, mostly out of shock than any real pain. Shifting his grip further up the man's arm, he spun Phil in an awkward pirouette and brought the forearm up behind him, forcing him to bend over. "You've got a couple of options here, Phil, and only one of them ends with you not going to the hospital for a couple of broken bones and a dislocated shoulder."

"You son of a bitch, I'll—"

Garrett yanked the man's forearm up even higher, the tension almost enough to make the man's arm pop. "Talking's done, Phil. Now is the time for a little listening, a little quiet introspection, and a whole hell of a lot of shutting the fuck up."

Claire burst out of the kitchen, her usually impeccably put together makeup smeared and running. He had to force himself not to do a double-take at her satin panties and midriff-baring tank top. God, those legs. It wasn't the time. "My God, Garrett, what are you doing?"

"I'm just going to have a little chat with your husband here. About manners. And respect for women. I've been trying to ignore your fights, but honestly, today, I'm just so damned tired of it all. First. Phil, apologize."

"I'm not doing shit, you psycho—" Garrett twisted the wrist up and Phil shouted. "Sorry! I'm sorry!"

"To Claire. With feeling."

Phil looked up at Claire, desperation in his eyes. "Baby, honey, I'm sorry, I'm sorry,"

"Second. You're not going to raise your voice again to her. You're going to use your big boy indoor voice and talk things out like a decent human being."

"Okay, okay!"

"Third. Right now, you're thinking you're going to call the cops on me. That would be a very silly thing to do. Especially since I know about the skimming you've been doing from that housing tract project in Harlowton."

Claire's jaw dropped. "You've been doing... what?" she hissed.

"Baby, he's lying—"

"The car. Check the car," Garrett said. "In with the spare tire. There's some paperwork there, and cash. You'll find something else there too, Claire. Something... well, extramarital. I'm sorry. I didn't want to get involved, but I won't let this bullshit go on."

Gable squirmed but couldn't break free. "No, no no, baby, it's not what it's going to seem like, I swear—"

"What?" she asked. "What will I find there, Phil?"

Garrett tapped the back of his head with his finger. "Answer the lady nicely. And truthfully."

"Panties," he said hoarsely.

After a long moment of silence, Claire shook as though she had a chill. Her eyes were dull and her hands clenched into fists. "Garrett, thank you, but please, let him go and get out."

"You going to be okay?"

She took a shaky breath and laughed. "Oh yeah. I'm going to be just fine."

Garrett nodded and released Phil. He cradled his arm and stumbled towards Claire. "Honey, oh God, I'm so sorry—"

Garrett shut the door on his weepy platitudes. The anger seeped out of him as he forced his feet home. Some tiny part of his soul wished he didn't take such savage joy in letting himself push past the point of losing his temper and into that destructive cold rage. It could be a tool—a powerful one—and in the cases of the Gables or Richter Haas, he didn't feel at all guilty about what he'd done. Still, he was glad he had Murphy to pull him back. Wondering how things were going at the hospital, he fell back onto his bed again, and this time, mercifully, he slept..

Chapter 3

Jamie Finson pulled up to the barbershop in his customary Lincoln Navigator. All black save for strips of chrome on the wheel wells, it practically growled for anyone who saw it to stay the hell away while provoking a natural desire to see who was riding in such an ostentatious SUV. Stenciled neatly on the back end was "Exodian Chariots," along with a number. It was a completely legitimate business, and if someone were to call up that number on that particular day, they would get a similar vehicle at their doorstep upon request, though not cheaply.

Finson was neither picking up nor dropping off a client, though he did insist on driving his passengers himself. Two of the local chapter's brightest minds rode with him. one tapping away at a laptop and the other flipping through photocopied pages of police reports from the early morning. Even when Finson rolled to a stop, he wasn't sure if they would have brought their faces up from their work if he hadn't pulled the keys and killed the heat.

He got out as the young hacker, a thickset woman who he'd only seen before that day in pictures, snapped her laptop closed and the man in the back slipped the copies back into a manila envelope. As they hopped out of the Lincoln, Dee asked, "Was the security gate opened?"

"No. Came and went by the side door," Markham said and brought out a cheap lighter and a pack of gas station cigarillos. He glanced questioningly at the other two. "Mind?" Finson growled a no and Dee waved him off. He tapped one out, cupped his hand around the tip and lit it. As he puffed a thin plume of smoke out, he knelt down to examine the security gate just to make sure. Satisfied, he shrugged and pushed himself back up.

Together, they walked as a group to the side door, Markham careful to blow the smoke away from the both of them. By the side door, he leaned down and nodded. "See here?" he asked, pointing at a faint scratch in the keyhole. "Picks. Cleanly done, but they still left a trace. You can just barely see the scratches on the metal."

Finson produced a key from his parka and offered it to Markham wordlessly. The middle aged man opened and held the door for them. Finson entered first, pulling his parka off and placing it neatly on the coat rack. Old as he might have been, the musculature underneath his long sleeve shirt was still impressive. Markham glanced back at the security alarm, turned off after the break-in. "The alarm wasn't tripped," he mumbled, thinking out loud about the packet of information he'd been given by Finson. "So the guy picks the lock but he knows the security code?"

"Could that have been hacked?" Finson asked Dee.

"Maybe," she said doubtfully. "But Occam's Razor and all, I'd bet he just knew the number. It'd explain the safe too."

Markham examined the room carefully. At the office door, he knelt and blinked. "No sign of forced entry, no pick marks. Huh. Both his guys said he was paranoid about locking the office."

"Haas kept a spare key on top of the locker," Finson said.

Markham grabbed a chair from the barbershop and put it in front of the row of lockers. He got up on it and examined the top, the cigarillo hanging out of the corner of his mouth at an angle. "Nothing up here."

Bewildered, Finson pointed at the door. "No access." He glanced at the alarm panel. "But he knew the codes and where he could find the key. Inside knowledge, but he didn't have access to the building?"

"Weird, right?" Markham asked. He put the chair back in the shop and grabbed an empty soda can out of the garbage to tap his ashes into. Dee watched this, her face wrinkling in disgust, but she said nothing.

Finson unlocked the office door and slipped under the yellow tape left by the cops. No one would be back anytime soon. Legion money had made sure of that. The legit cops working the case cared as much about Haas as they had a cockroach getting stepped on and wouldn't give two shits about the place now that the paperwork was logged. Dee brushed past Finson and Markham quietly and set up shop at the desk, leaving room beside her for the duo to case the room and continue their own step-by-step investigation.

The place looked like it had seen a war. Dried blood had been splattered liberally around a third of the room, with most of it concentrated in one vaguely man shaped area. Someone had rifled through the desk and safe, leaving papers and the contents of a cigar box scattered all over the big desk. The box was empty, as was the safe.

"So he comes to the door in the alley. He gets in with a minimal amount of effort. Our man is clearly a professional. What's the next step?" Finson asked Markham.

Formerly a detective once upon a time in Detroit, Markham had a reputation as being a real bloodhound until he'd been caught exchanging cash from a drug bust for gift cards from all over the city. His brutality when attacked in jail by a trio of convicts earned the admiration of his Legion cellmate. When the Legion arranged for a fine lawyer and got his charges all but dismissed, he signed on immediately and never looked back. Someday, Finson thought, Markham might have what it took to rise to his own level. Maybe not higher, since the man had been to prison and his face was too well known, much like Finson himself. But Markham's investigative skills and inside contacts had made him a valued member of their organization regardless. He circled the room, examining the damage done in the fight closely. The key was the minutia, the little things that didn't quite jive with the rest of the picture. He finally saw it on his third pass. "The lamp," he muttered more to himself than anyone else.

"Explain, please," Finson said, stepping forward to examine the remains of the desk lamp.

"Everything else tells a story about a fight that happened in that part of the room." He pointed at the door and the filing cabinets. "Haas comes in. He gets slammed up against those cabinets. Mystery man grabs the gun. Gun goes off—" here he pointed at the wall and the ceiling "-mystery man and Haas fight, but nothing gets touched on this side of the room. There's no blood, no piss—"

"Is that what the smell is?" Dee asked, grimacing. She was rummaging through the junk on his desk, looking for passwords or anything of interest to the Legion.

Markham continued on, ignoring her. "Nothing of interest here but that lamp. It's broken. I'm guessing Haas had it on that desk, and nothing else there looks like it had been knocked around."

"So?" Finson asked expectantly. Markham was brilliant, but he loved putting on a show.

"So. Our man robbed the place first, found something he didn't like, and got Haas's attention by throwing that lamp at the wall. The break-in was pre-planned, but our man either didn't know Haas was Legion or didn't know he was a recruiter."

Finson ran through the scenario, retracing the events with his imagination. The corners of his lips drooped in a frown. "That would rule out Haas's men. They'd have known. How certain are you of this?"

"There's always room for error, but... certain," Markham said and shrugged. "It doesn't entirely rule out them out, though. They might have called in an outsider, looking to make a promotion. Tip off the cartel, bring someone in, tell them about the codes and the key. But..."

Finson sat down on a chair and folded his arms across his knees. "But the Mexicans would have killed him. First thing or on the way out the door doesn't matter. And they certainly wouldn't have called 911."

Markham nodded and blew out another thin stream of smoke. "Bingo. I'm gonna head upstairs, see what I see." He didn't so much walk out of the room as swagger, impressed with his own reasoning.

Finson leaned forward, watching Dee work with sky blue eyes that seemed as though they'd been faded by too much exposure from the sun. He knew her by reputation only, but that reputation was glowing. She was pretty enough, he considered. Partly it was the unusual hairstyle, which she'd shaved closely on one side but grew long on the other, as though she were trying to show two distinct faces. Her clothes were pricey, but subtle—the cut of her slacks had to have been tailored, so well did they fit her, and her cashmere sweater almost hid the tennis bracelet and gold necklace she wore. They were not ostentatious choices, not chosen simply for the honor of working with one of the city's most preeminent Legion leaders, but worn with the casual simplicity of someone well versed in how to look good on a daily basis as though it were effortless.

Were he not taken, he might have asked her to dinner. It might have been bad form to shit where one ate, but Jamie Finson had spent twenty years in prison with only conjugal visits from Legion-sent prostitutes and cared little for what others thought when it came to getting his dick wet. Still, monster though he might be, he had principles and would not cheat on his wife. Dee caught his look and acknowledged the hint of hunger there with a smirk. This one had spirit, he thought to himself. She'd do well in the future. Aloud, he said, "What have you found?"

She dropped the smirk and focused back on the screen. "Bits and pieces. Mr. Haas liked to video tape some of his initiations."

Finson grimaced. "Those will have to go."

"Already on it. Some other stuff too. I found his passwords on a sticky note taped up to the top of his drawer. I went ahead and downloaded all his emails, his browsing history, and his documents. I'll sort through them all later, but it'll take time. There's one thing you should see, though. A guide to a cipher."

Finson got up, ignoring the slight twinge in his leg. It was the result of a weightlifting injury in prison, an "accident" brought on by four of the cartel managing to single him out. They had paid dearly for their slight, though not by Finson's hand. On the outside, their immediate families watched their houses burn. On the inside, Legion swarmed the four and with sloppy precision removed an eye from each. It had led to riots and months of tight lockdowns, but no one ever tried to mess with Finson inside again. He walked behind the desk and leaned over Dee's shoulder. His earlier introspection about her attractiveness evaporated before the need to focus on their work. He was all business as he read the words rapidly, his mouth forming each one as he went. Though remarkably clever, his formal education had been lacking and he had been a late bloomer to the complexities of the English language, so he often mouthed words aloud without a hint of self-consciousness.

"Clever," he said.

She nodded. "It kind of is. But there's nothing on the computer that it would have been used for."

Finson thought hard about the police report, about what had been taken. "We know what should be here that isn't. The police took his legitimate books and the cash from the filing cabinets that the thief missed. But there was nothing in the report about the numbers for the games."

She followed his logic and nodded. "Maybe that's how the thief knew him. Made a bet, it went south, he comes in, takes the records and the money."

"It makes sense. But... the kind of people that come here, to make bets... you think they're the type who could pick a door like that? Who could beat a man down so efficiently?" He shook his head. "He took the gambling books. The cash. No, he knew Haas was a bookie, but a customer... I don't buy it."

She brushed the long part of her hair out of her eyes and started shutting down the computer. "What, then?"

Finson drummed his fingers on the desk. There was a picture forming, but its shape was still unclear. "I don't know," he said, clearly frustrated.

Markham reentered the office, rolling his shoulders, only half the cigarillo left hanging out of the corner of his mouth. "Nothing upstairs. Doesn't look like the intruder made it that far. Gun goes off, he's probably thinking he's on the clock, has to race against the cops."

Dee checked a file on her laptop. "No one reported a gunshot here last night."

Markham snorted in derision. "Out here? Course not. Our guy didn't know it though."

Finson surveyed the business again, walking room to room with Markham, running the scenario over and over in his head. It was so damned nonsensical. It smacked of an inside job, but he knew in his gut that wasn't it. There was something he was missing. He felt like he was working a jigsaw puzzle and only had the outer pieces. Sure, there was a frame there, but the picture within was formless and largely missing. "I want the both of you on point for this. Follow every news story. Find us similar cases. If this guy was local, maybe he's got a history. Find us something we can use. We're done here."

Something about the job made him uneasy. Never in his entire career had he seen someone work a crime with such efficiency. It was almost as though the man were a ghost.

* * *

With every passing minute, Ransom Galbraith clinked his gold band against the lip of the tumbler. Ransom kept the time in his head, not bothering to look at his Breitling watch. He tracked the seconds in his head as precisely as any gadget. It was an old self-taught childhood coping mechanism for stress. Focusing in on the numbers calmed his often-burning mind and kept him sharp and focused. The ring against the glass was a recent habit, though. He was barely even aware he was doing it.

Another three minutes passed, another three clinks of the glass. He stared out the window, his face an unreadable mask, standing with his shoulders tensed and his back to the closed office door. Outside, snow swirled again, but not so much that he couldn't see the rooftop of the building across the street. It sat a story lower than his own office high in one of the cushier towers in a trendy part of downtown Rankin Flats. He could see every detail on their rooftop, from the stone angels on its corners to the access door. In just a few minutes, the janitor would step outside and light up. He had done this every day for months, a habit Ransom noted but never thought to capitulate on until recently. Ransom adored punctuality and habit as character traits and not just necessarily when he was planning to murder someone.

He sipped at the whiskey occasionally, letting the mellow burn warm him as he contemplated the snowfall and the streets below. It wasn't quite yet time for the five o'clock crowds to jam up the sidewalks on their way to the car parks and bus stops, but a few handfuls of people, hunched against the near-constant thrust of the wind, hustled as fast as they could manage to whatever was next in their insignificant little lives. One in a hundred would leave this world having actually impacted it in even the most minute of ways, Ransom thought. None of them had the guts to do anything truly of note. None of them had the foresight. They fell into mediocre jobs because they hadn't had the discipline to do the work to get a better education. They pumped out kids and paid an outrageous price for slum housing in a faceless suburb, content to live dull lives, drive dull cars, and make dull little conversations. Only a fraction of them could muster up the will necessary to not be boring. And of those, none of them could really see.

Ransom had the willpower and the sight. The monster in the reflection of the setting sun of the glass cooed silently at him, pressing flayed knuckles against the glass, its jagged teeth grinning at him. Without taking his focus away from the building, Ransom reached a hand out, letting his fingers trail down the glass in a loving, longing gesture. He hummed without realizing it, something tuneless and completely at odds with the Fanny Mendelssohn playing softly on the computer.

The anticipatory pleasure was a new development, one he pondered with vague unease. It was not a lust—there was nothing sexual about it. But it was certainly a perversion of the mind, and for a man with such a tight rein on his emotions, it was wildly out of character. The analytical part of his mind was breaking—had been broken. He was certainly rational enough to understand that. But it wasn't as though he could go speak to a shrink about it. Not unless he wanted to spend the rest of his days waiting for a last meal and a little poke in the arm to put him to sleep for good. He couldn't help it, though. With every passing day, he knew the next kill was getting closer and closer, and with it, the beauty of the colorful ephemera, so very like the thin paper streamers of his wonderful childhood birthday parties. He told himself the little pleasant shiver up his spine was from the cold and almost believed it.

The woman in the alley had been an impulsive mistake, one he wouldn't make again. She'd been so ripe and alive, the anger as she stormed away from the bar tight around her like a scarf. She hadn't bothered to turn around, hadn't seen him ease up behind her until it was too late and he was pulling her into the alley, his thick arm cutting off her air supply until he could fumble out his father's hunting knife ("Keep this sharp, Ran, and it'll never do you wrong," his father had explained, bewilderingly proud of the gift on his son's twelfth birthday as they prepared to gut a deer). Slitting her throat wasn't as easy as it had been in the movies. The knife stuck on something meaty and hard, and he'd had to make a sawing motion to free it. The arterial spray steamed a little in the air and froze as it hit the ground and her body dropped with a soft whup. Her ghost rose up out of her corpse immediately, the spirit strikingly vibrant and alive, the colors sharper and somehow more focused than her actual self, as though her body had been in standard definition and her spirit in 4K hi-def. She looked down at herself, bloody and empty, and said simply, "Oh," as though this were a minor inconvenience and not a terribly traumatic thing. Her ephemera were the color of milky coffee and a dark crimson, almost black. He had very little time to enjoy the show, however. The woman's friends were shouting drunkenly for her, laughing and calling her back. He walked to his car quickly, hearing the first of the screams as he pulled out into traffic, forcing himself not to gun it. No one had seen him, but the daring act had been too bold by far and he told himself there would be no more unplanned murders.

The thought of jail didn't terrify him as much as it might have before this had all started. In fact, the idea of the potential for violence in there captivated him. But he still valued his freedom and the little indulgences of his daily life, so for now, he was careful. Perhaps someday, if he grew bored enough, he might walk into a bank and cheerfully demand their money. Was that even a felony anymore for a white man in Rankin Flats? He wasn't sure. The prison in Deer Lodge was constantly past capacity, and the privately owned one in town stood unused and in disrepair after its owners declared that an agreement with the government couldn't be reached. He might literally have to admit to being a murderer in order to even see the inside of a cell. He allowed himself a wide smile at the callow humor of it all. The reflection of the creature, its skin split from the muscle in countless lashes across its grayish body, laughed with him, as though he were in on the joke too. It was one of a thousand such creatures Ransom had seen in mirrors, windows, and water, but this particular one was more familiar to him than most. Said familiarity had once bred a feeling of gnawing unease about something forgotten, some fleeting memory of the beast gone to him except perhaps in the midst of his darkest dreams, forgotten upon waking out of necessity lest his mind break.

Well, break more than it had, at any rate.

There. The door at the top of the opposite building opened and the short man tottered out, closing the door behind him only after carefully patting his pocket, making sure his keys were still there. Ransom noted the time on his leather-bound day planner. Exactly within the five-minute window, same as always. The janitor pulled a joint out of a baggie, cupped one hand over the end and lit it. Just like always, he meandered to the ledge, resting his elbows on it despite the snow and cold A regular clockwork man, so set was he in his habit. As he watched the janitor, Ransom wondered idly if a video camera could pick up on the trails of the dead. He wrote down "camera?" on the page next to the day's time. It was worth a try.

Ransom grinned and sat down at his desk. Time for part two. He called for his assistant Benjamin. Hardly out of college, the bright but awkward man was always eager to please. He hustled right in, his hands folded in front of him. "Sir?"

Ransom glanced up from his computer as though he'd been doing work. The truth was, the bit of coding he needed to finish for that week's patch remained untouched. "This code isn't going quite the way I'd hoped, Benjamin. I'm afraid I'm going to have to come in Saturday and possibly Sunday." That much was true. Sunday, he really would have to play catch-up if he wanted to continue this charade at work. His hours didn't matter—he was salaried—but results were expected and he'd been lagging behind a bit more than his company preferred.

Benjamin was quick to hide the consternation of having to work the weekend, but regained his professional mask almost immediately. "Sir, if you need me, I'd be happy to come in Saturday." He hesitated, and plunged forward. "But if you don't mind, sir, my girlfriend and I—"

"Oh, there's nothing you could do to help me here anyways." The comment was very literal. Benjamin was a fine programmer but lacked the older man's eagle-eyed vision for problem-solving and debugging without resorting to workarounds or tricks. It was why Ransom earned such a fat paycheck every other week. Ransom did not register the slight as he said it, but noted the quickly disguised wince on Benjamin's face. The boy was loyal, hardworking, and slightly less cumbersome to speak to than the rest of the staff at Agilumine Solutions. He certainly had the potential to become a fine businessman and manager someday, perhaps at that very company. Plus, and Ransom hated to admit this, he was rather fond of the boy, so instead of letting his blunt nature win out as he usually did, he tried to affect an air of softness. "I'm sorry, that wasn't meant as a slight."

"It wasn't taken that way, sir." Benjamin at least had the good grace to pretend the statement was genuine.

Ransom slid open his top desk drawer and pulled out an envelope. "Besides, I should think this might interest you and your lady friend more." He pushed the envelope across the desk with two fingers. Benjamin picked up it along with the proffered silver letter opener. He slit the envelope open and pulled out a pair of tickets.

Gaping at them openly, he said, "The Black Keys? Sir, we already have… oh." He'd noted the seating arrangement. "Oh!"

"Were your previous tickets front row?" Ransom asked with genuine worry. The whole plan went out the window if Benjamin thought he needed to be there that day and weren't otherwise preoccupied.

Bouncing on his toes, Benjamin ran a hand across his already-balding scalp and grinned widely. "No sir, they most certainly were not. I can't… these must have cost a fortune."

"They didn't. I'm friends with the venue's management." A half-lie. On his part, he thought of few as friends, but he supposed with the number of donations he made to the venue to bring in composers and music of real worth, the manager wouldn't exactly deny the lie either. At the very least, they were acquaintances who shared a similar taste in music.

"How can I repay you, sir? I'll gladly come in Sunday. Or whenever you need me."

Ransom shook his head. "No. Just let security know I'll be coming in and out over the weekend."

"Will do. Should I inform Barb to expect the code Saturday?"

Ugh. The thought of the annoying woman, theoretically his boss— at least, she signed the paychecks—pissed him off to no small degree. Her aggressive, no-nonsense demeanor seemed more suited to a man than that of a glorified secretary who didn't understand a line of Ransom's code. And yet she brought home nearly a full fifth again what he did. "That bitch," Ransom muttered darkly. His eyebrows shot up and he sucked in his breath. He genuinely hadn't meant to say that out loud. "That wasn't meant to be…"

Benjamin glanced back at the door furtively. Satisfied the coast was clear, he said quietly, "Never heard a thing, sir."

Ransom nodded. He wasn't worried about the possible repercussions, though he'd been warned before for his brusque demeanor to the women at work after his wife died. His resume was stacked well enough that he could stand on the rooftops shouting endless profanities at the women passing below and still quietly get hired by the first software company he applied to. But the loss of his temper in front of Benjamin had been unexpected and in rather poor form. He must remain, at all times, completely under the radar. "I'm sorry, Benjamin." He glanced at a photo of his wife, a staged maneuver he performed without a second's guilt. "It's just... some days are worse than others."

"I understand, sir." And he really thought he did, too. Benjamin knew the rumors floating around, that Mrs. Galbraith had been shacked up with another man when the little getaway house in Checkerboard went up in flames. That Mr. Galbraith himself hadn't known he was being cuckolded until it was too late. He knew her death had made him even more withdrawn and distant, though he seemed to be trying even harder to maintain the few connections he had. He knew his boss's mental state was fragile and that the man was in desperate need of both a vacation and a good rigorous session with a pretty thing or three. Loyal as always, he kept his mouth shut.

Ransom blew out his breath pensively. "Thank you, Benjamin. That's it for now."

"Yes, sir. And thank you again, sir. You are too kind."

When Benjamin shut the door and returned to his cubicle, he heard that clinking of metal against glass again and thought about his boss's out-of-character venomous response. Yes, a vacation, he thought privately to himself. Or an easy layup of a one-night stand. Just get back in that dating scene, take out his sexual pension on someone. It was a good idea. Maybe his girlfriend knew someone about Galbraith's age. A divorcee, maybe, someone who needed a good revenge lay as much as his boss. Flapping the tickets in his hand, his mind raced as he thought about how he could really help out his employer.

Galbraith returned to the window. How he wished it was Saturday. The beast in the window snapped at one of its brethren and turned back to Galbraith, chewing on newly rent flesh. Ransom smiled fondly at their play. Such lovely things.

Chapter 4

The last vestiges of the day's light flitted through the edges of the window not covered by heavy shades and stole across Garrett's face. As bright as it might have been, it wasn't the light that woke him up, but the buzzing from the end table. Caught in the fugue of a deep sleep and sure it was a bee, he swatted at the phone, knocking it off the table moments before realizing what he'd just hit. Scrabbling at the floor with his fingertips, he found the phone and brought it up to his ear just in time to avoid it going to voicemail. "Mm," he mumbled into it.

"What's up, dicksmoke?" The cheery voice of his sister on the other end brought him a little closer to lucidity, but not by much.

"Auggie." His voice was thick with sleep and unsure of itself, but he had enough presence of mind to call her by her most loathed nickname, practically feeling her sock his shoulder for saying it.

"You sleeping?"

"Yeah. No. I'm up now." He cleared his throat and pulled the comforter up over his shoulders, tucking himself in tighter. He always left the heat almost off in the bedroom, preferring to wrap himself in the enveloping down thickness rather than have a warmer bedroom and lighter blankets. That would change in summer, when he liked to lay atop the bed sans blanket altogether, letting himself roll into a little cocoon of sheets sometime in the night.

"Long night?"

"Poker. Good haul. Something like... I don't know, fifteen grand?" The practiced little lie hurt, but telling his youngest sister the truth wasn't an option. He didn't want to lose her too.

She whistled low. "Damn. That's... damn."

"Mm hm. So what's up? How's Florida?"

"Eh, beautiful, hot, full of crazy people. On the road to Mom and Dad's."

"Hm? On a weekday?"

Her voice lowered. "Has Dad called you yet?"

He rolled over onto his back and put an arm behind his head, wondering where this was going. "No. Why?"

She did that irritating little dramatic pause she loved so much and he ground his teeth together. "Gar, Mom had to go to the hospital last night. She had a stroke. They think she's stable for now, but it's... I don't know. Touch and go, I guess."

Anyone else might have thrown the covers back in a panic or shouted their indignation at not having been told sooner. All Garrett could say was, "Oh. Uh. Well, shit. Sorry to hear that."

Clearly pissed, Auggie said angrily, "You know, you could try to sound a little more worried than that."

"August," he started to say, but she cut him off.

"I don't give a shit what happened between you two, she's still our mom."

"Auggie—"

"And Dad, he's just fucking crushed. Stephanie too, and she hates Mom almost as much as you do."

The off-handed mention of his middle sister hurt, and hurt bad. It always did. She hadn't spoken to him in over a decade and a half, something he wished every day he could change. "I don't hate—"

"Bullshit! Bullshit bullshit bullshit!" Auggie screamed. She panted into the phone and he thought he could hear her thumping something. The steering wheel, maybe. All three of the Moranis siblings shared a temper, that much was certain.

Garrett waited until she had a minute to calm down, taking the time to slip out of bed and pad to the bathroom. "Aug, I am sorry. For what it's worth."

"Yeah, well," she said, sniffling. There was a long silence. "Are you pissing?"

"Yup."

She laughed shakily. "Jerk."

"Like you haven't ever talked to me while you were taking a leak."

"Yeah, but you know, I'm all ladylike and shit."

He breathed out a sigh. "August, what can I do?" He finished up and washed his hands, pointedly ignoring the figure in the mirror struggling to take shape.

"Right now? I don't know. The doctors say they caught it relatively early, but it feels like there's more they're not telling me. I don't think... with all her other problems, I don't think she's okay."

Garrett sat on the edge of the bed and couldn't believe what he was about to say. "Do you and Dad want me down there?"

August didn't hesitate. "Yes. Fuck. No. Yes, but no." She thought about it for a minute. "Let me talk to Dad. And Steph. And Mom, if she's having one of her good days. I've got vacation time saved, and Doc Henson told me to take all the time I needed. Steph's going to be there as much as possible too. She doesn't live all that far from them, and... well, she'll be there for Dad, you know?" She sighed again. "She doesn't hate Mom. That was mean of me to say."

"I know, Aug." He noted that she very carefully didn't redact her earlier statement about him hating their mom, which made him even more sad. There was a lot of anger there, that much was true. Unbidden, the memory of his head bouncing off the kitchen table as he fought against the restraining hands of the women from the church, his mother standing with her hands clasped as the preacher cast holy water down on him. He shivered, thinking about Yvette and his mother and their little circle of matronly church friends in their old house in Missouri.

But did he hate his mom? No. Maybe when he was on the bus, fleeing halfway across the nation from her, but as an adult, the things his mother—and his father, to a lesser extent—did just left him feeling exhausted, emotionally stretched thin. Hatred was not the word for it.

"I'll talk to them. I know Dad will want to see you. Stephanie wants to, she's just too stubborn to admit it. And Mom... we'll see how she is, I guess."

He rubbed a hand over his cheek, realizing just how badly he needed a shave. "All right, well, say the word and I'm on the next flight."

"Don't say that unless you mean it," Auggie said flatly.

"Cross my heart, August. Maybe not for Mom, but for you. Dad and Steph too."

"Thanks, Garrett. I appreciate—" She hammered on her horn and screeched, "You old asshat, it's the pedal on the right. Your other right! If you're over ninety, maybe keep your ass out of the damn driver's seat, you idiot! Garrett, I gotta go. Traffic's getting fun. Love ya."

"Love you too."

"Keep that pimp hand strong, motha fuckaaaaaa—" He cut her off in mid-swear, laughing softly despite his dark mood. August was always good for that.

After a long shower under his high-flow showerhead—illegal, probably immoral, and wonderfully soothing—and a shave done entirely by feel with his towel draped over the mirror, he felt more himself and ready for the gym. He tossed on a pair of sweats and a Kyle Gass Band tee. The gym clothes he wore home last night reeked, so he grabbed them up and stalked out through the living room.

Murphy sat on the recliner, deep in meditation. He claimed it was as close to sleep as he could get and that it helped pass the time. Garret tried to sneak past him, but like always, Murph immediately noticed him. He launched into what happened the night before without any preamble. "Well, he might be a vegetable, but we're clear on Richter. Looks like they don't know who did it. They'll be battening down the hatches, but nothing's coming back your way." He stood up and followed Garrett past the kitchen and into the laundry room. "Got a name for one of their boogeymen. Finson. Nothing more than that. There was a call, a real rough-sounding son of a bitch. Someone in charge. Maybe him, maybe not. Everyone was real careful about not using names, just like always."

Garrett tossed the clothes into the washer and started it. He rubbed at the backs of his sore knuckles. "I'll look him up, but a city this big…" He shrugged. "Anyways, good work. Thanks." He went back out to the kitchen to rummage around for a bite to eat and filled Murphy in on the meeting with Ed.

"Well, hell, thanks for the split. And the Ball Chomper? What'd she have to say about all this?"

"No mention of any blowback. She was pissed when she found out he was recruiting, but she knew more than she was letting on. I think maybe she came across one of the victims." Garrett flushed a little bit. "I, uh, ran by her place last night. And I showed her, you know, the uh, photos, and the ledger, and…"

His friend's sudden stuttering didn't slip by Murph. "No."

Garrett shrugged. He concentrated very hard on the sandwich fixings in front of him, trying not to look up at Murph, knowing his face would betray him.

"Shit, you did, didn't you?" Murphy started to laugh, then caught himself. "I'm sorry. I'm sure the two of you will make a fine couple. Tell me, though, if she went down on you, did she, you know, nibble?" Then he really started laughing while Garrett glared at him.

"It was a one-time thing. And no damn teeth were involved."

Murphy's laughs fell into little fits and he sighed. "Oh, man, that's… well, that's just definitely gonna come back and—"

"Don't say it."

"-bite you in the ass."

Garrett mumbled, "Prick," and immediately regretted his word choice.

"It'll probably bite you there too!" Murphy howled with laughter as Garrett returned to the living room, roast beef sandwich and a bottle of Pyramid in hand, and plopped into one of his overstuffed recliners. He turned on the TV for a minute.

"Want me to leave this on for you?" he asked. "I'm headed to the gym with Ed. Oh, he's going to try to break that code in Richter's book. I guess we'll see if it leads to anything."

Watching the channel guide attentively, Murphy said, "You sound doubtful."

"Honestly? I don't think it's worth the effort. Haas was lower middle management at best. That's his bookie business in there. A place like that, we'll be lucky if anyone put down more than a few hundred on a game." He stopped on a rerun of Joe Versus the Volcano for a few minutes, watching numbly as Tom Hanks raved about the lights sucking the light out of him and thinking about his mom. Finally, he sighed and told Murphy about the conversation with Auggie.

Murphy's grin disappeared. He folded a knee up towards his chest and wrapped his arms around—and into—it. "Wow, that's... complicated. I'm sorry. For what it's worth."

"Yeah, me too," Garrett agreed.

Murphy asked quietly, "Were you serious about going down there?"

"Mm hm." He paused and thought about it. "At least I think I am. Like you said... complicated." He finished off the beer. "So, the TV? Or I can set up a couple of audio books, or some music. Whatever."

Murphy got up and looked out the patio door. The view of the city was pretty okay from there, apart from a couple of taller buildings a block or two away that obscured parts of it "Nah. Think I'll stretch my legs, go see some of the regular places." By regular places, he meant some of the more frequent problematic areas for crime around town. In a place like Rankin Flats, nowhere was sacrosanct, but a few places usually got hit worse than others. He turned and laid a weightless hand as best he could on Garrett's shoulder. "You good?"

Garrett clicked the power button and brushed crumbs off his shirt. "Sure."

"Liar. Go punch something. I know you want to." It was meant as a joke, but they both knew the truth of it. "Catch up to you tomorrow morning. If your dick ain't getting mauled." He bit at the air several times as Garrett wished his friend was physical so he could cheerfully murder him.

* * *

Though not always by that name, over the last century the Hammerdown Gym had established itself as a fixture near the city's heart. After the first World War, a boxing craze swept through the roughly hewn city, and what had been a warehouse was soon converted to a full blown gym for pugilists and spectators, featuring weekly fights by local amateurs and semi-pros. In the twenties came hard economic times for the Flats and Prohibition nearly killed attendance at the gym. But with new ownership by the legendary gangster Flatface Freddy Dunham came deals with the police to look the other way while liquor from mountain stills was brought in by the truckload. Soon enough, the gym was back on its feet and its popularity soared again. The people, hard pressed to find work, found solace in the gym's cheap drinks and bloody spectacles.

The gym changed hands several times throughout the thirties after Flatface was gunned down outside a restaurant by a rival. Its fortunes rose and fell with the city's at large, but it slowly grew out of its former less-than-sterling reputation and grew into a legitimate business. In the forties, the second World War nearly forced the Hammerdown to close, but its owner, himself a former soldier, struck upon the idea of turning the place into both a gym for the inner city's teens and a recruitment center for the Army. Even after the war ended, the place remained a youth-focused gym, with many underprivileged kids finding a second home—or at least a place where they could punch things in a healthy way.

But with the sixties came a long economic slump for Rankin Flats, one from which the neighborhood never really recovered. Business after business shuttered its doors as the city's industries crumbled. The Hammerdown shifted hands as frequently as four times a year. No one was able to settle on a formula that worked. What little goodwill remained was ruined by the influx and sale of drugs within its walls, and the gym fell into disuse. No one cared about boxing or getting fit anymore. No one cared about much except their next meal. The only things they wanted to beat on were their wives or their kids Twice, the gym burned.

In the seventies, the gym was rebuilt from the ground up by an industrialist who simply wanted a place closer to his job where he could work out. He was by all accounts a lunatic with far too much money and not enough sense, but that lunatic had just enough capital to buy out some local muscle, enough to keep the junkies and firebugs from destroying his investment. And strangely enough, it worked. He offered up free memberships to anyone who helped the neighborhood clean up, buying the paint and supplies himself while getting the labor for a pittance. And what impressed them most was that this frizzy-haired, bespectacled toothy rich guy was in the trenches with them on a daily basis. True, it was mostly a means to escape his horrible, shrill wife and his floundering steel mills, but he earned their respect and kept it, even if he soon pissed away his entire fortune.

In the last few weeks of his life in the eighties, confined to a small cot in his one-bedroom apartment two blocks from the gym, the smell of mildew and mold heavy in the air, he told his grown son, fresh from the military, that he regretted none of it. Save for the infirm or those with the very young, every single soul for eight blocks showed up to his funeral. His son, Danny, confounded by the turnout, made a promise to himself to keep the doors open, to build on his father's legacy. And while not as wildly popular as his dad had been, Danny managed to keep his promise. He rechristened the gym and launched the place into a new era. Gone was the male-centric vibe, replaced by an open gender friendliness. He did have a lower tolerance for deadbeats than his dad did, but in time, that helped the gym develop a no-nonsense reputation that had been lacking for a while. Over the decades, he expanded, adding a tinted-glass enclosed yoga and pilates room, new equipment, and a larger workout area. He even brought back in a boxing ring, used nowadays for far more than boxing, what with the popularity of MMA and wrestling.

Three decades and change after her grandfather had died in that cot, Brianna Reeve walked through the doors and thought not for the first time just how much the Frankenstein's monster of a gym felt like home. She loved the piecemeal old building, patched together from decades of change and updates. The old building was decorated wherever there wasn't a window with pictures of the gym's best and brightest. No one's photo was ever taken down, no matter how far in life they fell. It was a reminder to all its patrons that anyone and everyone could walk in those doors and do something great, even if it was fleeting. On that wall were soldiers, fighters, boxers, teachers, janitors, criminals, preachers... everyone from all walks of life came in those doors.

Coming back hadn't been Brianna's plan. Fresh out of high school, she moved in with her mom on the east coast to go to school. She was going to be a Fortune 500 CEO, with her name a regular staple in yearly reviews of executives to watch. She was going to drive a Lexus, buy a two story house in Portland or the east coast, retire by fifty, and spend her golden years traveling the world. It was a good plan, a respectable one. But it never occurred to her just much she'd miss the city of her birth. How she'd crave a clubfoot sandwich from Staggering Ox or a pasty so scalding hot on the inside she always burned her tongue on them. How much she missed the gym. How much she missed her dad.

And so over the Thanksgiving break of her final push to get her master's degree, she sat with her father on her mother's front porch. He always made it a point to come visit over the holidays. They drank a third of a bottle of good bourbon between the two of them before she broke down and cried for no damn good reason. That was her, though. She cried unapologetically at anything and everything—if a sweet commercial came on TV, she cried. If she saw a cute pair of animals bonding together on a walk, she cried. When her mom surprised her with fresh wildflowers on her writing desk, she cried. Anything and everything could set her off and she didn't care. But that night, she did. Furious at herself, she rubbed hard at her eyes and refused to acknowledge her father's attempts to calm her down. He thought she was furious with him, so Danny got up to go for a walk, to let her have all the time she needed to cool off and tell him whatever she needed to get off her chest. She caught up to him at the end of the driveway and hugged him as hard as she could, which given her athleticism and ropy frame, was not an insignificant amount of force. She asked him if she could come home, to work with him in the gym. She stammered all over herself in the question, not wanting to put anyone else out or put her father on the spot. Danny agreed immediately.

It had been tough to break the news to her mom, who she'd lived with for all her college years, who had supported her both as a daughter and as an adult, giving her the space she needed in those socially blossoming years while still knocking her on the head with a plastic spoon now and then when she did something dumb. It had been an easy, comfortable living arrangement, but if both were being honest, by the end, they were both ready for their own personal space. So Brianna cried—again—and told the news to her mom as gently as she could. There had been some concern at first—mostly about where she'd live—

but her mom saw the need in her daughter's eyes and hastily agreed.

And in a couple of months, Brianna found herself home again in the gym. She worked long hours, observing everything that happened and getting to know the various trainers and coaches that rented space from them for weekly classes and even began to prepare some of her own. The day to day business was not difficult, but her father had never been great with numbers and computers, and she realized almost immediately she'd need to put her business degree to good use. It would never be the Fortune 500 company she dreamed of in her early college years, but it was spiritually satisfying work and Brianna was content.

On that particular night, she was impatiently walking her father through the basics of an Excel spreadsheet, vowing to herself and every deity she could think of that she wouldn't rest until she taught her dad how to add columns together. She didn't see the familiar tall, sinewy man come in with the titanic accountant she'd met a few days prior, not at first and not during most of his workout. Not until he stepped in the ring with the obese teenager and she heard snickering.

* * *

Ed gripped the handlebar of the treadmill as he trudged slowly up the brutal incline. "Legs feel like a pig at a... uh... pig roast... thing." he gasped.

Beside him, jogging up a matching brutal incline with his arms swinging freely and sweat rolling down his forehead, Garrett grunted, "That's a... terrible metaphor." He thought about it for a second. "But true. All I can think about... are my calves."

"Why am I doing this?" Ed asked, his head sinking almost low enough to touch the bar.

"Because we hate ourselves," Garrett responded, speeding up his treadmill. "Two minutes. Finish strong, buddy."

"Crap," Ed grumbled, but sped his walk up marginally. His eyes and veins bulging, he looked as though he might pop at any minute. His push lasted all of about twenty seconds before he slowed back down, sucking in great big gasps of air. Glancing over at Garrett, he said, "Running. The jerk's... running."

Finally, their timers beeped and they both slowed down and leveled out their treadmills. Next came a few minutes of cooling down, walking at a reasonable, sane pace to keep themselves from injury by stopping too quickly. From a small TV hung over the bank of treadmills, the tinny voices of the news anchors could finally be heard. They were just closing out the national news, remarking on another mass shooting and a somber speech by the President. Garrett wished there was some way he could prevent those kinds of tragedies, but he wasn't omnipotent and there was no way to predict crazy. Even with an army of ghosts at his back, someone was always going to fall through the cracks and he couldn't be everywhere all at once. It was almost a mantra considering how often he needed to repeat it to himself. If only he actually believed it.

Soon, they switched to local news. They led with the Secretary of Transportation's visit to the city. Her visit was mostly a photo opportunity—the light rail she was there to promote wouldn't break ground until April at the earliest—but that didn't stop the news station from speculating on potential ramifications, like the Canadian-Montanan bullet train, a perennial rumor not at all steeped in any sort of fact but the sort of thing that drew all sorts of viewers and attention. A murder-suicide by a Mexican immigrant and his wife was quickly glossed over. Ed shook his head and sighed at that, himself of Mexican descent and generally exasperated by the media's tendency to shoot right past stories about ethnic groups within Montana. Continued disappearances around the city persisted, with the faces of a couple of homeless shown just long enough to make the viewers aware without upsetting their delicate sensibilities about the city's unseen masses. Finally came a lengthy update on the story of a college woman murdered some days before, touching on her life, particularly her time at college and her success as an aspiring photographer. Police were still looking for details on the grisly alley slaying.

"That was something else," Ed said, finally catching his breath.

"That murder?"

Ed nodded. "What, you haven't heard about it?" Garrett shook his head, sending droplets of sweat splattering all over. "Huh. It's been all over the news. Woman—not much more than a girl, really—goes to a bar. Comes out alone, walks to her car, some guy drags her off to an alley and cuts her throat. Pretty brutally too." Garrett didn't think there was a peaceful way of cutting someone's throat, but he said nothing and Ed continued on. "No leads, no motive, nothing. Seemed to be completely random."

"Huh," Garrett said. "Had my head in the sand the last few days."

"This city, man."

"This city," Garrett agreed. Ed stopped his treadmill and grabbed his bottle of water on the weight bench where he'd left it. "Careful, you don't want to drink too fast. Make yourself sick."

"Mm. Not sure I care." Still, Ed capped the bottle regretfully and set it aside. "All right, it's the weights for me. You want to come?"

Garrett stopped the treadmill. "Sure."

As Garrett took a drink from his own bottle, Ed said quietly, "Hey, maybe that's something you could look into, you know? Do your thing there—"

"Not here," Garrett growled lowly at him. "Never here."

Taken aback at the flash of anger in his friend's eyes, Ed stepped back and held up his palms face out, a gesture of peace. "Hey, hey, sorry, I just forgot."

Softening his glare, Garrett sighed. He glanced around to make sure they were out of earshot of anyone. The gym had a handful of patrons that night, but none were near them. "It's okay. Not my thing anyways. If I knew someone was about to, you know… I could stop it. After the fact, that's mostly on the police." That wasn't strictly true, but without a ghost to speak to, there was no chance he could do anything about it. He wasn't a detective.

They started with dumbbells. Garrett didn't even bother trying to keep up with Ed. The man was a beast and trying to compete would have been foolhardy and downright dangerous. So Garrett focused in on his own workout, lifting the dumbbells slowly and assuredly, feeling the tension in his arms, chest, and core. When Ed switched to the bench press, Garrett wasn't offended in the slightest when his friend asked one of the squat-framed regulars to spot him rather than Garrett. It freed him up to work the weight machines, where he felt more comfortable than with free weights. There was something soothing about the mechanical nature of the push and pull of the weights, and soon he fell into an easy rhythm of pyramid sets, increasing the weight slowly while reducing the number of reps. He worked from his legs to his shoulders, finally ending with a series of chest presses. It was a good workout—not too stressful, but with enough force to it to help him get rid of some of that unspent aggression from the night before. He was careful not to take his emotions out on the weights in a dangerous way. A muscle tear was the last thing he needed.

A young man somewhere in his twenties, sat on a weight bench with a pair of light dumbbells, his arms extending from his waist to straight out from his shoulders. His lateral curls were a bit too fast.

Garrett sat up. "You mind if I give you some tips? Don't mean any offense." He hated giving unsolicited advice at the gym. Or anywhere else, really. His father had loved to offer his unwanted help at every passing moment when he was a young teenager and he'd grown to loathe the words "if I were you." Still, not saying something might mean the young man hurt himself or didn't get in as good of a workout as he could.

The man blinked at him "Me?" After Garrett nodded, he said, "Sure. Still kind of, uh, new to this."

"Bring your arms down slower. That's it," he said approvingly as the man slowed the drop of his arms to his side. "That's where the real burn comes from. Do that with all your lifts. Slow and easy sounds backwards, I know, but when you're working the weights, it's how you build muscle." He watched for a while longer. "Those lateral curls are a pain in the ass. I can't lift half of what I can otherwise with those."

"Me either," the kid admitted. He stopped after a few more and set the weights down carefully on the mat. He wiped at his forehead with the back of an arm, his long greasy blonde hair matted to the top of his skull. Within a few years, Garrett thought, the guy would be bald. "Thanks for the advice."

Garrett offered his hand. "Garrett."

"Wilfred," the young man said, and shook his hand, muscles quivering just a little bit from his workout. "Hey, uh, if you don't mind, would you show me how to use those machines? There was an old man here who was going to show me last week, but I think he got sidetracked. I don't want to bother you or anything, but…"

"No problem at all. Seen you around here a few times this last month." He got up and showed the kid to the chest press. "Here. Start light at first. Let's gauge just how much you can do. There's a notepad around here somewhere. Hang on." Garrett grabbed it from behind the stacks of dumbbells and showed it to Wilfred. "Here. You can keep track of how much you lift in here, at least until you get to know the machines well, you know?"

"Sure," Wilfred said enthusiastically. "My memory's crap."

"I hear you," Garrett said, smiling. He walked Wilfred through the basics, keeping his reps simple and short for the time being. They moved from press to press, and Garrett showed him how each could be used in separate ways to work different parts of the body. "Basically I'd adhere to the old KISS saying."

"The band?" Wilfred asked uncertainly.

"Nah. It just means keep it simple, stupid. You want to keep your routines simple until you get into a pattern and feel comfortable with it. Then branch out slowly—real slowly. You've got the rest of your life to work on this stuff and for the first year or so, it's going to be about developing good habits."

Wilfred nodded slowly. "Keep it simple, stupid. I like that."

"Right? So what got you here?"

"Oh, I, uh…"

"A woman?" Garrett asked, no trace of teasing the kid at all.

"Yes" Wilfred said, blushing. "Well, because I want to be more, you know…"

"That's as good of a reason as any to get out of the house, Wilfred, but when it comes down to it, you want to be here for you. At the end of the day, all that matters is your own opinion of yourself. You want to show up here, do it because you want to feel good, because you want to sweat a bit. You come here because of someone else, it's a whole lot harder to keep that in mind when you plateau out or life gets too hard."

Wilfred nodded, his jowls shaking. "Yes, sir."

"Knock it off with the sir shit." Garrett got up. "Come on. The ring's clear and you're gonna pay me back."

"Oh, I don't like fighting—"

"Good," Garrett said, and clapped him on the shoulder. "You can wear the punch mitts. Come on, it'll be fun."

Wilfred squinted at him, unsure of himself. "I've never, uh, been in that ring." He looked around as though he were seeking some kind of an escape. "Will it hurt? Getting hit?"

"Hang on," Garrett said and left Wilfred sitting there as he grabbed the large punch mitts, meant to help boxers work on their accuracy and in ring skills. This pair was old and frayed slightly at its rectangular edges but still well-stuffed and suitable for the kind of sparring Garrett had in mind. He came back holding them up cheerfully, glad to have someone other than himself to focus on and take the edge off the news about his mother. "See? I punch these, you're never even gonna feel it. Try one on. I'll show you."

Wilfred put one of them on, feeling just a little bit ridiculous and wondering if this was some kind of elaborate prank. The strange guy helping him seemed okay, but he could count the number of days of PE classes he'd spent without someone giving him hell on two hands. It was hard for him to trust the guy's intentions. Still though, if he was going to screw with him, he'd have probably done it by that point. Emphasis on probably. He slipped on one of the large gloves tentatively and stood up.

"All right, hold your hand up about this high. Ready?"

Wilfred nodded, and Garrett threw a right at it. Even at half speed, it still had some force behind it and his fist smacked the leather satisfyingly. Wilfred glanced at his hand, a grin spreading wide. "That's all I've got to do?"

"That's it."

"Awesome," Wilfred said. "I can do that."

"Great!" Garrett said enthusiastically. "Let's hop in the ring and we'll get started."

The two guys practicing takedowns finished up their sparring session while Garrett laced on his own set of gloves. As they got out, Garrett caught them glancing at Wilfred with raised eyebrows and smirks. Feeling a flash of irritation, Garrett had to refrain from saying anything to them. Wilfred's head sank, but he slid the punch mitts under the bottom rope just the same. Good man, Garrett decided. He climbed the steps and stepped through the ropes. He nodded down at Wilfred. "Water's fine, bud, come on up."

Wilfred climbed up the steps slowly and glanced at the edge of the canvas. It didn't seem like he had much room to walk. He lifted the top rope tentatively. There was a lot more resistance to them than he thought there would be. Cautiously, he raised one meaty leg up and over the middle rope, pushing the top rope up even further as he entered. But his other foot hooked the middle rope and he fell hard on his face. Watching from the pair of heavy bags by the front windows, the MMA guys snickered loudly and Garrett wheeled on them. "Could happen to anyone," he said angrily.

"Motherfucker fell like a pancake," one of them crowed. He was burly without any real definable muscle to him. Garrett had seen him work the heavy bag before. The guy had a punch on him, but couldn't go longer than a few minutes without wheezing like a geriatric smoker. He splayed his arms out and pantomimed falling forward, his head thumping on an invisible barrier.

Wilfred pulled himself to his feet. Wordlessly, he got out of the ring—this time without falling—and walked down the steps as fast as he could manage. Garrett hopped through the ropes and off the edge of the ring onto the mats. He caught up with Wilfred halfway across the room, almost to the lockers. "Hey, man, look, fuck those guys."

Wilfred just shook his head. "I just want to go, okay? Just let me go."

Ed was watching him silently, his eyes far off and his face unreadable. Murphy at that point would have said to him softly that he couldn't save them all. It was true. He couldn't force Wilfred to stay. Garrett pursed his lips and tapped the kid's shoulder. "All right, Wilfred."

He let the kid walk without another word. Turning to give the two assholes a piece of his mind, he was just in time to see a woman light out from the office behind the counter. He hadn't seen her when he entered. The office windows were seemingly eternally shuttered and the door half closed. He knew her. The scarred face was a dead giveaway. He'd never asked her or Danny about the marks and neither had offered up any mention of them, but they had been long healed when he knew her when she was eighteen or so. That had been just a shade over half a decade ago, he reckoned as she streaked across the room.

"Put up your fists," she bellowed at the two.

"What?" the other guy asked. He was thinner than his companion and more defined, but he was squeamish about getting really hit and had absolutely no future in the sport he fancied.

"Put up your fists so I'm not sucker punching a couple of tiny dicked wannabe bullying assholes."

The bigger guy laughed uncertainly. "Lady, I don't know who you are, but—"

"I'm the owner's daughter, that's who the hell I am." She stopped just feet short of them, her arms coming up. "You got two choices. You get out and never show your faces around here again or I break your jaws and you can explain to the doctors how your fat mouths landed you in the ER and just who put you there."

Garrett started across the room. From the office door, Danny, the old goat of the owner, leaned against the door frame, watching his daughter with a faint look of pride. He tipped an imaginary cap at Garrett and he nodded back, slipping his hands out of the boxing gloves and tossing them aside. He came to a halt just behind her, eyes steely and watchful Brianna glanced back over her shoulder, her brown eyes challenging until she realized who it was and then she nodded just slightly.

The big guy was starting to look angry. "C'mon, the guy took a fall, it was pretty damn funny."

"Yeah," his buddy agreed. "I'm really sorry we got a sense of humor."

"The door or my fists. You got three seconds to make up your mind or I'm going to get real antsy about making it up for you." She practically purred as she said that. Garrett could see the tension in her waist and hips. She was ready to throw a punch. Or ten.

"We've been customers here for a year, and this is how you treat us?" the smaller guy asked.

"You'll get a refund for the time left on your membership. But as of tonight, yeah, you're done here." A little louder so everyone in the gym could hear, she said, "That's how this place is run. Everybody's welcome. No one feels threatened or ashamed This is a community and if you can't behave, you're out on your ass. No exceptions."

The big guy glanced at Garrett questioningly, as though he were asking if he could believe this shit. Garrett could indeed believe that shit. He'd only known Brianna briefly before she left for college, but what he remembered about her was a lot of her dad's anger—and even more of his righteousness. He shrugged. "I'd do what the lady asks."

Biggun spat sideways and glared at him. "You gonna fight us too, Garrett?" It wasn't some question asked of bravado, but of genuine worry. Around the Hammerdown, people knew you didn't fuck with him.

Garrett stuck his thumbs in the waistband of his shorts where his pockets would be on a pair of pants. "Won't have to. You ever see Danny in the ring? Sure you have. She's Danny 2.0. Faster. Meaner. Prettier." She glanced back over her shoulder at him. He smiled at her and she looked back at the two guys.

"Time's up. You going now or are we throwing you out?"

The two men glanced at each other. "We'll go," the smaller guy mumbled. Returning from the lockers, Wilfred stared at the two oncoming guys, stiff as a board. They brushed around him, muttering apologies. He headed for the front door wordlessly.

Garrett came up to him and said quietly, "Come on back sometime. We'll work the weights and I'll show you some more basic stuff."

Close behind him now, Brianna chimed in, "Don't let those assholes ruin your time here. Any time you want to come in the door, you're welcome. Don't let them win. You are better than they are."

Wilfred looked sideways at them from hooded eyes. Finally, he mumbled, "I'll come back. Maybe… maybe you guys could show me a little bit about fighting."

Garrett slapped him on the back. "Good man."

* * *

Brianna watched the two dickheads leave and blew out a pensive breath. She turned back to Garrett Moranis. "So," she said.

He cleared his throat. "So," he said amicably.

He still looked good. Better, in fact. The gray at his temples and salted liberally throughout his hair contrasted well with his scarred, youthful face. He had a few more minute dents and dings and someone, somewhere along the way had broken his nose once or twice. But his eyes were still soft, a complete contradiction of the crags of his face and hard lines of his frame. Everything about him was clean-cut, professional.

As a teenager, she'd had her fair share of fantasies with him in a featured guest spot. She was young then and susceptible to his mysterious bad boy charm—not that he'd ever turned them on her, given her age. As a largely rational (well, part-time rational, anyways) adult, she had to admit Teenage Bri was pretty damn right. He was definitely not an ugly man.

Danny limped across the gym to join them. Before he could get there, Brianna asked Garrett quietly, "You're really going to throw in a compliment to a woman just before she's about to tear someone's nuts off?"

"Had to be said." Even as the corner of his mouth lifted, she could see him shuffle his feet. Was he nervous? Good. That made them even.

What came next was sheer impulse, one she had to act on before she lost her nerve. She stepped closer to him and brought her head up. Tall herself, she didn't have to stretch too high to kiss him on the cheek, flashing back to something her mother always said when she was a kid and had nightmares so bad she'd wake up screaming—when you're most afraid, that's the time to pretend to be brave and soon enough you'll realize you don't need to pretend anymore. She let the kiss linger just long enough to leave it an open-ended question, liking the mixed smells of his fresh sweat and the subtle last dregs of his aftershave. Citrus and something darker, she thought, something that reminded her of fine cigars without the stench of tobacco. Out of the corner of her eye, she could see the accountant grin a little bit knowingly, as though they were sharing a secret. What was his name? Crap.

He flushed. "Oh, hey, I'm all sweaty, and…"

"Don't care," Brianna said glibly. "You're getting a hug too. I'm a hugger. Deal with it.

Taken aback, Garrett didn't react except to bring a hand up to the top of her back, giving her an awkward, brief hug. Her eyes were like almonds swimming in milk, and he couldn't avert his gaze. He understood immediately what Ed had been talking about. She was not lovely in the traditional manner, but she was striking. When he'd known her last, she was just barely an adult and not really someone he'd have thought of as a sexual being—she was too young and he was in his mid-twenties. But now, he could appreciate the way the scars emphasized her squared face and slightly off-kilter eyes. Even her long bob seemed to emphasize the scars, not hide them. He liked the look. Not beautiful, no. But striking and unique in a way that drew him in like a magnet.

She pulled back slightly and smiled at him. "Thanks. For the backup, for the compliment. And for keeping an eye on this place for my dad," she said as her old man joined them. "I heard you helped him through a couple of tight spots."

He rubbed the back of his neck. "Well. I. Um."

Danny for his part really did resemble an old goat—his goatee was long and tufted, and his full head of white hair looked both shaggy and immensely comfortable, especially in the winter. He pretended not to notice the kiss. "Nice work, Bri."

She arched an eyebrow at him. It had the effect of drawing the white slashes of scars on the side of her face up. "Not mad?"

"At getting rid of those two lumps of shit? Nope." He patted her shoulder and glanced at Garrett. "Thanks for taking the kid under your wing. Meant to do it myself, but…" He tapped his temple, smiling grimly. Danny had once earned a fair chunk of change fighting in his own ring and across the States—even taking time now and then to do some fighting tours overseas in countries where the prize money was a bit higher and the rules a bit looser. Along the way, he'd suffered a few concussions, and sometimes his memory got a little bit fuzzy. It was usually limited to little things at first—leaving the lights on when he left, confusing birthdays, forgetting to pay his tabs, that sort of thing. But lately, his lapses came more frequently.

"No problem. Hope he comes back." He thought about it for a minute. "If he does—his name's Wilfred, but I didn't catch a last name—let me know. If he's serious, I'll spring for him a year's membership."

Brianna wondered if he was trying to impress her. She knew he had money—he'd helped her dad a few times making the bills, she knew that much, and her father every time had told her solemnly that Garrett had tried to swear him to secrecy on it. He wasn't the sort of guy who flashed money around just to brag about it. Maybe he genuinely was looking after the guy. She supposed it could happen, even in Rankin Flats. "That's kind, but really, we…"

Garrett clenched his jaw. "I'm not… look, guys like that, they're the ones that need to be here, you know? I don't mean him being out of shape. I mean, here's a guy who was deathly afraid of coming in here, and he does it anyways. That kid had guts, whether he knew it or not. The way things shook out, I hope he does come back and if he does, I want him to know he's got friends here." Looking her squarely in the eyes, he said, "I don't mean anything more by it."

If he was playing her, he was good. She nodded slowly. "All right. We'll give it a couple of days and if he isn't back, we'll reach out to him."

"Good. So Ed—"

That was the accountant's name. She wanted to slap her own forehead, glad he'd said it before she had to come up with the name.

"-tells me you're going to help out around here? Permanently, I hope."

She smiled. "Yes, and I hope so too. I graduated in December—"

"Congratulations."

"Thanks. I got real homesick, so I came back to work with my dad."

Danny puffed up when she reached an arm around him and squeezed him to her side. "Already getting the accounts straightened up and she's starting up a women's defense course soon."

"That's great," he said, and meant it. He wanted to see more of her. The thought made him flush a little bit as he tried hard not to glance down at the flare of her hips in those nicely snug jeans. He wondered if it would be too forward to ask her out in front of her dad.

"So I was wondering," she said quietly, a blush blossoming in her cheeks. "This Saturday, did you… that is, would you want to—"

"Maybe go to dinner with me?" he blurted out.

She laughed lightly and prettily and God he wanted her. "If you wanted to help us paint on Saturday."

"Swing and a miss, buddy," Ed said cheerfully. Garrett hadn't even noticed his friend walk up behind him. "Hello again, Brianna, lovely to see you. Danny."

"Hi again, Ed," she said, grinning at him openly and enjoying Garrett's uncomfortable stammering. She offered up Ed a hug too and he accepted gladly.

Garrett shifted uncomfortably. "I... oh." Painting? There wasn't much more he didn't want to do. Painting was about as dull a Saturday as he could have. He could be on a flight to Vegas or catch a marathon at the dollar theater that showed odd trios of movies that somehow all seemed to mesh together. Painting sounded like hell.

"But you could take me to dinner afterwards," she said softly, shooting her dad a glance and blushing even harder. Danny gave Garrett the type of murderous glare he'd seen in the old man's fight promo posters from his early years.

"Well, in that case, painting sounds great." Remembering Rose and Ed's invitation, he slapped his head. "I'm sorry. About dinner... I've got this thing at Ed's I forgot about. Ed..."

"Come along!" Ed said cheerfully. "My wife would love to have you. I know a double date might not be the most romantic first dinner together you could imagine, but Rose is making the best pasta in the world, I kid you not."

"That sounds lovely," Brianna said. "If I'm not imposing."

"Oh hell no," Ed said. "We'll be happy to have you."

"And what about you, Ed?" Danny asked gruffly. "Got any plans on Saturday morning? Come by, grab a roller."

"Oh, I... uh..." Ed scratched the back of his head. "Well, you know, Rose has been on an out-of-town thing for her work, and she'll probably want me home that day, you know, just settling back in."

Garrett winked at Brianna. "Oh, I'm sure she'd let you out of the house for such a good cause. They just added some new cell phone towers to that area. Hang on, I'll bet we can get ahold of her if she's out of the mountains." He darted off to retrieve his cell from the gym bag and came back, already talking rapidly into it. "...bring a guest to dinner? Oh you're the absolute best, Rose. And do you mind if we grab Ed that morning? They're painting the Hammerdown and... oh absolutely. Yup. He's squirming like a fish on the hook. I think he might actually try to murder me. Hey, yeah, come along too. Gotta imagine the more hands, the merrier." He raised his eyebrows at Brianna and she nodded, smiling. "Yup, just got the affirmative. We'll see you then. Thanks Rose." He hung up and grinned at Ed. "All square, bud."

"Thanks," he said darkly to Garrett.

Brianna saw the look and said quickly, "Really, if you don't want to…"

"Nah," Ed said, seizing upon an opportunity. "Just means Garrett volunteered to bring donuts and coffee. Good coffee, too. You skimp and bring some store-brand crap, I'm sending in your taxes with all the flags I can create."

"Thanks, man," Garrett grinned. He gave Brianna another hug while Danny harrumphed. "See you Saturday."

* * *

Before Ed could pull out of the lot, Garrett jogged up and he rolled his window down. "What's up?"

Garrett pulled out his wallet, dug through the bills, and tossed one into the open window. "Your bet from earlier." Ed's booming laugh followed him all the way to his own car.

Chapter 5

"I'm telling you, it could work," Murphy insisted with a poker face so solid Garrett couldn't decide if he was in earnest or not.

"Murph," Garrett sighed. "There's no way."

"Why not?"

Garrett tried to focus on the road. Thick traffic oozed through the shopping district like toothpaste being squeezed out of the tube. There had been a crash early that morning, some out of state idiot driving on the ice for the first time, and although it had been cleared, the traffic was still backed up. "How would the memory foam reshape itself to the cups after you had a bigger cup in there?"

"It's not a vagina, man," Murphy said with exasperation in his voice, as though he were explaining this to a child. "It wouldn't get ruined for all other cups if you put in a sixty-four ouncer. Oh shit, I'm sorry, I forgot you wouldn't know what that analogy means. Lemme explain. See, when a man with a big penis inserts it into a woman's—"

"You're the worst kind of asshole." Garrett laughed.

"Guilty. See, you'd make it square. Not round. That way, if you wanted to put something odd shaped in there, you ain't tryin' to figure out how to put a square peg in a round hole."

Garrett flipped off a car that wouldn't let him in. "No, then you're just putting a round peg in a square hole. You can't just change up the shape of it. Gas stations everywhere would have a fit."

"But that's why we use memory foam. It would still grip whatever you put in there. And if it was bigger than the hole, you could just sorta push it around, reshape it." He balled up a fist and mimed smacking it into his open palm, the gesture made a little weirder as the fist plunged halfway through the hand. "Bam. Game changer, bitch."

"Huh," Garrett said unconvinced. He took a right and almost immediately the traffic lightened.

"About twelve blocks up, stay to the right. So?"

Garrett thought about it for a minute, his fingers flexing on the steering wheel. "Do you know where we'd even get memory foam?"

"Well, we could maybe get one of those pillows or mattresses or whatever."

"Uh huh. And how would that work? We just cut it up and it's going to make perfect little cubes? We're not talking brownies here, Murph."

The trendy shopping area had given way to a string of cafes and small chain stores. Only a few cars lined their parking lots. It was too late in the morning for breakfast diners and shoppers and too early yet for the lunch crowd to start battering down doors. For Garrett and Murphy, this was one of their magic hours, those inauspicious times of day they could get their work done and fit right in with the rest of Rankin Flats.

Murphy glanced down his nose at him, a gesture born of his need in life to wear glasses and carried over into death by habit, one he'd been unable to break even three decades after he'd been buried. "Well, obviously we're not talkin' brownies," he said, exasperated, as though he were talking to a stubborn child.

"Besides," Garrett said, "you've seen me try to put stuff together before. Do you really think I could build something like this?"

Murphy snickered. "Good point."

"And who would we pitch it to? We don't exactly know a lot of Hudsucker types."

Murphy considered this. "Well, we find one. And by we, I mean I find one. And then we do a few of the old ghost tricks, you know, give him a real show, something to floor him. And when we got his attention, bam. We show him the cup holder. Wait. No. The stuff holder. Huh? Huh?"

Garrett sighed. "Well, it's no Segtrain, but it's got merit." The Segtrain had been the greatest of Murphy's ideas in Garrett's estimation, though he would have likely added quotation marks around greatest in derision. In Missoula for a Cat-Griz game, they'd watched ten or so of Missoula's yuppiest of yuppies, complete with smatterings of soul patches, skinny jeans, and leather thonged sandals, as they played what looked like a game of flag football on Segways in a dorm's parking lot. But even the football wasn't a football—they instead used a floppy Frisbee-looking thing that Murphy muttered was probably a remolded biodegradable, pressed hunk of cow shit. Both of them had to begrudgingly admit though that the Segways looked like a hell of a lot of fun. On the long drive across the state back to Rankin Flats, Murphy had come up with idea for the Segtrain, a long Segway that could be used to haul around people in pedestrian heavy areas. Step on, go up the block, step off. What could be simpler? Murphy had argued for hours while Garrett tried not to jump out of the car at a high speed after unsuccessfully trying to explain the power it would need ("Build bigger batteries!") and charging times ("Have three or four charging while you use one!").

As they got close to the coffee shop, Murphy started to pay more attention. "Okay, the Brisktro just has street parking. Grab a spot when you see it."

Garrett nodded and kept an eye out. "You're sure this place has no cameras?"

"Pretty sure." Murphy caught his glare and shrugged. "What? Who's to say they ain't hidin' one under the gluten-free, sugar-free, no-preservative—" Garrett made a gagging noise "-all natural, free range, raised-with-love-and-tenderness kale cookies?"

Garrett found a spot and slowed to turn in. "I hate Brisktros. Let's do this fast."

As they stopped and Garrett grabbed his baton from the back, Murphy said, "You're in a mood today. What's up?"

Garrett clipped the baton's sheath to his belt. "Nothing. Sorry. Just a long night."

They got out and started walking to the Brisktro. Part of a trendy coffee chain with baked goods aimed at the bandwagon that attached themselves to every latest health food scare, the Brisktro was exactly the sort of place Garrett dreaded with every fiber of his being. They feasted on the fear of hypochondriacs who wanted to be part of the in-crowd of people who really did suffer from celiac disease. The clientele and business reflected each other's douchebaggery and gave good coffee places a bad name.

Passing through a light pole, Murphy asked, "What, something happen at the gym?"

Garrett shrugged uncomfortably. "Kind of." A knot of people were coming so he held up his cell phone to his ear, pretending to talk into it so he didn't attract attention. "You really want to know?"

"Yeah, of course, man."

Garrett stopped. They weren't in a rush and the explanation needed more time than it would take to get to the Brisktro. "Danny's daughter. Brianna."

Murphy frowned and thought about it. "The one with the scarred face, right? Haven't thought about her in a while. She okay?"

"Yeah, she's fine." Garrett couldn't help but let slip a little smile. "She's great." He launched into a quick explanation of Brianna's return to town and the night's events. Murphy listened, his head half-cocked as he watched cars go by.

When Garrett wrapped up, Murphy frowned. "I'm confused. How is any of that a bad thing? You got a date on Saturday. It'll be good for you to knock the dust off that dick." His confusion turned slowly into realization. "Oh, you really like this one."

"Yeah," Garrett said softly. "And that's a problem."

"Shit."

"Yeah. Shit."

They trudged on a few more feet before Murphy stopped. "Hey."

Garrett half turned and kept walking. "Yeah?"

"Don't take it out on this kid."

Garrett should have been offended, but Richter Haas was still fresh in his mind. He nodded and tried on a sloppy smile. "I'll be as gentle as a kitten."

The first thing Garrett noticed upon entering in the Brisktro was a sharp vinegar-like tang, not at all the earthy, homey waft of coffee brewing he'd been expecting. Someone had gone massively overboard on the cleaning supplies the night before and no one had bothered airing it out. The place was nearly empty save for a couple huddled over their phones in a corner and a jittery, rail thin man behind a counter and a rack filled with plastic-wrapped muffins and fresh fruit that Garrett had to admit didn't look half bad.

The kid looked eighteen going on fifty. Though free of wrinkles, his face and arms were dotted with sores, some freshly scratched. Garrett wondered if the kid was seeing bugs right at that moment and had an idea the answer was pretty blatant. He watched Garrett like a hawk as he entered with eyes saddled with black bags underneath. He grinned nervously. He was too young or hadn't been using long enough for the telltale brown teeth. "Hey hey, welcome to Brisktro's we got a special blend today a Sumatran Arabica that'll just blow your socks off or maybe I can get you something to eat we've got some great muffins fresh made just this morning." He talked just like that, rapid-fire without any sort of pause. The kid was tweaked out of his mind.

"Mikey sent me," Garrett said quietly, and leaned in as Murphy took up a position near the door so he could watch both the street and the couple in the store. "Happy Times, right?"

The kid whipped a glance at the couple and shook his head. "Sorry man we don't carry that blend here."

"No?" Garrett asked. He pulled out his wallet and dug through it, making sure the kid caught a good glance at the fat sheaf of twenties he had in there. "How about just whatever you got cooking, huh?" He emphasized cooking and Murphy snickered.

The kid swallowed hard. The couple was completely absorbed in whatever game or conversation they had going on and didn't look up. He poured Garrett a go cup of coffee, rang him up, and wrote in a shaking hand on there, "Outback 5 mins." Garrett shook his head at the terrible spelling, but paid for his coffee and left.

Out back—and definitely not outback—he tossed the coffee into a dumpster, wiping his hands disdainfully on his pants. "At least the smell's better out here," he muttered to himself.

A few minutes later, the door opened and the junkie dealer stepped out, grinning nervously, and Murphy followed shortly The dealer reached up and scratched at a scab furiously. "Hey man not cool coming to my place of business you know—"

Garrett grabbed him by the throat and slammed him up against the door. "Last night you dealt to three college kids on campus."

The junkie slapped at his arm. "Hey man what the fuck?"

"Gentle as a kitten," Murphy sighed.

Garrett pulled the junkie forward just far enough he could knock the kid's head off the door again. The kid's hands, surprisingly big, slapped at Garrett's hands and forearm. "Shut the hell up and listen. You dealt them what you told them was a gram, except it wasn't. You kept a little rock for yourself, which you then smoked in your Ford Aerostar. You went home to your place at eleven fifty-two Hardy Avenue."

"Who are you a cop?"

Garrett smiled grimly, shook his head, and continued, "From there, you played your PlayStation 2 until two in the morning. You went to bed, but you didn't sleep, at least, not very well. You scream in your sleep, did you know that?"

"Who are you?" the junkie asked again, his dilated eyes wide.

"Stop. Dealing." Garrett emphasized the words with pokes to the junkie's forehead with his free hand. He extended his leg just a hair and pulled the teenager forward. Never seeing his foot, the junkie tripped and fell. Garrett rolled him over with his foot and planted it on the kid's chest, leaning hard enough to make it hurt just a little bit but not so much that he'd break something. "Or I'm going to come back here and—" His cell phone buzzed. Annoyed, Garrett took it out and glanced at it. "Hang on one second," he said to the junkie.

Gaping at Garrett, he said groggily, "Sure yeah take your time I can wait."

Garrett held a finger up to his lips and answered the call. "Kinda working here, man."

It was Ed. "Working? Working on what?"

"On a job," Garrett said with great emphasis on "job," shrugging apologetically at the junkie.

"Oh." Then Ed caught on. "Ohhhhh! It's about that ledger. Can you come by the office?"

"Sure. I'm about done, I think." Garrett shoved his foot down a little harder. "We're about done here, right?"

"Hey yeah why not."

Garrett grinned as though the junkie were a steak he was about to rip into. "Good man. Be right there." Thinking back to the muffins, he said, "Kid, you didn't package those muffins yourself, did you?" The dealer whipped his head back and forth like he was having a seizure. Back to Ed, Garrett said, "Hey, you want a muffin? I'm right here, and..."

"Nah I ain't hungry," the junkie said.

Garrett stomped down harder, forcing the breath out of the kid's lung's. On the other end, Ed said, "Yeah, sure, I could go for one."

"Be right there." Garrett hung up and returned his focus to the junkie. "Where was I? Something menacing, something threatening, yadda yadda yadda. Look, kid, just tell me who the hell your dealer is, and I'm out of your hair."

"He'll kill me man he's crazy."

"All right," Garrett said quietly. He unsheathed the baton and flicked it to its full length.

The kid stammered, "W-what the hell is that thing?"

"Steel baton," Garrett said. "Doesn't look like much, but I shit you not, first hit, it's going to hurt like hell, like if someone wound up and threw a baseball at you full speed. Second one might fracture a bone, but that's if you're lucky. See, I'm pretty strong. I'm guessing it'll full on break it, a skinny guy like you." He jabbed the end against the kid's chest. "Especially a soft spot like your ribs. Those'll snap like toothpicks in two, maybe three good hits. Then the little fingers on each hand. You'll still be able to do a lot of shit that way, but-

"Wait wait shit wait." The kid rattled out a name and an address, and a lengthy description on how to get there, more than Garrett needed.

Looking up at Murphy, Garrett said, "You think of anything else?"

As Murphy shook his head, the junkie looked at the blank space, perturbed. "Who you talkin' to man?"

Glancing back down, Garrett said, "Shut up." His foot still on the kid's chest, Garrett leaned over to look him square in the eyes. "You tell them I'm coming, and I come back here and force feed little broken pieces of your crack pipe to you. Quit dealing, kid. Go to college. Or high school. Just... clean up your fuckin' act before someone a whole lot less friendly comes around." He sheathed the baton and stepped off the kid's chest. He even offered him a hand to his feet, which the kid took with a look of dumb amazement. "Now... how much for a couple of muffins?"

* * *

On the road to Ed's office, Garrett called up Monica. "Tip for you. Meth dealer." He rattled off the pertinent details. "Do me a solid and wait a couple of days on him."

"Do I want to know why?"

"Going after his suppliers. You'll have them all tied up with a pretty little bow too if you give me until, say, Monday."

She sighed. "Fine. You've got whatever time you need. But if this guy bolts and rats on you, these assholes will be in the wind."

"And we lose a drop from the ocean."

After Garrett hung up, Murphy glanced at him, his cheeks sucked in slightly and fat lips pursed. "This girl—"

"Woman, if you mean Brianna."

"Mm hm."

Garrett sighed and rubbed at his jaw. "I know everything you're going to say. I've run it all through my head a hundred times since last night. I can't expose us. I know. The work has to come first."

Looking out the window, Murphy seemed troubled. "What we do is important. But the way you've been lately... I don't know. Maybe it's time we change some things up. Stare into the abyss, the abyss stares back, you know."

Garrett didn't, but he nodded as though he did anyways. "What are

you saying?" he asked as he made a turn a little too tightly, nearly sending the back of the Hyundai into a fishtail on the ice. He was still wound up.

"Maybe this bromance bullshit ain't enough anymore. We wrote these rules. Maybe it's time we change them." His clothes were changing rapidly now, from his suit to a pair of sweats and sandals with a brown UCLA sweater. It was an odd ensemble, one Garrett had never seen before. Noting Garrett's little double take, Murphy glanced down and sighed. "It's the outfit I was wearing the first time my girlfriend and I fought about getting married. I was high on something, heroin, I think. That dealer, this conversation… I don't know, glimmers of the past, I guess."

"You ever think about her?"

"Every day," Murphy said truthfully. "My boy's got her big ol' dopey crooked teeth. Like white picket fences, just jammed up in there and left in the sun a little too long."

"You want, I could call up a florist down there, have them deliver something yearly to her grave—"

"No." It was quiet but firm. "But thank you." It was a while before either spoke again. Ed's office wasn't all that far from the Brisktro, but traffic was still crazy on the main thoroughfares, leading to them having to go a few blocks out of their way and circle around. As they passed a lone figure wrapped up in a drab winter coat and snow pants at a bus station, Murphy said, "I think you should play it out. Saturday, I mean." He twisted in his seat and partially through the door to watch the person as they went by. Garrett pulled over a block ahead and spun a U-turn. Pulling into a parking lot near the bus stop, he called out to the figure to offer him a ride. There was no response except for a pair of middle fingers shot their way. Murphy couldn't help but bark out a laugh. "This fucking city."

* * *

Guzman Accounting wasn't advertised on the outside. Ed didn't need it to be. He worked for family and a few select friends, and oversaw the various accounts and businesses of one semi-retired professional poker player by the name of Garrett Moranis. That was enough for one man and a small crew. Over the years, smart investments by Ed (backed surreptitiously by some information gathering by Murphy and relayed through Garrett as "inside tips") had paid off handsomely and Garrett's fortunes had risen. Ed's need for other clients dwindled to the point where he could focus on Garrett's investments, though as of late, he'd started to talk about expanding to take on some charities and small businesses to Garrett's approval.

In the meantime, though, his small square building in the suburbs worked well for him. In the spring and summer, the walkway to the front door would be lined with tulips, usually nipped down by deer, and the weeping willow near the parking lot provided shade for the cars and pedestrians. In the last half of February, though, the ground was still crusted with snow and ice, and the walkway was made only slightly less treacherous with copious amounts of rock salt. It wasn't good for the concrete, but broken bones were more of an immediate threat. And although the temperature had dipped into the single digits just the day before, it was forty degrees by the time Garrett walked up the path. Fat sheaves of snow had fallen from the roof and onto the lawn. As he passed under the awning, a thick wet fist of snow splattered the top of his head, much to Murphy's crowed delight. He huddled closer to the door, brushing himself off and muttering vague obscenities about Frosty's no doubt sweet and undeserving mother before heading in.

Stamping his feet on the welcome mat, he wiped at his face with the back of his arm. Ed's secretary, Leila Graham, glanced up from her typing and had to stifle a giggle. That was unusual from her—she usually maintained a strict air of absolute, abject disdain for anyone who came in the door, regardless of their status. She allowed herself precisely two seconds of mirth before rising and replacing her smile with her usual mask of frowning disapproval. "My apologies, Mr. Moranis, let me get you a towel."

He knew better than to try to get her to call him Garrett. The white-haired woman was as firm about that as she was about calling her cousin by marriage "Mr. Guzman" instead of Ed. She brought him a dishtowel from the break room. "Can I get you a coffee, bottled water, or an espresso?"

"An espresso?" Garrett asked. It had been a while since he'd been to the office and that hadn't been an option the last time.

Ms. Graham permitted herself another brief smile. "Yes, sir. Mr. Guzman bought it for the office for Christmas. He asked that we request one thing, a sort of gift for the place aside from our individual bonuses, and that was what we picked."

"If you don't mind, I'd love one. Thanks." He thought for a second, wondering if he could score a hat-trick of smiles from her. That would be a first. "How are the college courses going?"

She sighed irritably. "Terrible. Latin is impenetrable. The verb structure is just..." She shook her head. "Go on ahead to Mr. Guzman's office. I'll be along with your espresso soon."

Damn. Well, he tried. "Thank you, Ms. Graham."

While the rest of the building was decorated with tasteful watercolor and oil landscapes and scenes from talented, largely unknown artists from around the United States, Ed's office looked as though a teenager had blitzed it in a mad shopping spree through a Spencer's. When he met Rose, he'd asked her to help him spruce up his old office, then a one room place in a really shitty part of town. Knowing he ran a very real risk of being robbed, Rose went on a tear with Garrett through a shopping mall and several online sites specializing in the sorts of things one might find in a dorm. She and Garrett decorated the office together during one of Ed's lunch breaks, and when he came back, he nearly doubled over in laughter. When he moved shop to the nicer location, he refused to change a thing, so enamored was he of Rose's gift for the madcap.

There were not one but three lava lamps of various sizes. A life-size cardboard cutout of Jean-Claude Van Damme stood in one corner, adorned with a Burger King crown that had to have been a decade and a half old. Atop a row of filing cabinets was one of those old pin art toys, with the outline of Rose's lips, perpetually blowing Ed a kiss. And everywhere there were photographs of the two of them and Ed's family, of whom several lived right there within the city. Had someone come in for a professional appointment who didn't know Ed—or more specifically, Rose—they might have thought it was a single bachelor's office, not that of a successful, happily married man.

Ed himself sat in his leather chair, flipping through documents and humming along to a country song on the radio. For a man with such a half-crazed office, he was as well put together as any other professional Garrett had met. Ed prided himself on looking good, even if he made most of his clothing purchases off clearance racks. He afforded himself a minimal salary for his position, opting instead to pump that money back to his employees. With what Rose made, they still lived a comfortable upper middle class lifestyle, but Ed himself didn't bring in much. It had been entirely his choice, one Garrett respected.

Ed glanced up from the papers. "You're wet," he said unhelpfully.

Garrett pulled out a plastic wrapped muffin and tossed it underhand to Ed, who fumbled it and fished it up off the ground. "Nice catch...

uh… famous… baseball person catcher guy."

Unwrapping his muffin, Ed raised an eyebrow. "Mike Piazza? Ivan Rodriguez?"

At the same time, Murphy, who was leaning against the door frame, said, "Berra? Campanella?"

Garrett waved Ed off. "I'm shit with sports." Checking behind him to see if Ms. Graham was coming, he leaned in and muttered, "I almost got her to smile three times today. Once when I came in covered in snow, once when she was talking about the espresso machine. Made the mistake of asking about her college classes."

The accountant whistled. "Wow, that's an accomplishment." Ed bit into his muffin and visibly gagged. "Ugh. What the heck is this?"

"Flax and almond seed flour with… I don't remember what kind of fruit. Orange rind or some bullshit."

"It tastes like… I don't know, like how I imagine bathroom spray would taste like if you squirted some on old moldy bread."

"Got it, it's bad."

"Like the water from a filthy hippy's bath after he's spent a year not using toilet paper."

"Enough," Garrett snickered.

"Like if you baked San Francisco in muffin tins. The entire city. That's what this would taste like." He tossed the muffin in the garbage. "Sorry, Garrett, can't do it. I hate to waste food, but that's not edible. That's baked mulch." He grinned slyly as Garrett laughed. Pushing forward a file on his desk, he said, "Here, sign these. Tax documents, some trust paperwork for your guy out in California."

"Eggar," Murphy said, all trace of good cheer lost. "His name is Eggar."

"Eggar," Garrett chided Ed gently. "That's his name."

Glancing at him curiously, Ed said, "Yeah, of course it is."

Ms. Graham knocked on the edge of the door and brought in Garrett's espresso, to his great appreciation. "It's in the job description," she said gruffly. "Is there anything else I can get the both of you?"

Garrett offered up the bag. "We've got a muffin here. Kind of a health food thing from the Brisktro."

Her eyes lit up, even if the rest of her face did not. "I love that place."

Garrett handed off the remaining wrapped muffin. "By all means." She took it as fast as a bird pecking at seed and shut the door behind her. "Just as well," Garrett said brightly. "Might have been made by a meth head."

Ed turned pale. "It... I... what?"

"Probably not. He said he didn't, but I had my foot on his ribs and I think he would've told me damn near anything. I think they have a morning crew that comes in, does the baked goods or brings them in from somewhere. But still, yeah, there's a pretty good chance a tweaker made those."

Ed shook his head. "You're unbelievable."

"I couldn't agree more. Also amazing, charming, handsome, a little gassy. Now, did you get the ledger translated or not?"

Ed leaned back in his chair, his fingers playing together like a mad scientist. "Interesting choice of words, my friend." He pulled the ledger out from a desk drawer and set it on the desk facing Garrett. he opened it to a random page and took out a notebook of his own. "I had some trouble at first. I thought, well, hey, this looks like a simple substitution cipher. The letters seem to fit a pattern, some of which look like vowels and consonants in the sort of usual places you'd expect. But—"

"Oh holy shit, how much of this do we have to listen to?" Murphy moaned.

"-no matter what letters I tried, nothing seemed to make sense. They almost seemed like words, but they weren't. Then I stepped away from it for a while and came back. First thing I read is one of those little notes on the edges of the paper. See those?" He tapped a couple of words on the side of the page. "I thought I recognized one of the words. "Arschloch. Luschel. They looked familiar."

Impatiently, Garrett made a "hurry up" rolling motion with his finger.

"German," Ed said, exasperated at having to cut short his cleverness. "The whole thing was in German. Arschloch means asshole, luschel as best as I can figure it means idiot or jerk. He couldn't help but make little asides to himself about all the people he didn't like, or the women he, uh, did. If he hadn't been such a prick, I might not have ever figured it out without help. But I think I did it." He handed over the other notebook. "Names. Dates. Betting figures, how much they owed, paid, the juice."

"Nice work, Ed," Garrett said, real enthusiasm in his voice.

"One other thing, though. There were a couple of names in there. No betting numbers, just their last names and a date."

Murphy stepped forward a couple of feet. "Hoooly shit."

"Holy shit," Garrett breathed in agreement.

"Did I do good?" Ed asked. He grinned. "I did good, right?"

Garrett slapped his desk and stood up. "Ed, you killed it. You didn't make copies? You deleted your browsing history and everything?"

Ed almost looked offended. "Please."

Garrett nodded and snatched up the books. "You're a good guy."

"Even if I am helping a filthy, lowdown thief?" Ed asked primly.

"You're the Little John to my Robin Hood," Garrett said.

"Speaking of," Ed said as he got up to show Garrett out, "You and your Maid Marian still on for Saturday?"

"I…" Garrett glanced back at Murphy, trying to pass it off as though he were looking back at the door. The ghost didn't meet his eyes. He turned back, trying to appear nonchalant. "Yeah. I think so."

* * *

One of Garrett's two spare bedrooms was made up into a small workout room. There wasn't much to it—rowing and bike machines faced a small television, and a set of dumbbells and a workout bench sat in another corner. A mattress was shoved up against one wall, his bed for when Auggie made her occasional excursions out to see him. He would take the mattress and sacrifice the master suite to her, despite her protests that she could afford a hotel.

The other bedroom was dubbed by Murphy as the War Room. To anyone entering the condo, it would look like nothing more than a simple home office. A sleek Origin gaming computer blinked at the room with sleepy red lighting. Seated next to it was a large office printer, one of the best models on the market for both regular paper and picture printing. The thickly padded office chair was luxurious, fitting for a moderately wealthy playboy who looked as though he enjoyed his gaming toys. A top of the line shredder sat next to the desk like a patient dog waiting for its master. Apart from the computer desk, a reversible rolling dry erase board took up residence along the opposite wall. Garrett updated one side with meaningless property listings once a week or so to keep up appearances. The other side, kept scrupulously blank most of the time, was dedicated to the jobs they pulled and the recon Murphy provided. Another wall was covered in city maps with colored pins as well as a large cork currently devoid of any notes or pictures since they were between jobs.

When Garrett came in, he immediately wiped the junkie's name off the board and replaced it with the address the Brisktro employee had given him. Murphy floated through the wall moments later and corrected him on the lane number he'd written down. Garrett didn't doubt him—death cured all ills for ghosts, including the decay of the human brain, and Murphy's memory, while not perfect, sure as hell beat his. He capped the marker and tapped his chin with it. "I think I want to bring on a couple of people for that one, have them watch the trailer twenty-four seven."

"I can do that," Murphy said, a little put out.

Garrett turned and smiled peaceably. "Don't think there's much money to be made on this one, buddy."

"Not all of them are about cash," Murphy huffed.

"I know. And I appreciate the offer. But we've been going non-stop. I want you to take some time, go see your son, get in a day or two to yourself. And besides, we have this." Garrett tapped the ledger and Ed's notebook. "If there's any usable information in there, I want you here to handle it."

"Don't put the cart before the horse."

"Fair enough." Garrett began tearing pages out of the notebook and pinned them to the cork board so they could both look at them. He worked from the end backwards, figuring that the most recent entries would be potentially of more use. Line after line was filled with small bets. "Nothing we can use," Garrett muttered. "Small bets, small payoffs. Just like we thought."

Murphy grinned. "So let's go over the big names."

Garrett read the first one and wrote it on the board. "Brennerman, A. No bet listed."

Murphy read the second one. "Finson, J. That was the name I heard at the hospital." He grinned. "And he was clearly the guy in charge."

Lost in thought, Garrett sat at his computer and started searching for names. The area was littered with dozens of Finsons and Brennermans, and those were only the listed ones. "All right, we've got four J. Finsons, at least in the city. Statewide, there's another eight. Brennerman, that's four total. And unless she's a ninety-year-old nursing home resident from Helena, that leaves three."

He put the names up on the dry erase board and started some research. Facebook helped them narrow down the Finson field—since it had been a man on the phone, they could obviously weed out the female half. Searches on the remaining male J. Finsons brought up a few normal looking guys with normal looking lives. All save for one.

He was old, that much was certain, but how old was unclear. Tall and leathery skinned, he might have been handsome if it wasn't for the severe cast of his face. He looked like he ought to be chewing a cigar and staring down some bandits in an old Western film. Instead, he was wearing a navy blue suit and standing in front of a trio of black Lincoln Navigators, the newest model. The picture was from a business website—Exodian Chariots.

Murphy leaned over and slightly through his shoulder. "The guy had a deep voice, kind of rough and slow. Less Sam Elliot, more… what was that guy's name from Jurassic Park? The dinosaur guy, not the old one, but the hero?"

"I don't remember," Garrett said, shaking his head. "But I know who you're talking about." There was a name there—Jamie Finson. He wrote it up on the board and circled it. A few minutes delving around the Exodian Chariots website didn't reveal a physical address for them.

"Well, that's easy enough to remedy," Murphy said. "We call them up, request a car, and I follow them back. Nothing to that. I stick to Finson like glue, make sure he's our guy, and we see what kind of damage we can do to this bastard and his organization."

Garrett nodded. It was a good plan. The fury from those photos of the branded women was still flitting through a dark corner of his mind. "We'll put Brennerman on the back burner for now. First things first, though, we get ready for this meth business. Let's go see the bums."

Chapter 6

Few sections of Rankin Flats were free of economic scar tissue. In some areas, they didn't even have the luxury of a Band-Aid. When the Holland Shelter for Hope opened its doors, its principle founders believed in the surrounding area and its people and invested that faith wholeheartedly into their project. Their bunks filled with the needy and they knew they'd done the right thing. What they hadn't counted on was the apathy of the city at large. The contractor took every available shortcut and within months they were plagued by burst water pipes and a heating system that kept them freezing in the winter. They tried to go to court, but their pro bono lawyer took a dive for a briefcase full of cash and a blowjob from the opposing lawyer. After that, their house of cards came crashing down and before a year had elapsed, the doors were closed for good.

The rest of the block seemed cursed too. A chemical plant folded just weeks later, leaving behind an industrial park the city had no interest in cleaning up or demolishing, and the handful of other businesses, mostly catering to the needs of the employees of the plant, moved on too. The entire block, despite its good location within the outer suburbs, seemed destined for abandonment.

At least by the living, anyways.

* * *

The snow plows hadn't hit the streets in what seemed like days, maybe weeks. Murphy wondered aloud if that was legal. Garrett didn't know, and it didn't matter anyways. This was Rankin Flats, after all, where municipal road maintenance was as mythical as a leprechaun shitting bricks of gold. And in any case, in four-wheel drive, the Hyundai was more than game for the snowy drifts.

The shelter had always reminded him of a high school in its simplicity and functionality along with its bevy of rectangular windows. The building seemed to slump under the weight of the untouched snow. Though in the colder months there weren't usually as many ghosts around as there would be come summer or Montana's beautiful fall, there still should have been a few poking their heads out of the building as they pulled up.

The age-old notion of ghosts haunting particular places wasn't entirely wrong. Often, they'd hang around to watch the lives of their loved ones, or they just found a place and a lifestyle they enjoyed. With the rise of binge watching TV shows online or gamers running marathon sessions and sitting in front of a console or PC for hours on end, there was no shortage of places and people they could trail to keep themselves entertained in the afterlife, and they often settled into those places and worked their way into the bones of a place. Blind people—and those who listened to books on tape in particular—were often targets of the bookish couch potatoes among them.

But that was only for some. For other ghosts who liked to get out and see the world, it was sometimes nice—and necessary—to congregate with their own kind. Someone, centuries before, had come up with the idea of centralized meeting places, usually run by a handful of local ghosts and manned in shifts much like a job. These were places where ghosts could leave or receive messages, find out any news on those who had ascended, or just generally spend some time bullshitting before they moved on to their next destination. The way stations were the hive brain of the ghost world and they were incredibly useful to Garrett—at a cost.

He aimed the SUV at what he thought was more or less the curb—it was hard to tell under those drifts—and slowed to a stop. They slid out of the car, glancing around curiously. If Padraig wasn't here, at least a couple of his people should have been. Garrett cupped his hands around his mouth and shouted, "Padraig!" He was unconcerned about noise. No one lived nearby—not for a good block and a half at least.

Murphy trod lightly over the snow and stopped at the door. "Hey," he shouted back at Garrett. "Door's been forced open." Garrett felt out the curb with his foot and trudged towards the building's front door. Murphy went inside. "Pretty dark. I think someone boarded up some more windows..." His voice trailed off. "Ah, shit."

"Murphy?" Garrett said, then repeated it again louder.

Murphy came through the walls in a hurry. "Shit. Shit shit shit. Gar, there are bodies."

"Fuck me," Garrett said and went back to the SUV for his rubber gloves. He slipped them on as he walked marginally faster to the shelter.

Someone had pried open the door to get in, and then wedged a rusted bed frame up against it on the other side to try to get it to close properly again. They'd done a good job, but the weight of the snow on the door must have glacially pushed the door back open. Garrett gave it a hard shove and pushed the frame out of the way just far enough to slip inside.

An acrid, horrible tang remained in the air, making Garrett's eyes water and his throat sting. Someone had burned something they shouldn't in a metal garbage can in the middle of the room. Three makeshift beds surrounded the garbage can, not much more than sleeping bags and grime-covered stuffed sacks meant to serve double duty as pillows. Two bodies lay entwined right next to the garbage can. A woman. A child. Near a pair of bathroom doors, a third body, this one a raggedly thin man, reached out towards the other two. Decomposition had barely started. With the fire out, their bodies must have frozen.

The stench of whatever had been burned was too much. Something bubbled volcanically in Garrett's throat and he lunged towards the door. He made it outside just in time to puke all over the snow-encapsulated shrubbery outside. He staggered further away from the building, his eyes watering. A form came up beside him, one he could barely make out. "Shit, Murphy, what do you think—"

"They wanted to get warm," a voice both slightly nasal and smooth, oil on water, said quietly. Padraig, not Murphy, watched him with a detached irritation. "That was all."

Garrett vomited again, this time mostly an acidic dribble. A few feet away, he cupped his hands and brought clean snow to his lips, not caring about the cold, just needing the liquid in his burning throat. Either the snow soothed the chemical burn or the cold numbed it enough that he didn't care. He took off the gloves and shoved them in his pockets. "What happened?" he wheezed. "Don't give me any cryptic bullshit. Just tell me."

The tears in his eyes were abating, and he could see the bulldoggish former Scotsman better. It wasn't just his voice that was a duality, but his looks, too. His features looked almost boyish, save for a little bald spot on the top of his head. Even his short scraggly beard looked more like the sort of thing a young college student would grow. But there was something about his deep-set eyes that looked exhausted even in death, and it made it extremely hard to judge how old he was. Garrett had him (or rather, the age at which his ghostly visage was eternally stuck) pegged at thirty, but Murphy bet it was somewhere close to fifty. Either way, both men knew the Scot was far older than that. He had once mentioned offhandedly of having last been in Paris during the Exposition Universelle with millions of other ghosts. Neither knowing what the hell that was, Garrett and Murphy had been shocked to discover after researching it online that it had taken place in 1900. Throughout their travels, they'd met only a handful of ghosts that could boast to be that old, but Padraig was never one to discuss it.

Padraig's greenish-gray and soft warm yellow ribbons of color flitted around his legs as though they were playing. He eyed Murphy as the ghost brushed through him and Garrett to sit atop the hood of the SUV, but said nothing to him. The two rarely could speak to each other without jabs and barbs, but neither seemed interested in baiting the other that day. "They came down the day before last. We looked for you. I thought you could call them in, get them somewhere out of our hair—"

"So humane of you," Murphy spat quietly.

"-and out of our lives," Padraig said, shooting Murphy a dirty look.

"I was working a job," Garrett said bleakly. "Wasn't home until yesterday morning."

"Hm. They came in with everything in a cart. Their bedding, enough wood to last them a couple of days, an axe, some other tools. While the man fixes up the windows, seals them as best he can, the woman goes dumpster diving in the afternoon, something to keep her busy. She finds some milk jugs in the trash left over at the chemical plant and tells her daughter the plastic will help the wood burn longer." Padraig smiled bitterly. "They settle in for the night. The wife loads up the garbage can, gets a nice homey fire going, and throws the jugs in. Except they're not milk jugs. Whatever was left over in there, it burned hot and fast and killed the mother and daughter in a couple of minutes. The husband was in the bathroom relieving himself in a hole in the ground where they used to have the toilets. He comes out and lasts just long enough to see his wife and kid are gone."

Garrett looked back at the shelter. "Hell." Murphy only shook his head, staring down at his feet.

"Their colors were beautiful," Padraig said softly. "The mother and child waited for the father. It was hard for the child, I think. She was clearly being pulled and didn't want to resist. But she did. They went together." He glared at Murphy. "My reasons for wanting them gone might have been selfish but these were my people. Living, maybe but still members of my tribe."

"I'm sorry," Murphy said genuinely.

Padraig's upper lip rose in a sneer. "You two want something. What is it?"

"It's not like—" Garrett started to say.

Padraig shook his head. "Save it. It's why you come here. You need something, we deliver. That's what we are to you. Your lackeys whenever you need us."

Garrett held up a hand and reached for his phone. He called Monica, and spoke quietly, as though his words might disturb the dead. He explained the details and asked her to give him an hour before she called a uni to check it out. "If you can," he said finally, "send me the details on where the bodies are taken. I want to arrange for a real funeral." He hung up and looked at Padraig. "That's taken care of whether you agree to help out or not."

"Thank you," Padraig said. He raised his hand in the air and made a come-hither crooking motion with his finger. From down the street, a pair of ghosts started walking towards them. Padraig turned his attention back on Murphy and Garrett. "What are you offering?"

"Standard deal, Padraig. I need two guys on one building, a meth lab in a trailer house south of town. It's way the fuck out in the boonies, so they'll need to be there all day every day. I'll want a full report after two days, namely if the people in the trailer are waiting for me."

"You think they've been tipped off?"

"Almost definitely," Murphy said. "Junkies, man."

Padraig rolled his shoulders and thought about it. "Two people for two days will run you a hundred for each of the men." He thumbed at the oncoming ghosts, a pair of brothers who had, in life, been a pair of kneebreakers for a loan shark business. "They'll pick who the money goes to."

Murphy hopped off the car and went to speak to the brothers, giving them all the details they'd need. Garrett folded his arms, still feeling a little nauseated, and said, "Might have more work for you beyond that, Long term. Tracking a man by the name of Jamie Finson. We think he's a local Legion higher-up, maybe one of their bosses, maybe not. Murphy will do the brunt of the work, but I'm gonna need people to trade off with him, maybe keep tabs on some of his friends."

Looking back at the building, Padraig said, "Sure. Moranis…"

"Yeah?"

"Let me talk to my people. Get a nice headstone for that family and maybe we'll do some of the work cheaper this time."

That took Garrett by surprise. With Padraig, there was always a cost. "Getting soft on me, Padraig?"

"Just getting tired, that's all," the ghost said wanly. And although Garrett knew ghosts didn't feel physical problems the same way the living did, he couldn't help but shake the feeling the ghost was telling him the truth.

* * *

Even with the scalding hot sandpapering the shower was giving him, he couldn't get clean enough. Armed with a loofah and a bar of soap, he kept scrubbing at his face, his neck, his back, everywhere until his skin was pink and raw. There were no tears, but he kept thinking about the way that woman and her daughter had fallen with each other and how man's hand lay outstretched towards his family. His cell phone buzzed on the bathroom counter and he shut off the water. Still dripping wet, he answered the phone, not liking the hoarseness in his voice. "Yeah."

"Fuck, Garrett…" Monica said simply.

"Yeah." He dug in the bathroom cabinet until he found an old bottle of saline solution and looked up at the recessed lights while he cleansed out his eyes.

"How the hell did you find them? What were you even doing there?"

"It's a little hard to explain, but it's job related."

"Oh." She sounded exhausted. "The bodies are going to the morgue. There'll be a story on the news—call down there then like you just heard the story and you can make the arrangements. Can't imagine anyone else'll step up." The bitterness in her voice mirrored his own heart.

"I will, Monica. Thanks."

"Garrett."

"Yeah?"

"Thanks. For doing this. And for all the times no one ever says that."

He hung up and grimaced at the gnashing figure in the mirror. He dried himself off with a towel and draped it carefully over the reflective glass. "You're welcome," he said to no one at all.

Chapter 7

Brianna was awake half an hour before her phone's alarm went off. From the apartment below, her neighbor Winnie's bed springs creaked rhythmically in time with the thump of a headboard or an odd-shaped bed leg hammering up and down. Reeek whap, reeeek whap. Brianna pulled her pillow over her face and giggled into it. The woman had to be pushing eighty. Good for her.

When her alarm did go off, she snatched up her cell phone and brought up her music mixes. She meant to set it to "Mackmistress Grooves," her ever growing get-up-and-kick-ass playlist, but instead she hit "Mortal Kombaaaaaat," an oldie but a goodie she used sometimes for the punching bags. The old, ludicrous theme to the Mortal Kombat movie pounded through her phone's tinny speakers and she shrugged.

A first date with a guy she'd kept in her mental "rowr" catalog for six years—Mortal Kombat seemed entirely, wildly appropriate for the day. She bellowed the iconic words in the shower and laughed wildly. She was nervous. She was Zen. She was going to paint that gym and then wallop that handsome son of a bitch with her gams and her awesome-tastic witty repartee.

Garrett Moranis was never going to see her coming.

* * *

Garrett sat on the shitter, rubbing his temples as he contemplated running to Mexico. Canada wasn't far enough. Maybe Italy. He'd always wanted to go and why not?

His stomach rumbled again and he moaned. It was only nerves. He knew that. He'd go to the gym, help Brianna and her dad paint, and make a complete jackass out of himself. He'd be such an asshole that she'd be happy to ditch him for their date that night. And if, for whatever reason she still wanted to go on the date, he could run. Mexico. Italy, maybe. The middle of a barren field in Russia. Anywhere to get away from her and those beautiful eyes and the flare of those hips. Not to mention the way she'd stood up to those douchebags. That had been it for him, he realized.

He could do this. He could be a horrible person. It was for her sake, really. He was a monster and she'd be better off knowing it early. What was left to think about?

* * *

She unlocked the door for him. Her certainty disappeared and she smiled tentatively, honestly, openly. His need to push her away dissolved and he smiled back. There were no shots fired. The day was won and they were doomed.

* * *

He set the boxes of donuts on a plastic folding table. "Mountie Moose, best in town. In the state, really. I guess they started in Townsend," he rambled, his eyes never leaving her. Even without makeup, in a pair of ratty jeans and a flannel shirt that draped over her slim chest like a cheesecloth, she fascinated him, taunted him, drove him to stand a little straighter and fumble for words a little harder.

"Better than June's?" she said disbelievingly. She took up a yellow-frosted cream filled and took a bite. Her eyes lit up. "Oh my God, yes, yes it is. I've never had a banana-cream donut and this... this is my everything." She eyed the insides of the donut and wagged a finger at it. "Hello. You are my newest favorite thing. I will eat you up I love you so."

Amused, Garrett said, "Did you just quote Where the Wild Things Are to a donut?"

She tilted her head, jaw jutting out, trying to look serious and failing wildly. "Why, yes, I did."

He tried and somehow succeeded in not kissing her right then and there. He wasn't entirely sure she would have stopped him. The eye on the unscarred side of her face jumped with a nervous tic whenever he looked at her for longer than a few seconds, and was her breathing a little erratic? Maybe she'd just gotten in a workout. "I, uh, I got coffee. In the. Um. Car. Thing," he said, hating words and their stupid way of fighting it out in his throat in a battle royale of stupidity.

She nodded, her eyes bright. "Go. Me and Mr. Bernanner Cream here are going to get very cozy together." She mock kissed the donut and he banged into the table as he attempted the newly-difficult task of walking and thinking. Behind him, she laughed gently and all coherent thought was lost to him.

Outside, he sucked in air and rubbed his eyes with the back of his hands. Murphy came out through the wall. "Yeah, you're really showing her what a terrible jackass you really are," Murphy said. His tone wasn't quite as mocking as Garrett expected. Instead, he sounded... sad. That was odd.

"I can't do it," Garrett said as he walked to the SUV. "I can't. I cannot be a jerk to that woman."

"Garrett—"

"I mean, Where the Wild Things Are. How am I supposed to not fall for that?"

"Gar—"

He yanked open the SUV's back door. "I know everything you're going to say. I can't fall for her. I know. I fucking know."

"You can," Murphy said softly.

"I... what?" Garrett turned around, confused and angry. "How would that work? Me coming home at odd hours, fresh new bruises everywhere? Just out for a stroll and I fell on a pile of fists? Or, hey, honey, how would you feel about running to a country with no extradition laws because, boy howdy this is funny, I kind of—"

"Tell her."

Garrett's laugh was brittle and short. "Right." He turned back to grab one of a pair of cardboard boxes. Two coffee urns jutted out like a pair of steely nipples.

"Does she look fragile to you?" Murphy asked as Garrett slapped the door shut with his hip. "Made of glass? How disrespectful of her is that kind of thinking?" A pair of people Garrett didn't recognize were walking towards the gym wearing ragged painting clothes. He nodded at them and was unable to speak to Murphy as they held the door open for and blathered hellos. Murphy went on in a rush. "She's strong, Garrett. And she's capable. In there with her, I see something in you I've never seen with anyone but your sister. You're happy. And you deserve to have someone in your life, someone other than an old ass ghost from the ghetto to talk to."

Garrett set the box down on the table and pointed the pair to the donuts. He smiled at Brianna—seemingly couldn't help himself—and stormed back out into the early morning light. Alone again, he muttered, "And what happens when I do tell her the truth? She runs? Thinks I'm crazy?"

"Probably," Murphy said truthfully. "In fact, almost definitely. But we make her see. We run some tricks."

Garrett thought back to the last time he'd tried to convince anyone he was telling the truth about Murphy. His mother, flinching away from him when he'd tried to touch her shoulder. Her sitting on the ground one afternoon when he'd come home from school, pictures of the family everywhere, cutting him out of each one and humming to herself. His father and his fists. It had been the only time his father had ever struck him. Only the once. And he'd laughed. Garrett shivered, but then he thought about Brianna. Thought about the way she'd stormed over to those guys in the gym, ready to tear them a new asshole. And he'd believed she could do it, too. She was tough. But could she believe?

He pulled the second box out of the backseat and locked the SUV up before closing the door. "I don't know. I need to think. You gonna go to the movies?"

"Been thinking about hitting up the college." Murphy liked to go up there and sit in on the lectures. Despite his love of books, he'd never had much of a formal education growing up, but as a ghost with a like-new brain, he soaked up knowledge like a sponge and loved hitting up the local colleges. He particularly liked history and literature, but he was developing one hell of a taste for theater too.

"No classes today. Saturday."

"Right, but there's a theater production dress rehearsal today."

Garrett baited the trap. "Oh?" he asked innocently. "Anything I might want to see?"

"Nah, you know, a dry stuffy arty thing. Some stoic playwright, something you wouldn't like."

"You sure it's not that musical version of Bridges of Madison County?"

Murphy reached up and scratched at where the back of his head had been. "...the lead actress is really, really good," he mumbled sheepishly.

Garrett grinned. "Go have fun. I'll meet up with you tonight."

"Or tomorrow morning," Murphy said, making an upside down V with his fingers and licking at it lewdly.

"Oh fuck off."

* * *

The security guard slept with his feet crossed on the wide desk in the lobby, his double chin tucked down into his chest. His snores were quiet but audible. Ransom cleared his throat, startling the man and nearly sending him sprawling. He pushed himself to his feet—no easy task—

and fumbled for the clipboard on the desk. "Mr. Galbraith, hey, Benny said you'd be in today."

"Not a lot of traffic today, huh?" Ransom asked with a little bite to his question. He abhorred laziness.

Red-faced, the guard shook his head, sending his jowls jiggling. "Nope. Got a few people up and about, mostly the cleaning service." He swiped Galbraith's ID card and handed over the sign-in clipboard. Ransom glanced at the names as he twirled the pen in one hand. Nobody he recognized. Good. The only thing he couldn't account for was someone from his office—apart from Ben—coming in on a Saturday. Given the improving weather, he wasn't surprised. He scrawled his name and the time.

He thought about saying something to the guard about his nap, but thought better of it. He needed the man friendly later and it wouldn't do to go off the rails at him. Besides, one word to Barb on Monday and the dumb fuck would be gone. It would be less satisfying, but that was a small price to pay for the kill. He grinned at the guard, trying for disarming and mostly succeeding. "Don't pay me any mind. I never saw a thing."

The guard grinned at him. "Thanks, Mr. Galbraith. Lemme know if you need anything up there. I was thinking about ordering a pizza later if you want a couple of slices."

Garrett wanted to throttle the man. Pizza would throw his entire plan out of whack. Instead, his smile widened again. "Appreciate the offer, but I'm gonna have my nose to the grindstone today. Have a good morning, huh?"

"You too," the dope said, watching until the good guy went up in the elevator, then settling back in for another fifteen minutes of sleep. Half an hour, tops.

* * *

The picture frames on the walls were hung according to age. The newest photos hung closest to the front desk, where Danny presumed people would want to see pictures of more recent fighters and boxers who had frequented the gym. The oldest, which Garrett found the most intriguing, were hung by the weight machines, dating back an entire century. They worked in teams to pull down the frames—Danny and Garrett tackled the oldest pictures, while Brianna and the pair of volunteers whose names Garrett couldn't remember worked at the newest ones. Garrett pulled down the pictures while Danny followed along with a box for the frames and a jar for the tacks and nails. In no hurry, Danny paused frequently to show Garrett who a fighter was, or the name of some celebrity who had come by the place. He knew some of them already—not because he had any real knowledge about century old boxers, but because Danny had told him a lot of these stories before over the years. Still, he liked hearing them, and didn't mind the old man talking animatedly about Jack Dempsey coming to Rankin Flats and visiting the gym or the busload of young men from the gym standing in front of a ring where Joe Louis had just destroyed Gus Dorazio. That story Garrett particularly liked, especially Louis's later comment on Dorazio— "At least he tried."

But as they went along and the two groups got closer, Garrett caught himself glancing over at Brianna more and more often and paid less attention to the old man. Danny caught his looks and said nothing for a while. Eventually, though, he snapped, "If you check out my daughter's ass one more time, she'll be going to dinner tonight with a Greta, not a Garrett."

From across the room, Brianna sighed heavily. "Thanks, Dad. Not at all crapping on my mojo."

"You're welcome, hon," he said brightly, ignoring her sarcasm. "I'd be happy to do it anyways. Just say the word."

"Nope. All good, Dad. But I'll keep it in mind if he gets handsy."

Garrett said weakly, "Um."

Danny mulled that one over. "Got a pocket knife in the desk drawer. Kind of dull. And rusty."

Brianna scratched her chin. "Hm. Maybe keep it handy. Just in case." She winked at Garrett, who stared dutifully at his feet and decidedly not at the open button on the top of her flannel shirt and the little hollow at the base of her throat that he couldn't help imagining kissing.

Someone knocked on the front door, and Garrett muttered, "Oh thank God." The others in the room snickered and Brianna darted to the door to let in Ed and Rose.

Where Ed might have easily been an extra on Spartacus, Rose might just as easily have been the leading lady in an alternate world's version of Friends. She was always impossibly, breathlessly at ease with her looks and comfortable with her body. Her makeup seemed minimal because it was—she recognized her blemishes and didn't seek to hide them. The moles by her ear, the wrinkles at the corners of her mouth, the little hint of shadows under her eyes, they gave her a reality that other women blessed with such looks and wrapped in pancake makeup lacked. Her long dirty blonde hair saw a lot of love and a comb, to be certain, but she wore it in a loose ponytail, practical but still the sort of thing that set a man (and more than a few women) to dream. She loved her curves, too, embracing her solidity with clothes that flattered her large frame rather than hide it away in a sea of thick, formless outfits.

Ed played at being miserable, but his wife always brought out the best of him and he beamed when he introduced her to everyone. "Rose, everyone, everyone, Rose."

Without hesitation, Brianna swooped in and hugged Rose, who only took a moment to adjust to the taller woman's affection. Eventually, Rose leaned back and looked her up and down, not shying from giving her scars a once-over. She scanned Brianna's eyes. "I'm so happy to meet you. It always sounds so fake when women say that to each other, doesn't it? But it's true. Ed told me about the other night, the way you jumped in and threw those two dillholes out of here. I knew I'd love you right then."

Brianna worked at trying to say something, but Rose shut her up with another hug. Finally, as she blinked away the tears forming in the corners of her eyes, she squeaked out an awww. She sniffed and dabbed at the tears with the arm of her shirt. Looking over at Garrett, she said, "I cry. A lot."

"Okay," he said agreeably.

"Like... rivers." Turning back to Rose, Brianna said, "I hope I'm not imposing tonight. I didn't mean to interrupt anyone's plans."

"Oh, honey, no, you're not imposing at all." Rose glanced over at Garrett and smiled sweetly at him. "Garrett's like our idiot brother—"

"I'm right here," Garrett said testily.

"-even if he's technically Ed's boss. If he likes you, you're something special. Believe me. And that means you're more than welcome at our place. We'll get down the details later, but no, Brianna, trust me, we're looking forward to it so much."

And with that, Brianna felt the waterworks really come on. She hugged Rose again, hugged Ed, and for the hell of it, hugged everyone else in the room too. When she hugged Garrett, she let the hand her father couldn't see trail down his arm just a little bit, sending goose pimples up and down his skin. "Thanks everyone for coming." She clapped her hands. "Let's get this knocked out."

* * *

When Ed stopped to grab an apple fritter and a cup of coffee, Garrett split apart from Danny and told him he'd be right back. Ed looked up as Garrett came over and raised his cup. "Hey, man, good coffee."

Garrett looked through the near empty boxes of donuts and found a cherry frosted monstrosity. "Thanks. You got a minute?"

Glancing back at the rollers and paint awaiting him, Ed shrugged. "I suppose I can make time."

They sat in the office and ate quietly together for a minute. Ed found some paper towels and handed one over to Garrett as they finished up. "What's up?"

Outside the office, Brianna folded the flaps on one of the last boxes of photographs and knelt to write a rough approximation of the years the photographs spanned. Her marker was out of ink and she grumbled as she got up. There were more in the office. She told her partners she'd be right back and darted towards it. As she drew up close, she could hear Ed and Garrett inside talking. She should have pushed right on in. Would have, except for the strange hush in their voices.

"...see that news report last night about the homeless people being found out in the shelter? Near the chemical plant?" Garrett's voice was practically a whisper. He'd tried to shut the office door behind him, but unless it latched properly, it would swing back open an inch or two.

"Yeah. Why?"

Garrett sighed heavily. "I found them."

She raised a hand to her mouth.

Ed sucked in a deep breath. "Oh holy crap."

"They were... God, I don't want to go into the details. It was bad. They burned these plastic jugs in a fire. The jugs came from the chemical plant, and something in them just...." Silence for a brief moment. "Don't say anything to anyone else, okay? Especially Brianna. I just want to have a fun time tonight. I'm not going to bring anyone down with my bullshit."

"Sure, man, but... crap." Brianna was inclined to agree.

"Yeah. Oh, one other thing. I got ahold of the mortician. I want to handle the funeral costs anonymously. I gave them your office number, so if you get a call, that's what it's about." Brianna smiled at that. Oh, he was definitely getting a kiss goodnight later.

"Okay, yeah, sure. What brought you there?"

There was a brief pause. "A job. It was unrelated. Something I need to do tomorrow."

"Anything I can help with?" The question seemed perfunctory as though Ed knew the answer.

"No. Bad people doing bad things." That was curious. Was he the bad person doing bad things? Someone else? Huh. She wondered what he meant but the squeak of leather inside meant someone was getting up.

She backed up a foot or two and dropped her used marker into an empty garbage can then walked forward and pushed the door open. "Hey, you two little lovebirds, what's going on?"

Ed tipped his Styrofoam cup of coffee at her and grinned. She thought his expression was a little bit forced, but would have never noticed it if she hadn't overheard the conversation. No, they hadn't been putting on the little show for her amusement. Ed was genuinely concerned for Garrett. "Well, howdy, lil lady. Just grabbing a quick bite and talking shop. Tax season is always so much fun."

"Ugh," Garrett grunted. "It's just never ending paperwork from here to April."

Ed shot him an amused glance. "You don't even do any of it."

"Yeah, but it's all there, isn't it? All those folders and binders and calculators and Steve Urkel suspenders."

"You have no idea what kind of work I actually do, do you?" Ed asked as Brianna dug in a drawer for more markers. She grinned at Ed.

"No, I do not, but I most definitely feel your pain," Garrett said, without a trace of seriousness. He held up his left hand and raised his ring and middle finger while holding down his pinky with his thumb. "Scout's honor."

Brianna eyed him, smirking. "Isn't a scout sign with the right hand?"

"And with three fingers raised," Ed added.

"I mean, well, yeah, sure, if you're getting all technical about it," Garrett said and sidled out the door, ready to get back to work.

Ed paused by the doorway on his way out. He glanced back at her, face serious, and opened his mouth as if to say something. She wished he would. But then the moment was gone and he went back to work too.

* * *

The second the lead actor fell, Murphy knew the play was done for. The arm was broken, no question about that. The director fainted at the sight of the impossibly bent angle of the bones. When he was revived by a dour-looking woman, he got up and left the building mumbling to himself and shouting back over his shoulder that the play was cursed. Murphy thought that was Macbeth, but he might have been wrong. He was still pretty new to the theater lifestyle. Still, he supposed maybe the man was right about there being supernatural forces in residence. He was, after all, there haunting the place.

The stage manager tried to put it all back together, but after two hours, it was clear the lead actor's understudy was woefully unprepared and opening night would have to be delayed. With a different cast and crew, maybe it could have been pulled out of the fire, but not this time. There was even a grumble or two about canceling the whole show, which left the lead actress in tears.

Murphy thought about sticking around to watch the fallout, but he had no particular love for anyone in the cast apart from her, that onyx-haired beauty, whose voice drilled home to him just how much he missed having a backbone so he could get little chills up and down it. He intended on following her for a bit, but when everyone else had left, the seamstress for the show pulled her into the dressing room, their hands all over each other. Murphy was many things but not a pervert and so he left the lovely young couple to it.

He meandered for a while, thinking he might go see the bums and find out how things were going. But Padraig was nowhere to be found and none of the other ghosts had spoken to the two at the cook site. He thought about going to the movies, but he wanted to be near people. Something raucous, something alive. A bar, he decided. That should do nicely. Maybe a sports bar. There were plenty of games on that day and the multiple televisions would be bound to have something he could watch if he got bored. Perfect.

He started towards one not all that far from the college. The sun was out, his friend was on his first real date in a decade, and he had nothing pressing going on. It was a good day to be dead in Rankin Flats.

* * *

With one last lick of the roller, the primer was set and ready. By then, the atmosphere was almost party-like. Classic rock blared out from Danny's old CD player in the middle of the ring and someone had ordered in Chinese for Danny and the helpers not going to dinner. They sat around for a while afterwards, laughing at Danny's tall tales about his fights overseas, including one whopper of a story about him taking on eight—no, nine—fighters in a row in a seedy little town in Asia. It sounded a lot like the plot to Diggstown to Garrett, but he played along and said nothing, catching Brianna's wink halfway through and smiling back at her.

One by one, the helpers left, making promises to return the next day to get the actual painting done once the primer had time to dry Ed, Rose, and Garrett pitched in and helped clean up. They agreed an early dinner was in order—the tempting smells of the Chinese food had almost been too much to bear—and that they'd meet up at Ed and Rose's at six. Garrett and Brianna insisted on bringing something, so Garrett was to bring wine (and a six pack for Ed and himself) and Brianna agreed to a dessert.

In the parking lot, as they got into their respective cars, Brianna flashed Garrett a brief, hesitant look, unsure as ever as to who he really was, but dying to find out.

* * *

Ransom paced the confines behind his large L-shaped desk, his arms folded across his chest. He could not think beyond the rage. Where was he? Where was the stupid little man? His fingers flexed and straightened. He wanted to choke the little bastard out. He wondered what it would feel like to crush a man's windpipe. Wondered if he was strong enough.

He grimaced. Don't get sloppy. Don't get sloppy. Don't get sloppy.

Forcing himself to calm down, he stopped pacing and stared out the window.

Late or not, the janitor would go up there. He always went up there.

Ransom's hands flexed again, and he shivered with rage and anticipation.

Chapter 8

Ed and Rose's home lay at the end of a cul-de-sac in a modestly well-to-do neighborhood. Garrett liked the place, particularly around Christmas, when the entire neighborhood banded together and decorated. Up and down the cul-de-sac, paper bags would be lit with electric candles (it was too windy in the plains east of the mountains to bother with the real thing), and neighbors competed on a yearly basis to see who could do up their home in the most fashionable or fun ways possible. Even the non-believers joined in with lit sacks. It was the sort of thing that might have been written into the area's bylaws or something. Garrett had no clue about that sort of thing, but it was lovely.

In February, the street wasn't quite so festive, but that didn't diminish the beauty of the homes by one bit. Lit by the glow of ornate street lamps, the Victorian and colonial homes seemed nestled in for a long winter nap, their windows glowing with an inviting warmth. Though their lawns were still blanketed in snow and sheets of dangerous ice glimmered under the lamplight, the winter had started to recede little by little, revealing the hedges and lawns that would be so cautiously maintained come the late spring.

Ed and Rose's good fortune helped raise Garrett's spirits whenever he visited, though it sometimes made him a little forlorn for a normal life. Garrett had often thought about buying a house on a street like that, maybe even that very specific area when a particularly lovely Victorian came up for sale (complete with handcrafted latticework and a stone retaining wall). But that amount of space would only serve to emphasize how very little he had to do with the living. His only company was Murphy, and he didn't need for anything—the ghost could live anywhere and didn't have any use for material goods, so that left just Garrett. The thought of being that alone in a four or five-bedroom house with nothing but his thoughts to keep him company scared him in ways that taking down the city's worst elements couldn't even touch.

He pulled into Ed's driveway, careful to leave plenty of room for Brianna's car. A pair of snowmen had been erected beside the icy sidewalk on their lawn. One was dressed in a threadbare Russian trapper cap with a nubbin of a carrot for a nose. Its smaller companion had a pink and blue frilly scarf wrapped around its neck, this time with a much larger carrot. Both stared into the others charcoal eyes, their spatula hands locked together, lovers quite literally frozen in a passing moment. He ran a finger down each of their faces, marveling at the strangeness of the last few days and the normalcy of that moment, staring at a pair of snowmen in a beautiful neighborhood. The following night, he'd have nothing but this memory, he thought, as he and Murphy took down a meth lab in the middle of the plains. A few hundred feet away, one of the streetlamps grew brighter and hummed audibly.

A pair of headlights flashed onto the street. The driver slowed way down at the first couple of houses. Garrett thought that had to be Brianna, so he walked down to the street and waved at the Aztek. A few moments later, she pulled up alongside his Hyundai and got out. "Hey. I feel under dressed. Am I under dressed?"

"Hi," Garrett said, smiling gently.

"Hi," she said, blushing. "No, really, though, am I?"

She most certainly was not, but Garrett made a show of looking, his finger tapping on his freshly shaved chin as he examined her. Her black skirt and leggings accented her calves nicely, and her hip-length coat made him wonder what was underneath. It was almost a crime that her beautiful hair was tucked under a beanie. "I see. Hm. Points deducted for a lack of fluffy slippers. No clown nose, either, that's not good." He sighed. "I suppose you pass muster." He rolled his eyes. "Okay, so I suppose you look absolutely lovely."

"Apart from the missing clown nose."

"Well, yeah."

They walked together up the icy cobblestone sidewalk, her coat brushing against his sweater, the fabrics saying hello. Before they got to the door, she grabbed his elbow. "Garrett…"

He turned. Her eyes sought his, her breath catching in her chest. If he could have felt her heartbeat, it would have echoed the jackhammering in his own. She was better than beautiful. She was unique, she was alive, she was his and he was hers. The humming lamplight died on the street and she shivered. He reached up, his thumb rubbing gently across the scars of her cheek. "I'm scared too," he said, and leaned in. His lips brushed against hers, her eyes half lidded and fluttering.

"Then why are you smiling?" she whispered, her forehead pressed against his and her voice almost lost in the wind.

"Because isn't it fun?"

* * *

They sprawled out in the living room contentedly, their bellies full of gooey, spicy baked ziti and garlic bread. No one had been able to touch the key lime pie Brianna brought. There just wasn't enough room in their bodies.

"Oh God, it looks so good, though," Rose moaned as she plopped down on the couch. Ed joined them a few minutes later, doling out glasses of wine to Rose and Brianna, and tossing a beer to Garrett. He ducked back out to the kitchen to take care of the leftovers and put the dishes in the dishwasher.

"Right? But that ziti was amazing. Ed said you made the absolute best and he wasn't lying," Brianna said truthfully. If she was on death row and had to ask for a meal, she'd be hard pressed to think of one so tempting as the meal she'd just finished.

On a loveseat next to Garrett, Brianna sat with her legs curled up underneath her. His toned arm draped across her shoulders as though it had always belonged there. She could get drunk off the rich, musky sandalwood cologne he'd dabbed on the insides of his wrist. Her head nestled against his chest, and she thought she could feel his heart thump. She was not given to whims or fancies, and she knew she had to find out answers to her questions about that conversation between Ed and Garrett if this was going to go anywhere. But she knew what she wanted—who she wanted—and she couldn't help but feel safe with him in that moment. Maybe it was an illusion. Maybe she was being an idiot. But sometimes, she decided, you have to fake brave to eventually be brave.

The blouse she wore was so thin it was almost sheer. Silky under his touch, he had to fight the urge to caress the length of her arm and still caught himself doing it once or twice anyways. "That really was great," Garrett said, rubbing his hand up her arm again. Damn. To distract himself for a minute, he lifted his arm off her and cracked his beer open. That task finished, Brianna shifted her wine to her other hand and pulled his arm back around her. "My arm now," she sighed.

"I'm okay with that," he said, a little loopy, and kissed her forehead.

Rose beamed at them both and set her own glass down on the table. "All right, we've got the Wii hooked up, pool table upstairs, or we can just go ahead and rent you a hotel room right now, you two."

"The room?" Brianna asked Garrett, arching her eyebrows. She somehow managed not to blush.

He grinned down at her. "Sounds good, but I know they have Mario Kart."

Ed poked his head out from the kitchen. "Are you crazy, you idiot? You want to wreck your relationship before it starts?"

"That's the essential first-date game!" Rose protested.

Ed snorted. "For the Manson women and their man, sure. She loves me, she loves me not, she loves me, she hits me with a shell and all of a sudden we're going at each other with knives."

They all looked at him and Garrett said in amazement, "What the hell kind of games of Mario Kart have you been involved in?"

Rose cleared her throat. "I, uh, I get a little competitive," she said. "I mean, it's not like I was actually really going to cut him. Or you guys, for that matter," she added quickly. "I promise, I'll be sweet and kind unless Ed knocks me out of first with that bullet thing. Then you might have to hold me back."

"I still think you're playing with fire," Ed said cautiously. "She bites."

Rose got up and knelt in front of the TV, setting everything up. "Do you hate romance, Ed? Do you hate fun? Did I marry a fun-Nazi?"

After heading back into the kitchen to start the dishwasher, he sighed and joined them, wiping his hands on his pants leg. "If I wake up tomorrow and she's sitting in the corner holding a certain body part of mine and a knife, you two are to blame."

* * *

Ransom shut down the computer, his mood black and his temper rising. The janitor hadn't shown. He wanted to punch something hard. No, he wanted to kill someone. That was very specifically what he wanted to do and he knew he wouldn't be sated until he did. For his research, of course, he told himself. He wanted to study the colors more. It was all for that.

Something glinted off the computer screen and he ignored it. Where was the demon? he wondered. It should have been there in the screen. He could see his own shape in it and so the other thing should have been there too. Had it abandoned him as well?

The only light on in the office was a soft lamp in the far corner. It couldn't reflect off the screen from its angle. Something was off. Or on.

The reflected light winked out. It hit him in a rush. He stood up, knocking over his chair and turning rapidly to the window. The man was out there. The light had been the faintest reflection of the stairwell door opening and closing.

Showtime. He had only minutes.

He raced for the elevator banks, wondering if it would be faster to go down the stairs. That was risky, though. There were still a couple of people working throughout the building and if they saw him running down the stairs they'd inevitably ask questions. Instead he waited impatiently for the ding of the elevator and its interminably slow doors. Even more intolerable was the slow ride down, where he had to listen to a feeble instrumental version of an old REM song. When the elevator finally opened on the ground floor, he had to stop himself from running. He nodded at the same security guard from that morning. "Decided on dinner after all. Back in a flash."

By the time the guard started to mention the pizza he'd talked about earlier, Ransom was out the door and headed towards the alleyway across the street. It wasn't out of character for him to go that way. It was a faster route to get to the Subway and Jamba Juice on the next street. But instead of going for a sandwich or a fruit smoothie, he ducked around the corner and entered the office building from its rear doors.

There was a long moment when he thought he'd forgotten his balaclava. His heart stopped and he felt at his pockets. No, it was there, rolled up in his sport coat pocket where he'd left it. He took a moment in the stairwell to put it on, rolling it up almost to his ears. He'd look just like any other person wearing a wool cap in February- sensible and not at all out of place.

He climbed the stairs quickly, ready to explain himself to anyone who might get in his way that he had seen someone up on the roof and meant to talk them down. An easy, inelegant explanation that had the benefit of being partially true. Nearly out of breath by the top of the stairs, he stopped for a moment to pull the balaclava down. He grinned fiercely, stepped through the door quietly (making sure to prop it open with the cinder block left by the door for that purpose) and looked up to see the little man puffing on a joint, staring at him.

"Hey, are you the guy Candy was sending over?" His voice was lazy and light. Whatever green he was smoking had obviously already kicked in or he might have been wondering why the man wore a ski mask out there.

"Sure am," Ransom said, his lips peeled back from his teeth. He walked forward rapidly.

"You're a day early," the janitor said. "Smoke?"

He closed the gap rapidly. "Never touch the stuff. But let's talk about you. You're fucking late." The janitor frowned questioningly at him, never thinking to bring his arms up. Ransom grabbed him by his shirt and lifted him up, a much harder thing to do than he'd imagined. The janitor gave one impulsive kick, and then he was over the side and falling.

Not daring to look over the edge, Ransom ran back to the door, glad that the janitor or someone had cleared a path to it. In the snow, the cops might have seen two pairs of footprints, not one. He pulled the cinder block back into its place and closed the door gently behind him before he sprinted down the stairs the same way he came in, only remembering at the last second before he hit the street to pull his balaclava off and stuff it back into his pocket.

Outside, he walked unhurriedly to his car to grab the Subway bag with a sandwich and chips inside. It would be frozen and inedible by now, but it wasn't meant to be eaten. He bought it the night before and ditched the receipt. It was his alibi. He came back down the street as though he were returning to the office. When he encountered the first rapidly gesturing group of people, he asked what happened. They told him, and he faked horror and sympathy and the same morbid curiosity that he saw on their faces.

After a while, he returned to the office with that same shell-shocked look on his face and told the security guard he'd be back upstairs, that he needed a drink and some time to sit down. The guard nodded sympathetically and shared his sentiment that it was a tragic thing, that no one should take their own lives, and certainly not like that.

Back in his office, he plunked down heavily in his chair. The reflection in the mirror was that of a lipless, hairy thing with incisors as long as a man's finger. It snarled and smacked at the screen with a warty, hairy palm as though trying to high five him. Ransom high-fived him back and laughed and laughed and laughed until he bent over and dry-heaved into his garbage can.

For just a moment, the toxins in his mind cleared and he wondered what he'd done. He closed his eyes and saw a clawed hand reaching out of smoldering rubble, a spear of wood jammed through the wrist and propping it up. When he opened his eyes again, he turned to the window to watch the aftermath and make sure he'd gotten the whole thing on tape.

* * *

Rose sliced into the key lime pie and slipped a spatula under one end. She almost managed to scoop it all onto a plate in one piece and whooped. Brianna grinned and raised her wine glass in a toast. After sipping, she looked around and said, "You've got such a lovely home here." And they did. Though the home was clearly large and nice enough to be worth a good chunk of change, it had a lived-in, homey appeal that she found greatly endearing. The furniture might have come straight from a craftsman's shop, but draped across the chairs were handmade quilts and throws. The carpet in the living room and hallways was thick, plush, and immeasurably comfortable under her feet, but it also bore several stains and signs that people actually could live and walk through the place without feeling like they were setting foot in a museum. That duality extended all throughout the house. For every beautiful little piece of artwork, there was a picture or three of Rose and Ed laughing, smiling, poking fun at each other, making silly faces and snarling at the camera. Matte honed granite counter tops were spotted with boxes of kids' cereals and shot glasses from various places around the globe. It was, she decided, eclectic and lovingly weird in all the best possible ways.

"Thanks!" Rose said contentedly, darting her tongue out of the corner of her mouth in concentration on the pie. The second piece wasn't quite as successful as the first, but she mashed the fallen glob of lime in with the rest of the piece and estimated that it looked all right. She set down the spatula and drank from her own glass. She eyed the pie and sighed. "So many calories today," she said, then shrugged and served up two more pieces. Brianna reached for two of the plates but Rose waved her off. "C'mon, sit down for a minute and talk. The guys can sweat it out a minute without us."

Rose pulled out a pair of stools and offered the spatula to Brianna. Brianna took it and wiped a piece of key lime off there. "Mm. Not too bad," she said, happy with her choice.

"Believe it or not, you picked one of my favorites," Rose said, taking the spatula back and trying a little for herself. "Oh yeah, that's the stuff." As Brianna poured the last of her bottle of wine into their glasses, Rose eyed her. "You've had something on your mind all night. Is everything okay?"

Brianna held her glass to her lips a moment longer than was

necessary, more to contemplate how well she knew this woman and how much she could trust her. Maybe it was the wine, maybe it was her need to have a female friend in a town where most of her high school friends just sort of faded away. Or maybe it was that she recognized something in Rose and Ed, some kind of honesty and goodness that brought her in like a magnet. Stupid or not, she leaped. "You're perceptive," she said, smiling tentatively. "Look... um... about Garrett."

Rose tensed up just a little bit on the stool. It was almost imperceptible, but there it was. "Yes?" she asked, gently.

"You two know him a lot better than I do. Is he... is he for real?"

Rose's shoulders seemed to deflate and she relaxed. "That's an interesting way to put it." She sipped at her wine thoughtfully. "That's probably really more like three or four questions, isn't it? Do you mean is he looking for something quick and easy?"

"That's part of it. I don't exactly have the best history or judgment in that department. I think a guy wants something serious, and bam, he's out the door."

Rose nodded. "First thing you should know – he and I had one date together, before I met Ed. Actually right before, like... days. That might make things weird between us and I'm sorry, but I swear, there was so little chemistry there. Not that he's not a handsome guy, but I'm not into the tall, dark, and mysterious type and he clearly was bored as hell talking to me. He's not that way with you, not in the slightest."

"Good to know."

"I've seen him with a few women here and there. His relationships with them were pretty short." Seeing the grimace on Brianna's face, she hurried on, "Oh, no, hear me out. That sounded worse than I meant. He... with all of them, they knew. He knew. It was an implied short term thing. I wouldn't worry, though. He never once looked a hundredth as happy with them as he does with you. He can be so... isolated."

"Isolated?"

"Mm hm," Rose said around a mouthful of wine. "With the others, it felt like he was... I don't know. Going through the motions? I mean, he tried to make their dates as pleasant as possible, but he was always so detached and businesslike with them. I never saw him play them. He never promised them anything and they never expected it from him. They were just..." She laughed. "It's stupid, but it felt like he was with them because it was expected of him. They were window dressing, some obligation he felt he had to make to society. I don't know if he ever even slept with any of them. He didn't even kiss me good night, not that I really would have let him. You, hon, you've got him. All of him. I can't predict the future, but… I don't think he'll go anywhere if you don't want him to."

"I hate feeling so self-conscious," Brianna said.

"It's okay, hon, believe me, I understand. He's a catch, no two ways about it."

"Ed seems great too."

Rose gave a deep, appreciative hum and said happily, "He is." She drank the rest of her wine in one gulp and got up to get another bottle from the cabinet. "But there was more to that question. About his realness."

"Yes. And I'm not even sure what I'm asking."

Rose glanced back at her, a bottle of red in her hand. She tapped her lip thoughtfully with one well-manicured finger. "Um. Hm. You remember what I said about his defenses with those other women? Like he had walls up he didn't allow anyone to look over? Well… here's the thing. I've always had the feeling he does the same thing to us. I don't think it's anything bad." She brought over the bottle and uncorked it. "I think maybe it's some secret, something he thinks he can't tell anyone. I think if he offers that up to you, you know he's for real, as you put it. And if he doesn't…" She poured herself a liberal amount of wine. "I think he will," she said, thoughtfully. "Yes, I'd almost bet on it. I think I've almost said too much already, but… I'll tell you this. When you can, get Ed alone, ask him how he met Garrett. I think that's really the story you want."

Mystified and feeling even more uneasy, Brianna nodded and accepted a bit more wine. They grabbed the plates and made their way upstairs with the slices of pie.

* * *

Murphy came within a heartbeat of choosing another bar and missing the news. Three college kids pounded down the house special, a drink called the Chumbucket. Each night, any bottles nearing emptiness were dumped into a big plastic jug, thoroughly mixed, and served up the next night for fifty cents a shot (with the order of anything on the menu). The greasy, undercooked chicken fries they ordered to go with the drinks didn't settle well at all, and six shots in apiece, all three were feeling it hard. The bartender should have cut them off long ago, but they were friends and he didn't Instead, he brought them one last shot—

this one a Prairie Fire, comprised of whiskey and hot sauce. He paid for the drinks himself and laughed when they chugged it down without knowing what they were getting into.

When Murphy walked in, the bartender was sheepishly cleaning their vomit off the floor five feet from the bathrooms. The three man-children were in various states of misery on the bench near the door, ready to be hauled away by Uber. Murphy shook his head and sighed.

It wasn't exactly the most welcoming scene and he thought about walking on to the next sports bar a dozen blocks down. But the Polecats were playing against Mizzou and he wanted to plant his ass down and watch. So he did, and he was there later when the game broke for a brief news update about an alleged suicide downtown.

Except it couldn't be a suicide. Two things happened to suicide victims. Sometimes, a person who was in too much physical or mental anguish just couldn't help themselves and opted for a quicker end. Instead of just a ghost popping out of their shell, something curious and inexplicable would happen instead. Their ephemera exploded into a cloud of particles and swirls, as though a disco ball's colors had become corporeal and infinite within a contained area. The ghost would ascend, almost immediately, but it lacked the joy of the darting ephemera. The colors would coat everything around them for weeks. As people came and went through the area, they pulled little bits of the miasma to them, absorbing it into themselves without even realizing it. Spirituality's nature, reabsorbing its own. It was a beautiful, tragic process, one that haunted Murphy every time he came across it.

The second thing that could happen was if a person was guilty—truly guilty—of something terrible, and took the coward's way out rather than paying for their actions. Those poor bastards got a ghost too—for all of about a minute. The specifics changed from person to person, but whenever someone was taken to hell, it was always gruesome. Sometimes it was as though black ribbons cut them apart and dragged them down while they remained completely aware. Once they'd seen a man erupt into a dark blue sickly pulsing light, only to explode into a gooey phantasmal liquid that was then slurped into the earth like a child sucking up spilled soda through a straw.

No, this guy couldn't have committed suicide. His ghost was still there. This was murder. Murphy knew he should let it go, that his friend deserved a night off. But the man in the video was staring straight at the camera and talking over the reporter. "Hey, if you can hear me, someone get here fast. I'm freaking out. Holy shit, I think I been murdered."

Murphy sighed regretfully as the game came back on. Garrett was going to kill him for interrupting his date. Well, kill him even more.

* * *

"What do you think, us versus them?" Rose asked Brianna.

"I'm not great at pool," Brianna admitted. "You might want to rethink that."

"Oh trust me, I'll more than make up for Garrett." Rose grinned at Garrett's glare. "He's awful."

"Oh, just for that, we're going to destroy you," Garrett said.

Ed rubbed his chin. "I don't know, man, you really are terrible at pool."

Garrett sighed. "Smack talk, Ed. It's smack talk."

"Oh right, yeah. I mean, rowr, we're going to destroy you." Ed tried his best to look threatening and wound up looking more like he really needed to use the bathroom.

"No, I just said that… you know what? Never mind."

"Oh, uh, we'll obliterate you?"

"Nice one, love," Rose said and kissed his cheek. "Now, Brianna, how about we take these little pantywaists and kick 'em right in the grapes they call balls?" She shrugged at their stares. "What? I call 'em like I see 'em, boys."

"Just because I can't make a stupid arch right," Garrett grumbled.

Ed clapped his shoulder. "I got you, buddy."

Hoping her grin masked the nervousness at asking the question, Brianna asked, "So… what else about Garrett don't I know?"

Ed snickered as he broke and sent a billiard ball straight in. His wife slapped his butt on his way around the table. "Well," he said as he leaned over for another shot, "he's the most uncultured guy I've ever met."

"Oh come on, that's not fair," Garrett protested. "I've… you know. seen stuff."

Ed made a sucking sound with his teeth as he missed an easy shot. He settled back onto a stool. "Name a movie from the last fifteen years. Go on ahead."

Brianna thought about it "Um. Eternal Sunshine of the Spotless Mind. I think that was the last fifteen years, right?" Ed shrugged and Rose nodded.

Garrett made a face. "Uh, try another one."

She pressed a finger to her lips. He shivered, wishing he could be that finger for just the briefest of moments. Her eyes lit up. "Lord of the Rings." Seeing his look, she gasped. "Oh my God, we are so doing a movie night soon." Catching herself, she blushed lightly. "Ah. You know. That is… if you, ah, want to."

He grinned at her. "I'd love to."

Rose swore as Ed tapped her side with his cue as she shot. She turned and blew him a raspberry. Turning to Garrett, she asked slyly, "How about The Dark Knight?" Ed sucked in his breath and Garrett's face lost all color.

Brianna looked at everyone in the room, confused. "What?" she asked. "Did I miss something?"

Garrett shook his head. "No, I just, uh… no. I saw part of that one," he said to Rose, his voice quiet. "Never got a chance to finish it."

Hastily, Ed jumped in. "Books."

"Now those I do read," Garrett said, shooting his friend a grateful nod.

Ed scratched his head. "You? Come on now."

"I'm cultured!" Garrett protested again. "I even know some poetry."

Now the whole room was silent again, but this time, it was pure disbelief on all their faces. Brianna cleared her throat. "Poetry me. Now."

"I'm not sure you can use that as a verb," Garrett said.

"Pfffft," she said, waving him away. "Hit me."

Ed shook his head. "Nah, he's bluffing."

Garrett drank deeply from his beer and spoke before he lost his nerve. He recited a poem he remembered from his youth, something he'd liked so much he'd committed it to memory. It wasn't Shakespeare or Rumi, but Shel Silverstein, and he repeated it fast, mumbling the finish and looking sheepishly down at his feet, realizing how silly it sounded coming from a grown man. Rose and Ed looked at each other, astonished. Brianna put her pool cue very calmly down and walked over to Garrett. He shrugged. "I know, it's not… you know, a great classic—"

She pulled his head down and shut him up with a long kiss. Surprised, he almost didn't react, but then he wrapped his arms around her and returned it. Her lips tasted like cinnamon and God she felt good in his arms. Ed wolf whistled and Rose elbowed him. He pulled back a little and asked, "Not that I'm complaining, but what was that for?"

"Oh, just… because," Brianna said, her face crimson.

Then he looked up and saw Murphy coming through the wall, a serious look on his face. "Garrett, we gotta go. Now."

* * *

Garrett ran the tap so no one could hear him and think he was talking to himself. "Your timing. It's just fucking perfect," he snapped.

Murphy very literally ran a hand through his hair. "Look, I know. But it's a murder. And the police and news think it's a suicide."

"So we look into it tomorrow."

"The ghost is still there," Murphy hissed. "Or he was, ten minutes ago. But we have to move, now."

Garrett balled up his fist and fought the urge to punch something. "This is going to destroy her," he croaked. Finding the truth of it, he said quieter, "No. It's going to destroy us."

"I'm sorry."

Not caring about the burn, Garrett splashed steaming hot water on his face. "It's not your fault. It would have happened sooner or later, right?" He looked up at the mirror, at the eyeless, noseless thing staring at him with barbed wire looped around its neck. "Meet me there. Keep him there and tell him I'll be along as fast as I can."

He looked so damned tired. Not on a physical level, but on an emotional one. This was a mistake. "Garrett, I…"

"It's not your fault, Murph. This is the life we chose. Both of us." He shut off the faucet and dried his hands. Murphy slipped through the door and was gone from the house in seconds. Garrett sighed, wishing he could slip through the walls too.

His feet dragged like concrete to the game room door. He stood there watching three of his closest friends laugh and shoot the shit. Something cloyed in his heart and he selfishly thought, no, not tonight, the dead can handle themselves tonight, they don't need me. But that wasn't true. This wasn't something he could set right later. Murphy could get all the information from the ghost, but if the man knew who murdered him, Murphy couldn't do a damn thing about it. He could. So he watched Ed try a stupid little trick shot off the chalk and laughed a little when he actually made it. Brianna heard him, turned, and smiled.

Oh God, he cried out inside, why?

Because he could. That was why.

She walked to him, those magnificent hips swaying just ever so slightly. He lost his smile and something in her face changed. He saw the nervousness that she'd been fighting break through. He laid his hands on her shoulders, more to keep her away from himself than to comfort her. He didn't trust himself to do the right thing if he caught a deeper whiff of her perfume again or the citrus scent of her hair. "Brianna, I'm sorry. I have to go."

Her scars creased with her searching look. "What? Now?"

"Yes. If you want to be with me, this is going to happen. A lot."

She pulled away from him and folded her arms across her chest. "Oh?" she said, deadly quiet.

"It's not... I can't..." He ran a hand through his hair and blew out a pensive breath. "I am falling for you. Hard. There's something between us and I want that so damn bad."

"I won't put up with being second fiddle to another woman if that's what this is," she said, the fury rising up in her.

He recoiled from that. "It's not another woman."

"Then stay," she said. "Or let's go talk somewhere about what all this is."

He wished he could tell her yes. Wished it maybe more than he'd wished anything. But all he could say was, "Someone needs my help." The words were stronger than he expected. "I can't." He pulled her to him, feeling her tighten and tremble against him, knowing she was gone already. He kissed her forehead and released her, going for the stairs and what he knew was out of her life.

* * *

Ransom watched the video for the umpteenth time, his excitement no less abated. The quality was amazing. He could see himself in the video, just a man in a suit like a thousand others around that area, approaching the janitor like a man possessed—and oh how he giggled at how close to a truism that really was. Then the man was soaring over the top, lifted and thrown like deadwood. The silent slap of the body against the pavement was his favorite part. At one point, Ransom owned a wood pellet stove. The way the body had fallen, it reminded him of the way he'd use to throw around the forty pound bags of pellets for that old thing. There was a rippling jolt through the body as it smacked into the pavement, and that was it.

Except he hadn't died, not right away. The man had lasted a full minute, maybe two. Just as Ransom saw himself come around the building, people gathered around the body and started shouting for help and pulling out cell phones, both to call 911 and take photos, an act of morbid obscenity Ransom completely understood.

Then the ghost had come out. He'd wondered if the man would remain as short as he had in life, or whether death would correct this too, the way it had a tendency to do. He'd killed a man days after his wife's death, an old bum with a bad leg who hadn't been able to hobble away from the gun he'd pulled. But in death, the old man straightened up as straight and firm as an oak. He wondered if death had fixed his wife's problems. An image rose unbidden in his mind. A hand jutting out of the rubble of a burned house. A face in the water. The taste of ash in his mouth. He shivered and shoved the thoughts away from his conscious mind.

The ghost rose up again on the video. Ransom grinned wider, his eyes bulging, and he took another long drink of scotch.

He looked up to see if the ghost was still there across the street. Sure enough, he was. Another ghost had joined him, a black man wearing a nice suit. The new ghost's curly haircut and shirt collar had come from the seventies or early eighties and firmly died there. Probably literally, he thought, and grinned even harder. His face was starting to hurt from all his new-found good cheer, but he didn't care. It was good to smile. He lifted the camera and zoomed in on the talking ghosts. The black one's gray and blue colors seemed subdued. They didn't play around his legs the way the janitor's ghost's ephemera did. They just sort of flopped out behind him. Did that mean something? Ransom didn't know. He recorded and said so the camera could hear him, "I wonder if the death ribbons—oh, that's a pretty good name, death ribbons—reflect a ghost's mood? His actions? Or are they sentient things at all? Hm."

After a few minutes, he set the camera back down and yawned. He was tired and he had no particularly good reason to keep watching. Ten more minutes, he promised himself. Then he'd go home, get some sleep, come back, and finally knock out that coding tomorrow.

Except the thought of doing real work bored him. He didn't think it could ever excite him again the way it did in high school and college, when the formulas and numbers sang out to him. Instead, he caught himself wondering if all the whores still parked their asses near the city park on Murrell Street. One of them would be really easy to do in, he thought. Hell, the city would probably thank him for it. Not tonight, he thought. It was too quick. He was still riding high on the emotion of the fresh kill. Best to prepare. Take precautions. Maybe look into a different car. His BMW would draw too many eyes.

He raised the camera up again, musing on his thoughts out loud as he watched the two ghosts below talk. So they could see each other. It was all so damned fascinating.

Chapter 9

"You're staying here tonight," Rose said adamantly.

"Agreed," Ed said, twisting the lid off a bottle of beer for his wife and handing it over to her. He opened his own and drank half in one go. He tried to hide a belch in the elbow of his arm. "We can't apologize enough."

Brianna sat with her arms wrapped around her knees on the same loveseat where she'd curled up with Garrett. Her own mostly untouched beer sat on a square coffee table in front of her. "Thanks," she said distantly. "I should turn you down. It would be the polite thing to do." She sniffed. Her face was red from crying and she knew her makeup was a mess, but she didn't care. Fury mixed with embarrassment in a strange cocktail of emotions. "But I could use the company tonight, I think. I really hope you don't mind."

"We wouldn't offer if we weren't serious, hon," Rose said gently. "I've got some old pajamas that are too small for me. When you're ready for bed, I'll grab them for you. You have such a lovely frame, they'll be too big for you, but there's a drawstring on the pants so maybe that'll work."

"You're rambling, Rose," Ed said, squeezing her palm.

She nodded. "I know. I just..." She punched her leg with her free hand. "God I hate this. Why don't you just tell her?"

Ed sighed. "Because it's not my place. You know it's not."

"Tell me what?" Brianna asked. "He said he runs off a lot like that." She glared at Ed. "He's not a criminal, is he?"

Rose shot him a look. Ed finished off his beer in another long drink and set it down on the table. "Look. I..." He rubbed his jaw.

Brianna got to her feet. "This was a mistake," she said angrily. "I'm sorry. I appreciate the hospitality, but I... I don't like being lied to." Shit, crying again. She rubbed at her eyes furiously with the same soiled tissue she'd been using, despite a box of fresh ones right at her side. "Or having the truth kept from me like I'm some sort of... I don't know. Like I need to be protected. Like you think I'll break or faint or some other bullshit sexist thing."

Ed shook his head. "It's not…"

"Tell her how you met," Rose said firmly, rubbing her husband's tense back. "Tell her now. It's what she needs to hear. Hon, please. Listen to him. Just let him tell one story and maybe you can infer what you need to know." Now Rose was crying. "Garrett needs you so so much and we love him but he's so pointlessly stupid—"

"Then tell me," Brianna said, crossing the room and pleading with him, looking him straight in the eyes. "I think I'm falling for him, God knows how I know that after one day together but it's true and—"

"Sit down," Ed said. "If you care for him, I'll tell you the truth. All of it, so it pertained to me, anyways." He looked at Rose, eyes pleading. "I know you hate the first part. I'm sorry. I swear, I'm so much a different man—"

"I know," Rose said, and traced the back of his hand.

Brianna sat back on the loveseat, her eyes glimmering. Ed cleared his throat and started talking. His voice was so low Brianna could barely hear him. "I very nearly killed a man once…"

* * *

When Ed Guzman finished with his education, he realized very quickly he was the enemy. Fresh faced and naive, he'd believed the economic crisis would work itself out, that things would improve and his chances at a job would open up like the parched earth to the rain. He was wrong. He was an average student coming out of an average college and there was nowhere that would hire him in Rankin Flats. Not unless he was willing to work for the wrong person.

The wrong person turned out to be Dante Jackman. On the books, he owned a legit laundry service catering to some of the shittier hotels around town, the kind that still accepted cash and let a guy pay by the hour. Off the books, Jackman wasn't much of an inventive guy—he laundered money, plain and simple.

The amount he offered Ed was outrageous for that particular business. It didn't take a genius to figure out the guy was really asking Ed to cook his books and help him run his little criminal enterprise. Desperate, hungry, and about to miss his bill payment window for the second month in a row, he accepted, telling himself he would work there just long enough to find something real.

Jackman wasn't a real hardcase himself—he didn't do the jobs, he just laundered for the people who did, taking a large percentage for himself. With Ed's help, they found all sorts of ways to hide the money and recirculate it. With it came the cooked books—Ed filled ledgers with fictional shipments, chemical expenses, profits, the works. He found his financial calling, though it wasn't as a real accountant. He was a damn good criminal.

He was getting paid, but the work got to him. The angry, vicious bastards who came in the door each day scared the hell out of him and Dante's mood swings ground him down. He'd hear a car door slam and jump a foot in the air. It was too much. He wanted out.

But Jackman didn't want him gone. At first, he consoled the nervous accountant, telling him he needed him for just a while longer, that they were almost good to go. Then it devolved into threats of violence. Ed recorded those little pep talks on a digital recorder, figuring he could take them to the cops if he needed to. That time came one day when Jackman threatened to break every bone in Ed's body with a hammer if he didn't shut up and keep his nose to the grindstone.

In Rankin Flats, there was a fifty-fifty chance of getting an honest cop who stayed true to the badge—and that was on a good day. The guy Ed spoke to took his statement, heard the tapes, and told Ed to get back there and pretend like nothing was wrong for his safety and that of his family. Ed agreed blindly and returned to work. An hour later, the cop showed up and ratted out Ed in exchange for two fat stacks of clean money.

With the cop gone, Jackman said little to Ed. He even poured him a cup of coffee. Then he got up, grabbed a folder from his desk, and threw it in front of Ed. Inside were pictures of his family, his friends, everyone he was close to, along with addresses and the hours they were at home and at work. He very quietly and calmly explained to Ed that if he ever went to the police again, he'd execute one of them at random.

Ed didn't sleep. Didn't eat. Didn't hardly dare breathe, so great was his terror. So the next day, he stopped by his cousin Julian's house to ask him for a gun he could use. He needed it for self-defense, he explained, hating the lie but knowing Julian or his pregnant wife might very well be one of the ones in Jackman's crosshairs. Julian gave it to him freely, only asking if he needed his help. Ed smiled and shook his head. It was one of the easiest lies he ever told.

He drove to work and got out, tucking the gun in the back of his pants. His oversized sport coat was plenty long enough to conceal it. No one should have known what he intended. No one. But a man stopped him on the sidewalk. Ed tried to push past him, but the man did some kind of weird arm grab and he found himself with his elbow up in the air, grunting in pain as the man took the gun from his belt and stuffed it into his own. The stranger told him that he knew who he was, what he was facing, and how bad things had gotten for him. If he really wanted to change, to be a better man, the stranger said calmly as he pressed the gun back into Ed's hand, then he wouldn't use that. He'd put it back in his car and trust in him for ten minutes. After a long moment of hesitation, Ed dropped the gun under his driver's seat and agreed. The man grabbed a folder from a nearby parked car and they entered the laundromat.

Dante demanded to know if the man was another cop. The stranger dropped the folder on Jackman's desk and waited for him to finish reading it. Irritation became curiosity, curiosity became dread, dread became terror. Jackman looked up at the stranger and asked him what he wanted.

Three things, the stranger said as serenely as Mother Teresa. Apologize to Ed. Never so much as think about him or his family again. And what else? Run, the stranger said, far less serenely. Run as far as you can as fast as you can. And never look back.

The launderer got on his knees—literally, on his knees—and begged Ed for forgiveness. When Ed said yeah, sure, whatever, get out of here, Jackman bolted for the door and never came back to the place.

The stranger was Garrett. Ed asked if he was going to kill him. He just looked horrified at the question, as though it appalled him on some instinctual level. Instead, he offered to buy Ed a bagel at the place next door. As they sat and ate, he explained that he'd been observing them for a while, long enough to know Ed was a decent guy who wanted out of a bad life. He asked Ed if he would consider working for him. Ed could walk away if he wanted and so long as he lived on the straight and narrow, Garrett would never bother him again. But if Ed was willing to take another chance, he could help the world in some small ways. It was a good sales pitch—quiet, straightforward, honest. It had only taken Ed long enough to finish the bagel to agree.

* * *

Ed tried to pull away from his wife in shame, but she kept a grip on his arm and he glanced at her gratefully. To Brianna, he said, "I know you've got a thousand questions," Ed said. "I wish I could answer all of them, but some of them are Garrett's to tell and some I just plain don't know the answers to even today. I have no idea what he showed Jackman. He took the folder with him. Dante was picked up by the FBI a few weeks later in Idaho. As for the rest…" He shrugged and gave her a small smile. "I know right now it's hard to swallow, but Garrett Moranis is the best man I've ever known. If he had to leave tonight, he had a reason. And like he told you, it will happen again. Often. But I promise you, you stick with him, he's worth waiting for."

Brianna turned her glass in her hand, the wine long gone. "Ed, I—"

"It's okay," he said. "I can't blame you. Any decision you make, I can't. He would be a hard one to date, I think."

Brianna blew out a breath. "I think I might take you up on the offer of those pajamas now, if you don't mind. I think… I think I'd like to think." She tried to grin at her own little joke, but the humor just wasn't there, even if she was good and buzzed. Rose got up, and she did too. Ed just sat there, looking out their back porch, a lost expression on his face. She walked over and grasped his arm. "Thank you. For the truth, what you can tell, anyways. And I respect you for not saying anything but what you can. I hope whatever happens, the three of us stay good friends."

Ed smiled at her distractedly. "Me too. Thank you." But then he was back to staring out the window, lost to memory and time.

* * *

Garrett pulled up into a parking garage a block away. There was no point in trying to get closer—though traffic had thinned and the news teams had left, there was still no way he was going to get parking any closer. He handed the attendant a bill and told him to keep the change, not bothering to look or care about it. The astonished, very happy man let him through and Garrett found a spot on the first floor.

He walked down the street, slightly hunched over, playing those last few awful moments with Brianna over and over again in his head. It was only a first date. It should have been like ripping off a Band-Aid. How often had he done it before? "Oh, hey, look, I had fun, but I just don't think we're compatible." Why hadn't he gone with that old chestnut? "Oh, Bri, you're great, it's not you, it's me. I'm just not interested in you. Sorry. You'll find someone great. I know you will."

He knew why.

Because she'd cried when she'd met Rose. Because she'd stood up for that boy at the gym without question or hesitation. Because she'd kissed him first, no matter how brief. Because she'd shaken like a leaf when they walked up the sidewalk to Ed and Rose's. Because she was afraid and because she fought through it. He'd never find one like her again.

He thought of how those lips had felt against his, how her eyes flitted like a bird's wings, how her tongue had just barely darted inside his mouth, how delicious the curves of her ass and hips were when she leaned over that pool table, how she'd captured him with that easy smile that made her scars shimmy up and down, how naturally they'd fit together on that couch.

He turned and punched the building next to him, shouting a grunt of pain, not caring that there were people who saw him and avoided his gaze. He licked blood off the back of his knuckles and muttered to himself, "Fuck. Fuck fuck fuck!"

Then he started walking again. Towards Murphy. Towards his old friend, the best friend he'd ever had, really, and the only one he could keep.

At the alley entrance, Murphy pretended not to see his friend punch the wall or hear his outburst. He looked pointedly away until Garrett drew near. "Thanks for coming, man."

"Is he still here?" Garrett asked, the anger leaching out of his voice.

"Yeah. Down the alley. He was about to take off when I got here."

"Good." They walked together. "I'm sorry. About anything I might have said back there at Ed's."

"Forgiven, man. Always forgiven," Murphy said dismissively.

Garrett nodded and rubbed at his eyes with his palms. The ghost of a man, about as tall as his belly, stood by a dumpster, muttering to himself. "Hey, guy. I'm Garrett." The ghost ignored him, thinking he was talking to someone else, or maybe he didn't hear him. "Hey. Ghost guy. Did you—"

The ghost looked up. "Hey, asshole, you told me ten minutes, max," he said to Murphy.

"Charmer," Garrett said drolly.

"Holy shit, you can really hear me?" He glanced at Murphy. "Guess you were right. Been shouting at cameras all night and no one else showed."

"Not sure there's anyone else who can do what I do," Garrett said. "C'mon. I'm going to attract attention down here. To anyone else it'll look like I'm talking to myself." As they walked back down to the entrance of the alley, Garrett brought his cell phone up to his ear. "This is how I camouflage myself when I need to. Not talking to anyone else on the other end, so you've got my undivided attention. What's your name?"

"Foster."

"I'm Garrett. Tell me how you were murdered. Every last detail."

* * *

Ransom gaped at the window, not believing what he was seeing. The ghosts had been joined by a man, a living, breathing real person, fully aware of the two ghosts and interacting with them. "Holy shit," he said softly. They were coming back down the alley. He realized he had only moments to act. "Holy shit!" He grabbed the camera before he sprinted for the stairs. He took them two or three at a time, leaping down the stairwell so fast that if he fell, he was almost sure to kill himself. He didn't care. By the ground floor, his lungs burned and his legs screamed for him to stop. Instead, he barreled out the door, not bothering to explain to the guard about his hurry. He whirled around. "Where are they," he chanted to himself, "where the fuck are they, where are they, where are they?"

There. Down the street, the flicker of colors just turning a corner. Gray and blue. The car garage, not the one he used but one he was familiar with nonetheless. They'd have to turn out his way. The median wouldn't allow a left. He flicked the record button on the camera and zoomed in down the street. A white SUV pulled out of the lot only a moment later. He could see three people inside when anyone else would see one. He fell back into the shadow of the entrance, recording them as they drove by. He zoomed in even further and caught the license plate. It was a good shot, clear as day. And it was all he needed.

He tugged his overpriced cell out of its holster and called his friend at the police station. "Mike. Your loan. It's wiped out tonight if you run a license plate for me. I just need an address. It's nothing bad. The guy just nearly ran over my feet and I'll admit I want a little petty payback. Nothing more than a little soap on his windows, I assure you."

After rattling off the plate number and waiting a few minutes, Mike fired him off a text message with an address. He thought about going there that night. He wanted so very badly to talk to the man, to find out his secrets and how he'd come to have the gift only Ransom thought he had. But he thought back to the way that ghost had sat there waiting impatiently for his companion. They had known each other. How intimately he couldn't be sure, but they looked like they'd known each other well. It was apparent in the way they fell into step together, their pace matching, one never getting further ahead than the other. They seemed close.

He wondered if he might not be able to find out more with a ghost companion of his own. Where would one get such a wonderful thing? he wondered. A morgue? Would ghosts really go to their own coroner's inquest? Watch their bodies be cut open? He didn't think so. Where then? Someplace people died in droves. Someplace he hadn't thought of before. A hospital. Too late tonight for visiting hours, but tomorrow, surely.

He laughed delightedly. Oh, this was going to be fun. The world seemed at that moment infinitely larger for Ransom Galbraith. Maybe he wasn't so alone after all.

* * *

Not even partway across town, they hit a wall.

"You're sure you don't remember anything else?" Garrett asked, clenching his hand and trying his damnedest not to punch the steering wheel.

"Run it by us again," Murphy prompted the man. "One more time. Step by step."

Foster sighed dramatically. "Okay. I live in that building, down in the basement. Not supposed to, but the boss, she was fond of me and we were fuckin' on the side. She wasn't much to look at and just happy to have a little dick in her, know what I mean? Little dick? You guys got no sense of humor. So I do work for the building too, cleaning toilets and what not. It ain't a dozenth what those assholes pull in there, not on a bad day, but hey, I'm a manual labor kind of guy and there's not much more out there for a guy with no GED and shit-all for references other than the prison."

"Go on," Murphy said encouragingly for the second or third time.

"So I get a call late this afternoon, that one of the toilets got plugged up. I was just getting done with the day and this woulda been overtime, but the boss lady, she okays it so I suck it up and deal with it. Real bastard of a clog, had to bring in a snake, then I still couldn't get it. Took me I don't know how long. But I finally fix it, clock out, and I head up top like I do every day."

"For what? The view?"

"Yeaaahhh, that, and some bud," Foster said, grinning. "Shit, I

113

guess ain't no gettin' high no more, is there? Gonna miss that. Ah well. I feel sharp, like I could fuck for days."

"Yeah, about that," Garrett started. "You can't—"

"So I get up there, I light up, and I hear the door open. I figure it's this guy the boss lady is bringing in to do up some of the electrical, but he ain't supposed to be there until tomorrow night and the guy don't know me for shit. He sure wouldn't have known I was up there, but I wasn't thinking straight on account of I was high as fuck. I turn, ask him if he's the guy, he says yeah, then he charges me and throws me off the building."

Garrett asked. "That's it? That's all he said to you?"

"Yeah. No. Wait. You're late. That's what he said to me. Like he was real angry at me about something. Except I had nowhere I was supposed to be. It don't make much sense."

"You're late? You're sure that's what he said?"

"Mm hm. Clear as day. Well-spoken dude, eee-new-cee-eighted."

"Enunciated," Garrett and Murphy said together.

"Like a damn old married couple," Foster muttered. "Anyways. Guy had on a suit—go figure there, right? And a ski mask, but one of those ones where you can kinda see the forehead. His eyes kinda reminded me of that old comedian, uh, the Caddyshack guy."

"Chevy Chase?" Garrett asked.

Murphy shook his head. "Rodney Dangerfield."

"That's it!" Foster snapped his fingers, or would have if they didn't go right through one another. "Damn, that's gonna take some getting used to. Yeah, eyes like Dangerfield, but he was tall. Big, kinda. Looked maybe a little flabby but still powerful, like maybe he worked out but didn't give a crap about his diet, you know the type? Oh, and his skin. It was white. Real white. Like glue."

They grilled him for a few more minutes, but there was nothing else. He hadn't paid any attention to anyone coming and going, and there was nothing else they could pry from him, they offered to drive him anywhere he wanted to go.

"Yeah, the strip club down Lincoln and 44th. Figure now I can do anything I want, go anywhere I want, I'm gonna do a titty tour. Hit every place from here to Vegas, then out on the east coast," Foster said, rubbing his hands approximately together. He stared at them, annoyed that there was no friction.

"You won't be able to—" Garrett tried again.

"Sounds like a hell of a plan," Murphy said, shooting Garrett an amused look. The guy was a real work of art. Let him figure out the rest on his own, the look said.

"Strip club it is, then."

As they drove, Foster seemed to bounce in his seat. "So... like... am I stuck here forever?"

Murphy took that one. "No. There's a heaven, or what we think is heaven, anyways. The best of humanity pop out of their shells and ascend within a few minutes. Everyone else hangs here in the afterlife or gets a ride downstairs."

That didn't seem to faze Foster. "So what do I gotta do to get out when I want?"

"There's no set rule as to how long a ghost stays here. Everybody here's paying a price, but it's more than that. We think people gotta learn lessons, too. It ain't just about the reward of heaven, but figuring out something about themselves, maybe. Gotta learn to be a good person for the sake of being good, you know?"

"Nope," Foster said, snickering. "But I think I get where you're goin' with this. And hell is real too?"

"Yeah," Garrett said. Neither of them said anything else about it and Foster was smart enough not to bring it up again.

"So... what about other religions?"

"Well," Murphy said, "we got it figured like this. There should be millions of ghosts walking around, right? Most people who die, they stay here for a while. I mean, most people are essentially good, but well, most of us got a little extra work to do for the shit we caused. But sometimes they just sorta fade out. Ghosts, I mean. If you ever get a chance—and I hope to hell you don't—watch some coverage of a war zone sometime in the Middle East or someplace with distinctly different religions. There should be tons of ghosts there and you can almost feel them, even through the TV. We think they're still there, but it's a different realm of perception. Since Garrett and I are essentially more or less Christians, this is our version of that. So we—"

Foster shook his head. "You lost me."

Murphy sighed. "People from other religions are out there. We just can't see them."

"Why didn't ya just say that?"

"Yeah, sorry about that," Murphy said. He glanced over. Garrett's hands around the steering wheel were bone white and the muscles in his neck tightened from gritting his teeth. "Any other questions?"

Foster thought about that for a minute. "Yeah. What'd you do? You seem old. I don't know how this works, but shouldn't you have had a chance to, ah, what'd you call it, ass end yet?"

"Ascend," Garrett growled.

Murphy jumped in, giving Garrett a placating glance. "I got some selfish reasons for staying here. That gets a little easier to do when you've got some years on you. New ghosts, if they're ready, they get pulled up without a choice."

"And you? You have a choice?"

"No," Murphy said colorlessly. "No, not really." He pointedly tried to focus his attention on the blur of neon lighting from the fast food chains and gas stations outside rather than looking at Garrett again. His guilt for the way his friend's life had turned out was his own business. No one else's.

"Huh. So what are these things that fly around us?"

"That's maybe the best question of them all, and unfortunately, one we don't know a damn thing about," Garrett said, a little less surly. "I think they're kind of like personal ID tags, except they're sort of sentient. Uh, alive. I mean."

Murphy nodded. "Like, they're both part of us and not, all at once. Sometimes it feels like they're watching, other times it just feels like they're following us. But it's just that. Feelings. No one knows what they are."

There was sweet, blessed silence the rest of the ride. They finally pulled up in front of the club and Garrett stopped. "Hey, Foster, if—"

"Look, kid, it's cool you're lookin' into my death and all, but there's tits to see and asses to bury my face in." He shrugged. "Don't get me wrong. I was panicking. I mean, bad. And I sure appreciate you fellas showing up and telling me what's what. But I gotta do me, you know? Lived my life tethered to that building and now I can go anywhere I want, whenever I want. And I'm gonna. Good luck guys." Foster slipped out through the door and jogged towards the strip club. At the last moment, he turned back and gave them a little wave.

"What a guy," Murphy muttered, scowling. Garrett couldn't agree more.

They drove a little ways and talked about it. Neither of them could figure out a logical next step. Maybe ask around, but there wasn't much to go on. White guy with big bug eyes. Great. That could be a thousand people. They agreed to bring it up with Padraig, to have him keep an ear to the ground for similar cases, but there wasn't much either one could do. Monica would have to be brought in, but she'd have even more limited options without any proof a murder had been committed.

Finally, Garrett pulled over and sank his head against the wheel. Murphy said nothing, letting his friend work it out. He'd given up on a great date, an amazing woman, and a probable future with her for no payout whatsoever. No justice would be done. Nothing they learned over the last hour mattered.

He put it in park, got out, and leaned against the car. Murphy slid through the door and stood beside him. They could have left it that, Murphy knew. They could get up in the morning and keep on carrying on. It was what they did—what Garrett did, really. He might have taken more beatdowns than anyone else Murphy had ever met, shit so hard it would have driven a lesser man to take a real swan dive off a building. But he hadn't and he wouldn't. No, life would go on. But it would be miserable for him, Murphy knew. The not knowing about his and Brianna's possible future together. That would be the worst.

And it would be miserable for her too.

"Call her," Murphy said suddenly. "Do it right now." He laughed crazily. "Let's do it. Let's fucking throw the dice."

Garrett glanced over at him. "Do you not remember my mom? What happened to her mind?"

"Do you honestly think there's a weak bone in that woman's body?" Murphy laughed so hard he snorted. "She's waiting. You know she is. And she'll wait forever and she'll hurt. Oh God she'll hurt. And we're sitting here…" He laughed even more hysterically. "We're sitting here playing what ifs when what does it fucking matter? We're cliches. We're walking, talking emo clichés who are playing a game of will they, won't they, and by God Garrett you can be happy, do you understand me?" He laughed harder still, great whooping cries of laughter. "All you have to do is be what you always are. Brave."

"And what if she believes me? Where do we go? How is she safe?"

"We figure that shit out tomorrow, man. And the day after. And the one after that. No. You figure that out. With her." His laughter faded away. "You're a brother to me. And my brother's happiness is all I want in this world. Take the chance, Garrett. It might be the dumbest thing we've ever done. But do it anyways. Because doing dumb shit is kind of our thing, ain't it? And because she's worth stupid risks."

Garrett got back in the car. He hesitated only a moment, then he pulled out his cell phone. In the seat next to him, Murphy pumped his fist through the roof and whooped.

* * *

She lay in a strange bed in a strange house, the heater ticking and a down comforter folded around her knees. She didn't cry. This was not her fault, and she wouldn't pretend it was. She wasn't sad, she wasn't upset, she was angry. And not just with him, but at herself. For not being able to get him out of her mind. For wanting him, even then. And most of all, she was furious that the hand—her hand—wandering south along her skin under the pajamas wasn't his.

She thought of his little knowing smile and the steel tension in his muscles when he'd had his arm around her earlier. Damn it, she didn't want to, but she couldn't help it. And sleep was not going to be easy. She leaned back, her hand playing, teasing.

Her phone rang. Of course it would be Garrett. Damn him. She punched the ignore button and stared up at the ceiling, her fingers working a little harder, the anger and lust building. The phone rang again. She grabbed at it with her free hand.

"What?" she snarled.

"Where are you?"

"I'm in bed. At Ed and Rose's. Doing something, uhm, you should be, you ah-asshole."

His pause made her grin ferally. "In their guest bedroom?" There was more silence. "Fuck. That's hot."

"Goodbye, Garrett. Fuck you very much."

"How badly do you want to know what it is I really do? And how I do it?"

She hesitated, her hand still.

"If you're still there, and God, I hope you are, meet me outside in twenty minutes. I'll show you everything. And if you don't... I won't ever bother you again. I swear."

Her fingers slipped away, drawing up across her soft folds and out of the silk of her panties. She wouldn't play this game, she promised herself. She wouldn't. She wasn't his to call at his command like some obedient dog. But... she thought of him, between her thighs, her fingers digging into the gray hairs at his temple. His smile. That kiss. How her heart knew what her mind didn't want to admit. And most of all, even beyond the yearning, was simple curiosity. The story Ed had told her

118

was something else, but left her as full of questions as she'd started with. Put plainly, she wanted to know the truth. "Fuck," she whispered softly into the night, and got up to get dressed.

Chapter 10

She slammed the door purposefully as she got in. The Hyundai didn't deserve her rage, but she couldn't help but feel a little satisfaction with the heavy thunk of the door. She blinked back furious tears. "You're an asshole," she said loudly.

"I know."

She turned in her chair and glared at him. "Let's get something straight. I'm not here at your beck and call. I won't be your girlfriend on the side. I won't put up with that kind of crap."

"I know. And I don't expect you to be. But like I said earlier, there are going to be times when me leaving isn't an option. That's cryptic but I'll explain everything. You've just gotta give me a minute to do this in my own way." He reached a hand out. She flinched, thinking he might be reaching for her. She wasn't ready for his touch. But it wasn't her he was reaching for. Instead he grabbed a backpack from behind her seat and handed it to her. "Open that up. Inside is a notepad and a pen. You're going to need those. There's some, uh, other stuff in there for you too."

"Can you just tell me?" she asked. "I don't want to play games like this." But she turned on the dome light and looked in the bag anyways. She pulled out the notepad, with a pen clipped in its rings. She hefted something else out too. "Is this a Taser?"

"Yeah. Well, a homemade Taser anyways, kind of a specialty of an acquaintance of mine. It's a bit more powerful than a normal one, so be careful. If you believe me, you'll want it later." He shifted the SUV into reverse and hesitated. "Want your seat warmer on? We're going to take a bit of a long trip. It might get kind of dangerous, I'm not going to lie."

She dug out her cell phone and took his picture. She tapped away on it for a minute then held it up so he could see. "I'm sending this to five of my friends so if you murder me or something, they know who to look for."

He dug in the console between them and handed her a piece of unopened junk mail. "My address is on there. If it makes you feel better, send them that and my license plate number too."

She hesitated a moment. He was serious. "You're really not going to do anything to me, are you?" It was less a question than a statement.

"No," he said flatly.

She was no idiot—she sent the original text with his picture on it, but modified it to say "I'm with this guy Garrett Moranis tonight." That was all. It was enough that if something happened, they could find him. She shut off her phone and put it in her purse.

* * *

As they rolled down the block, Rose pushed the curtain from her window back into place and sprinted back to the king sized bed. She crawled over her husband, planting her knees on either side of his stomach, practically giggling with excitement. "They're leaving together."

"I know," Ed said, smiling fondly at his lovely wife, his hands roaming freely around her waist.

She rocked on her knees and traced the sparse hair on his chest. "He's going to tell her."

"I know," he said again, loving the warmth of her on him.

She covered his face with kisses and pressed his hand to her chest. "I love you."

"I love you too."

* * *

Half a block away, Garrett said, "Okay, pick a spot. Anywhere that's open. It'll help show you what I need you to know."

"What? Why? Why not just tell me right now?"

Garrett rubbed the back of his head and grimaced. "Because you'd laugh, demand I stop, and get out at the next corner."

"Try me. Complete honesty, Garrett, or I walk anyways." Her heart hammered in her chest. Was she lying to him? No. No, she knew in her heart she could walk away, even if it killed her to do it.

He closed his eyes briefly, as though he were praying. then he opened them and stared straight ahead, his face resigned. "I see ghosts."

She shot him a blank stare. "I. Huh?"

"I see ghosts," he repeated more firmly.

"Shut up, stop the car, and let me out here."

He did all three of those things. She backed out of the car slowly, as though he were a snake that was going to bite her. Ice thatched the sidewalk and she slipped a little before righting herself against the

Hyundai. The lights were terrible here.

Crazy. He was fucking crazy. That was his big secret. Awesome. She'd fallen for another nutbar. Terrific with a side of woo-hoo. She dug out her cell phone, about to call a friend to pick her up. Or Uber. Or anything. Ghosts. What kind of psycho bullshit was that?

Completely insane.

She hesitated. He was still sitting there, watching her, his face screwed up in sadness and pain. She could walk away now and tell her father that he was no longer welcome at the gym. She'd never have to see him again in her lifetime. Ghosts. What kind of idiot did he take her for? Ghosts... she turned and glanced at him again. Ghosts. Damn her curiosity. Damn her need to know how far gone he really was upstairs. Even if he was crazy, even if she was in danger being near him, it still didn't explain what he'd done to save Ed from murder. And she still wanted to know. Damn it all, there was a story here, and she loved stories.

She treaded carefully back to the SUV and got back in. "You what now?" she said huffily.

"I see ghosts."

"Like Sixth Sense ghosts?"

"God, I hate that movie. But yeah, sort of, I guess. They're not as gruesome, just kind of like normal people wandering among us, but... yeah."

"You're crazy. You are batshit bananas crazy."

"You asked for the truth. I'm giving it to you. All of it."

"Like What About Bob levels of cuckooness."

He blinked. "Sorry, I don't know what that is."

"You really need to watch more movies," she said. She waved the Taser at him. "I'm keeping this right where I can use it. You understand me? I catch one whiff of you going psycho on me and I'll zap you."

"Yes, good. Honestly I'm surprised we made it this far in the conversation."

"Yeah, well, there are some stories I'd kick myself for not hearing." She tucked herself into the corner as far as she could fit, her shoulders wedged into the edge of the chair and the door. "You asked me before to pick a spot, any spot. Why?"

"I want to show you that I'm telling you the truth. If you pick the place, maybe you'll believe me a little more easily. I have a few ideas on how to do that I'm telling you the truth, but... well, it's going to be weird." He started driving with nowhere in particular in mind. Not yet, anyways.

"But you said we were going to take a long trip."

"If you believe me, yeah. First though let's get the demonstrations out of the way."

"And if I don't believe you, you'll let me just walk away."

He nodded. "Yeah."

"Just like that. I'm out of your life. No stalkery bullshit?"

"No. Nothing like that."

She studied him carefully. "You really would let me go, wouldn't you?"

He glanced at her. "Complete honesty?" She nodded. "It would hurt. A lot. I enjoyed our date tonight way more than I hoped to. I want to see where things could be between us. But… if letting you go is what you want and need, I'm prepared for that."

She chewed her lip. "You'd really be okay with not seeing me again?"

"No. I'd be heartbroken. But if that's what you wanted, I'd respect that."

"Hm." Somewhere inside, something let go. In for a penny, she thought. She reached around and tugged on her seat belt. "What kind of demonstration are you talking about?"

He pulled back out onto the street. This part of Rankin Flats was quiet, dark, and deceptively dangerous in its tranquility. The upper middle crust still lived out here, but the economic divide didn't make it any safer. "That notepad. Hold it away from me so I can't possibly see it. It'd help if there's a bit of light shining on the paper, but so long as you can see the writing, so can he."

"He?"

"Murphy. He's a friend of mine. Has been for a very long time. He's going to see what you write, tell me, and I'm going to tell you. It's a dumb little parlor trick, but we only had about half an hour to think this through."

She choked out a desperate laugh. "And he, what, rides shotgun with you?"

"Yeah. Well, usually. He lives with me and we work together on… that'll come a little later. Sorry, cryptic, I know, but let's just get this out of the way first."

She thought about it for a minute, but that odd feeling of letting go hadn't left her. This was weird and goofy and she felt like she was being put on, but in a way, it felt like being a part of an audience to a magic trick. She knew it was all make-believe but she wanted to be dazzled anyways, to try to see where the wires and the mirrors and what not were. She turned in her seat so the notepad was between her and Garrett, and wrote out a single sentence.

From the backseat, Murphy said, "I fell so hard for you."

Garrett smiled sadly at her. "I fell hard for you too."

She nearly dropped the paper and whipped a look at the glass. At the mirror. "Where's the mirror control? Oh, here it is." She moved the mirror so it was facing upwards.

"That's kind of dangerous—" Garrett protested.

"Hush." She scribbled again on the notepad.

"She doodled a flower. Don't know what kind it is, sorry, but it's got six of those little flowery half circle things around it."

"Flower. Six half circle petals around it. Murphy doesn't know what kind of a flower it is."

Her mouth worked open and closed. She twisted in her seat, looking for trick mirrors or a camera or something to explain it away. There had to be something. "This is crazy," she muttered. "How are you doing this?"

"There's no trick. No reflection. Nothing."

She wrote more words, phrases, and doodles. Each time, Murphy told Garrett what they were. Apart from a dog which Murphy called a horse, they were spot on. She shook her head in disbelief. "What's the other part of the demonstration. The one where you wanted me to stop?"

"We kinda thought maybe you could go in to some random place where I couldn't see you. You would do whatever in there, Murphy would follow you, and tell me exactly what you said or did."

"OK, the gas station. Coming up on the corner. Stop there."

He pulled in. She unbuckled and shot a finger at him. "Stay. Here."

She left the notebook behind and walked into the store. Other than the bored clerk reading a paperback, the place was deserted. She stormed through the store and at the back cooler, she grabbed a bottle of Pepsi. Then she swapped it out for an iced tea. She made her way back to the front, touching various products on her way through the store. When she paid for her drink, she said to the clerk, "Good evening, Mr. Caldwell" to his confusion and left. When she got in the car, she said,

"Tell me everything I did in there."

Garrett turned and listened to what she assumed was absolutely nothing and nodded. "You went in, got a Pepsi from the cooler, put it back, got the tea, then touched two bags of chips, a thing of jerky—oh, teriyaki beef sticks, sorry—and a twelve pack of beer in a display in the middle of the aisle. Full disclosure though, I did see you touch the beer. And you paid for your stuff and told the clerk good evening Mr. Caldwell." He searched her astonished face. "Is that about right?"

White as a sheet, she nodded. "How?" she squeaked out. "How are you...?"

Garrett rubbed the knuckles on one hand then repeated the motion with the other. "It's too much to ask you to believe. I know."

She licked her dry lips. "It's a trick. It has to be."

"No," he said gently. "It's not a trick. And if you're willing to go a little further, I'll explain why it was I had to leave and what I do."

She clutched her purse, needing something real to grip. Something solid. She'd looked around in the store. A big round mirror in one corner might have given her away, but there was no way he could have seen it from the car. A camera? Where would he hide it on her? She scraped at her clothes with her fingertips. No. Nothing. He watched her, bemused and a little sad. "All right," she said, sucking in her breath and letting it out slowly. "There's no camera. There's nothing obvious here." She rubbed at her temple with one hand and wheezed out a laugh. She was terrified now, almost-pissing-her-pants levels of scared, but she was excited too. She had him stop again at a big box store, this time touching dozens of things, not even remembering what she did or said but heard it recited back to her verbatim. Maybe he'd followed her. A thousand maybes—a hundred thousand, a million—couldn't stop her from wanting to know.

"Tell me the rest of it." She eyed him carefully. Very carefully. "Garrett, who the hell are you?"

He put the car in drive and cleared his throat. "That," he said, "is a very long and strange story."

* * *

In a town in rural Missouri nearly a decade and a half before Garrett and Brianna drove for the plains south of Rankin Flats, a grumpy boy got into his car. He was irritated because a cute, slightly older girl had shut him down past second base and he was young, very stupid, and impatient. It wasn't the sort of night to be driving angry—the wet weather left the roads covered in a layer of ice as fat as the joint on a finger. But he had no grasp on his own mortality, and he roared down the streets, fiddling with his radio. He listened to everything for only a minute at a time, flip flopping from old country to heavy metal to a modern hits station. For a while, he left it on a college station. The DJ played a good mix of blues rock, and Stevie Ray Vaughan came on.

From the seat right next to the boy, a man spoke up. "Finally, some good music."

The young man looked across sharply. A black guy sat in his passenger seat, bobbing his head, his eyes closed as he took in the awesome sounds of Vaughan's guitar. He seemed vibrant, his substance somehow more alive than the world around him, but there was a flimsiness to him too. Like if the boy blew on him, the man might burst apart into nothingness. And there were these ribbons. Strange, beautifully colored things, one a blue about the color of the sky, the other gray and faded. They flitted about his lower body playfully. "Who are you?" the boy asked.

The ghost whipped his head at the young man and started to say, "You can see me?" Except that the boy, who hadn't paid any attention to the road in seconds, crashed into the ass end of a parked van.

That sexually frustrated idiot was Garrett. The ghost was Murphy.

* * *

"You saw him before you crashed?"

"Yes. I distinctly remember that. He does too. I know—if it was a brain injury or something that caused all this, you'd think I would've seen him after the crash, not before it. But..." he shrugged. "There's a lot of this we don't understand."

Maybe that did rule out a brain injury. Or maybe it didn't. Who was she, House? "Keep talking."

* * *

Though by all outwards appearances he only had a cracked rib and a broken leg, the hospital insisted on him staying for observations. They were concerned about Garrett's rambling, they said. He might have a concussion they couldn't see, or worse yet, brain damage.

He tried to make them understand. He did. His mom, his dad, his two younger sisters, the nurses, the doctors, all of them listened to him about the ghost from the crash and the ones wandering through the hospital, but no one would believe him. Through it all, Murphy stayed near the teenager, thinking it was his fault for causing the wreck somehow. The boy was terrified of the ghost at first, but that quickly changed to curiosity. After all, ghosts were supposed to be scary or cute and not look like they came straight from the seventies. He liked the ghost's short stylishly curly hair, the way his shirt collar looked vaguely piratey, his slick black suit, the dress slacks, the sleek leather loafers. He liked the colorful but intelligent speech, the way the man composed himself. And after a while, the two began talking when no one else was around.

He learned a lot about Murphy. How the man had been a bit of a criminal's criminal in life, dealing drugs, breaking a bone here and there, how he'd eventually-

* * *

Garrett glanced up at the mirror. "Is it okay if I tell her about your past? I didn't even think to ask."

"You're talking to him?" Brianna said, a little faintly.

"Yeah. Hang on, he's… we gotta work out the logistics of the three of us talking all at once. Oh, that's a good idea. Murphy says when he and I are talking, I should hold up my fingers or something, like a sign." He held up his pointer and middle fingers on the right. "Yeah, okay."

"Well?"

"He says it's fine. Anything I need to tell you about, he says he's an open book to you."

She laughed shakily. "Great."

* * *

-eventually started to hate the life but felt trapped by it. It was what he knew. He couldn't stop and suddenly become a banker or something. Funny enough, it wasn't violence or the life that killed him, but cancer.

He left behind a kid, and for a long time, Murphy watched over him. But when he became a man and started living his own life, it became hard and not a little lonely. So Murphy started traveling a bit, mostly to his old haunts and favorite spots. That was why he was in Missouri, for some music in St. Louis.

Garrett tried to convey all this to his family. The two of them even came up with some simple tricks to show them he wasn't lying, like the whole "guess how many fingers" bit. Stephanie, one of Garrett's sisters, thought it was cool and believed him. She even told the kids at school about it—for a while, at least, until she was laughed at and bullied to the point where she became a social exile, growing to despise her brother.

His youngest sister Auggie always seemed a little doubtful. She'd figured out Santa and the Easter bunny before she'd even entered kindergarten, and she figured there was some angle straight from the beginning. Her Teflon disbelief spared her from the same social pariahism as her older sister.

But their parents... well...

* * *

"Can I have a drink of that?" Garrett asked her. She handed over the untouched bottle of tea wordlessly. He sipped it. "Thanks. This next part... it's hard to talk about."

* * *

His mom was religious. Not crazy religious, but she went to church every Sunday, and she helped host a lot of the functions the church ladies loved to put on. Bake sales, bingo games, holiday parties, that sort of thing. His father wasn't particularly religious, but he believed, mostly out of a desire to humor his wife, who he loved more than anything else in the world, even his children. It was natural that when Garrett told her he could see ghosts, she would turn to religion. He even went with her to speak to a preacher, Yvette. She was a large woman with an indefinable eastern European accent and she stared at Garrett with the deadest eyes he'd ever seen as he explained to her just how everything had happened.

Yvette had tried a few tricks there in the church—prayer, dabbing his eyelids with holy water, giving him a cross to wear. Nothing took away his vision of the man standing beside them, looking bored and a little put out. His mother invited him back to church several times after that, promising him they'd fix what was wrong with him with the power of healing, but Garrett didn't feel broken. He felt perfectly normal—he could just see more, that was all. And eventually, as his and Murphy's friendship solidified, he stopped believing he needed to be fixed at all.

And so he tried to continue on with his life. Being an outcast at school irritated him until Murphy spotted a douchebag dealing weed from his locker during a basketball game. Garrett blackmailed the kid— not one of his classier moves—into giving him both the weed and the two hundred bucks he had stashed in a copy of a Robert McCammon novel in the back of his locker. That night, as he lay under the stars smoking a joint and talking to Murphy, he realized they could make a go at little jobs like that. It was going to be fun, they thought. Take revenge on the assholes who mistreated Garrett and Stephanie, and make a little money on the side.

Those first few weeks, they rolled through the school. The school's biggest, meanest junkyard dog of a bully soon found himself expelled for the discovery of a crack pipe and several ounces of meth in his locker. A stuck-up prig of a girl who made Stephanie's life particular hell had her diary stolen from her locker, photocopied, and the juiciest pages slipped into the lockers of all her victims. A shitty teacher who liked to look down the blouses of the girls in his classes as he leaned over them in computer class was kicked out when a video tape surfaced showing him jerking off in the women's locker room.

But then there was Bruno. That wasn't his real name, but that was what the kids called Barry, the hulking star running back for the high school. Garrett had never really paid him any mind—in fact, they'd been teammates for a couple of years and they'd once shared a beer together, snuck onto a bus in an empty Gatorade bottle. But Bruno got on Garrett's bad side by hurting a girl Garrett fancied. When she reluctantly told him what had happened—Bruno had dumped her for a math whiz—Garrett promised her he'd get even.

And he did. Murphy tried to talk him out of it. Tried to convince him it was a petty dick move. But three days later, Bruno was suspended when they found the stolen answers to an upcoming math midterm in his locker. He was well known for having problems in math, and no one believed his pleas of innocence. The girl thanked Garrett in a very enthusiastic, physical way. But afterwards, he felt no pleasure. It had been wrong, deeply wrong, all of it. Murphy wanted out if they were going to keep doing that to normal people, and Garrett agreed. It had been a stupid, childish thing to do.

The next day, of his own will, he walked into the principal's office and admitted his guilt. He showed them how he'd broken in, where the papers had been stashed, and everything they needed to know to prove he was the guilty party, not Bruno. He was suspended for a week, his parents were called, and he was told to spend the time rethinking his entire life.

When he got home, his mother was sitting on the floor, all the family albums neatly beside her and dozens of pictures splayed out around her in a wide half circle. She was humming, something pleasant he remembered vaguely from his early childhood. A pair of scissors in her hand went ssskit ssskit ssskit and half a picture fell on the floor. The half still in her hand went back into a photo album. The half laying on the floor was of Garrett. She was cutting him out of all the pictures. He choked out something unintelligible, and she finally noticed him. Her vapid good cheer melted away and she cried out. She darted to her feet and ran for her bedroom door, slamming it shut behind her.

She didn't come out for days.

When his father came home and Garrett explained what happened, he went back to check on her. When he came out, he was grinning, his face as red as a fire truck, and when Garrett asked if she was okay, his father laughed and hit him twice, hard in the gut, shots that doubled him over and left him gasping for air. He knew his father had been a bad, bad man in the service but this was the first time he'd ever so much as raised his voice to his son, let alone touched him. His father stumbled back, horrified at his own actions, but didn't apologize.

For days, they said nothing to each other. Stephanie and Auggie tried to bring them all back together, tried to keep the family from imploding, but the clock was ticking. When his mother finally emerged from her room, she seemed normal, happy, and loving. She acted like herself for the first time since his accident.

He went back to school. Bruno beat the shit out of him in the locker room. Garrett didn't put up a fight. He knew he deserved it.

And when he went home that night, his mother was waiting. With friends.

* * *

"Garrett, I—" Brianna started, eyes glistening a little.

"If you want out, I'll stop," he said kindly.

"No," she said firmly. "I don't know if I believe you, but I want to hear the rest of it."

He nodded. "It's a long roundabout way of getting there, I know, but you'll see where it's going soon."

She surprised him by reaching over and squeezing his hand. "I'm glad you did the right thing for that boy by telling the truth."

"I sent him some money later on. A lot later on. I found out he had a kid, and I sent him enough to get her a college fund started. I hope that's what he did with it. He's a coach, still in Missouri. I hear his team went to state last year." He shook his head. "It doesn't matter. Sorry."

"It does matter, I think," she said softly. "You kept track of him. How many other kids from your class did you do that with?"

"I..." There weren't any. "None, I guess."

"You took responsibility. That's... well, I heard what you did for Ed. At least up until the point when you offered him a job. He won't say

130

a word about what you do, but... you look after people, don't you?"

"I try."

She nodded. "Finish your story."

He rubbed his jaw. "My mom, she—"

* * *

She stood there in the kitchen doorway, smiling at him happily, but her eyes were vacant and dewy. Medicated again, he thought. Oh joy.

Then the door closed behind him and someone shoved him forward. They came out of the bedrooms and kitchen. How many, he couldn't remember. Murphy said six, but it seemed like a whole army. Women, all of them. They pushed and pulled him towards the kitchen table. He thought maybe he could have broken free if he was really willing to hurt them, but he wasn't and didn't. They shoved him back on top of the table, and he banged his head back against the wood grain hard enough to that red stars flashed in his eyes.

That was the part he remembered the most—his head striking that table where he'd ate meals, played games, and talked with his parents on long nights about problems at school. It had always been a symbol of a good family life, and he wasn't even aware of it until it also became a symbol for his mother's mental break.

Yvette strode down the hallway from his parents' bedroom, a bottle of holy water in hand and a cross in the other. Garrett pleaded with his mother that this was crazy, that they needed to stop, that he was telling her the truth. Some of the women looked uncertain, but Yvette convinced them this was the devil talking through him, tricking them. Garrett cried for the first time in years and years, since he'd lost his dog as a child to a drunk driver. Yvette tried to call out the demons in him, tried to cast out Satan. He realized the fury welling up inside was with himself for so horrifying his mother, not the preacher and he wept like a baby, knowing his mother hated him. With absolute certainty, he knew he was no longer her son but something else to her. Something to be excised.

He broke free then, twisting off the table and falling to the floor. He stumbled to his feet and despite the women yanking at him, he managed to make it to the front door. He cast one terrified, ashamed glance back at his mom and tried to tell her he was sorry. She just shrieked at him and he fled.

* * *

He pulled over and rubbed his eyes for a minute. "That was the last time I saw my mom," he said quietly. There were no tears.

* * *

Even with a ghost at his side, he wasn't prepared for the world without the shelter of his parents.

The earliest days were terrifying. He did nothing but run as far away as he could. Still raw from Bruno, his father's punches, and his mother's breakdown, he refused to steal until he was sick from hunger and exhaustion. After that, they broke into vacant houses, stealing food and taking what cash he could find until he'd amassed enough small bills to get free of Missouri and hop on a bus to Vegas.

Card games, even for a sixteen-year-old, were everywhere if a person knew where to look, and with Murphy searching, they found plenty. Within a few weeks, Garrett made enough money nickel-and-diming rich kids that he could afford a couple of months on a hotel room downtown. One evening, drunk off a game with a bored contractor's kid, he called home. His sister Stephanie answered, but wouldn't speak to him. He couldn't blame her, and still didn't fifteen years later. She pawned the phone off on his dad. Garrett explained where he was, that he was okay, what had happened with his mom and that he understood why his father hit him but that he couldn't come back. His father pleaded with him, but only half-heartedly. Before he hung up, he made Garrett promise one thing—he'd check in with a couple of his service buddies out there now and again. He just wanted to know he was safe. Garrett promised, and surprising himself, he did.

Joshua Tree Security took up a former storefront downtown. They specialized in short term protection for the city's lucky gamblers. Their shifting staff was largely comprised of former military types. His dad's friends were the only constants, seemingly always arguing with each other and never standing still for too long. They took to him like a pair of eternally pissed-off uncles.

Froggy and Blake became his mentors. They didn't once offer to let him stay with them—they were a couple and valued their privacy—but they made sure the boy could not only survive but kick plenty of ass doing it. Between the two of them, they taught him a lot about self-defense, and when he took to it naturally, they opened doors with various other combat instructors from their own business and elsewhere. It became clear when he turned eighteen they expected him to join them in their private security firm, but he politely begged off. By that point, he and Murphy had enough of a foothold in Vegas making some serious money. It was time to start figuring out th

For the last two years, while he'd been training, Garrett continued doing his odd jobs, as he referred to them. He'd built up a sizable bankroll, nearly ten thousand in cash. Fake ID in hand and never staying in one casino too long, he upped that slowly to a hundred thousand by the time he legitimately turned twenty-one. Then he started to work the big money tournaments.

Years of keeping his head down taught him to play well, but not well enough to draw a lot of attention. With a simple lifestyle and a quiet stoicism, he was just another better-than-average player in a sea of other faces, well known to some in Vegas but rarely drawing anyone's ill will. And slowly, his bank account grew to the point where he could legitimately semi-retire. All before his twenty second birthday.

All the while, they kept doing their real work. Poker attracted a lot of assholes, and while dealing with the ones he knew directly would bring hell down upon them, he could safely take down their contacts and associates. But Vegas wasn't real to him. There was violence and corruption to be fought there, but it wasn't a place he could care about. Everything about it felt temporary and superficial, and while they did good work there, it was hard to find a reason to stay. He traveled the States, and fell in love with Montana. With the mountains, the people, everything. And when he came to Rankin Flats, he realized this was a place where he could try to make a difference. Where he could help people.

* * *

"And that's what we do," he said, his voice dry by this point from talking. "We help people. It's not always by punishing criminals. Sometimes it's other things, legal stuff. I've had Ed buying up businesses in town for years now, trying to keep jobs here. I don't know much about that aspect but I think it's working."

"So he knows about you being a criminal?"

"Yeah. He runs my money into those businesses. How much did he tell you?" She told him in broad strokes and he nodded. "Okay, good, yeah, I didn't want to tell you about his past if he didn't tell you himself. I sort of figured he would. Rose and Ed are keen on us."

"I noticed," Brianna said dryly.

"Anyways, I didn't want to drag him right back into the life after he just wanted out, but once I told him what I wanted him to do, where I wanted to take things, he agreed. It kind of surprised me, but I think Ed's always wanted to make a difference too."

"He never spoke a word about what you do now, just about how you saved him from murdering that guy, uh, Jackson?"

"Jackman," Murphy and Garrett said together.

She fidgeted in her seat. "So, you're, what... a vigilante?"

"Of sorts, yeah. Still mostly a thief. I try not to get physically involved if I don't have to, but we do our homework on someone and we figure out what we can do. That's where we're headed tonight. We had a job lined up for tomorrow or the night after, depending, but I wanted you to see what I am. All of it." He reached for her hand, hesitated, and brought the hand back to the steering wheel. "I'm not a saint," he muttered. "I won't pretend I don't want a comfortable life. But we're trying to be better people."

She looked out the window at the pitch-black night. Out this far south, there was nothing but the occasional light of a distant farmhouse or trailer. There might have been anything out there. If Garrett was insane and planning to do her harm, this was where he'd do it. Just pull off somewhere on a dirt road, pull her out, and... she shivered. "Have you ever murdered someone?" she asked quietly.

"Yes," he said softly. "Two men who deserved it. I—"

She held up a hand. A murderer. A strange sort of vertigo struck her, like she was a child again, fearless, staring down into the Grand Canyon and realizing that even without a fear of heights, you respected the hell out of the potential fall. "I don't know if I want to know more than that."

"Okay."

Fake it until you're brave, she thought. "I have questions."

"Sure." He waited for a long time. "You can ask me anything."

"I know, I just... it's like seeing a mountain you need to move and figuring out where to start digging. Um. Your family. Do you still keep in contact with them?"

"Kind of. Auggie, yes. She always was there for me. My dad sneaks a call to me now and again. Things between us are... well, weird, but he tries to be kind, I think." He hesitated a moment. "My mom, she's sick. I just found out the day we bumped into each other at the gym. I think she might be dying. Auggie won't say as much, but... it's there."

"I'm sorry," she said automatically, and found she really was. Crazy or not, she still cared for Garrett. She glanced over at him "That must be…"

"…yeah," he said, agreeing with her in a vague sort of way. For a while, there was just silence. Finally, he said uncomfortably, "Okay, hey, I think we're getting pretty close. I promise you, if you still want answers, I'll tell you everything you want to know tomorrow, next week, whenever. But right now, we've gotta get ready and that means there are a few things I need to tell you."

"Where are we going?"

"There's a trailer out here. It's really a meth lab. Or it was, as of a couple of days ago. Murphy and I have some friends out here watching the place. Other ghosts. I know, more crazy talk. But these cooks are bad guys. Maybe they've packed up and moved on—there's a big chance that might be the case because the information came from a junkie. But if things haven't changed, this is going to be pretty simple. I'm going to go in there, take down the cooks, and smash their lab up and burn it to the ground. Not with them in it," he added hastily. "I'll be only as violent as it takes to get them out the door."

Confused, she asked, "Why burn it? Why not take it to the cops?"

"This stretch of road, this is all Legion, cartel, or redneck territory. They've all got their hooks into something. There's maybe about a fifty-fifty chance you call the cops and wind up with one not on someone's payroll. I'm not willing to risk that. I've got a friend on the force, but she works mostly in Rankin Flats and the suburbs. Out this far, it's anybody's guess who they'd send. It's better to be safe. Plus, these chemicals and that kind of equipment and setup isn't cheap. It'll set someone back and send a message."

She nodded sagely, as though this weren't the most insane conversation she'd had in, well, forever. Still, there was something about his assurance that reminded her of that bed and her fury. And her fingers, sliding down across her skin. A tingle shot up her spine. "And you're not going to kill them?"

"I can't promise no—if they look like they're going to go for you in the car, I'd kill them in a heartbeat, even if that meant prison down in Deer Lodge the rest of my life. But no, I don't intend on it."

"So what do I do?"

"Stay in the SUV. Be ready to take off if anyone other than me steps out of that trailer. Honk if someone's coming."

"I'm confused. If you wanted me in the car, why bring me out here?"

"Because this is what I do. Take earlier tonight, when I left. If I told you, oh, hey, a guy's been murdered but the cops look like they're about to write it off as a suicide—"

"Wait, what?" she exclaimed.

He nodded. "There was a murder downtown tonight. A janitor at an office building, made to look like he jumped."

"But he didn't?" She pulled out her cell phone and started looking it up.

"No. There are certain, um, signs that a person's committed suicide, usually. Or no signs at all. It's complicated. But the guy's ghost was on television, trying to get someone's attention. It worked. Murphy saw the feed and grabbed me out of the house."

She read the story aloud from the Observer's website. Even to her, something felt wrong about the man's death. "Isn't there supposed to be an investigation into suicides, that sort of thing? A coroner's inquest? Isn't that what it's called?"

"Yeah. They'll go through the motions. But they won't find anything. The guy who did this was good. Covered his tracks. If we hadn't caught the break on the news, we'd have never known. The part that killed me was even after we talked to Foster, there wasn't anything we could do. He didn't see the guy's face, didn't give us anything to go on. My cop friend will make some inquiries around the building but that's about it. But I had to try to set things right." He looked at her. "If we become a thing—and I don't want to try to push you, I know how crazy this all is—but if we do, that sort of thing is going to happen. I hate it, but I can't promise you'll be first in my life. And I can't promise you'd be safe, either."

She thought about that for a while. The blunt honesty might have stung someone else with a lower self-esteem, but honestly, she understood completely. She'd always felt a degree of irritation with the tried-and-true TV storylines about an ER doc or a cop getting called in and the wife or husband getting selfishly pissed. She understood their reaction but their significant others were saving lives, making a difference larger than themselves.

But with that understanding came the realization she was buying into Garrett's crazy world. And was she okay with that? She bit her lip in contemplation. She liked Ed and Rose. Well and truly, they seemed like wonderful, kind people. They trusted Garrett implicitly, and he'd clearly inspired some sort of hero worship in Ed. Her father cared a great deal for the man too and had been speaking fondly of him for years, ever since he helped bail the Hammerdown out of a few bad situations. He might have acted gruff around Garrett, but she knew better. Had that all been some kind of long, strange con? Was he leading all these people on, inspiring them with some sort of cult leader charisma, driving them to like him even as he went mental?

Or... was there a chance he was telling the truth? His tricks with the notepad and at the gas station were beyond bizarre, but not definitive proof. Then again, what constituted definitive proof? Her actually seeing ghosts? She'd been raised to believe in God, had even made a point of taking courses on religion and still occasionally made it to church on time. Was it so hard to believe in belief? Tea didn't help her suddenly dry throat. That precipice seemed even more daunting, the fall even more brutal, but there was a giddiness springing up too. She wanted to fly and this man told her she could if she grabbed hold of his hand. She already knew she cared for him more than any other boyfriend she'd ever had (was he her boyfriend, her mind wondered feverishly, was she okay with that, was there ever really a choice?). Was she willing to take a chance on him? On something equally parts insane and amazing?

She shivered. "I'll stay with the car. I can do that," she said. Not a leap. A tiny step forward. But still, her heart thrilled to it.

He glanced at her. "You seem oddly okay with this for someone who just found out from a guy who claims to see ghosts that we're going to destroy a meth lab."

"I had a cousin. Some of her problems were her own doing, some weren't. But she was an addict. I don't know about the rest of it, but this? If this really is a meth lab, I'm a-fucking-okay with it."

Garrett noticed the use of the past tense in regards to her cousin. "I'm sorry. About your cousin. But this too. All of this. I just..." he sighed. "I tried to walk away, but I couldn't. I had to tell you, to try to at least make you understand."

She reached over and touched the back of his hand, surprising not just him but herself too. "I'm glad you did. You're scaring me, but... I'm glad you're being honest."

"Do you believe me?"

Did she? She hesitated. "Let's see how the next part goes," she said finally. Her timing was excellent. The turnoff was only a half mile later.

* * *

He pulled off on the side of the bumpy snow-packed dirt road and turned off the engine. He thought they were far enough away that he could have left it running without anyone hearing them, but better to be safe. He dug around in the back and pulled out a couple of ski masks from his duffel bag. He handed Brianna one and kept the other one for himself. He also dug out the rubber gloves. "If you want to come in after we finish work in there, you'll want to put these on."

She did as he asked, pulling off her knit gloves and slipping on the rubber ones. "Um, why are we stopping here?"

"Murphy's going to go ahead and grab our two scouting friends. They've been out here a while. We were supposed to meet up tomorrow to do this, but circumstances being what they are, we're gonna get it taken care of tonight. He'll grab them, we'll talk here, and we'll figure out what we're going to do."

"Oh. So... do these other ghosts hang out with you too? Like Friends, but with... you know... dead people?"

Garrett laughed at that, delighted. "Oh, Murphy will hate that. It's perfect. No, no, these guys... well, there's a group of ghosts at an abandoned shelter." He grew serious, reflecting on something. "We go out there when we need them. This last time, there was... well." He looked off into the darkness of the night.

Gently, she said, "I heard you and Ed talk about the bodies."

Startled, he whipped his head to gaze at her. "You did? I swear, I didn't have anything to do—"

"No, I believe you. I heard enough and I saw the news." Her eyes moistened. "That must have been..."

"Terrible," he croaked. "There was a kid and she..." He shook his head. It was a while before he cleared his throat and spoke again. "Anyways. There's a group of them that usually hangs out there under better circumstances. We call it a way station, it's sort of a meet-up point for ghosts traveling through the area."

"They travel? Never mind, I'm having so many side thoughts here." She wrote down the question for later, not even realizing as she did she was taking another cautious step forward towards that gorge. "Sorry, keep going."

"We sometimes hire them out to do work for us. We can't actually pay them, but we offer up a cash reward to someone they choose, someone living. On occasion, it's a charity or someone who could really use it, but they're assholes, all of them." He said that with a funny little smile on his face, an old inside joke she wasn't a part of. She wrote down assholes on the pad with a question mark. "So the money usually goes to a former mistress or… what's the male equivalent of a mistress? Mister?"

She thought about that. "I don't think there is one," and wrote that down too. What the hell, she thought, drunk off the absurdity of the moment.

"Anyways, you get the point. They pick, we pay."

"It sounds expensive," she said, shivering as the cold outside started to settle in.

"It is," he admitted. He shrugged out of his coat. "You can use this as a blanket, if you want, or I think I've got the real thing in the way back."

She took the coat gratefully and spread it over her chest. It didn't help much. She wanted him to drape his arm around her again, pull her close and cuddle there among the sea of wheatgrass and brush. And maybe do something else too, some not-so-small part of her mind whispered. She shivered deliciously He confused it for cold and smiled apologetically at her.

"Sorry. I'd run the heat, but we definitely don't want a dead battery out here."

"It's fine," she mumbled. She noticed the callouses on his hands. Wondered what those would feel like on her skin with nothing between them. What was wrong with her? she screamed inwardly. This man was a self-admitted murderer and some kind of Robin Hood wannabe, and she was ready to jump him? "Garrett, the people you said you killed. I guess I do want to know."

He nodded. "The first was in Vegas. He was our last job there. James Pitt. He was a rapist and he sold women and children. Skin trade. He was brought up on charges, ones we helped set up, and he was let go on a technicality. He went right back to doing what he did. Or would have." He stopped there. "I don't recommend it, but if you want to know how…"

"No," she said firmly.

He nodded again. "The second one was a mild-mannered guy, worked two jobs as a waiter and a grocery clerk. By all accounts a nice guy, except he was taking photos of people's IDs at the bar when he could get away with it. Then he'd sell the driver's license numbers for a pretty good profit."

"Not much of a crime," Brianna said, her brow furrowed.

"Right? We figured we'd confront the guy, give him a chance to go straight. We did and he promised he would. Very next day, he's right back at it. I confront him outside of his house and he pulls a gun on me. We struggle and it goes off."

Considering, she said, "That doesn't seem like you murdered him though. Manslaughter, maybe."

"I don't blame myself, if that's what you mean. Under the circumstances, I think I did the right thing—I tried to get the guy to see reason and he went off the deep end instead. That could've been a cop or someone else instead of me, and that thought scares me more than any sort of guilt I might have about it. He was a bomb waiting to go off. But I still murdered him. I can't deny that. The crazy thing is, in both cases, I felt okay about it. I wasn't happy it needed to be done or that it happened, but apart from some what-if nightmares about the stolen ID guy, I don't think it changed me in the way Hollywood tries to tell you it does. If I had to do it again, I would. I know that, and I hope that doesn't scare you off. It's not something I look forward to or anything, but..."

She tightened the coat around herself. "Just... you know, try not to. For me, okay?"

"Of course." After a moment, he pointed at something in the darkness. "The ghosts are coming now. They're hard to see in the dark, but their colors are sort of luminescent."

"Where did you get such a big vocabulary, if you didn't finish out high school?"

"Murphy, mostly. He's a smart guy. And I did get my GED, I just... hang on, they're by the car now. And they're in the backseat." He glanced at her. "It's okay. I'm just going to talk to them for a minute and we'll plan this out, okay?"

He held up two fingers and she shrank back into her chair, a little lost and not a little excited.

* * *

Bjorn and Stansen filled him in quickly. Since he relayed everything spoken to Brianna, it took a while.

The trailer was a double wide. The two cooks inside slept in the spare bedrooms and cooked in the former master suite. Some of the cough medicine was stored in the living room, but by and large, they kept their supplies in a laundry room between the kitchen and master bedroom. One man had opened a back door off that laundry room for a cigarette break while cooking, so they knew it wasn't jammed up.

The two men inside worked in shifts. One was watching a movie on his phone in one of the bedrooms, the other was in the middle of a cook and had his music on with the door closed. Miracle of miracles, the junkie dealer hadn't called them. Sometimes the universe was kind. It was a rarity, but it did happen.

"We can stick around," Bjorn offered, his eyes beady and glinting over his hooked nose. "But we think it's gonna cost you."

"Yeah," his idiot brother said, chuckling. "Cost you."

"Nah, we're good," Garrett said abruptly.

Murphy nodded. "Yup. Adios."

The two ghosts glanced at each other. "But you need someone to, you know, keep an eye on the one Murphy ain't watchin', right?"

Garrett twisted in his seat. "Don't ever try to blackmail me. Get out. Murphy and I got this."

"Fuck you then," Bjorn said crossly. "But we still get paid for the work we did."

"Yeah," Stansen said, nodding his big head slowly. "We did work."

Murphy shrugged. "Leave the name with Padraig. I'll come by tomorrow and we'll take care of it. Now get out."

The two ghosts slipped out of the car, grumbling. Garrett sighed and Brianna finally spoke after minutes of silence. "Ghosts are assholes?"

He nodded. "Yup." He rubbed his face. "Hm. Okay. Two guys."

Murphy thought about it. "You go in the back, you can maybe take out the cook."

"And you watch the other guy? That's solid." Garrett conveyed all this to Brianna.

She scratched her head. "What if the one guy in the bedroom hears you with the cook?"

"With the music playing, that's probably not going to happen."

Murphy considered this. "She could watch your back, Gar, in a way I can't."

"No," Garrett said flatly.

"No what?" Brianna asked.

"He wants you in there with me. As backup. In case you're right and he does wind up hearing me."

She hefted the Taser. "If I stood by the wall next to the hallway leading to the spare bedrooms," she mused.

Garrett looked at her, horrified. "You can't be serious."

"I'm not going to be one of those women who sits around and waits for you to go play hero," she snapped. "I wouldn't be out here if I was. You wanted me in on this? Well this is me, all the way in. I want to see what the hell it is you do."

Garrett lifted his hands off the steering wheel and flexed them, thinking. "If I shout run, you run. You do not hesitate. Murphy's going to be with you all the time."

"Gar, I can slip between—" Murphy started to say.

"All the time," he growled at his friend. "Do we understand each other? Because otherwise we all go our separate ways right now." To Brianna, he said, "Don't be a hero. When we're in there, you do not take unnecessary chances."

They glared at each other, her eyes a fiery challenge, his steel and cold. Finally, she nodded. "How do we do this?"

* * *

They circled around the master bedroom at a distance. Garrett punched through the drifts first, trying to push a path through the snow rather than raise his feet and bring them down in a heavy crunch in the off chance the cook's music stopped. And in fact, in one heart-stopping moment, the twang of a Creedence song died and the radio was silent. Garrett masked the flashlight with his hand and they both held their breath until the upbeat piano keys of a honky-tonk old rock song started. Then with a little more fire in their step, they hurried to the northeast corner of the trailer, where a large blind spot made it easy to slip next to the trailer.

Moments later, they were testing the stairs wordlessly, Garrett first. He clicked off the flashlight, stuck it in his tool belt, and drew out the picks. He glanced up at Brianna questioningly. This was her last chance to not get involved. She made a rolling "get on with it" motion with her finger and he glanced back at the lock, amused.

The locks were old and simple to get open, and by the time the song on the radio reached its zenith of honking and tonking, Garrett was sliding the door open, the picks back in his work belt, baton at his side. Brianna, behind him, raised the Taser and took a deep breath. This was crazy. This was exhilarating. This was the best, weirdest first date she'd ever had, bar none.

The laundry room was a tight fit. He let her slide by him to get to the living room. She took the opportunity to graze his abs, not entirely sure herself if the motion was deliberate or not. He grinned at her with that lopsided smirk, but she could see in his eyes the concern and fear. It was cute, but irritating. She was Danny Reeve's daughter, damn it, and she could go toe to toe with some meth-dealing dickweeds.

As she swerved into the living room and took up her place next to the corridor, Garrett took a deep breath and exhaled gently, focusing his mind. Murphy took up a point next to Brianna in the hallway. "All good here, Garrett. I'll watch her, man."

Garrett nodded, though the ghost couldn't see him in the laundry room. He flicked his baton to its full length and crept to the master bedroom. He twisted the knob, pushed the door open, and the biggest Native American he'd ever seen stared right back at him, dressed in cargo pants, a sweater, and a pink apron that read Number One Mom. "Who the—"

"Oh fuck me, you're a big one," Garrett growled, and flew at the guy.

* * *

The crash down the hallway drew her gaze only for a second. From the pair of bedrooms, she heard a man shout, "Bill?" She brought her Taser up, ready to strike, not even realizing how hard she was grinning in anticipation of the fight.

The door to the master bedroom crashed open and Garrett was thrown down the short hallway to the laundry room. He got up to his feet, gave her a shaky thumbs up, and was tackled from behind by one of the biggest men she'd ever seen. He roped his arms around Garrett, squeezing him tight to his chest and he had just enough air to gasp, "A bear hug? Really?" He whipped an elbow into the man's face, again and again. Then Brianna had her own fight to worry about.

The man came down the hallway fast, almost darting past Brianna before she did the most natural thing in the world and tripped him. The man fell flat on his face, and she grunted triumphantly. But the wormy little guy was up on his feet in a flash and turning. She didn't hesitate and brought the Taser up in an arc, aiming for the side of his gut. The zap paralyzed him and he fell to the floor in the fetal position. She zapped him again for good measure and whooped.

The big man had Garrett beat in terms of reach, but in the narrow hallway with no room to negotiate, Garrett's blazing fast fists were too much for the man to keep up with. He had lost the baton somewhere in the struggle, and was snapping straight solid jabs right into the man's solid gut and jaw. He might as well have been throwing bees at a rhino. The big man charged him again and he ducked into the laundry room, twisting at the last second to shove the cook down the hallway and into the kitchen. The cook turned on his feet pretty fast for a big man, but Garrett was already there with a flying elbow to the face that shattered the big man's nose and sent him reeling against the kitchen wall where the stove should have been. Garrett didn't let up, kicking the man's knees out from underneath him and taking short, measured shots at his face and thick square jaw. The cook batted at him ineffectually and Garrett caught an opening. He grabbed him by the hair and slammed his head against the edge of the counter. Once, twice, three times and the big man was swimming in a punch drunk haze. Garrett hauled back and punched him one last time, a solid haymaker to the temple that dropped the big man. Breathing hard, Garrett looked around wildly for Brianna.

She was just getting up off her knees, the zip-ties he'd given her in her hand. "Already got mine tied up," she said as though she were bored. "You sure took your time." She tossed him her ties.

They hauled the two men outside and tied their hands together tightly. After checking an old Bronco for knives and sharp edges, they shoved the two still-groggy men into the back Garrett would have let them suffer in the cold, but Brianna hauled out a blanket from the bedrooms and tossed it over them. "I'm sure they'd thank you if they were at all coherent," Garrett said.

"I know, I'm such a saint," she said lightly.

They went through the trailer house fast. Garrett found a few hundred bucks in a cigarette carton, not enough to make the night financially viable but enough to put a little grin on his face as he gave Brianna her half. They took to each room, smashing up bottles, vials, and beakers with wild abandon. They dragged sheets and blankets to the master bedroom, tossing on everything flammable they could find along with the boxes of drugs and supplies.

Back in the living room, giving the place one last look for anything they might have missed, Brianna tugged her mask up. Her cheeks flushed and her eyes twinkled with excitement. Every part of her tingled. Laughing, she gasped, "Oh my God, this is incredible. The rush, it's…"

"It's insane, isn't it?"

"Is he gone?" she asked breathlessly. "Your friend?"

"Out by the car, watching those two."

She pulled him to her, hands clasped around his head and neck, seeking his lips with her own, their breath mingling together. She let him push her against the wall, her fingers knotted in his hair. One of his hands roamed down her spine, down across her butt, and lifting her hip so that her leg wrapped around his. His other hand cradled the back of her head as they kissed. He drew her hair away from her ear, nibbling at her lobe, and she was gasping for him, whispering his name as she kneaded the muscles in his back. Her foot rubbed up and down the back of his ankle and she could feel his need pressing against her thigh. She ground against him, and he made a fist and pounded it against the wall, pulling back slightly, gasping. "Tell me you don't believe. Tell me and I'll go."

Her hands felt for his zipper, brushing up against his hardness. She moaned wordlessly as his hand splayed over her rear, squeezing, teasing. She finally got his pants down and his other hand was up under her blouse, finding a hard nub through the silk of her bra and rubbing gently. "Tell me you don't believe," he said hoarsely. He pulled his hand out of her blouse so he could lift up her skirt, skimming the backs of her thighs.

She tugged down his boxers and he groaned with pleasure as she brushed against him. Fingers flitted against her sex, rubbing her through her panties and they were gone, just gone, torn out of the way and she didn't care, he was making her feel so electric, so alive. He pressed against her but wouldn't enter. He stared into her eyes and she knew if she wanted this to end, he'd be gone in a heartbeat. "Tell me," he said, pleading with her to end this madness, to be free of him. Instead she kissed his neck, kissed his cheek, kissed his mouth, and she was being lifted up and pushed against the wall again as she wrapped her legs around him. Carefully but forcefully, he entered her and she cried out.

Holding her up by her hips, he built up a steady rhythm. She gasped erratically, sucking in breath and hiccuping it back out. She scratched at his back through his shirt, and his hot breath tickled as he whispered her name and nuzzled her neck. Her moans turned into a wordless shout as she shook and writhed and rode out her orgasm, her fingers tensing and clenching the back of his shirt. He slammed into her with abandon, loving the feel of her ass in his rough hands, loving the flutter of her eyes, the little involuntary nip of her teeth on his neck. And then he was over the edge, shoving into her one last time, gasping her name and kissing her neck, her chin, her forehead, her lips, feverish little butterfly kisses, knowing this could be their only time, knowing she was the only one he'd ever want. "Tell me," he begged. "Tell me to walk away. Tell me you don't believe me and you can have a normal life."

"I believe," she gasped.

Chapter 11

The roughness of his five o'clock shadow tickled as he kissed her thighs and slid upwards. She arched her back and moaned, crushing the thick sheets between her fingers as he worked magic down there, slowly, teasingly. She pleaded with him softly, telling him what she wanted, and he began in earnest. She pressed him down, her head twisting back and forth slowly, tingling from her head to her toes. Release, sweet release, and she shuddered and moaned wordlessly.

Then he made love to her, slowly this time, studying her face as she stared back up at him, loving the soft smile, his mussed-up hair, the way his muscles clenched and loosened with every stroke. And he looked down at her, and loved the way that dark hair spread on his pillows, the secret little smile he'd never seen before on her face, the quiet sighs and moans. And although she didn't orgasm that time, it was still sweet for both of them, perhaps even better than the frenzy of the night before. He lay beside her after, hand tracing the side of her face. "Good morning," he said, grinning.

"God, you can wake me up like that anytime you want," she said, laughing.

He kissed the hollow of her neck. "I will. What time is it?"

She reached for her cell on the nightstand and swore when she looked at it. "I promised my dad I'd be in an hour ago," she said as she swung out of bed. He laughed. "What?" she asked.

"Your back. I'm so sorry. It looks like someone rubbed it with sandpaper after what we did last night."

"Yeah, that was... intense," she said. She got up and pranced into the bathroom, knowing his eyes were on her naked ass. She flicked on a light. "Hey, there's a towel covering your mirror."

He rolled his eyes. "Hell, I have so much I still need to tell you. Go on ahead and take it down. I don't like mirrors." He grabbed his own phone off the end table and started browsing it for the previous night's news.

She pulled it off and examined her back as best she could. "Ouch," she said. "Boy, you really did a number on me."

"Um, yeah. Sorry about that."

"Don't be," she called, now out of sight. He pretended not to hear her go to the bathroom. She flushed and poked her head around the corner. "Shower?"

He dropped his phone and practically leaped off the bed.

Sometime later—much later—they finally managed to get dressed. For the first time, Brianna really paid attention to the condo. The stark walls, blank and angry as an empty canvas. The massive monolithic safe in the bedroom. The comfortable, but completely bland furniture. This was the apartment of someone who'd been alone for a very, very long time and the emptiness of it brought her to tears.

She sat on the edge of one of his recliners in his living room and let herself go, the exhaustion of the last day finally catching up to her. She cried for Garrett, for the loneliness she felt in that place. There were no photographs. No artwork. Nothing but a sterile cleanliness. There were things in his house, to be sure, but they felt as though they were window dressing. What was it Rose had said about the women in his life? That he'd felt obligated to have them there? That felt like his entire place. Fifteen years, he'd been alone. She couldn't have lasted a tenth of that, she knew. She needed people the same way she needed water or food. How hard it must have been to reach for her last night, to admit his own need and tear down these walls he'd so carefully constructed. She cried at that, too, and for herself a little bit, because she was happy and the tiniest bit scared, not of Garrett but at what they were quickly becoming, at the speed and ferocity of her own heart's feelings.

And most of all, she cried because between his kitchen and his living room, where most people would have set up their dining area, there was nothing but a pair of metal folding chairs.

Garrett let her cry, watching her from the door frame. After a while, she looked up and blinked away the tears. He took her hand, pressed it against his cheek, and kissed it gently. She took out her cell phone, pulled him in beside her on the arm of the edge of the chair, and took a picture of the two of them, her with glassy trails of tears and a smile, him with amused bafflement. "That computer in your spare bedroom, does the printer work?"

He nodded. She got up and pulled him in there along with him. She connected her phone to the printer, something he didn't even know could be done, and soon they had a beautiful black and white photograph of the two of them. She asked him for a pin, and stuck the photograph up on the wall in the living room.

"There," she said happily. "Now you're not alone anymore."

From behind, he wrapped his arms around her. He brushed the side of her neck with his lips. "It's perfect," he said.

She could feel him stiffening as he explored the contours of her body, his rough hands amazingly gentle. "You like my ass, don't you?" she laughed.

"Mm."

His hands moved to her hips and she tried not to suck in a breath. "You know we've gotta get going."

"Mm."

She shivered against him as he unbuttoned her blouse and tugged it a little out of her jeans, giving his fingers access to her waistband. Finally, she pulled his hands away and smiled. "Later. I promise. But we need to go and besides, I'm a little, um, tender."

"From me?" he asked, surprised. "It's like a thumb down there."

She laughed, liking this, her back pressed up against him as he held her gently. "Yes, from you. Besides," she said, grabbing his hand and kissing it, "it's more like a middle finger."

"Ouch," he said, snickering. "You're great at the post-pillow pep talks."

She turned and pressed her head against his chest, sighing. "Your friend Murphy, is he here? Gone?"

"Gone. He went to talk to our friends at the shelter." He pulled away from her gently. "Wait, does that mean you actually do believe me?"

"Yes," she said simply. "I don't know why—God knows it seems crazy—but yeah, I do believe you. I think it just boils down to wanting to."

He pulled her close again and crushed her against his chest. This was not a hug born of desire but of plain human need. He held her to him, not wanting to speak, not wanting to dare breathe, for fear that it was all some trick of the demons in the mirror. He let her go only when he was sure she would not fade away. "Thank you," he said simply.

* * *

Three very different expressions greeted them when they got to the gym. Ed seemed largely amused, Rose shone as bright as a lamp, and Danny just seemed mildly put out. "Thought maybe you two numbnuts got lost," he grumbled.

"I, uh… sorry," Garrett said.

"Well, grab a damn roller and get to work," Danny said. Then, almost as an afterthought, he said to Brianna, "And don't you get any thoughts about playing grab-ass in the gym. Keep it in your pants for a few hours, huh?"

While Garrett just gawped at Danny, Brianna rolled her eyes and sighed. "Yes, Dad."

The work went much faster than the previous day, since they didn't have to move equipment or pictures, and they were done by noon with all the help they had. Even Wilfred stopped by to help, though he mostly stood around and held down the fort near the bagels and coffee. Still, Garrett was glad to see the kid there. Brianna and Danny gave him a free six-month membership, on the house, and he walked out of there with his head held much higher than when he entered.

With the painting done and nothing left to do but let it dry, the bulk of the volunteers left by noon. After thanking her for bringing her car to the gym, Brianna kissed Rose on the cheek and the two hugged like old friends before the Guzmans departed, bound for home. That left Danny glaring at Brianna and Garrett.

"You're buying lunch," he said, and stumped towards the office to lock up.

* * *

The hospital couldn't have been more of a wash, Ransom thought, as he bit into a ridiculously overpriced BLT from the cafeteria. The two ghosts in the ER had given him shell-shocked stares and begged him to talk to their families for them, that there were things unsaid they needed to talk about. Then, inconveniently—but still rather fascinating—one of them started to flake apart, his colors swirling around him as the particles of his existence rose up and through the ceiling in that familiar passage of death.

He tried the cancer ward, but the lone ghost there told him to piss off as he watched the children play a video game in a common area. Children with video games in hospitals, Ransom thought with contempt. No wonder his bills were always so astronomical. They had to pay for Halo somehow.

He strolled down to the long-term care ward, but the lone ghosts he saw in there were sitting with family members and he couldn't see a way of approaching them without drawing unwanted attention. The nursing home was a complete bust, apart from a hot little housekeeper who gave his suit an appreciable glance. Her wide, slim eyes seemed to promise a good time if he wanted it. Her pussy was probably ground zero for a plethora of venereal diseases, he mused, but he got her number anyways, thinking back to his idea about the hookers.

To get back to his car, he had to go back through long term care, but the smells wafting out of the cafeteria reminded him he hadn't eaten anything since yesterday. He stopped in, got the sandwich, and decided against the nearly three-dollar minute bag of chips. As he ate, he tapped his fingers on the table, trying to keep a beat in his head to stave off the frustration and anger rising up in him. This was a good plan. He just had to be patient.

After he finished his sandwich and left the cafeteria, he plodded down the long term care hallway. He flapped the piece of paper the housekeeper gave him against his palm, idly remembering the taste of ash in his mouth and wondering why. Lost in thought, he was startled when a ghost walked through a wall and into the hallway. The brown streamers looked nothing so much like shit and baby shit respectively, he thought, snickering. There were too many people around to get her attention, so he trailed her around the hospital. Her walk seemed aimless and bored, the sort of thing a living person would do in just that sort of place after too many hours of sitting. In an indoor atrium (yet another example of wild extravagance), she stopped by a monstrous cactus and sat on a bench, swinging her feet through the floor as she watched small groups of people go by. He sat down next to her.

"I can see you, you know," he said quietly and calmly. She thought he was talking to someone else and ignored him. "You. The ghost. Right beside me." She shot him an astonished stare and he grinned. "Yes, hi, hello." Still she said nothing, just watched him, her eyes huge. "Weird, I know. I saw you in there earlier. In the long-term care section. Family member?"

She didn't speak, just nodded.

"Shame. What happened?"

She worked her mouth as though she were a fish. "Car accident," she said finally.

"That's terrible. Not much of a talker?"

She shook her head.

He raised his palms up. "It's okay. I don't want to make you uncomfortable."

"I was born mute. It's... strange to talk. She's my daughter." The admission seemed painful. There was history there, something bad or she wouldn't be stuck here. He seized on it.

"I know something must have happened between you. But what if I told you that you could help set things straight between the two of you? Her bills must be insane—I mean, look at this place, it's a temple to money." She laughed nervously at that. He leaned in closer, smiling, one friend to another. "See, there's this person I saw yesterday, a guy not entirely unlike me. He can see ghosts too. I want to know more about him. Everything I can, actually."

The look she gave him was calculating and wary, but she wasn't walking away.

"If you help me, if you follow this man around and come back to me every night to tell me what he does, I'll cut your family a check—"

"Not my family," she said firmly. "My daughter's caretaker."

His grin faltered for a minute as the urge to punch her for interrupting surged, but then it returned even wider. "Sure, yes. I'll pay them a grand for every week you work for me. But if I sense that you're stretching it out or test my patience in any way whatsoever—" the grin disappeared and his eyes went deadly cold, "-then they'll never see a penny. Sound reasonable?"

She thought about it and nodded.

"Good. It'll require you to be a bit more talkative than I'm sure you're used to, but I think you'll like working for me." He grinned and for a crazy moment she thought he might bite at her. "I'm a likable guy."

* * *

Less than a block away, a balding doctor pushed his glasses up on his nose and told Jamie Finson just how long he had to live. He registered the news, processed it, and shrugged it off, wishing he could be free of the intolerable little room with its dry, boring decorations and this overstuffed little prick of a doctor. It wasn't so much the man's bedside manner that irritated him as it was the man's mucus voice. He couldn't wait to be out of there and done with it, and then he realized, well, why not just get up and leave?

So he did. The doctor stopped in mid-sentence, startled. "Mr. Finson?"

Jamie opened the door and glanced back. "Buy yourself some fucking Mucinex."

He strode out to the sunlight, what little there was of it on that dreary day, trying not to wince at the pain in his leg. His stomach roiled too, but that was to be expected now, he guessed. His cell phone buzzed.

"How'd it go, grampa?" His granddaughter never sounded anything but cheerful.

He tried to smile, knowing she'd feel it through the phone if he didn't. "Just fine. Doc checked me out, says I've just got some indigestion and some ulcers."

"Liar." Her tone was blunt and there was no playfulness to it. She knew him better than he knew himself.

He grimaced and reached in his pocket for a baggie of antacids. "It's nothing, sweetheart. I've fought through a lot worse than this."

She sighed. "Cancer, right?" His silence was all the evidence she needed. "Shit."

"Yeah. Shit."

"Did he talk treatment?"

"He did," he said honestly. The doctor had talked about it and told him with no degree of uncertainty it was almost too late for any of it. "You know, so much of that is worse than the disease."

"I guess," she said doubtfully. "What are you thinking?"

"What we talked about," he said, trying to sound as though the pain in his gut wasn't like a liquid fireball burning him from the inside out. "The exchange with Hamber and your little party."

She sucked in her breath. "Grampa, we can take care—"

"I'm not going to be talked out of it," he snapped. "I'm too old, I don't want to spend what time I have left thinking about what I can't change." he added gently.

"I just wish... I wish you'd focus on yourself for once. Not me. Not our... friends."

"Thank you, sweetheart, but that's not my way. Our people out east need a certain... delicate touch. Do you understand?"

"Yes, grampa. For our friends."

"For our friends," he said back, prouder than ever of his blood. Every day since she'd taken that young mechanic, pumped him full of cocktails loaded with party favors, rode him like a cowgirl and branded his ass, she kept impressing him. She would leave him a fine legacy, he knew. Not like his ingrate son and that common whore teacher he'd married. He had a few regrets in life—any man who didn't was lying to save himself the pain of having to own up to his mistakes—but ordering that hit to have his granddaughter raised the right way wasn't one of them. His son was his greatest failure, but his granddaughter? Far and away his greatest success.

He got to his feet, feeling better than he had in ages. His cell buzzed again. Markham, this time. "What is it, Markham?"

"We just got a tip on a weird one. You read about that trailer house that burned down south of town?"

"The meth lab. Sure."

"One of my guys in lockup just told me they brought in two men last night. One of them was beat all to fuck."

"So?"

"So. Two people beat 'em down, but they weren't cops. One masked man, one masked woman."

Markham's smugness was irritating, but Finson couldn't help but feel the excitement build in him. "You think it's the same people that did up Haas?"

"Yup. I'd almost bet on it."

He reached the Lincoln and got in, sighing with relief as his leg eased. "See if we can find anything out on these people. Who they're working for, what they're after. Do we know whose lab it was?"

"Independents."

Markham turned on the heater to full blast. "Excellent. Then your man can pull anything he needs to out of them." He thought of his granddaughter again and said, "Bring Dee in too. I want you both working on this full time. If Anny tries to pull you away, tell her tough tits."

"Got it."

Finson hung up and sighed. "Who are you?" he asked no one in particular.

* * *

The Overhang was exactly the sort of bar that exemplified why Garrett was so fond of Rankin Flats, even under its layers of metaphorical and literal grime. Not much more than a square box with a couple of filmy, opaque windows set like the last few remaining teeth in a redneck's mouth, the bar and grill was situated a few blocks from the gym and both Brianna and Danny's respective apartments. The owners lost the fight to taggers years ago, but the exterior wasn't what brought its loyal customers in. It was the sort of place anyone not familiar with the intimacies of the inner city might have avoided like the plague, leaving it almost pure for the locals.

That was a damn good thing, as far as Garrett was concerned, because the minute the Bozeman hippie or Missoula yuppie transplants caught wind of the place's interior, he had no doubt they'd popularize the place within weeks and ruin it with requests for kale instead of lettuce and tofu instead of beef. Anyone who came in there concerned about their cholesterol or whether or not the buns came in gluten-free varieties could turn their asses right around. But they wouldn't have left once they caught sight of the magnificence of the bar's centralized stone fireplace, open on four sides and blazing on that dreary day. The stonework for the fireplace was inspired by the Castle Museum in White Sulphur, and the original owners had spared no expense when it came to getting their own stones from the Crazies brought in. That might have been one of the many reasons they'd gone bankrupt within a year and had to sell the place to a string of new owners. Regardless, the fireplace and the cheap drinks made it one of those rare finds—a bar both cozy and easy on the wallet.

Though it was the sort of place where most its patrons usually huddled over cheap drinks rather than lunch, they still served up a pretty decent meal. The food was the usual bar fare—burgers, fries, chicken that came in greasy or extra greasy varieties—but that was sometimes the best kind of comfort food, especially after a crazy night. Danny ripped into a chicken leg, coming away with a bit of deep fat fried skin hanging from his lips as he chewed happily. Brianna might have said something about it to him if she wasn't halfway into a cheeseburger herself ("And load that thing up with all the pickles," she'd told the waitress. "All of them!"). A spot of ketchup fell on her jeans and she couldn't care less, so hungry was she from the previous night's exploits.

Garrett was mowing down the house's special for the day, a batch of French fries slathered in steaming nacho cheese—the good, wildly unhealthy kind that came from a tin can—and crumbled hamburger. It was, in his estimation, possibly the least healthy meal he'd eaten since… well, last night, but he was enjoying himself anyways, despite waiting for the inevitable earful from Danny about dating his daughter.

But that earful never came, despite Garrett's rising tensions about it. At one point, finally pushing aside the last quarter of her burger, Brianna scooted closer to him and reached her hand out. She glanced at him questioningly and he smiled, going to take her hand in his. Instead, she snaked three of his fries from his basket and grinned at him.

"You have your own," he protested.

She shrugged and popped one in her mouth. "Yeah," she said, chewing, "but nacho cheese."

"Fair point." He nudged his fries closer to hers and took the remains of her hamburger from her. She glared and he arched an eyebrow at her mockingly as he polished it off.

Soon they started to slow down and finish up their meal. After he patted away the grease on his mouth, beard, shirt, hands, pants, and pretty much his everything, Danny leaned back in his chair and laced his hands behind his head. "So," he said, face dead serious, "you were in my daughter last night."

"Jesus, Dad!" Brianna exclaimed.

Garrett was damn sure glad he had nothing left to drink because he would've choked on it. "I. Uh."

"No use trying to deny it," Danny said. "You two've been looking at each other like you might run off and knock one out in the bathroom. Don't, by the way. It's clean enough, but when I was in there, I did something unholy to that crapper."

"Dad!" Brianna shouted.

"It was basically a war crime. Tears. I had honest to God tears."

Brianna smacked her dad on the shoulder. Garrett cleared his throat and repeated stupidly, "I. Uh." Dazedly, he shook his head. "Wait, no talk about what you'll do to me if I hurt your daughter?"

"Moranis, if you hurt her, she'll be cooking your balls for breakfast. There's nothing I could do that she couldn't possibly do herself." He sipped at his beer and considered it. "That said? If you do hurt her, when she's through, I'll kill you. With a spoon. A very rusty one."

"I wouldn't. Won't."

"And if you get it in your head to start calling me Dad, you'll find that spoon in your anal cavity."

Fresh drinks in hand, the waitress overheard that last bit and turned right back around for the bar.

"Graphic, but agreed," Garrett said.

Brianna touched her dad's hand. "You're okay with this, Dad?"

"With you and him?" He popped a lemon wedge out of his water and sucked on it a moment. "Could do worse."

"Thanks," Garrett said, genuinely.

"Don't let it go to your head. Could do better, too. There's a single janitor comes to the gym. Could hook Bri up with him instead."

"Again. Thanks," Garrett laughed.

"Don't mention it." He raised his empty bottle of beer and shouted across the room to the waitress, "Gonna need another one of these."

Garrett asked Brianna, "You sure you're his daughter?"

Watching as her dad shoved a handful of French fries into his mouth, she nodded. "We just haven't gotten to the point of the relationship where I tell you how he taught me to chug a beer and belch loud enough to rattle the silverware."

"Hah. Wait," he said, squinting at her. "Are you serious?"

Through another mouthful of fries, Danny said cheerfully, "She sounds like a bellowin' gassy moose doin' it, too, Moranis. Got that from her mother." He reached over and squeezed his daughter's shoulder affectionately.

"Hot," Garrett said dryly.

"Right?" Brianna asked. "Got that to look forward to."

* * *

She grabbed a stack of folded clothes from her laundry basket and said, "You're sure this isn't freaking you out a bit? I mean, we've been officially dating less than a day."

As she handed him clothes, he slipped hangers into the tops and hung them up in the closet on the opposite end of his own meager assortment of clothes. He didn't even have to think about his answer. "I think once we've gotten past the whole I-see-ghosts part of the relationship, moving some clothes and bathroom stuff into my condo isn't such a big deal."

"Good. Because I really like your bed."

He smirked at her. "Oh really?"

"Simmer down. Well, for now, anyways," she said, trying to wink at him.

"Are you having a stroke?"

"Shut up."

"What's happening with that side of your face? Do I need to call an ambulance?"

"Shut up."

When they finished hanging her clothes and she littered his bathroom liberally with her personal stuff, she clapped her hands. "Okay. Show me the rest of it. Show me what you guys do. Step by step."

So he showed her what they did in the War Room. He explained that once they found someone who might be a likely candidate for their particular brand of snooping around, they researched the person thoroughly, not just with Murphy checking them out, but via the Internet and good old fashioned legwork too.

"There's a certain amount Murphy just can't account for," he explained. "He sees pretty much how you and I would see, so if, for example, we were robbing someone with a vault, there's no way he could see in there if it was completely dark inside. Like the job we're doing now. We think we know who it is we're after—" he showed her the picture of Jamie Finson, "-but we don't know much about him. So tomorrow, I'm going to call up his car service from somewhere downtown, request him specially, and then walk away. When he shows up, Murphy will jump in and follow him wherever he goes."

"And he'll, what, stay with Finson for however long it takes?"

"If it's just Finson we need to tail, yeah. In this case, since he's a big Legion guy, we're probably going to need to bring in a few of the bums from the shelter. I mean, the ghosts. Not a very nice name for them, I know. It was their nickname first, what their head guy—"

She waved that away. "Okay. Tell me about Jamie Finson."

He explained everything from the job they'd pulled on Richter Haas to the research they'd done on Jamie Finson and A. Brennerman. She was absolutely fascinated by their process. "You could've been a real detective. Or some kind of super spy or something."

He smiled without any real humor. "Imagine me getting found out by the government. Imagine what they'd do with that. No, I'll work on my own."

She nodded. "I see your point." She gestured at the computer. "You've got time until you call this Finson guy, right? Let's work it through together, see what we see. Is your ghost friend here? Can I call him Murphy too, or is it Mr. Murphy?"

Garrett grinned. "He is, and he says Murphy's just fine."

She shook her head ruefully. "This is going to be weird."

* * *

After a while, he brought in one of the folding chairs from the kitchen and watched her work quietly. She was blazing fast on a computer, much faster than his own henpecking allowed, and he enjoyed watching her speed through pages and pages of information. She had a habit of sticking her tongue out of the corner of her mouth when she was deep in thought, and any time she thought she found something interesting, she would trace the lines on the screen with her fingernail.

And she did find something both Garrett and Murphy had missed. One of the Finsons they looked up and crossed off had the same name as Jamie Finson, but this other one was young, maybe twenty or so, with blue streaked hair and a bizarre taste in clothing. Brianna tapped her finger against her mouth thoughtfully and held up Garrett's printed photograph of the old man next to the screen. "Bingo," she said excitedly.

"What?" Garrett asked, not seeing it.

"Oh shit, she's right," Murphy breathed. At the exact same time as Brianna, he said, "Look at the eyes."

Garrett leaned over Brianna's shoulder and squinted. "They could be related," he said. "That's... holy crap, that's incredible."

"Is it something you can use?" Brianna asked.

"If she's not involved, we'll leave her be. We're not going to go after anyone's family for no good reason. But if I'm right, this guy's old school Legion. They brought in a lot of family back in the day because they thought they'd be more loyal, make better soldiers." He rubbed his jaw. "Could be she's got something to do with this. If that's the case, we take her down too."

Murphy said, "You know, this Jamie's young. Should be easy enough to tail while I'm off chasing the older Finson. If Brianna wants to learn some of the less violent parts of what you do, might be a good field trip for her."

"What'd he say?" Brianna asked as Garrett lowered his fingers. He relayed everything back to her and she grinned. "Oh hell yeah, a stakeout sounds like fun. High five, Casper." She held up her hand expectantly.

Murphy slapped it, his hand passing right through. She sat there waiting to feel something. Finally, Garrett said, "Um, he slapped it. Like a minute ago."

"Ass. You could've told me sooner."

"Probably," he grinned.

Chapter 12

While Brianna worked, Garrett prepared.

It wasn't just for the Finson case—not all of it, anyways. He spent most of the morning trying to write a letter. The right words always seemed just out of reach, like he was grasping at the tendrils of color that fluttered around Murphy as he sat in the next room watching the latest Robert Downey Jr. movie. He balled up and threw away half a dozen sheets of paper before he finally decided one was good enough. He folded it and slipped it into an envelope with a key, then sealed it and wrote Brianna's name on the outside. The letter went into his bedroom safe atop nearly a hundred grand in cash wrapped in rubber bands and plastic. He'd teach her the combination later. Maybe tonight, when they had time, he thought to himself. He pulled out one of three burner phones in the safe, kissed his fingers, touched the cross hanging on the inside of the safe and closed it tight.

Then came a call to Auggie, who seemed exhausted but otherwise okay. She talked about their mom with monotonous banality, giving him the same reassurances he was sure she'd been feeding the entire extended family for days. When he asked her how she was doing, really doing, she broke down and cried, and he wished he could be there for her. Instead, when he hung up the phone, he made some calls to delis and restaurants around the Pensacola area, explaining his family's situation and making appointments to have food delivered to his dad's door. Whether or not they accepted it didn't really matter to him. He needed to make the gesture. To try. He texted the details to Auggie and she didn't reply. He didn't expect her to.

He sat down next to Murphy and watched the movie for a bit. They were in no rush and it was good to have a few minutes alone with his friend. He didn't understand the plot of the movie, something to do with a rift between him and Robert Duvall, but Downey's quick wit was always appreciable. Halfway through, Brianna texted him a picture of half the walls at the gym covered in pictures again. It was strange how much like a normal life the morning felt like.

When the credits rolled, he got up and stretched. "Murphy, there's no rush on this. We've been going so non-stop lately and—"

"Ah, shut it, man," Murphy said kindly. "You and your lady friend need some time and my boy will be fine doing his thing. He always is. I'll be by in the mornings to check in with you, same as usual. You good with it if I need some help and get ahold of Padraig?"

"Do it."

"Cool." Murphy stood up. "All right, let's go make a phone call."

They settled on making the call from the airport to make it seem legitimate. Garrett hated that drive—no airport in America seemed to have figured on actual traffic coming to their terminals—but having no specific destination in mind made it easy to just pick a spot where lots of people where coming from and pull in to its short term parking. He could have made the call from his own home if he'd really wanted to, but he had nowhere else to be and wanted to see Finson pull up for himself.

In a restaurant inside the terminal, he ordered an overpriced bottle of water and dialed. A friendly, professional female on the other end asked for his payment information. He rattled off the information of one of his fake IDs and the prepaid credit card that went with it. The payment went through, nearly as much as if he'd just gone ahead and bought a junker off a lot. It didn't matter much to him. This was an investment.

She gave him the estimated time, and he requested one other thing—a specific driver he'd had previously, Jamie Finson. Her tone changed instantly, more guarded and colder. He realized that was a mistake, that he should have opted for any of their other drivers and let Murphy do the legwork. But he was hungrily curious and feeling a little bold. Murphy made a cutting-his-won-throat gesture, and Garrett shook his head, grinning. "Tell Finson it's the man who wrecked Richter Haas's shop."

The woman hesitated. "I'm sure I have no idea what you're—"

"Tell him. And point out that my money's good. I want to have a sit down with him."

Murphy's eyes bulged. "What the fuck are you—"

Garrett shook his head. "I'm gone in half an hour. If he doesn't show, he doesn't get another opportunity to talk to me again."

The woman hung up and so did Garrett. He sipped on his water while Murphy called him all sorts of things. Finally, he could take no more and said, "I don't actually plan on meeting him. Are you crazy?"

"Are you?" Murphy snapped. "You just played our hand at least a month early."

"We'll still have our month," Garrett said calmly. "But think how much damage control Finson's going to do after today. Phone calls. Meetings."

"Yeah, and he knows you're coming for him!"

"Good. Let him. It'll be fun to have the odds a little more even this time," Garrett said as he got up. "Time for you to go keep watch."

They agreed on a meeting spot, but Garrett stuck around the restaurant for a while before he moved to a gift shop nearer the terminal where Finson would hopefully show. He smiled at the clerk and told her he was just browsing for something for his girlfriend. With a little shameless flip of her hair, she told him if he needed anything to just ask. Within fifteen minutes, Murphy walked through the wall, still bristling with anger. "He's out there, and so are three of his friends. Keep your head down, you stupid idiot."

Garrett picked up a newspaper, the Diana Francis novel he'd been thumbing through, and a pair of sunglasses, paid the clerk, and left. He pulled out his cellphone as he walked, faking a conversation so he could talk to Murphy as he went.

"Okay," Murphy muttered, "first guy's on the left up here, inside the terminal doors. The guy that looks like he's a shitty hipster college professor."

Garrett snickered at that, and kept walking right past the man. "You're right," he said into the phone. "I can definitely see that now."

"Second one's seated outside, bus stop, looking straight at you."

Garrett shifted the bag and pulled the cell phone away from his ear a moment. "This reception's terrible. I'm gonna be in the car in a minute, hon. No, I can still hear you, just... shit," he muttered, pretending to dial the number again as he walked. The thuggish looking kid in the ball cap looked away from him, no longer interested. To him, Garrett was just another asshole.

"Finson's by the SUV. Look slowly to your right, like you're looking for the right parking area. There's one up there. Start making your way to that."

Garrett spoke back into the phone. "Baby? You hear me? Yeah, I got you now."

He walked on, pretending to feign interest in what he considered was Fake Brianna's conversation. "Whatever you want, baby, I'm good for anything. Sushi sounds great." An old man stood by a black SUV, watching everyone pass around him. Garrett was struck by how much the old man's face looked like a skull, his cheeks hollow and his skin stretched thin across his forehead. Ten or fifteen years ago, he might have been handsome, and even then still had a hell of a physique. He scanned Garrett as he walked across the busy terminal's drop-off zone to the short-term parking garage. It would lead him further away from his car, but in a way, that helped sell his paper-thin cover. Who knew where the hell they parked in an airport?

Finson's gaze still on him, he almost smiled with wolfish anticipation. He could take the fucker down right there, cut off the head of the snake. But there was no play there that didn't end with him going to jail or winding up dead. Nothing he could see, anyways. So he walked on, continuing to talk to Fake Brianna until Finson's gaze fell to someone else. Later, while watching Lord of the Rings with Brianna, he'd have nightmares of Finson, except his face was Sauron's eye and it fell upon him and he burned. But for that moment, he swaggered on, swinging his bag of goods and talking nonstop.

"Last one's here, by the entrance," Murphy said. A full figured woman leaned against the wall next to the opening leading to the parking. She looked bored and disinterested in what was happening around her. Her right arm was tucked under her left elbow. Murphy got a closer look as Garrett almost stepped into her line of sight. The ghost whipped a hand up, a halting gesture, and shouted, "Phone, she's got a phone and she's taking pictures of everyone."

Garrett stopped dead, looking up at the terminal signs, then his parking ticket, and turned around. He broke out into a cold sweat. Had she managed to get his picture? By itself it would have meant nothing to the Legion as it was, but what if someone matched up his photo to another job? Like that junkie? He walked a little faster, feeling like the walls were closing in and it was his own damn fault. Stupid, stupid, stupid. Finson's head swiveled back towards him, and he grimaced at the phone. "Look, I'm going to get there when I get there," he snarled. "I'm just a little lost here, okay?"

Murphy said quietly, "You're clear. She caught your back but that's it. Finson's looking away again. You're a moron, brother. I'm going with him. Get to your car and get the fuck out of here."

Garrett sighed. "Love you too. See you soon."

"Aw, he loves me," Murphy crowed. "So sweet."

As Garrett got back into his car, he allowed himself only a minute to breathe deeply before he started it up. He reversed out of there, waited impatiently for the three or four cars ahead of him to get through the exit, and practically threw his money at the toll booth receptacle. He caught himself doing nearly fifty in a thirty on his way down the street nearby, stopped at a gas station, and rested his head on the steering wheel. He thumped it softly with the palm of his hand, muttering, "Vanity gets you caught, you stupid idiot." He got out, gassed up, and as he got back into his SUV, a black Lincoln drove by, speeding down the street with four very irritated, confused people inside—and one ghost mooning him through a tinted window.

* * *

They found the younger Jamie Finson through her Facebook page, which she kept updated almost to the minute with where she was and who she was with. Brianna's eyes practically went white from rolling them so hard at that, but it was a lucky break for them. They caught her at the college's indoor basketball courts playing a pick-up game with some of her "sister squad," as she appeared to call some of her friends. They stood inside just long enough to watch Jamie play. She had fast hands and could sprint up and down the court effortlessly, but she was an abysmal shot and kept mostly to defense. After watching her play for a few minutes, Brianna and Garrett wandered back out to the parking lot. Her hand found his, surprising him just a little with the natural way she went about joining their bodies together. Such a simple gesture of warmth and caring had been absent from his life for so long that it felt almost alien to him. Not that he minded it a bit.

Mostly, they talked as they sat on a nearby bench. Sometimes too there was companionable silence, but there was so much between the two that they had to catch up on, both simple and complex. It was the sort of getting-to-know you stuff that would have happened in the first few dates of any budding relationship She was mildly liberal. whereas he hadn't thought about politics at all beyond what was of immediate concern to him. She liked video games. He mentioned he owned several, but he very rarely played them except for Murphy's entertainment. She loved fantasy and science fiction in just about any medium; he'd never seen or read any of the names she rattled off but promised to try some of her recommendations. She wanted to run the gym but only when her father was ready to retire; he thought a good life would be wherever she was. She kissed him for that. She didn't like any of the presidential candidates—that, they agreed on. They disagreed on little initially, but she found his diffidence or straight up ignorance on some of the most basic questions almost astounding.

The game wrapped up and some of the women started streaming out, laughing and talking. They got up unhurriedly—Brianna was still young enough to look as though she belonged at the college and fit in nicely, and on her arm, Garrett drew little attention either—and got in the Hyundai. Jamie came out the doors, her phone at her ear and swinging her keys in one hand. Garrett began running down his tips on following people to Brianna's amusement. As Finson got into a CR-V and cut off someone as she pulled out erratically, Brianna said, "Not sure we'll have much trouble losing her if she plows into someone in the first few minutes."

They followed at a leisurely distance a few cars behind her. She wound through the college complex carelessly, driving well past the speed limit and taking corners with only a hint of slowing down. It made it hard to follow her without risking being seen, but she didn't have to go very far, just to a large, off-campus apartment building that looked as though it had last seen a fresh coat of paint sometime in the seventies. As they passed, they could literally feel the thump of the beat from whatever was playing in her car. Garrett and Brianna drove past and doubled back a block later, just in time to see the blue-haired teen visibly cuss out a roundish boy holding the door open for her. "Oh, I hate that," Brianna said. "The guy probably holds the door open for everyone, not just women." Apparently satisfied with her tongue-lashing, Jamie pushed past the boy, who looked back over his shoulder and snapped a quick pic of the blue-haired girl's ass in her basketball shorts. "Oh. Well. Yeah, screw that guy."

Garrett pulled into the parking lot of a mirroring apartment building across the street. Though not right on the street, they had a good, unobstructed view of the entrance. "Do we go in there?" Brianna asked.

"For now? No," Garrett said as he wrote down the address. "No point in us risking being seen if Murphy can go in." As Jamie came back out, hurtling towards the passenger side of her car, Garrett leaned forward. "But we can maybe narrow it down for him. She forgot her cell phone, what do ya want to bet? C'mon."

As Jamie did grab her cell phone, they got out and hustled across the street. They got to the door just as it was about to close. Through

165

the glass, they could see Jamie wait for the elevator, tapping her cell phone against her hand impatiently. When she got in and the elevator doors closed, Garrett and Brianna darted inside to watch the numbers above the elevator door. "Fourth floor," Brianna said.

"Feel like being a little daring?" Garrett asked.

She grinned at him and they ran for the stairs. It was a good thing they were both in good shape because they sprinted up those flights, racing each other and laughing madly. Garrett won by a full half flight, but ever a gracious winner, he made only the slightest wah-wah sound when she joined him.

She poked her head in and looked up and down the hallway. No one was coming. She tugged Garrett's hand and they went from door to door as Garrett cocked his head towards each one in kind. "What are we listening for?" she asked.

"A shower running, or maybe—"

Another blaring beat started thumping in an apartment close to the elevator.

"Music," Brianna and Garrett said together. They took down the apartment number and rode the elevator back down. Garrett couldn't keep his hands off her and she didn't want him to. He was kissing the back of her neck, hands wrapped around her waist, when the doors opened and they had to reluctantly make their way back to the SUV.

And then they waited. They wanted to play, to do all the things a newly minted couple wants to do when they're alone, but there was just no way, not with the erratic stream of traffic and their need for invisibility. So instead Brianna reached for the radio.

Garrett gave her that cocky little lopsided grin of his. "I'll bet a dollar Lusty Gallant comes on."

"Big fan of theirs?" she asked, thinking maybe he meant he had their music plugged in or something.

"No, just wait. Any station you pick, I'll bet you one of their songs starts playing."

"Hm." She turned on the radio and turned it to a modern pop and rock station. As Adele's beautiful, introspective voice faded away, a DJ came on, "And now, a little blast from the recent past for ya, some Lusty Gallant."

Brianna sat back in her chair and blinked at the radio. "Well, that's weird. How'd you know?"

"I have these funny little things happen to me. Murphy and I call them curses, but they're really minor stuff. Whenever I turn on a radio, so long as it's more than a couple of seconds, I'll always hear Lusty Gallant. Any station, doesn't matter."

She turned off the radio, turned it back on, and switched it to an older country radio station. Merle Haggard sang about being a lonely fugitive. The audio quieted and fuzzy static hissed as Lusty Gallant played something perky and upbeat she didn't recognize. Within a few seconds the hissing stopped and the music returned back to Haggard. "Bizarre," she breathed. She turned off the radio again and twisted in her seat to better look at him straight on. "What other kinds of curses?"

"Oh, uh, street lights. One will pop off temporarily if it's nighttime and I get out of my car or come out of a building. They don't burn out, they sort of just buzz out for a minute or two."

"What else?"

"My Chinese fortune cookies are always blank. That one creeps me out. I won't eat them. Oh! Here's another good one. Every time I open a fresh newspaper, part of it's out of order."

She shook her head in disbelief. "That's beyond weird. Sometimes I feel like I'm about to get real lucky or something when there's a raffle or a drawing, or I walk by a gas station and I think I should buy a scratch 'em."

He looked at her curiously. "Do you ever win?"

"Eh, not really," she laughed. She turned back on the radio to a modern hits station. When she started humming along with a song he didn't recognize, he wrapped his arm around her shoulders and thought for about the thousandth time that day that he must be dreaming.

* * *

"Favorite hot dog toppings," he said.

"Ooh, getting into the relationship-killers now. Um, it's all about the bun. Gotta be sesame, but they're so hard to find cheap. Mayo—"

He gaped at her. "Mayo, are you crazy?"

"Hush," she said, pressing a finger to his lips which he took to kissing. "Mayo. Spicy mustard. Those dry fried onion things. Dill pickles, not sweet, sliced lengthwise. How about you?"

"Not mayo. I'm not a lunatic," he muttered. Then he sat up straight and grew serious. "There she is."

She seemed ready for a night out. Her blue hair was done up with an intricate braid and it looked like she'd added about a pound of makeup. "Girl has style, I'll give her that," Brianna said. "What do you think, Garrett, should I dye my hair blue?" She laughed softly at his horrified expression.

They followed her again. Her social media pages had been silent for a while, which seemed like an oddity for Jamie. With that same blatant disregard for traffic laws or human safety, she barreled down a series of series, carving a pattern Garrett could barely keep up with. They wound up in a residential area he was unfamiliar with, populated with small bungalow style homes and the occasional double-wide. She pulled up in front of a small dilapidated house with an old Ranger in the driveway and hammered on the horn. Garrett and Brianna parked a half block away and observed.

He wrote down the address while Brianna fumbled in the back for her old digital camera, a model her father had given her one Christmas ages ago when she'd taken up photography as a hobby. It hadn't panned out—she realized the technology was now good enough that anyone armed with an SLR could take award winning photographs and her playful kitty photos weren't going to cut it—but she was grateful now she'd kept the camera. She zoomed in, sweeping the camera back and forth between the house and Jamie Finson Jr.'s car. A doughy man in a white tank top and sweatpants hurtled out the door, holding a stuffed manila envelope. He leaned into the car for a long, hungry kiss with Finson. As she snapped picture after picture, Brianna muttered, "I feel like a perv."

Finson crooked her finger at him and handed something off, too small for Garrett to see. He pushed it into his pocket. She kissed him one more time and took off.

"Did you see that?" Brianna asked excitedly. The man stood on the street and pulled out the something. "Cash," Brianna said. "He's counting it."

Garrett rubbed his chin. "A fistful of cash and a manila envelope. All right, I think we come back to her place and here with Murphy. He'll be home in the morning and we can... hey, what are you doing?"

She was, in fact, getting out of the car. "You're thinking about this too hard," she said cheerfully, and walked towards the man's house. Garrett caught up with her and she whispered into his ear, "Follow my lead." She pounded on the guy's door. "Open up."

The door opened. Upon closer inspection, Garrett realized the guy couldn't be any older than Brianna. Ill-dressed as he might have been, the man was well groomed. His five o'clock shadow had been neatly trimmed, his fingernails had clearly seen a manicure recently, and when his teeth were revealed when his jaw hung opened, they gleamed white as the snow outside. He stared at them, confounded. "Can I help you?"

"Rankin Flats University, sir, would love to know just what the hell kind of drug deals you've been making with Jamie Finson."

Shocked, he took a step backwards. "D-drug d-deals?"

Garrett snapped, "Own up to it. We just saw you exchange a manila envelope for cash. It's better for everyone involved if you just come straight. Maybe we won't have to involve the authorities."

The man blinked. "Oh. Oh! It's not drugs, I p-promise!" He opened the door wider. "Come on in, and I can c-clear this right up."

Brianna marched in after the man and Garrett followed suit, slightly more hesitant. The inside of the place was as neat as the man's appearance. Most of the furniture looked cheaply built and well used. A smattering of pictures hung on the wall, mostly of the man and Jamie Finson Jr., though a few were of some monuments and landscapes. Vacation photos, Garrett assumed. Everything in the place seemed just precisely so, and the faint chemical smell of cleaners hung in the air. A neat freak, he thought. He could relate, if not quite to this degree. The smells were almost overpowering.

The man sat at a desk in front of a small computer and started pulling up a file. "Jamie, she's my guh-girlfriend, she's smart, but she's not so g-great with proofreading." He pointed at the screen. "This is her original th-thesis. I have her email if you need to see that too, there's an at-attachment there…" He pulled up a different file. "This is the one I just g-gave her. See, I didn't change any of the c-content, I just sort of help her with her muh-mistakes, and—"

"It's okay," Brianna said soothingly.

"No, it's not," Garrett said flatly, picking up on Brianna's good cop vibe and playing off it. "The money. What was that about?"

"She insists on p-paying me for my work. It's how we met. I tutor sometimes for the p-professors on campus. I don't like it and I know it's shameful but I'm kind of down on my luck right now," he said, hanging his head. "I'm not proud about it, but she knows t-times are t-tough and I'm between jobs right now." He looked up, a sheen in his eyes. "Look, if you need to punish someone, don't punish her. She's had a tough life, you know, and she's a g-good person."

"So you're a tutor?" Garrett said. "And we can check that?"

"Here, I've got some b-business c-cards for the professors I help out," he said, and dug out some cards from a drawer. Garrett stuck them in his wallet without looking at them. "They can v-vouch for me."

Garrett glanced at Brianna. She shrugged, so he stuck out his hand to the young man. "We've taken up enough of your time, mister...?"

"Nolan. Nate Nolan." The man shook Garrett's hand. Surprisingly, Nate's hands were rougher than he expected and his grip strong and firm. "And I d-didn't get your names."

Already headed for the door, Brianna tossed an exasperated look over her shoulder. "No," she said. "You didn't."

* * *

Brianna made a sour face. "Ugh, I couldn't get out of there fast enough."

"The chemical smell, right? It was going to give me a headache. I mean, I'm kind of nutty about cleaning, but come on." He had to guess at what direction they were headed and pulled back towards the Interstate. "But I believe him." He sighed. "And unless Murphy finds something else out about her, I don't think she's anything but what that Nolan guy said. I'll bet money on her just being a college kid, born into the wrong family."

"So..." she said. "Our first movie night?"

"Sounds great."

As they drove off, Nate Nolan locked his front door, kicking himself mentally. He'd left the damn trap door in the pantry to the basement open. if either one of those two university dipshits had wandered through the kitchen, they might have seen it. Had he not been so anxious to return to work, he might have questioned their story, but he'd never set foot on the campus and had no idea what he should expect from their people. He checked the locks, slipped downstairs, washed his hands thoroughly in the sink, and put on his apron. He'd left his work in a good spot, thankfully. The two skinned bodies swinging from the meat hooks in front of him were ready to be sliced into some nice cuts of meat for the boss's exchange and his girlfriend's ritual. One had been homeless, the other a runaway. Both of them were too thin by far, but he could still pull some good meat from their bones.

He whistled as he sharpened his knife.

Chapter 13

He recognized the dream for what it was, but still Garrett stared at the size of the tree, utterly dumbfounded. Miles wide, maybe dozens or hundreds—his perspective was skewed with that drunkenness of dreams. He didn't know dendrology from dentistry, but he had the unshakable feeling that this tree might be some giant version of Missouri's cherry trees, given the swirl of pink and white blossoms twirling around it. Its branches spread out and upwards like countless upturned arms asking the heavens for reason. Millions upon millions of barely-visible specks, all people and animals, moved upon its surface together, a vast network of life and liveliness that barely covered a fraction of the tree's surface area. He moved closer, taking the distance in three impossibly long bounds, and found the sculpted foliage was, in fact, moving to accommodate the people.

Something spattered across his feet. He looked down and realized it was dirt, flung from a skeletal hand as it tried to pull itself from the ground. Twisting, he looked all around and saw hundreds, thousands of them, the mirror-things, flesh rent and torn and burned and chewed. He tried to shout a warning to the tree dwellers, tried to get them to run, but run where? Nowhere was so beautiful, so why would they go?

So he stood between the tree and the rising horde, the blossoms whipping against his back and cutting him open, and they came for him. He gritted his teeth and shouted, a wordless cry to the joys of the fight, of a life spent waiting for this moment. He would die and it would be pointless, but he would go on his feet.

They stopped and opened ranks to let three figures pass through. An old man, a woman wrapped in a cloak, and a feral, grinning child whose face had been sculpted by someone's hand. He could see where the fingers had plied at her skin like wet clay. As one, the three opened their mouths. Frogs squirmed their way out and fell to the ground with wet plops. They were horrifically large, gray green things with milky white eyes that looked upon nothing and everything.

And then the three came not for him but what he guarded, and he woke up screaming.

* * *

He stumbled out of the bedroom for the kitchen, sweat dripping down his nude form and hitting the floor in fat drops. He fumbled a drinking glass out of the cupboard, one of four very basic ones he'd bought from a discount store upon first buying the place. Every bit of kitchenware he owned came in fours. There had been no point in owning more until he'd fallen for Brianna. He never entertained. Not even Ed and Rose came to his condo.

He ran the tap for a few seconds, letting the water chill before he filled the glass and drank it all in one long go. He filled it one more time before cupping his hands under the flow and splashing his face. God, he was running hot. A fever? Had he gotten sick? He'd been going non-stop so it wouldn't surprise him. But no, he suspected the heat was something else. Maybe some reaction, his body warning him about something.

Like the strange ghost standing in his living room, maybe.

He shut off the faucet and took the glass of water in the other room. She stared at him openly and he stared right back, sipping at his water. Her ribbons of color reminded him of a campground in late fall, when the foliage turned from those magnificent yellows to the dull, dead browns. She herself was a relatively unremarkable woman, maybe in her twenties, wearing a long tunic that hid most of her figure and a pair of jeans.

"Help you?" he asked.

She pointedly averted her eyes away from his nakedness but said nothing.

"You one of Padraig's? Tell him and those idiot brothers I sent on the money."

Still nothing. He was starting to get annoyed.

"Okay, well, suit yourself."

He finished off his water, rinsed out his cup, and meandered back to bed. As he slipped under the covers, Brianna reached for him and murmured, "Who were you talking to?"

He kissed her forehead and whispered, "Just another ghost thing."

"Okay." Already losing herself in sleep, she snuggled closer and murmured something about blueberries. He thought sleep wouldn't come for a long time, but with every breath, her gardenia and vanilla shampoo fogged his mind, and soon he dreamed of little at all.

Chapter 14

Instead of forcing Jamie Finson Sr. into action, Garrett's antics at the airport sent him into a tight, paranoid lockdown. Few came into or out of his office, juxtapositioned next to the car service's garage, and no one visited him in his Victorian home in the suburbs. He spoke of no business on the phone, only in person, and even that was with his hand leisurely stroking the butt of the Sig Sauer in his shoulder holster.

Only one man seemed to come in with any regularity, Murphy learned, and that was Markham, no first name given. If ever there was a mold for a dirty ex-cop, Markham fit it. He wore a loose fitting, frayed black suit jacket over untucked button downs, and always black or gray slacks that never seemed to fit him quite right. His constant five o'clock shadow seemed a good match for the rugged look of his face, but it was the hollows of his eyes that gave him away. This was a man who'd sold his soul and knew it, despite his constant smirking demeanor.

They were searching for Garrett. That was no surprise. What was surprising was that they knew about Brianna, or at least that Garrett had a female companion. They had little information on either, aside from vague height and weight approximations from the meth cooks at the trailer. Markham scoured the streets for leads on Garrett, trying to pull together a pattern for the man and sift the truth from the bullshit. Garrett hadn't come face to face with a criminal in months before Richter Haas, so there wasn't much for him to find. Still, his bulldoggish approach to the matter worried Murphy.

He learned about the day to day operations of Exodian Chariots. As had most of the other major criminal organizations who wanted to remain in power without drawing too much heat, the Legion had set up any number of legitimate storefronts and businesses, all of which would continue to function well without underhanded backing. Exodian did a lot of business with execs passing through the area—even the company Rose worked for used them regularly—as well as a handful of celebrities. When he found out Bruce Campbell was one of those celebrities, Murphy made a point of traveling with the driver just in case his most beloved B-movie actor just happened to be a maniacal Legion leader. He was happy to report to Garrett that he was not.

The drivers also picked up some Legion intermediaries. Legion leaders were notoriously private and paranoid after nearly three quarters of a century of hard-taught lessons, so they didn't travel by driver. At least as far as Murphy saw, anyways. Most of the Legion men and women the drivers picked up were middle managers, the sort of earners who the Legion wanted to keep happy. Even with occasional help from Padraig and his crew, it was impossible to follow all of them through their daily criminal exploits, but they managed to collect a nice pile of names for Garrett and Brianna to add to the War Room board.

Finson spoke to his granddaughter only sparingly. There was no mention of the Legion in their talks. As for her apartment, a brief run through her things and an hour of listening to her talk to friends was enough to convince Murphy she was a slightly daffy, vulgar, and completely ordinary collegiate. Had he waited around another couple of hours, he might have seen her sample her boyfriend's latest wares, but he didn't.

Finson's wife was also a bust. She was practically a vegetable and spent her days mostly camped out in front of a blaring television. She took calls from her sisters and chewed listlessly on whatever food Jamie put in front of her, but she walked the house almost like a ghost. Hell is murky, Lady Macbeth, Murphy thought to himself grimly.

This was not a job to be pushed quickly, Murphy realized. It was going to be their longest game yet, even more so than their last Vegas job. And unless they were very, very careful, nothing good could come of it. And there was a small part of him that wanted to protract things, that selfishly wanted to give his friend time to grow into his new relationship. He liked Brianna well enough—she was an open book, a woman who let herself feel her emotions entirely and didn't let things like logic or common sense get in the way of what she wanted. And then there was the fact that she liked movies and games way more than Garrett ever did, so he had that to look forward to when the job was over.

But would this job ever really be over? They were going up against some heavy hitters. One slip, one stupid mistake—and they'd already made plenty—and Garrett's face and name would be circulated through the criminal underworld with all the horrifying speed of a text message. And after that, there would be nowhere they could run that the Legion couldn't find them. Their resources were as vast as their name and they had people everywhere. They really were legion.

Both men agreed that the rewards outweighed the risks—for now. They had a golden opportunity to study the organization, something maybe only the FBI or Homeland Security had the power to do. But in an early morning talk while Garrett got dressed for the homeless family's funeral and as Brianna powered through her daily squats, leg lifts, and crunches in the workout room before she prepared for work, Murphy swore to Garrett that if he pulled any more stupid stunts like at the airport, he'd quit. He was no longer playing for one, Murphy said with real anger in his voice, and he'd been stupid and careless in a way that appalled him. There was nothing for Garrett to do but agree.

Garrett wasn't idle either. Auggie, back at her own place at least until there was a marked downturn in their mom's health, called him one day and he introduced his lover to his sister via Facetime. Brianna, who seemed to like everyone on general principle, had a hard time talking to Auggie. She didn't know what to think about Garrett's family, how to react, what to say. But Auggie, being oh-so-colorfully obscene and witty, soon won Brianna over and they promised each other to keep in touch. Garrett later texted Auggie and thanked her profusely. She responded with— "needs boob job. tell her i said that. you did ok bro. she quoted an anime. cool in my book." He had no idea what she was talking about when it came to the anime—he'd never watched a single episode or movie of it—but when he showed Brianna, she laughed and texted Auggie deliriously long rants about their favorites at random times in the days to come.

During the days when Brianna worked, he went over all the websites and information he could find on the Legion. The lowest levels of their organization were well known and documented. The organization was broken up in an indeterminate number of ranks, each signified by a rite of passage or initiation. The public was well aware of the first few ranks and initiation rites—he found dozens of pictures of the burns left by initiates on their victims' skin. The next rank—murder or utter humiliation of a Legion enemy—was easy enough to track via newspaper articles and crime scene photos. After that, the ranks became more mysterious and harder to pin down. It was known that to advance one in the Legion had to perform a great service to the organization, but how and what the service was seemed to be up to their higher-ups. Beyond that, there was nothing.

At night, he and Brianna spent some time driving by houses, offices, and frequent hang-outs to get pictures and videos of the surroundings. This was by and large make busy work, but they took down a couple of wanted initiates who had orchestrated a bunch of stupid, random thefts at small businesses in the area. They were holed up in a safe house, waiting for a ride to Sioux Falls. The fight didn't last long—the two men were huddled over bags of fast food when Garrett and Brianna crashed in, and stood absolutely no chance without their guns. One anonymous call to the cops later from a burner phone in the apartment and they were out the door, hands all over each other like a pair of kids.

And then there was the silent ghost woman. She'd taken to following Garrett closely, though she'd taken some time to follow Murphy, too. He tried to dodge her, but he didn't think about how easy it would have been to avoid her until he tried to turn the tables. When Garrett figured out she usually disappeared at night for an hour or two at a time, Murphy hatched a plan to follow her and try to figure out just who the hell she was. He managed to, for a while. But at a busy intersection downtown, she glanced back at him and waggled her fingers in the air in a wave goodbye. Then she sank down through the earth. He dove in after her, but in the pitch blackness of the earth, it was impossible to see where she went. He resurfaced, spinning every which way to try to spot her, but she was gone.

* * *

Jade hated using the trick. Not only did the earth bring about a dark bout of claustrophobia, but below the surface of the earth, there should have been silence and peace. Instead, in the dark, things moved and stirred, whispering at her to sink lower, to go just a little further. For just a moment she thought she felt one of them caress her leg but that was crazy. She couldn't feel a thing, she assured herself. She sprinted forward through the dirt, running what she assumed was about a mile before she popped up through the dirt again and hopped into the back of a passing car. Murphy, that strange ghost, was nowhere to be seen, but she kept her head down anyways. It wouldn't do to be careless.

Her arrival coincided with the departure of a young, well-dressed, guilty-looking man. He cast one last worried glance back at the luxurious A-frame home before he got into a Ford Taurus and sped away. She slipped into the front door of the house. Ransom sat on his couch, a glass of something amber in his hands, a crystal decanter and another half-filled glass sitting on the coffee table in front of him. He stared blankly at the large mirror hanging on the wall above his fireplace, which she'd never actually seen lit. He wore that same off-putting smile of his, the one that said he wasn't quite all there, but she affixed in her mind the image of her daughter in that hospital bed and stepped forward.

Ransom didn't notice her until she stood right in front of him. He jerked, splashing a little bit of alcohol on his shirt. "Don't you know how to knock?" he snarled, then grinned like a junkyard dog given a nice juicy T-bone, extra rare. "Get it? You? Knock?"

She watched him carefully. The rosy bloom in his cheeks was new. He hadn't seemed like a sloppy drunk, but here he was. He motioned at the chair across the table, but she preferred to stand. She didn't want to hang around that house any longer than necessary. Everything about it felt wrong in a way she didn't understand. It reminded her of rot, plain and simple, almost disturbingly like the madness under the earth. Ransom owned nice things, had a nice wardrobe, seemed nice on the surface. But beneath the skin, things weren't right.

Focus. Her daughter's listless eyes watching the television, not really seeing anything at all.

He grimaced at her. "It's a joke. A little humor."

She nodded patiently, thinking about something her sister used to say about their daddy. If you're the one laughing hardest at your own joke, you're the asshole. He'd overheard that one once and beat her black and blue. It was funny, wasn't it, how the loudest laughing people were always the ones most likely to turn that laughter into rage?

Ransom sighed. "My employer is less than satisfied with my recent absences. I'm having a drink to calm my mind."

"I'm... sorry," she said finally.

He snorted. "No, you're not. But all is not lost. I have a date tonight. A lovely young thing, ripe for the plucking." He giggled at that, a high little laugh that didn't touch his eyes. "But let's get to it so you can get back to our friend, shall we? We shall."

Her mind kept straying to his turn of phrase. Our friend. It felt like the house when he said it. It felt wrong. No, it felt worse than that. It felt filthy. Every day, with every story, his obsession with the man seemed to grow by leaps and bounds. She wasn't sure what Ransom wanted with Garrett Moranis or Brianna Reeve, but she couldn't afford to stop. So she spoke.

* * *

The women gathered around the apron of the ring, most already dripping with sweat after the brutal exercises Brianna led them through. She promised them they'd go home sore every week, and she delivered. A thumping, high energy Pink song blared and she stood in the middle of the ring, grinning ferociously. "Okay. So. Who's ready to learn how to not be afraid anymore?"

Some of the women cheered halfheartedly. Brianna slapped her hands together and shouted, "Who's ready to not be afraid anymore?" They seemed more genuine this time. "Good! We're going to get started in a minute, but I want every single one of you to know this important basic." Her voice dropped and she spun slowly in a circle. "Maybe you can win. Maybe you can't. Maybe you can run. Maybe not. But what I'm going to teach you here today is going to be the difference between them swaggering away from a fight and them crawling, do you understand?" This time the cheers were way more genuine. She liked this first batch in her self-defense course. Most of them took yoga, pilates, or spin at the gym regularly. For a lot of them, this would be their first time in the ring.

"First things first. We do not strike each other inside this ring, not in this class. Everything we do will be done safely and according to my rules, understood?" They nodded their assent and she ran them through the basic safety guidelines, about running everything at half speed and never coming closer than a half foot beyond arm's reach. She paired them off, keeping the ones she knew were friends separate.

Then she began showing them the soft spots on a man's body. They laughed a bit at the obvious one and she quieted them with a harsh warning that it was also the part that would be of most concern if a man really did attack one of them. They didn't like that. It sucked the fun out of the room. Good. Then she showed them the eyes, the ears, the instep, the toes, even the fingers.

And then she started to show them how to strike those parts, how to break them, jab them, smash them, and cut them given the right positions. They didn't laugh very much at all.

She let the pairs work on their basic self-defense strikes, working slowly with each body part and not rushing things. Some of them took to it instinctively, others needed a little more encouragement. These last she took special care with, adjusting their arms, standing side by side with them and running through the motions as she showed them how to send a knuckle into a man's eye or the right spot on the ear to clap.

Finally satisfied with the night's progress, she outlined her plans for them for the coming weeks and months ahead. For those willing to go the distance, there would be sparring, introductions to weight lifting, and eventually the basics of krav maga. Her father was more familiar with the form and had agreed to help teach the class when it came to that, though they both agreed that anything more than the basics would require an outside trainer. They'd have to wait to gauge the class's long-term interest for it, but given the gleams of savage pride in the eyes of most everyone there, she hoped it would come to fruition.

She unlocked the doors for the class after they'd had a chance to hit the showers. Most of them thanked her somberly but seemed thoroughly excited for the next week's class. A couple of the meeker ones might not make it back. There were always a few, her father had told her, and she shouldn't take it personally. She locked the door again behind them, shut off the music, and started picking up the gym.

Something thumped against one of the large mirrored windows near the door. She glanced up, thinking maybe one of the women had left something behind. Instead, a man in a hoodie stood there, looking in, his middle fingers raised. She recognized him. It was one of those MMA dipshits that had laughed that boy out of the gym. The smaller one. She tried to think back on his name and drew a blank. He couldn't see her, of course, but that didn't put her at ease. If he was out there, was his friend?

The guy licked the glass and humped it. He balled his fists and started hammering at the window with every thrust. Judging by the contorted face and manic expression, he was high as hell. She thought about calling Garrett and her dad. And in fact she did—she'd be foolish not to tell someone about the man. But first she went for the gun.

Her dad kept a revolver in their office, locked up in a desk drawer with a handful of ammunition, kept in a plastic baggie. She unlocked the drawer, calmly loaded the gun, and texted her dad. It was a matter of who was closer—Garrett was halfway across town and her dad was right there. The thumping on the window was getting worse. The man was in a rage now, but she did not scare easily. Her dad responded immediately—be right there—and she finished loading the gun. Six bullets. One man, probably two, maybe more. All she had to do was wait him out.

But this was a different world, a different Brianna. She did not want to wait in the office with the door locked. She did not want to play at being scared. She wanted to eviscerate the bastard.

So she walked out of the office to the main door. She unlocked it and stepped outside. The man was standing not ten feet away, staring at her with a clear erection in his pants. "Yo, hey, baby, you saw what you liked... wait, liked..." He had to think about that a minute. "Liked what you liked. Liked what you saw." He tittered and took a step towards her. She brought the gun up and he stopped. "Whoa, hey, you wanna be wit' me, you don't gotta do it at gunpoint."

"Get the fuck back in your car and get out of here," she snarled, "or I put one in your kneecap. And if you ever come back—I mean ever—I dig out your personal information from our computer. I take a little trip to your place, I maybe put a little something in your protein powder. Something to make you a little sleepy. And when you wake up, you'll have your tiny little dick on a chain around your neck. Are we abso-fuckin'-lutely clear?"

"You wouldn't shoo—"

She aimed the gun at his feet and fired. The bullet screamed off the pavement a mere two feet from the man and he shrieked in surprise. "You've got ten seconds. Go." As he bolted for his car, she shouted after him, "And tell your friend the same."

As he screeched away, she stepped back inside and calmly leaned against the edge of the ring, the gun on the canvas next to her. Her father pulled up a minute later and rushed inside. "Bri! Brianna—oh." Danny caught sight of her next to the gun and felt relief spread through him. He limped towards her. "Are you okay?"

"Never better," she said, and actually meant it. "Might get a noise complaint from the cops about a gun going off."

"Did you shoot the bastard?"

"No, just the pavement to show him I wasn't screwing around."

He hugged her. "My girl."

They put the gun away and locked up together. He insisted on walking her to her car, despite her protests that she'd just handled the situation. He told her he was old and farty and didn't give a shit about feminism and would sub in decaf for the morning coffee if she didn't let him. So she gave in. His decaf sucked.

Back at Garrett's condo, she let herself in the building with her keycard and combination. It was strange but she was already considering his place as theirs. It had been less than a week but it felt right. She marveled at that. She rode up in the elevator, humming to herself, and smiled at his pretty neighbor as they passed each other. Candy? Cara? Claire. The poor woman looked slightly despondent. Brianna wanted to stop to ask her what was wrong, but she hurried into her own condo without saying a word to Brianna.

Garrett looked up at her as she entered, deep in the research he'd printed off on some of Finson's closest associates. She leaned in and kissed him. He smiled and asked her, "How'd the defense classes go?"

"I think I understand something," she said calmly. "Your demons in the mirrors. I think I get why you don't like them so much. They're horrifying. But…" she said as she walked for his bedroom, already stripping out of her clothes for a nice long shower, knowing his eyes were locked on the sway of her hips, "…in the end, all they want is to be something more than a reflection. To be noticed. They're kind of sad, really."

Mystified, he stared after her until she crooked a finger at him from the bedroom. Then he found it pretty easy to put it out of his mind.

Chapter 15

The little drops of crimson stained the water an almost pinkish color. Jamie Finson leaned over the toilet, trying to put his pecker back in his pants with hands shaking too hard to manage it. He finally knocked the lid down and sat on it heavily. He knew he couldn't wait much longer. A month, maybe two at the most.

He drew in deep, ragged breaths and brought his hands up to his face. It was almost over. What lay beyond didn't much bother him. He had never shared much of Brennerman's breathy enthusiasm for the dark mystical aspects of the Legion, content to remain nothing more than an obedient servant. Her enthusiasm on the subject had been infectious, especially after her trip to Hamber, but he'd never gone and had no intention of it, now more than ever.

He wondered what she was up to and wished they could talk again. They would before this was through, to make final arrangements, but he'd like one more day with her. She might fight him tooth and nail on policy, but they'd made a good team, splitting the duties across the city. He had little doubt she'd be brought into the uppermost crust of the Legion. If he were well enough, she'd make a token gesture to try to elevate his position too, but they both knew the truth. In the Legion, twenty years in the pen put an unbreakable glass ceiling on one's progress and with the cancer… well, no one was going to promote him even as an honorarium.

Not that he was complaining. He had everything he wanted and then some. His granddaughter would be guided. Given her skills at subterfuge and her unbridled passion for the organization, she'd be a shoe-in someday to replace him. Maybe not for ten or fifteen years, but she'd still be one of the youngest in the history of the organization. of the line. That was what was important now. His legacy, his family's continued service to the organization he loved so much.

It was time to start planning for the exchange. His hands trembled only slightly now, so he reached into his pocket for his cell phone and tapped in a number from memory.

"Hello?" The youthful voice on the other end belied the cool depravity of the man. He knew his granddaughter was sleeping with the Butcher. That was a good choice. They would make an excellent power couple within Rankin Flats.

Without any preamble, Finson Sr. said, "How are we coming along on the exchange?"

The Butcher finished chewing on something. "City's been on lockdown with the cold, but we're making do. We'll have enough for the quarterly tribute."

"I want better than enough. I want at least a hundred pounds more, ready for the party. Do you have that much on hand?"

The Butcher thought about that. "No. But give me maybe a month or so?"

Finson's stomach rolled again and he winced. "Make it three weeks and I'll send some manpower your way. Jacobs. Phelps."

"That could work. But what we'll need to do, it'll draw some attention."

"It's fine," Finson barked. "Just make sure it's done, Butcher."

There was a pause. "She told me about the cancer. I'm sorry. You've been an inspiration."

Finson's head pounded. He wanted nothing more in that moment than to take a long nap. "Thank you," he said blearily. "Get it done. And not a word to my granddaughter about her party."

"My lips are sealed, boss."

Murphy watched this entire exchange, completely baffled and more than a little irritated. He'd never heard Finson talk to this man before, nor had he ever heard of an exchange. Padraig had never mentioned this Butcher in his people's reports either. An exchange clearly sounded like code and a hundred pounds sure sounded like drugs. This sounded big, but they had so little information to go on. Whatever Finson had planned, without some specifics, there wasn't going to be any way they could stop him.

* * *

The flowchart of the power structure within the Legion's local chapter was woefully incomplete. There were few names listed—Finson, Markham, a tech expert named Dee who seemed to be a rising star and on good friendly terms with Finson, a dozen or so soldiers—but, for the most part, they had been treading water until Murphy's iceberg. Now they were sinking rapidly. They came up with plan after plan and discarded them immediately as foolish or needing too much time. The silent female ghost watched them the whole time sitting in the corner.

"What's our play?" Garrett muttered to himself. "Who's Butcher?"

"Padraig doesn't think it's a name, but a title. He heard Finson refer to him in passing once before but didn't think much of it. The Butcher."

"Well, that's a bit of a clichéd name, isn't it?" Brianna asked after Garrett relayed what he'd said. "Might as well call yourself Mr. Murderer or Shooty McShootem."

Garrett rubbed his chin, ignoring her. "Hm. I don't know that we have much of a leg to stand on here. Not yet anyways."

"Does it have to be drugs?" Brianna asked suddenly.

Garrett and Murphy turned to look at her, surprised. Garrett held up his fingers as Murphy spoke. "She has a point. We don't know for certain what it is.".

She got up and flipped rapidly through the notes on each of the three biggest names on the board. "No priors for drugs, save for a couple of misdemeanors for carrying."

Garrett examined the notes with her. "Huh. You're right."

She shrugged. "I don't know, I thought maybe it was a smart idea, not jumping to conclusions." Garrett's cell rang in the other room. "I'll grab that. I'm not much use here." The silent ghost woman followed her out, ignoring Garrett's glare.

"Maybe she's right. Not about being of no use. She's thinking outside the box and that's exactly what we need. Maybe we're assuming too much," Murphy said. "Let's pull Padraig in, get him to go over the conversation that he heard. Maybe there's something there we missed. Something that got lost in translation."

Garrett rubbed his eyes. "Agreed. I think we're spinning our wheels here for now anyways. Have Padraig keep watching. Shit, this is going to be expensive." He studied the names. Finson. Markham. Dee. He tapped their photographs one by one, then looked at the soldiers again. "You said Richter Haas's men were back in town, right?"

"You think they got an invite to this party? Whatever it is?"

"I think... hm." The beginnings of a plan were starting to come together. "Padraig's got people on Dee, Markham, and Finson? Let's run a call-home-to-mommy."

Murphy laughed, then his face grew serious. "Wait, you actually think that'll work?"

"Shit if I know. But it's as good of an idea as any and it's been at least, I don't know, a week since I punched someone. Gotta work the rust out somehow." From the other room, Brianna laughed sharply at something and Garrett raised an eyebrow. He leaned against the War Room's door frame, watching Brianna. She grinned at him wickedly, her hand over the receiver, and mouthed, "Monica Ames."

"Oh, this can't be good," Murphy said, snickering as he leaned against the wall to watch the fireworks.

"Sorry to interrupt, Monica, but he just came into the room. Let me put you on speakerphone." She punched a button and Monica's voice filled the room.

"-so I looked back over my shoulder and said, hey, is that thing in yet? Turns out he'd been finished for minutes."

Garrett rolled his eyes. "Hi, Monica, how are you, how's things, et cetera et cetera." To Brianna, he said, "Don't believe a word she says."

"It's so much fun to watch him squirm," Brianna said at the phone.

"Oh, I like this one, Garrett," Monica said. "Brianna, I hate to cut things short and I really want to meet up with you some time, but can I speak to Garrett alone? I promise, it's a, um, work thing."

Seeing Brianna's discomfort, Garrett jumped in hurriedly. "It's okay, Monica. Anything you have to say she can hear. Anything," he said with meaning. Brianna pointed at the phone, then pointed at the air behind him, then made a question mark in the air. Realizing what she meant, he shook his head firmly no and pointed to her then himself. The only ones that knew about his ghosts were in that room—well, and his family, more or less. She nodded.

Monica cleared her throat. "Um, are you sure?"

"Yes, absolutely," Garrett said. "She knows about my side work."

"Oh good. It's better she knows what she's getting into with you. Uh, welcome to the fold, Brianna. He must think a lot of you."

"Thanks," Brianna said cheerfully. "He's bananas but I like him." She winked at Garrett.

"Garrett, I ran some of those names you gave me. There's not much here that might help you, but I put together some case files and got copies. At the very least, you'll have some background information. I'm headed to work in a while, but if you can meet me at the Coffee Can near my place, we've got just enough time to meet up. Brianna, you too. I want to meet you."

He glanced up at Brianna, who was grinning like a shark about to devour a tasty bit of bloody leg. "Oh yes, I'd love that," she exclaimed.

"We'll see you there in a few."

"Great," Garrett said weakly. "This should be awesome."

* * *

As it turned out, it kind of was.

As Brianna held the door for him, he leaned in and kissed her cheek and whispered, "Bull testicles." She fought the wild gales of laughter that had overcome her when he'd told her the story of the Ball Chomper's nickname in the car, and managed this time to just let out a tiny little giggle. The corners of her eyes still leaked tears from laughing so hard. Inside, the silent ghost and Murphy sat at opposite ends of the room, watching each other guardedly.

Next in line at the counter, Monica gave them a little wave and said loudly, "You guys want something?"

"Whiskey," Garrett muttered. Aloud, he said, "Black coffee."

"Maybe a tea?" Brianna asked.

"You like chai? They got a killer chai here," Monica said as she moved forward to order. "Never mind, you're having chai tea. Two of those and a black coffee. And..." she looked over the food, "Three of those homemade granola bars." She waved away Garrett's attempt to hand her some money. "I'll shoot you if you try to pay. Not really," she said quickly to the barista. "Well, maybe if they'd tried to order decaf or a soy nonfat bullshituccino. Am I right?" The barista shrugged a little fearfully and set about to work. Monica turned and offered Brianna her hand. In typical Brianna fashion, she ignored it completely and hugged Monica. "Oh, yep, we're hugging, we're... yep."

"Get used to it," Garrett said.

Brianna pulled back and smiled. "Sorry, it's just... you know, I noticed he trusts good people. So you get hugs instead of handshakes."

Garrett halfway expected Monica either shoot her or poke fun at Brianna, but instead she eyed her, making a clucking sound with her tongue. Finally, she said, "You're pretty. I mean, not that I had any doubts, it's just... nice pull, Garrett."

"Um," Garrett said eloquently.

"Thank you," Brianna said, brightening immensely, her smile much more natural now. "You're lovely too."

"Pfft. I look like a loaf of bread with tits and a gun." Monica grinned despite herself. "But thank you anyways." After they got their drinks and sat down at a table where Monica had left a stuffed folder, she leaned in and said in a hush, "So you know about Garrett. And me. I mean, not just, you know," she made a circle and pushed a finger into it as Garrett swore and turned beet red, "But what we work on together?"

"Yes," Brianna said, just as quietly. "You point him in the direction he needs to go and he does what the police can't. I know it's uncomfortable and bad that he told me, but the circumstances were…" She shrugged. "If he hadn't told me the truth, I think I wouldn't be here."

Monica nodded. "It's okay. Wasn't thrilled about it at first, but he trusts you and I trust him. Implicitly. As for what you said, I tell him about a few cases we get, and what he does with the information, well, that's his business, not mine."

"Meaning she keeps her nose clean," Garrett said softly.

Brianna sipped her tea and gave Monica a pleased thumbs up. It really was fantastic. "How'd you two meet up in the first place?"

Monica settled back. "Caught a body out at the pond at the city park one day. A prostitute nobody but me gave a shit about. I had no leads and the case was going nowhere. And then I get a call, telling me to lean on the alibi of one of her johns. It crumbled, fast. You can guess who the tipster was."

Brianna squeezed Garrett's hand and smiled.

"So I start getting more of these calls. Nudging me in the right direction, never much more than a sentence or two. And the caller is always right. But one time, he calls about a corrupt detective. My partner."

Brianna's eyebrows shot up. "Oh no."

"Mm hm. Said he was shaking down some people in the area for protection money. I had no idea. I thought Donald—that was my partner's name—had to be innocent, so I went to talk to him at home, try to figure this thing out. He cold cocks me, knocks me out. Next thing I know I'm being dragged through his house to his garage, and there's this sound like wood cracking because, well, wood was cracking. My mystery caller was kicking down the door."

"Wish I'd gotten there faster," Garrett muttered darkly.

Monica gave him a halfhearted smile. "Wasn't any fault of yours. You saved me." She sipped at her tea and stared at it. "So they fought. Mostly a one-sided affair. Moranis, he's the best I've ever seen in a fight. And I've seen some, let me tell you."

"What happened to your partner?"

Monica took a deep breath and exhaled through her nose. "He went to prison. A cop on the inside, well…" She shook her head. "He was stabbed in the prison yard. Shouldn't have even been in gen pop, but there was a severe fuck-up or someone got bribed or… it doesn't matter. Bled out in seconds."

"I'm sorry," Brianna said, and took one of Monica's hands in her own. Surprised by the gesture, Monica tentatively squeezed back.

"Anyways," Monica said, "your man is a good one. Little bit rough around the edges and lousy between the sheets, but he's fighting when no one else has the balls to. Plus, he's almost as good a shot with a pistol as me, so he's got that going for him too."

"Really? I'd like to get out to a firing range sometime and try some target shooting with a pistol," Brianna said, thinking about the way that shot had pinged off the pavement. "I used to go deer hunting with my dad, but that was with a rifle. I could use some pointers."

"Oh hey, I'm a member of a good one. We could go sometime," Monica said pertly. "I could show you. I mean, if that's not too weird. I need to get up there and test out a new .45."

"Well, if it's not too weird for you, it's not too weird for me," Brianna said. "I'd love a chance to get to know you better."

Monica grinned. "Settled then!" She banged the table with the palm of her hand, causing the barista to shoot them a look of indignant irritation.

"Two of the women who've seen me naked, firing loaded pistols next to each other at a gun range. That's great," Garrett said. "Just great. Uh, so… the folder?"

"Right," Monica said. She pushed it across the table. "Here."

He opened it and flipped through it quickly. It was full of photocopies of case files, pictures, mug shots, and short dossiers on Jamie Finson Sr., Markham, and Dee. A sticky note in the back of the folder said only, "J.F. Jr., two misdmnrs., traffic violations."

"Your guy Finson's a bad man," Monica said. "Gets sent to prison after he takes the rap for a Legion big boss man. Does twenty years. He orchestrated a retaliation from inside the pen against the families of some men who beat him up inside and it was brutal. No one could pin it on him, but he did it, sure as shit. He gets out in his forties, gets rewarded with control over the city. Got ties to a hundred different crimes since then, at least, but he's a careful man. And he's protected from on high."

"What do you mean?" Brianna asked.

"I mean, someone—or a lot of someones—is getting paid to look the other way while he runs this city. Judges. Police."

"And nothing on this Brennerman?"

"Nope. One of the women, a professor, was arrested some time back for protesting, but that's about it."

Garrett sighed. "Then it looks like it's just Finson, Sr. for us."

"Sorry," Monica said. "Markham's interesting too. Guy was a cop, turned dirty and wound up in jail. He miraculously gets out with a new lawyer, and he's kept his nose clean ever since. Dee's a new Legion hire, but she's sharp. Programmer, techie, has a prior for assault and battery and was picked up on, get this, a rape case."

Surprised, Brianna reached over and flipped through the photos. She doubted that pretty woman could have any trouble landing a date, even with the extra weight. "No kidding?"

"No kidding. Held down a freshman at the college, tied him up, left him there afterwards. Her lawyer had the case thrown out." She leaned forward. "So which one are you going after?"

That was the million dollar question, wasn't it? He finished off his coffee and grimaced as he flipped through the folder one more time. "All of them."

* * *

Soon. Soon. Soon.

The word thumped in Ransom's head as he tried to avoid breaking the speed limit. His ring tapped on the steering wheel every time he said the word. The camera was on the seat next to him, ready to record his next kill. He wasn't sure anymore if it was for research or for his own pleasure. The thin veneer of civility he'd felt by studying his murders before had worn thin by now and he was starting to recognize himself for what he was. A monster. A murderer.

And he didn't care. He reached up to the mirror with one finger, crooning softly at the patchy-furred snarling beast on the other side of the glass.

The first date had gone almost exactly as he thought it would. There had been flirting at dinner. She rubbed his leg a little under the table with her foot, he brushed the back of her hand with his fingers, soft little strokes as light as spider's silk. Her mouth worked magic on the drive back to her place, and when she'd invited him in for more, he'd accepted with a sneer. He'd taken her hard and rough, and she'd loved every second of it. He made sure to spill into a condom and flushed it away.

He left her place a few minutes later without a word as to why. She couldn't call or text him to ask—she never even had his number in the first place, since he'd called her from a hotel bar.

This time, he hadn't called at all. He knew where she lived. He put on the plastic gloves and fitted a baseball cap over his enormous skull. It was too tight, but if he kept his head down, no neighbors would be able to make out his face. Buying the junker of a car from the shady discount dealership had been a good call. He paid the man extra for his silence and the plates that came with it, all in cash.

Her outdoor security light came on as he walked up the drive and he pulled the cap lower. He knocked politely, holding the flowers he'd brought with him and tucking the video camera under one arm. The door creaked open and peered out myopically, dressed in a bathrobe, her hair a wild mess. She wasn't nearly so sexy as the last couple of times he'd seen her. "Harold?" she asked. That was the name he'd given her, under the guise of being a criminal defense lawyer. Then angrily, "Where the fuck did you go?"

"I'm sorry. There was an emergency." He tried to look sheepish. "I had a client, he's special needs, he got himself in a bit of trouble and needed me right away. You were so beautiful there resting and I just…"

It worked. Holy shit, it worked. She was still pissed, but she opened the door wider. "You didn't call. You didn't text. Nothing. I'm not your booty call, asshole."

"I know," he said, pushing past her into the living room. "I am so very, very sorry. Here, I brought you flowers." That would occupy her hands. She took them and sighed. With his hand behind his back, he hit record on the video camera and set it on the bookshelf next to her door. That would give him a good angle of what he was about to do next. She lifted the flowers to her face and inhaled as he stepped in closer. Thinking he was going to kiss her, she started to fold her arms and tell him off, but instead he punched her hard across the jaw and she stumbled away, falling across the coffee table. One leg broke under her weight and she rolled onto the floor. She only had time for a short scream before he wrapped his hands around her throat and started choking her. She flailed at him, hitting him without any real force, then trying to scratch at his hands, his face, his neck. He picked her up by the throat and slammed her head against the ground. That helped.

He leaned over her, his lips peeled, white teeth dazzling. Images of Queen Bitch from work rose unbidden in his mind, and he thought about her words on the voicemail she'd left him. Erratic behavior. His hands tightened even harder. Sub-par performance lately. Give her ten minutes with him and his dick and he'd show her that all the other men in her life gave her a sub-par performance. Not him. He laughed giddily. He knew who would be next. Oh God, yes.

Her eyes bulged, irises flickering to and fro. She bucked her back, kicking and trying to worm her way out, but he was too strong and she was losing strength. Her eyes focused on the ceiling above him, and her spasms settled into tremors and then into nothing at all. He kept his grip on her another minute, maybe more, enjoying the feel of the pliant flesh and hard muscles and cartilage under his fingers.

Her ghost slid up and out of her body and she stared at him in shock, green and violet streamers fluttering behind her. "You fucking bastard!" she shrieked. "I'll kill you!"

Finally letting go, he got up, panting, feeling as though he'd just run a marathon. He pointed at her body and said, "Try it, bitch."

She turned and looked and gave a very soft, "Oh." She backed away from him, from her body, and kept repeating that single little word. "Oh. Oh." Then she was turning and racing, running for the door, through it, and out of his life.

He checked the backs of his hands. She managed to make some small impressions on his skin but nothing deep enough to draw blood, and he grinned even wider. He thought about what Jade Gibbons had told him about Garrett Moranis, about the way he described his work to his girlfriend. How he claimed he took what he wanted and gave back to the community. Ransom had no doubt the man's humblebrag—as his acquaintances on social media called it, a delightful newly coined term he'd liked immediately—had been intended to keep the fair lady's nether bits wet and were complete bullshit. Everyone took. No one gave except when they thought their soul was on the line.

Looking around the house, it wound up being a moot point. She had nothing of value, unless one valued dirty bongs. But the temptation to do as Garrett did was alluring, too much so to resist. From a box in her kitchen, he found all sorts of prescription bottles, from penicillin to muscle relaxants. He took the muscle relaxants and painkillers, but left the rest. It seemed like the sort of thing Garrett would do. Hell, given his tension lately, why not pop a muscle relaxant tonight? He deserved a good night's sleep. He wondered vaguely if Garrett would approve. The thing reflected in the glass, with teeth growing out of an open, festering wound between its neck and its shoulder, seemed to think so. It slathered the glass with its lengthy, acid-spotted tongue as though it were trying to give him a kiss for his work.

Feeling satisfied with his work, he grabbed the camera, turned off the outdoor lights and walked back to his car, humming a made up tune, never noticing once the scratch on the back of his neck and the tiny smeared beads of blood.

Chapter 16

The bartender thought about wiping down the bar and even gave it a tentative licks with the towel before the idea of work overwhelmed him and he sat back down on his stool. No one else was in the place. Typical. He dug out his dip and smacked the can against his index finger to pack it. He shoved a fat wad of the shit in his mouth and nearly choked when someone jerked open the door. The juices ran down his throat and he had to lean forward and hawk the crap out into the garbage can before he retched. Holding a hand on the bar for support, he blinked up at the newcomer. "Help you?" he croaked.

"You all right there, partner?" There was something familiar about the man's voice, but he'd seen a lot of people come through and it could have been any one of them. "Know plenty of people who've died from that shit, but never by choking on it."

The bartender poured himself a shot of whiskey and downed it in one go. He spat into the wastebasket, then spat again. "Yeah, good. Now whaddya want?"

"Bottle of 151 rum. Whatever's cheapest." The man seemed to be listening to something behind him, but there was no sound other than what they were making. Something about that rang a bell in the bartender's head. "Matches, too, if you got 'em."

"Bar doesn't carry matches no more."

"C'mon. You don't have a lighter or a matchbook anywhere in the place?"

"Throw in another buck and I'll give you mine."

The man slapped the bar. "Done."

The bartender set the bottle on the counter and dug out his lighter from his pocket. He flicked it on to show the guy it worked. The customer nodded and tossed a couple of bills on the counter without looking at them. He did that odd head-cocking thing again and asked for a couple of bottled sodas too.

The bartender added those and turned to punch everything into the register. The way the man tossed the bills down. He'd been the same guy as before. The one who'd left him the monster tip for the bottle of beer he never drank. He turned back to the man, grinning, halfway expecting him to be already on his way out the door, leaving behind his change. But this time the man only stood there staring at him, visibly annoyed. "Well? You going to ring me up?"

Fuming, the bartender turned back to his work, made change, and tossed it on the counter. Scooping the money up, the man muttered irritably to himself, "Everyone expects a bigger and bigger tip these days."

* * *

The hair fell away from the teenager's head like wheat falling before the blade of a scythe. "You ain't gonna ask me why I want a faux hawk?" the kid asked.

Mullet shrugged and said nothing. He didn't really give a shit. The kid was a nobody, not even Legion. He recognized the type, though. This kid was a wannabe banger, the kind who dug his daddy's pistol out of the back of his closet and played el bandito with it until his buddies texted him for another game of Call of Duty. Just another punk kid, not worth his time. He was tired, annoyed, and he just plain didn't feel like talking.

The kid, of course, took no notice. "Got school pictures tomorrow. My grans, she told me to go get my hair shredded, but she at the Lucky Lil's tonight spendin' that skrilla."

Freckles dropped his phone on the chair next to him with a sigh and glared at the kid from across the room. "Man, what the fuck is skrilla?"

"The lettuce, man!" The kid slapped the back of his hand against the other repeatedly. "Cash money?"

"Why not just say cash then? Or money?"

Mullet snickered and tilted the kid's head down. With a couple more zips from the electric razor, he was done. The kid examined his dome carefully. "I don't like it," he said sullenly.

"You're not trying to get out of paying your bill, you little turd," Freckles said as he stood up and cracked his knuckles menacingly. He stepped forward and looked right into the kid's eyes, giving him what he called the asesino glare, the one that told motherfuckers they'd better make peace either with him or their maker.

The kid snickered. "Man, you look like you 'bout to go tellin' me how life is like a box of chocolates or something. Back off my ass with

194

that bullshit."

Mullet's snort prompted Freckles to fold his arms across his chest and glare at his business partner. "Not helping."

The kid counted out the exact change carefully, then got up and ran for the door. "Y'all get back to your bumpin' and grindin', y'hear?" He cackled wildly and slammed the door behind him, sending the shades on the door clattering down.

"Stupid little…" Freckles muttered as Mullet set about to sweeping. He walked over and drew up the blinds again. He turned back to Mullet and said, "Can't we close up early?"

The door opened and shut behind him, lock clicking, and Mullet had just enough time to say, "Ah, hell—" before Garrett—masked and gloved as he tended to be in these little outings—zapped Freckles with the Taser, dropping him immediately into a spasming little ball on the floor. Mullet scrambled for the gun in the bottom drawer of his cutting gear, his fingers kissing the cool barrel before Garrett tased him too. Unlike his companion, the shock only staggered the bull moose of a man. He fell to one knee, fighting to keep his balance, hands searching for purchase. After he set the bottle of liquor on the counter, Garrett snapped a knee up and into the man's jaw, sending him sprawling backwards. The fight wasn't out of Mullet yet, though. He grabbed hold of the metal armrest of the barber chair and started to pull himself to his feet, until Garrett pried up his pinky finger—and kept going. Mullet's yelp of pain turned into a shriek as the finger bent too far backwards and popped audibly. Broken or dislocated, it didn't matter. He fell to his knees, cradling his hand.

Freckles tried to push himself upright, but that was easily solved by grabbing him by the shirt collar and shoving him halfway across the room into the counter top beside a wash basin. His hair was stiff with gel, perfect for grabbing, so Garrett took full advantage and used it to slam his head once, twice, three times into the wash basin's ceramic lip. Freckles dropped, completely dead weight.

Mullet screamed at him, "Shit, man, that's how you get concussions!" as though this were news to Garrett. Thanks to the smashed nose, it sounded like he was fighting a cold. The big German stared at him as he approached. "You're late, asshole. We just got robbed."

"I know," Garrett said, and offered him a hand. "I was the one who did it." Annoyed with the man's gawping silence, Garrett snapped his fingers. "C'mon. You can get up and get into the chair or I can beat you up some more. I've got all day."

"Just, shit, don't hit anyone's head anymore. Do you know what you even did to my boss?" He let Garrett help him up and sat in the chair complacently. "He won't do math that isn't harder than two plus two the rest of his life."

"Good. You raping fucks deserve whatever you get." Garrett worked zip ties around his hands, binding him to the chair securely. Then he patted the man down. Nothing except his wallet which he threw aside after fishing out the few bills inside and stuffing them into his pocket. He checked Freckles too, who had a little surprise strapped to his ankle. Garrett undid the holster and examined the gun. It was an expensive-looking little holdout piece, a sleek black semi-auto. "Nice gun," he said appreciatively.

"Gift from his mother," Mullet said.

"No shit? Huh. Last thing my mother ever gave me was... eh, let's not go into that." He put the pistol and the holster on the counter. Then he drew the blinds and contemplated the German, tapping his fingers against the counter. "So, you don't like having your head messed with. All right, that's gonna make this simple then. Won't even probably need the demonstration."

Mullet spat out blood. "Demonstration?"

"Yeah. See, this is 151 proof rum. Hugely flammable." Garrett uncapped the rum. He took a sip and grimaced. "Disgusting stuff. Want a drink?"

The Garman shook his head. "Sixty days sober, last Wednesday."

"Oh yeah? Mazel tov." Garrett poured a little bit of the rum on the counter. Flicking the cheap lighter to life, he lit the rum. A line of cool blue flames shot down the dribble of liquor. "See, I was gonna threaten you two dickheads with fire, then pour just a little bit in the space between your fingers. See?" He dribbled a little on the fatty tissue between Mullet's pointer and middle finger. "It wouldn't burn very hot, at least not with that little liquid, but it would irritate the ever loving crap out of your skin. Enough to get my point across." Then Garrett's easy-going smile disappeared. "And then I'd pour a little on one of you sons of bitches' eyes. I'm real curious about what the fire would do to them. Surface vision would be wrecked for sure, but what would it look like, you know? Would they boil? Pop? Cook like meat? I'd start with his, probably. He's out cold, so, you know, that'd be pretty easy." He nudged the man with his foot. "Aren't you, buddy?" Freckles did not disappoint him by responding.

"I... I'll talk," Mullet said, swallowing hard.

Garrett laughed harshly. "Yeah you will. Just a matter of how much truth I'm gonna get out of you without a little pain."

"No, I swear!" Mullet shrieked as Garrett flipped Freckles onto his back. He turned back and glanced at the German. The big man blubbered, "Please don't hurt him. Please. He's... I..."

"Oh..." Garrett said, finally understanding. "I won't," he said gently, then he dumped half the bottle of booze onto the man anyways. "So long as you hold absolutely nothing back, understand?"

"Yes," Mullet sobbed. "Just please, don't."

"You're going to tell me about this little party Jamie Finson's planning."

Mullet blinked at him, once, twice. "Party? I don't—"

Garrett clicked the wheel on the lighter. "Damn thing," he muttered cheerfully. "Might take it one or two clicks before I get a spark."

"No, just stop! There's a... handoff. I don't know where it is."

This was the gamble, the only line in the whole charade that mattered. "I know where it is, asshole. That's not what I asked. I need to know who's coming," Garrett growled, "what kind of security, who brings the punch, that sort of thing."

"I, ah, shit. Haas knew all this, him and the boss were tight. Uh. Finson. The Butcher, most definitely. I don't know who else, I swear."

"Who is the Butcher?" Garrett asked, his eyes laser focused on Mullet.

Mullet shook his head side to side. "No. I tell you, he'll do worse things to us than you can imagine."

Garrett flicked the lighter and Mullet yanked at his restraints, eyes bulging. Garrett hissed, "One more time. That's it."

"I can't tell you!"

After staring at the flame for a long minute, Garrett realized Mullet couldn't or wouldn't tell him anything more. His role in this was done. He let the lighter go out. "I believe you." He slapped Mullet's cheek lightly a couple of times, a mockery of a friendly gesture. "Oh, I'm taking that little pocket pistol and the holster too. That's cuter than shit." He took them off the counter.

"Enjoy," the man said weakly.

Garrett grabbed the rum and the Taser on his way out as well as a nice bottle of shampoo. Saved himself a trip to the store. That was forward thinking.

* * *

He picked Brianna up at the gym. "Have fun with the boys?" she asked as she got in. The bottle of shampoo rolled around by her feet. She picked it up and opened it, sniffing at the scent. "Ooh, Manly. Not your brand, either. A little present from your friends?"

He nodded. "That's not all I got, either." He held up the holster and the gun carefully. "This is for you. I didn't check the safety on it, so be careful."

"Oh, that is the coolest thing ever," she gasped, then scratched her head. "You're a bad influence on me. I don't think a month ago I would have considered a… what do you call this?"

"A holdout gun. Or a pocket pistol. Don't ask me what type specifically."

She giggled. "Pocket pistol. Dirty." He snickered as he pulled out onto the street. "Anyways, I know on a basic level guns are just guns and it's weird to say they're cool, but… this is pretty cool."

He glanced at her, grinning. "It's a neat little pistol."

She checked the safety to make sure it was on, reholstered it, and put the gun carefully in the back. "So, do you think he bought it? That you really knew where the meet was at?"

He blew out his breath. "I'm no actor, but God, I hope so. Otherwise, I mean, I guess we could follow Finson until the day of, but that leaves us with no room for planning. I don't know that I'd go up against the Legion without something in mind. If that happened, I guess I'd call it in to Monica and hope the cops could do something about it."

They cruised through the city, a little aimlessly. They weren't in any rush to get anywhere—Padraig would meet them back at the apartment if and when he got news, and he'd be paid to wait. Murphy sat in the backseat, content with the way things had gone, and so they enjoyed a few minutes of quiet normalcy. Garrett and Brianna sipped their sodas, stopped for a shared bag of Town Pump popcorn, and decided it was warm enough to walk through a local dog park and people watch while they snacked.

At that point in the evening, the park lights were just coming on, casting the tall, winter-bald foliage, weeping willows, and pines in a warm light. They passed a few dog owners out for their evening walks and soon fell into an easy debate over the best dog breeds when Brianna

198

stopped to fawn over a German shepherd and boxer cross puppy. As she wiped away dog kisses, Brianna remarked that she had made up her mind and boxers were indubitably the greatest breed. Garrett shook his head and sighed, pointing out the unassailable position that pugs were, in fact, at least three point four times better because of their crop dusting ninja skills.

By the time they reached the end of the path, they agreed between them that a boxer pug mix would be the best way to settle their differences, and set about naming their theoretical future dog. "Farts McKenzie," Brianna said matter-of-factly. "Farts for the pug side, McKenzie for the nice, normal, sane boxer side of things."

"You know, if we had two, we could name them Riggs and Murtagh."

"Oh my God," she laughed. Her cell phone started buzzing. "That's perfect." She smiled apologetically and took the call. "Hey Dad, I…" After a minute, she rolled her eyes at Garrett. "Yeah, I can fill in. Tell Terrence this is the last time, though. Dad, I know you like him. That's beside the point. I've looked at his time sheets for the last year and the man can't keep a schedule for…. look, can we argue about this tomorrow? I'll be there in, I don't know, fifteen or so." Another pause and she sighed heavily. "No, Dad, you didn't catch us in fragrant delectable. And it's in flagrante delicto. No, I'm sure." She raised her eyes to the sky as if asking for help. "Dad. Dad! I'll be there soon and I'll show you the spelling tomorrow. Okay, love you, gotta go, going through a tunnel, bye." She hung up and grumbled irritably. To Garrett, she said, "Our trainer for the joint senior citizen and extra lovin' course for the evening crapped out on us. Again. I need to head back there."

He thought about it for a moment. "Why don't I come with? I'm due for some cardio."

"Don't you have to get back for your Finson thing?"

He shrugged. "Murphy can go back and talk to Padraig. It doesn't really matter if I'm there."

"This is huge, though. This is like your whole battle plan."

He wrapped his arms around her and kissed her nose. "You're cute. You win over old grumpy Scottish ghosts. Or English. Whatever. The point is, let's go whip some old people into shape." Since Murphy was half a football field away and he couldn't call him without drawing attention, he whistled as though he were looking for a dog. "Hey, Murphy, c'mere, buddy."

"Where is he?" Brianna asked.

"See that old barking sheepdog?"

An old shaggy dog seemed to be barking at absolutely nothing at all, joyously and to the consternation of its owner. She gasped. "Can dogs see…?" She cut herself off and glanced back and forth. "You know. Them?"

Garrett shrugged. "Murphy thinks the old ones can. And the very, very young. Like just barely opening their eyes young. I don't know, though. I adopted one once from the pound, this old pitbull mix. It seemed to bark at Murphy on occasion, but it also barked at the wind blowing, cars going by, nothing at all. He'd spend half his time looking at a wall and chuffing at it." They started walking together towards the exit. "But dogs can sense a lot of weird stuff, you know? Who knows? You're talking to a man who's been cursed with Lusty Gallant. Who has any idea what's possible?"

* * *

The class was pleasantly energetic and low stress. Everyone there was out to have a good time or learn the basics, and Brianna had a lot of fun with that. There were a handful of couples there, either young and a little out of shape or older and looking to stay active. Curiously, there didn't seem to be any middle-aged folks. The other half of the class were singles or friends dragging each other out. Wilfred even showed up, and when he started making sweet eyes at a neighboring woman with a kind smile, Garrett knew the kid was going to be okay.

The class talked a bit together afterwards, laughing and breaking apart into smaller groups and couplings. Some went home, some did some cardio, all of them seemed satisfied. After a few minutes spent talking to his new female friend, Wilfred came over and asked Garrett shyly if he'd show him the sparring moves he'd talked about. Garrett was happy to oblige. As Brianna and the young woman worked some basic core strengthening exercises together, Garrett bounded up the steps and got in the ring. He beckoned Wilfred up and smiled to himself when the kid, hesitant at first to go through the ropes again, glanced down at his new friend, blushed, and swung his legs through the ropes like an old pro.

They started and finished with simple boxing fundamentals—the jab, cross, and the hook. Once Wilfred starting pounding the boxing mitts, Brianna and his friend cheered him on. It wasn't long before Wilfred tired, but by the end of their session, his confidence had skyrocketed and he finished strong with a set of ten simple combinations Garrett drilled into him. "It's going to be footwork and repetition, day in, day out. When you've got time, come in here and hit the treadmill. Cardio's gonna be your best friend. Strength training's part of it too, don't get me wrong, but you want to learn more than just how to punch a guy, you gotta learn footwork. We'll get you started on jumping rope in a few weeks."

When Murphy popped through the mirrors of the outside wall, Garrett finally clapped Wilfred on the shoulder and told him he'd had an excellent first session. Brianna took advantage of the opportunity to tell him and his female friend about their sparring and self-defense classes, both of which she thought they'd be excellent candidates for when they had a few weeks of gym basics under their belt. They left together, on a mission for a late dinner and maybe a movie. Garrett stood in the ring after they'd left, feeling pretty mellow and happy. Brianna joined him and he whispered in her ear so the few remaining people couldn't hear, "Murphy's here."

She kissed his cheek, liking the combined smells of sweat and deodorant rising off his body. "Use the showers to talk," she whispered. "All the guys have left."

He nodded and she swatted his butt as he climbed through the ropes. That got a few laughs from the customers left. She laughed too and hollered at them to all get back to work. Garrett snuck off to the showers. He checked all the aisles to make sure they were alone, just in case Brianna had been wrong. Finally, he sat on a bench and looked at Murphy squarely. "Did it work?"

Murphy couldn't hold his somber look for very long, his face like the sun breaking through a very long fog. "When Mullet got free, first thing he did was call Markham. Markham flipped. He grabbed Finson and took him out to the middle of a parking lot, completely paranoid. Wouldn't allow his boss to say a word. Not a single one. They got out, walked a hundred yards, and started planning changes to the location immediately."

Garrett slapped the bench. "All right, shit's finally looking up."

Murphy nodded. "You think Finson was paranoid before, he's gonna clam up tighter than shit on this one. Markham suspects someone is feeding you information on the inside, just enough so you know where to show. He thinks you're someone's hired gun, that someone's making a power play. Maybe we can use that. I'm focusing everything on him now."

"Anything more on that Butcher guy?"

"No, nothing. I'm still not sure about this party, either. It could be the same thing as the exchange, but they make it sound almost like one of their initiation rites. It's something else to keep an eye on, anyways."

"Okay, good. Thanks, Murphy."

"You can feel it, can't you? We're close. We went from nothing on this one to everything."

"Don't get cocky," Garrett warned. "We take it slow. We prepare. We make contingency after contingency. We do this completely by our playbook."

"Yeah, yeah, you're excited. I can see it."

"I am," Garrett admitted. And he was. Whatever was going down was big. If they weren't about to cut off the head of the snake, then at least they were doing a fair bit of damage to the body. But there were still so many unknowns. Whatever this Butcher was peddling required an incredible hush of security. The planning had been going on for weeks before they'd arrived on the scene and it was clear nothing would be spoken about aloud unless it was absolutely necessary. That cut their information down to a trickle. And Padraig's people were getting bored and antsy. They would make mistakes. He didn't know how much longer he had them for, money or not.

At the entrance to the locker room, Brianna cleared her throat and shattered his concentration. She said loudly, "Uh, Garrett? There's a man here to see you." She sounded scared. Terrified, even. Garrett jumped up. "Says it's about your friend. Murphy."

* * *

The world faded away and all he could hear was a steady thump in his ears—his heart beating. It was shockingly slow. It should have been racing. Should have been just about ready to leap out of his throat. In fact, every movement he made felt as though he were trying to do it underwater. This was not possible.

He took one unsure step after another. Out of the corners of his eyes he could see Brianna hustling the last two remaining ladies towards the women's showers. The pistol he'd given her and the Taser were still in the car. If this man was Legion, if he knew Garrett's secret, he was dead. And God knew what would happen to Brianna. He forced himself to breathe slowly. Unhurriedly. He tried not to think of all the horrible things he'd read about the Legion doing to those who betrayed them.

Murphy fell into step beside him, his eyes locked on the man in the suit leaning against the mirrored windows.

He was big and not just in a single form of the word. He looked as though he had some muscle to him, sure, but there was a hint of a sedentary lifestyle there too, especially in the smooth skin and business attire. His suit looked tailored, though it seemed ruffled and more than a little lived-in. He saw Garrett and smiled widely, showing a hint of teeth. Beside him stood the silent ghost, who had been gone since the morning. Curiously, it wasn't Garrett she watched warily, but the stranger.

"Garrett Moranis. Been waiting a while to say hello to you." He motioned towards the women's locker room and said in an amicable tone, "We'll wait for our other friends to leave before we talk a little shop."

Brianna re-emerged from the locker room and headed straight for the office, glancing at Garrett worriedly. He tried to convey confidence to her with a tight lipped smile, but his hands were trembling. "You know Murphy?" Garrett asked innocently enough.

"Oh right, proof. Well," he said, lowering his voice and whispering theatrically, "there's a large black man straight from the seventies standing right beside you. And on my side, lacking the delightful curly hair and style, is the chatty Miss Gibbons. Have you introduced yourself?" he asked, turning to Jade. "No? Didn't think so. She's particular about when she talks." She glowered at him but still said nothing. "See what I mean?" To the locker room as the last customers emerged, the man tipped them a bow and said cheerfully, "And a lovely night to you ladies!"

They giggled a little at that and left, the doorbell jangling above them. Brianna came out and locked the door behind them. From behind her back she produced an old pistol, cocked it, and darted towards them. "Whoever you are, whatever you're here for, don't imagine I won't shoot."

The stranger held his hands up, still grinning. "I'm going to lift up my coat very slowly and show you I'm not carrying a gun, okay?" Brianna waved him on with the point of her pistol and he did just that, lifting his coat up tall and spinning around slowly. "Feel like I'm a ballerina on one of those old wind-up musical toys. Sing for me, won't you, Ms. Gibbons?" She didn't comply and looked even more put out by him. "Oh well. Had to try."

Brianna lowered the gun hesitantly, but Garrett noticed she didn't take her finger away from the trigger guard. Good woman. To the stranger, he said, "You know who we are, everything we've done thanks to her. But you still have us at a disadvantage."

"Oh! That. I'm... whoops, spoilers!" He tittered, showing even more of those teeth. "For right now, let's just call me Mr. Specter, shall we? We shall."

"Uh uh," Brianna said. "We don't talk without—"

"Don't be rude." The man's grin disappeared and for a moment, his eyes seemed to take on the coldness of a snake's as he squinted at her. "Mr. Moranis and I have so much to talk about and you, you're not even in the clubhouse, are you?" Garrett saw her muscles tense and thought she might shoot him right there, just on principle. A light broke behind the clouds and he smiled again. "Sorry, how rude of me. My temper seems to get away from me more and more these days." Then the man snapped his attention to the boxing ring. "You know, I've never been inside a boxing ring before. You mind?"

"Be my guest," Brianna said sarcastically, but the stranger took it as a serious go-ahead and darted towards it. He thundered up the stairs and stood on the canvas.

"This is a real treat!" He lowered the middle rope and slipped through. "Wow. I mean, it's a little low rent, but still, an honest to goodness boxing ring. That's incredible."

Garrett followed him up the stairs. Brianna circled around on the ground, ready to shoot if necessary. As Garrett slipped in the ring, he said casually, "So. You can see ghosts too."

"Yes, my good friend, I can. And that's what I'm here to talk to you about." Mr. Specter—or whatever he was really called—danced in the ring, bouncing foot to foot like he'd seen on TV. Garrett tried to keep from laughing. The man was horrendously uncoordinated. He stopped and threw a couple of looping punches in the air as he talked. "I'd like to meet with you. Soon. I have so much I want to discuss with you." He turned to Brianna and dipped his head. "Come along too, if you'd like. You, though, Murphy... what say we leave the ghosts at home, hm?" Turning his attention to Murphy, he rolled his shoulders. "My assistant never seemed to catch a first name. Or a last name, whichever the case might be." When no answer was forthcoming from either Murphy or Garrett, he shrugged. "Murphy it is then."

Garrett's cell phone buzzed against his hip and he silenced it, annoyed. "Why not talk now?"

With a smirk to Brianna, the stranger said, "While the atmosphere here seems friendly enough, I think I'd like to meet somewhere a little more… neutral and slightly less murdery." Garrett's cell phone buzzed again and the stranger's smile dipped. "Preferably then you'll have less distractions."

From the front desk, Brianna's cell went off. She lowered the gun hesitantly and backed towards it. "Don't think I can't make the shot across the gym."

The stranger's smile grew tighter around his skull and Garrett shivered. There was no humor to the man's perpetual grin. It was more like a rictus of agony, like his muscles had been forced into that position. This guy was not dealing with a full deck. "Like I say, we'll talk more when it's more convenient for us both." From his pocket, he drew out a fine leather-bound day planner and wrote down a number on a sheet of paper within. He tore it off and handed it to Garrett. "Call me at that number when you're ready to meet." From behind them, Brianna stifled a cry. Garrett darted to the ropes immediately, leaving Murphy hissing that his back was completely exposed to the strange man. But Mr. Specter did nothing, just climbed out of the ring. He jumped to the ground and slapped the canvas with his palm. "Right then, this was…. unproductive. Well, good luck to you both and I hope next time we can actually talk."

The man strode towards the door and his ghost friend followed him. "Hey. You. Gibbons," Murphy said sharply.

The woman stopped. She turned around and stared at him as though she were a deer on the middle of the highway, seeing an oncoming semi and powerless to do anything about it.

"Whatever leash he's got on you, it's not worth it. If you're willing to talk sometime—"

Mr. Specter turned and said cheerily, "Ms. Gibbons is free to act in whatever manner she chooses, of course." She looked at him reluctantly and maybe a little fearfully. Murphy didn't like the sickly pallor of the stranger, nor the way his eyes bulged.

Gibbons gave Murphy and Garrett one last look. Despair filled her eyes and she hesitated. "I'm sorry."

Murphy nodded at her and followed them out. Brianna slowly walked towards Garrett, holding her cell phone out. Tears streaked down her face, giving her cheeks a glassy, doll-like look. "I'm sorry, I'm so sorry."

His heart hammered even harder in his chest. He didn't have to guess at who it was. He took the phone and held it to his ear. "August?"

"It's Mom, Garrett," Auggie said, her voice hoarse. "She's going. And she wants to see you."

Chapter 17

He'd never believed it was possible to find a position sleeping with a woman in which he was always a hundred percent comfortable. Someone always wound up with a mouthful of hair or a numb arm. He had no doubt at some point he and Brianna would probably come to some sort of gentle debate over how she managed to wind up with ninety percent of the bed and the comforters all in one night. But that night, his arm draped around her as they spooned, he thought he'd never be more comfortable again. She felt good pressed up against him, her frame both soft and sinewy. And she was so warm. He took back the thought of arguing with her over covers. If they could lay like that forever, he'd never want for warmth again.

Though they were naked, there was no lovemaking that night. There would be, in the morning before he had to leave, but not then. A little after half an hour from the point when they laid down, she relaxed and started to snore. He liked that about her and wondered how he could ever sleep apart from her snorting for breath. He waited a while longer before kissing the back of her shoulder gently and regretfully slipping out of bed.

He pulled on a pair of boxers and crept out to the living room. She stood there, watching him silently, always silently. He crooked his finger and led her into the War Room. He sat on the edge of the computer chair, sweating lightly.

"I can't stop you," he said softly. "I'm going to leave for a while. And Brianna, she's too stubborn to go. She thinks she can handle your acquaintance if he comes by again. Maybe she can. I don't know. But I saw you looking at me in that gym. You want to be decent."

She said nothing, only watched him guardedly.

He got on his knees. "Please. I'm begging you." He was not crying, she thought, but hoarseness crept into his voice as though he were on the edge of tears "If he tells you to follow her, don't. Give him the wrong information. Tell him she's gone with me to Florida. Or that she's in a hotel. Or anything. Something is wrong with him. Something bad. I could feel it coming off him. You know it too. I'm scared."

She still said nothing.

"I love her."

After a long minute, the ghost woman sank to her knees too, looking down at his hands in his lap. "I will lie." Her voice was halting, the cadence strange. Some speaking problem in life, he realized. That was why she was so silent.

He put his hands out, as if to touch hers. "Thank you."

She brushed his hands with her own, and acted as though she might speak for a moment. But then she stood, walked through the wall, and was gone.

* * *

At Ed and Rose's, Garrett stalked back and forth, scratching at his arms and glaring up at Ed on occasion. "You need more. I should go get my guns."

"Garrett," Ed said reasonably, "We've got the hunting rifles in the safe down here, and there's a pistol in the bedroom in a lockbox on the shelf. The last thing I need is more guns."

Garrett, haggard despite Brianna's insistence on helping him shave and clean up that morning, nodded, not really hearing him. "Monica will come by as often as she can. you don't know her but you will. She's a friend. She's about yay high, kind of looks like she's seen the shit because, well, she has." He snapped his fingers. "Photograph, I'll have her send you a photo."

"Garrett, I—"

"She'll be by. And she's going to take Bri to the shooting range a few times. That'll be good." He looked up, his eyes bright. "I could call up Froggy, get him up here with a couple of his boys. I should've thought of that—"

Ed had no idea who Froggy was. He took his friend squarely by the shoulders, stopping him forcibly. "Garrett. Stop." The other man's eyes darted back and forth. His breathing was shallow and ragged. He slapped him, hard across the face and Garrett's recoiled, shocked. "Stop. This. You realize how tough she is? This motherfucker—" Ed's swearing caught him by surprise more than the slap. He rarely swore. "-should be so lucky as to stay away. We'll handle him. I swear. We'll be so bored this week I guarantee she'll jump into her car when you fly home and scream out of here for joy with how dull it was."

His breathing still rough, Garrett stared at his friend, almost unseeing. "I love her."

Ed crushed his friend to him in a huge hug and released him. "I know, buddy."

Rose and Brianna thumped down the stairs and entered the kitchen. Rose smiled at Garrett comfortingly. "All set to go for however long you guys need."

"Thank you, Rose," he said, so grateful it hurt. "I'll pay you back. When all this is over, a trip, cash, something."

"Garrett?" Rose asked. "Shut up. Seriously. Shut. Up. We are happy to help, more than happy. This is a drop in the bucket compared to what you've done for us. And besides, we love you two, you crazy, crazy kids."

Brianna hugged Rose and started crying again, and Garrett had to admit he was touched too. He grabbed Rose after Brianna let her go, clutched her to him and kissed her cheek before he finally let her go. To Brianna, he said, "I've got one more thing for you." At Ed and Rose's catcalls, he rolled his eyes and pulled her into the next room. He dug out a scrap of paper. "The code for the safe in my apartment. If something happens—"

"Nothing will happen."

He smiled fondly at her and repeated himself, "-if something happens, not just this week, but ever, get to that safe. Memorize this." He looked at her as sternly as he could muster. "There will be a quiz on the code later. There's money and something else for you. A letter. Maybe you'll never have to open it, but if the time comes—"

She stopped him with a kiss, a slow, burning one that shut him up completely. Her hands ran through his hair and she wished they had time for a quick roll around upstairs. Instead, she settled for a loving exchange of their warm breath as she leaned her forehead against his, her eyes closed, much like the aftermath of their first kiss outside that very house.

Outside, a horn honked. Danny. He held her cheeks in his hands and kissed her tears, not willing them away but encouraging them. He loved her tears. Loved her quick emotions. Loved her fire that never seemed to burn out. He wanted to tell her then, the three little words that meant everything, but cocooned in the emotion of the moment, he just held her until Danny honked again.

"We've gotta go," she whispered.

Ed and Rose circled around the corner slowly. Ed smiled at Garrett almost apologetically, hefting his overnight bag in one hand. Garrett nodded at him and took the bag. "Ed..."

"I know, buddy."

Garrett nodded. Then they were out the door.

* * *

They huddled together in the backseat of the Aztek as Danny drove, like survivors clinging to each other after some terrible plane crash. To Danny, he said, "I'm sorry. I brought this to your door."

Danny glanced up at the rear view mirror. "You've got a nutjob stalker and you're the one apologizing?"

Garrett nodded. "I need to tell you about what I do, Danny. Not all of it, but..."

"You a bad man, Moranis?" Danny asked.

Garrett blinked. "I... what?"

"Because I don't think so. Unless I really missed the mark. Did I miss the mark, baby?"

Brianna smiled and clasped Garrett's hand tighter. "No. I don't think you've ever been more right, Dad."

"No, didn't think so."

"Danny, I—" Garrett started.

"You help people," Danny said simply. That was word for word what Garrett told Brianna. He looked at her questioningly and she shook her head, totally surprised herself. Danny snorted. "I'm not an idiot, Moranis. You chase off the bad element from my gym. You bail me out without taking any of the credit for it—hell, if I didn't have a friend at the bank, I'd have probably never known it was you. You did all that shit before you even had an inkling you wanted to put it to my daughter."

"Dad!" Brianna said without any real fire in her voice.

"And I've seen the scars. The days you've come in looking like hamburger gone bad. And I look in the news and I see some asshole's got what's coming to him. So I think, hm, two plus two equals four. I'm an old bastard but I'm not stupid."

Garrett stared at him, still shocked. Brianna unbuckled her seat belt, leaned up, and kissed her dad on the cheek before settling back in. The old man looked mighty pleased with himself. "Truth is, I wasn't sure until right now. Kinda thought maybe you were into underground MMA shit. Woulda made more sense but the way you two been acting, ain't no MMA asshole that's coming. I'll keep an eye on her and the gym, no worries there."

"And whatever you do," Garrett said firmly, "be careful. Two to

210

your cars. Always. You see a hint of this guy, you get to a gun or you get gone. Understood?"

Danny nodded. "Okay."

They rode in silence a while, Garrett and Brianna holding hands and staring out the windows at the city going by. Danny turned on some music and for a while, they listened to John Mellencamp singing about life going on. When the station faded and fuzzed into Lusty Gallant, Danny whapped the radio with the flat of his palm. "This damn station's gotta get that reception fixed. Happens all the time at the gym."

Brianna and Garrett just looked at each other, letting smiles creep across their faces for what felt like the first time that day.

* * *

She blew her nose noisily into the toilet paper. When she looked up, a little bit of mucus dribbled out of her nostrils. He brought her hand back up and helped her dab it off. She slapped his chest with the palm of her hand and wailed, "This is supposed to be all romantic, damn it. I'm not supposed to... not supposed to have s-snot b-bubbles." Garrett tried to kiss her and pull her against his chest. She struggled free and sobbed, "Stop, you'll get my grossness all over your shirt. Damn, damn, damn it, I already have." She wiped furiously at his shirt until he took her hands in his and forced them down to her sides. She glared at him, half furious, half embarrassed.

"I love your grossness on my chest," he said, smiling. "It's a mark of pride. Someone cares enough about me to see me off, fungus and all. And when I come back, someone will be here."

"Says y-you," she said. "Dad still says the janitor's s-still available."

That got a surprised laugh out of him and she started laughing too. Then she was kissing him, hard, her hands scrabbling for purchase around the back of his head and someone in the distance muttering about PDA. The kiss helped kickstart her memory.

"Oh!" she gasped. "Before you go through security, check your bag. Rose and Ed sent you something and you need to check it before you get too far."

Garrett knelt and grabbed up his carry on. They sat on a pair of plastic chairs while he opened it. A card had been added to the top of his clothes. He slid it out and ripped it open. The card depicted a field of poppies, maybe somewhere in the Death Valley, he thought. He opened it and read Ed's handwriting:

Garrett,

I made your reservations for you like you asked and you're still on the same flight, but the ticket we gave you wasn't the real deal. Rose and I wanted to do something special for you and upgraded you to first class. It's not much but I hope it helps you have a better trip.

You're a good man, brother.

-Ed

Then just a little further down, Rose added:

Gar-
Ditto to what Ed said. Not great at these things but...
You. Are. Loved.
-Rose

He looked up, blinking away tears. Brianna dug in her purse and brought out another ticket for him, smiling and crying again. They exchanged the fake one for the real thing and he tried to say something, anything, but couldn't find the words.

They sat together for another five minutes before she stood up and pulled him to his feet. He looked so lost, then, as she led him to the security gate. She brought his head down for one more brief kiss before she pushed him back. Her eyes were dry and she pleaded quietly, "Go. Please. Go now."

He nodded uncertainly and forced himself towards the gate. After he'd gone through and pulled back on his shoes and belt, he looked back. Had she still been there, he didn't think he could go through with it. He would have rushed back through, guards be damned, and ran with her for the mountains, for the west coast, overseas, anywhere to be with her.

This was her parting gift to him, he realized. Letting him go. Making him go.

* * *

While Rose and Ed meant well, it made Garrett uncomfortable to sit in first class, so when he saw the little old lady in the thick reading glasses wheeze her way into the boarding area, he made arrangements with the gate clerk to switch her places anonymously. That won him some ferocious flirtations from the clerk which he batted away uncomfortably.

The look on the old woman's face when they told her what had happened made the wait bearable.

After he boarded and shoved his overnight bag into the overhead compartment, trying not to punch the impatient asshole waiting beside him, Garrett squeezed into his window seat and Murphy stood in the center of the aisle as people passed unknowingly through him.

"Don't speak out loud, Gar, but did I ever tell you about my boy's momma? I know I told you that she died, but… I ever tell you how we lived?" Garrett shook his head just slightly. Murphy continued. "When I was slinging, she worked these long hours at a restaurant. Nothing fancy and sure as shit no place where people were gonna tip her, you know? So she took all the hours she could, worked even more on weekends helping stock shelves at a grocery store. I'd be out there, on my feet maybe two, three hours of the day, the rest on my ass in some strip club or on a chair on a corner, doing jack shit and talking game about how I was going to change the dope trade. I didn't make crap, didn't change crap. But her, she came home every night, gave me a little kiss, made dinner for me, fed the boy, and cleaned the house. She got maybe four hours a day of sleep, six max. And all she ever asked of me, every night seems like, was for me to rub her feet. She had these big ass corns, her feet stunk, and she had these thick yellow nails, they looked like little baby onions." Garrett turned his laugh into a cough to keep up appearances. "And every night, I'd tell her, no. Ten minutes a night, Gar. I ain't gonna tell you she was the sweetest woman in the world, but she never asked for anything more than that on principle." He watched fondly as two children climbed into the seats two rows ahead. "There's a point to all this. You're not me. That woman's your life and you're hers. But someday, she might ask you to rub the corns on her stinky-ass feet and you're gonna recoil like she told you to stick your dick in a toaster. Don't ever take her for granted, Gar."

* * *

At Ransom's place, Jade watched him chew on a painkiller like it was candy. He washed it down with a tall glass of water, gulping it down like a man dying of thirst. She cleared her throat and he turned and stared at her, no humor at all on his face. She jumped right to it. "His mother's dying. They are flying to say goodbye." The words were coming easier and easier for her these days. At least Ransom had given her that much.

Ransom watched her carefully. "The phone calls at the gym last night, I take it."

"Yes."

"Hm." He paced the room slowly, touching things at random and caressing the mirror. "It's unfortunate. I'll have to send flowers. But it's all right. I have other things that need my attention this week. I've worked you hard, Ms. Gibbons, and I know things have been strained. Why not take the time and be with your child?"

She hesitated. Sometimes, the man seemed so downright normal it scared her. Scared her even more than the grinning manic mask he put on sometimes, like last night at the gym. But his offer seemed... genuine? He was looking at her with eyes that swam with friendliness— real honest friendliness and a hint of concern. "Thank you, sir. I will check their condo every day to tell you when they're back."

He poured himself another glass of water and sat on his couch. "That sounds like a plan," he said, sounding exhausted. He hoisted his feet up and wiggled a pillow under his head. "Me, perhaps... perhaps I'll take a little nap and say goodbye to the world a while."

Florida

After the dreary cold and smog of Rankin Flats, the peaceable sunshine was a splash of water to his soul. Knowing what lay ahead, he felt a little guilty for enjoying the feel of the warm sun on his face, but enjoy it he did, taking a full minute of holding his chin up to the sky, eyes closed, just breathing in the humid air and feeling the tension of the tight seating seep out of his body. Then he called Brianna and checked in. Their conversation was brief, but sweet. When they said goodbye, both left something hanging in the air unspoken and incomplete.

The call left him with a profound sense of emptiness, and the sunshine no longer felt so wonderful to him.

Accompanied by Murphy, whose suit had shifted into a bowling shirt and white dress slacks, he walked to his rented car, a white Camry. It reeked of berry air freshener, the spray type from a can people so often used those days in lieu of actual cleaning. At least someone had taken the time to vacuum it out a little bit. Crumbs lined the floor mat and a sizable stain on the backseat made him a little green. Murphy pontificated on its origin at great length to Garrett's feigned annoyance.

He programmed the hospital's address into the requested GPS and drove out of the airport, realizing a little too late the car's air conditioner only seemed to have two working settings—ice cold or room temperature. He settled for room temperature, and traveled with his window down and the radio blasting a mix of aughts rock and roll and hip hop—and yes, the DJ threw on a quick Lusty Gallant oldie.

The drive to Pensacola wasn't terrible. Traffic was thick but sloshed along at full speed, like water down a sluice box. He caught occasional glimpses of the Atlantic, gleaming blue and dark as the Montana sky after dusk, but could ill afford the luxury of staring at it from the freeway. Murphy did plenty of gaping, though. He'd seen that ocean before, many times, but that never stopped it from being stunning and he too was just as susceptible to the pleasantries of warmer weather, despite not being able to feel it.

The city looked beautiful in that late afternoon. Garrett liked the low-key architecture, the sort of yawning, relaxed atmosphere it gave off without being so hipsterish or touristy as some of the places he'd seen in California and certainly not as grimy or industrial as the coastal cities of Texas he'd visited once on a whim with Murphy. But there again, he didn't have much time to see the ins and outs of the town before he'd arrived at the hospital. It was a fast trip, disappointingly so.

He turned off the radio and pulled the keys out of the ignition, but didn't move for a long few minutes. Sweat beaded on his forehead as he sat there and thought about how easy it would be to just turn right back around and get on a plane home. Beside him, Murphy said nothing, just sat there wishing he could offer his friend a pat on the shoulder.

"I wanted you to stay with her," Garrett said, his voice sounding very small and afraid. "But for what it's worth, I'm glad you're here."

"Of course," Murphy said simply. "You ready?"

"No."

They got out anyways.

The receptionist pointed them towards the right area. It was a long walk to the ICU, made even longer by Garrett's dragging feet. At any moment he expected Yvette to barge out of a room with her little army, push him onto a gurney, and strap him down. He forced himself to keep moving, willing his breathing to remain calm and even. The numbers on the doors ticked upwards and he counted each one of them like a thief in the old west must have counted the seconds until the floor dropped under him and the noose snapped his neck. He stopped at a fountain to splash cold water on his face and mop the sweat off his forehead. It wasn't from the heat this time.

And in another minute or two, he was there. Room 414. A little window on the door looked inwards. His mother lay in bed, but he could not see her face. His father sat in front of her, back hunched. It was impossible to see anything else but his father's wild white hair, once as thick as a damn forest on his head, now thinned to the point where Garrett could see splotches of color on his scalp. Garrett scooted a little further to the right and there Stephanie and Auggie huddled together and talked quietly. Stephanie, sweet Stephanie. August had sent him digital pictures throughout the years, but seeing his middle sister in person for the first time in fifteen years shredded his emotions. She'd put on weight—a lot of it—and she looked as haggard and unkempt as Auggie beside her. But oh God, she was still his beloved sister, the one that had told him and him only when she'd had her first kiss as a fifth grader, relating the story with eyes so wide that he'd thought they might pop right out of her head. He remembered sitting on the couch with her, laughing at Leslie Nielsen and wishing aloud together they could be detectives in a slapstick world. Going together one Halloween as Beavis and Butthead. Helping her make egg nog one weekend—she'd drank so much she puked. Her coming in and sleeping beside his bed one night when she'd had a nightmare, afraid to wake him but wanting him near. Teaching her how to dive on a lazy summer evening at the community pool. Her teaching him spades.

And he remembered too how she'd come home, crying furiously because she'd stuck up for him after a particular fender bender left him seeing peculiar little things. About how she'd believed him until it broke her and nearly ruined her life. He remembered the silence on the other end of that phone call from Vegas, when she'd picked up the phone and simply handed it off to their dad.

He remembered all of this in a flash, in a single second out of time, and he cried out with the weight of his sorrow. Auggie jumped to her feet. She rushed the door and pulled it open. He grabbed her in a bear hug and she was crying and he was crying.

His dad got up shakily and joined them too. Landry Moranis saw the gray at the temples of the man before him, saw the hard lines of his face and the signs of a thousand fights. Saw the jackrabbit like glances of his eyes as he debated whether to run or to embrace him. This was the child whose ass he'd wiped clean. Who plucked at his fingers when he was only knee high to his father as they walked across the street. Who he had caught in the back of his minivan with a cheerleader, his look both apologetic and deeply satisfied with himself. Landry reached out to clasp his lost child to him.

And his son flinched away.

Garrett couldn't help the reaction. Saw the hand come up and thought for a brief, insane moment his father was going to hit him again. He recoiled back, his teenage instincts kicking in before he even had a chance to mentally acknowledge the act. His father's eyes closed slowly, gasping out an apology with a voice as thin and exhausted as the man himself. "I'm sorry, I'm so sorry." Then Garrett swept forward and hugged him, pressing the old man to him, feeling like a child again.

When they pulled themselves apart, Landry's hand clinging to his shoulder like a man holding onto a life preserver at sea, Auggie wiped her tears away on her shirt and said quietly, "She's been asking for you."

"How is she?" Garrett asked.

His father glanced away, his eyes haunted. August touched her dad's elbow and smiled sadly. "She's... well, she's fighting." He could read the unspoken words on her lips. She's dying, you idiot.

"Any signs she might, you know, improve?" he asked awkwardly.

"No, she..." Auggie sighed. "I'm just really glad you got here when you did."

His dad's grip on his shoulder tightened. "Are you okay with this?"

Garrett nodded, fighting the urge to say no, no he was most definitely not okay, would never be okay, but thanks for asking. Stephanie poked her head out and started to say something to her dad. Instead, she stared at Garrett for a long moment, working out something in her head, fighting some sort of internal battle. He knew the feeling. Finally, she whispered, "Hello, Garrett." He wanted to rush to her, to hug her too, to apologize to her for the rest of his life, but he didn't. He had the feeling what was going on now was the full extent of her olive branch. That was fine. He still got to see her, share the same air as her. That was enough for now. Then his sister glanced at his dad. "She's awake."

* * *

They shuffled into the room before him. His father took up a position near his mother's head, kissing her gently on the cheek and taking up her hand. His sisters took up positions on the other side of the bed, with a space between them for him. He crept into the room, his sneakers squeaking a little on the glossy waxed floor. He stood between his sisters. Auggie sought out his hand and clenched it tight. His other arm brushed Stephanie's and he sensed her pull slightly away.

His mother lay with her eyes fluttering against the light. He'd expected the almost white hair, but what shocked him most was his mother's once-beautiful skin, so smooth and soft, was now as thin and see-through as greasy paper. Blue veins poked out against her skin and she'd lost so much weight that he could imagine a breeze picking her up and carrying her away. "Hey Mom," he said uncomfortably, reaching forward to take her unoccupied hand in his, carefully minding the needles and tubes jutting out of the back. "It's me. Um. Garrett. I'm... I'm here."

His mother's eyes tried to focus. His father squeezed her hand. "Megan, honey, it's Garrett. He came to visit you, just like you asked."

With a huge amount of effort, she opened one eye and trained her

218

gaze on her son. Her chin dipped down and she started to shake her head gently. She squeezed back against his hand and for a moment he thought this might go okay, that maybe this wasn't going-

Then the wet murmurs started. "Nn. Nn. Nn." She tugged her hand away from his and scraped along the railing of the other side of her bed. She started to convulse. "Nnno. Nnno. Nnno." Her eye went wide and she started to see-saw up and down in bed, biting at the air in between every weak protestation. Her mumbling took on a higher pitch. He realized she was trying to scream.

For the second time in his life, he fled from his mother. Behind him, Auggie shouted his name. By the time he hit the reception area, he was sprinting for the doors.

* * *

He jabbed the key into the ignition and it wouldn't turn. He screamed out fifteen years of fury and pain and starting hammering the steering wheel, the radio, the dashboard, the seat beside him, anything he could punch.

Then he tried another key. This one wouldn't even fit into the hole. Another. Same.

"Gar—" Murphy said quietly.

"Not now."

"Those are the wrong ke—"

Garrett shot out of the car and slammed the door shut. Murphy didn't try to follow. He just sat in the car as Garrett kicked the tires as hard as he could. Several people stared at Garrett and he flipped them the bird, then felt immediately shitty about it. He stumbled away from the car towards a pretty little park area. The grass was absurdly green for the time of the year, his feverish mind thought.

A stone bench was unoccupied so he occupied it. He sprawled across it, letting his anger and his pain fire through him. But in that funny little way fate had of messing with him, a man walked two dogs in the park that day—a boxer and something more or less resembling a pug. Transfixed by the dogs at play, he felt the pulse of the strangeness of the universe before him, as though something out there knew he needed just the slightest, most bizarre reminder of the best part of his life. The dogwalker didn't have them leashed, and at one point, the boxer trotted up to Garrett, tongue hanging out of the corner of its mouth in a happy little dog smile. He reached out to scratch between its ears, and the boxer closed its eyes to receive some top-quality petting.

And then it peed on the bench, ending the moment pretty perfectly as far as Garrett was concerned. After the dogwalker called back the beautiful dog, Garrett pulled his cell phone out and called Brianna. She answered on the first ring. "Gar? Is everything okay?"

Her voice made it easier for him to breathe. "What are you up to?" he asked finally. His voice was surprisingly calm, he thought.

"Oh, Ed's showing me some of his accounting software. I think I can use it at the gym, make up a new master list of the customers. My database at work is garbage and this is… well, it's boring, but for a math nerd, it's crazy cool." From somewhere in the background, Ed bellowed something indistinguishable. Auggie walked towards him from the hospital, hands in her pockets. He gave her a little tentative wave. "Ed says hi. How's your mom? Did you get in yet to see her?"

Garrett didn't say anything for a while. Then, finally, "Tell me a story about you. Ever since we started dating, it's felt like this whole thing is all about me. Tell me something about you. Anything."

"Oh, I don't know, I'm such a boring person," she laughed. It was forced, to be sure, but it warmed him anyways. "But I'll try anyways. Um, let's see."

Auggie settled on the bench next to him and he wrapped an arm around her, hugging her close. His kid sister draped her own around him and leaned her head against his shoulder, sniffling.

"So. When I was ten or so, my dad, mom, and I went on this shopping day, you know? We had lunch, bought some clothes for me for school, that sort of thing. It was a lot of fun, but we ate at this really bad Chinese place. Just heightened levels of awfulness. Like the guy behind the counter, the cook, I think, he was just openly belching and picking his nose. That kind of grossness."

"Eurgh," Garrett said, trying to smile.

"Right? We ate there anyways because my dad loved their hot and sour soup. And it being my dad, once he has something in mind he wants to eat, we're having that or he'll be pissed for days. Literally. Days. So we're shopping. My mom and I feel fine, but my dad is getting greener and greener. My mom, she's gone to find some antacids for him, so it's just my dad and I standing in the middle of this aisle, surrounded by like eight or nine people.

"So my dad, who's sweating just tons, lifts his leg and lets loose this godawful honk, all wet and as loud as an elephant bellowing. And it reeks. I mean, really, really reeks." She started giggling. "And these people around us, they're sniffing the air and gagging. Some of them. Oh, oh," she laughed so hard she snorted, "oh, some of them are looking at us and just forming this huge circle around the edge of the farts. And. And. My dad, he looks around at all these people, and he says to me, real loud, hon, when we get home, I'm checking your pants!"

Garrett laughed so hard he missed her at first, just out of the corner of his eye. It was a good laugh, a real one, and it made Auggie laugh too. The woman drew closer, unsure of herself at first but emboldened by that lovely sound. It had been so long since she'd heard him laugh. When he could finally speak, he said happily, "Thanks Bri. I can't tell you how much I needed that.".

Then he saw her. His phone fell from his hand and bounced off the bench. He swallowed hard, the laughter immediately gone. "August," he said very quietly. "You need to go be with Dad and Steph. Right now."

She pulled away from him, giving him a questioning look. "Garrett, what's wrong?"

"I need you to trust me right now, okay? They need you. Go."

She stood up, fumbling for something to say. "Garrett, don't you leave. Please. Just stay for a while longer, okay?"

He smiled faintly at her. "I will," he said gently. "Hurry." When she left, running for the ICU, he picked up the phone. "Brianna, I'm sorry. I need to go."

"Is it your mother?" Brianna asked. "She's gone, isn't she?"

"Yes," he said, swallowing hard. "And she's standing right here."

* * *

"May I sit?"

The phone still in his hands, he stared at her, not daring to breathe. This was his mother from his earliest childhood memories, so vibrant and rosy cheeked. She was thinner than he remembered. He thought maybe her visage was her from the days before he was born. She wasn't quite beautiful, not in the way all young boys think of their moms as beautiful, but she was realer in a way than his memories allowed. A blue floral summer dress draped across her thin frame, tied off around her stomach with a black sash. It was a nice look on her, one that he thought he vaguely remembered. Finally, he patted the bench.

She sat and watched the colors at her feet swirl around her. "I guess I know now you weren't lying about any of it," she said, without any real humor.

He cleared his throat. "I like the violet," he said, "but the pink

221

doesn't suit you."

"No," she said, amused. "I never was much of a pink person, was I? I'm surprised you remembered."

Stiffly, he said, "I remember a lot of things. Your favorite food was lasagna. Lilacs always made you sneeze but you loved to smell them anyways. You crushed hard on Dan Aykroyd. I could never figure that one out."

"It was his enthusiasm," she breathed. "No matter what role he was in, he was all in. It was cute."

Their attempt at a cheerful moment faded. "I remember other things too. Slapping me when I first tried to tell you about the ghosts. Cutting me out of the family photos. You, Yvette, and the others holding me down and performing an exorcism. On your own son," he said loudly, loud enough to draw the attention of a couple on the lawn. They looked at each other and walked back towards the hospital, slowly and casting glances back over their shoulder. He hissed, "Do you know what happened to me afterwards? The things I started to see besides ghosts?"

"Garrett, I did what I thought was best for you," she said as though she were explaining this to a child. "I won't apologize for that. My mind was not right either, but that's no excuse."

"You could have listened to me. You could have had a little bit of faith in your child. You were so ready to believe in that freak of a woman and not at all ready to listen what your own flesh and blood was telling you. You know I never meant to hurt you. Not once. All I ever tried to do was tell you what was happening."

Her gaze was intense. She didn't so much look at him as peel him apart like an onion. It was her "we need to talk" look, the one he both feared and respected as a child. But it melted away into something softer as she fiddled with her hands. "I'm sorry. I was wrong."

He rubbed his face. The heat was making him a little ill now. "The funny thing is, I don't blame you. If I had a freak kid like me and I didn't know what I know, I'd have hated me too."

She recoiled from that, gasping, "Garrett, I don't hate you. I never did."

"Try telling that to a kid sobbing because he's stealing a can of chili from a stranger's house and sleeping on their couch while they're gone. Tell it to him when he's alone in a Kansas City bus station and some fucked-up pervert tries to get him to blow him for ten bucks." He cut her off. "No, don't. I know you didn't hate me. You were afraid of me."

There was a faint quaver to her voice. "I don't know what I thought back then. I believed you, I think. And that terrified me. I thought…" She laughed shakily. "I thought it was some great sin I'd committed. That you'd been infected by the devil and it was all my fault. And I didn't know what I'd done or why this had happened to you, but that's every parent's fear, right? That it's their fault how a kid turns out?"

"You picked your faith over your child," he said softly.

"I know. And given the chance again, I don't know if I'd do things differently. I was trying to save your soul, Garrett. In my own way, I was trying to help you."

He thought about getting up and going. Just leaving her there on that bench. The bitterness welled up in him and he came very close to doing it. But wasn't that why he'd come there? To excise that like an abscessed tooth? He could hold it in and keep it with him, letting it poison his life and spread, or he could deal with his pain right there. "I know, Mom. I was so alone for so long," he whispered.

"And you're not now?" she asked hesitantly.

He smiled. "No." He dug out his cell phone and pulled up the photo of him and Brianna on the second day of their relationship, the one she had printed out and put up on his wall. "Brianna Reeve," he said gently. "She runs a gym with her dad. We've only been dating a couple of weeks, but I love her, Mom."

"She's striking. And she's a good person?"

"The best. She cries at the tip of a hat. She's a complete nerd and loves it. And when I told her, she didn't run away."

"She knows?" his mom asked, surprised.

"Mm hm. And not just about the ghosts. I… do other things, Mom. Stuff you probably wouldn't be proud of, but I'm trying to help people who need it. And she wants to be there for it. All of it." His hand reached out for her, tentative and shaking. "Mom, I'm sorry. For scaring you, for… everything."

She tried to grasp his hand in hers, settling for putting it roughly on top of his. "I'm sorry too. For… well, all of it. You deserve to be happy, Garrett. I'm glad you found someone. She was the one you were laughing with?"

He hung his head. "Yeah. Sorry, I know it was disrespectful—"

"Don't be. It was the sweetest sound in the world, hearing you and your sister laugh like that again. They love you so much. Stephanie and August. Mend your fences with them. Please."

"I'll try," he said awkwardly.

She laughed gently. "I'm so glad I had one last good day with Stephanie a while back. With Auggie, it was always easy, but Stephanie's always so reserved. She blamed me for a lot of things. And she was right. But a month, maybe two or so ago, she showed up at our door. Maybe she was lonely, maybe she just needed some mom time. She took me out for dinner at my favorite little bar, the Fat Parrot, and we ended up singing karaoke together."

Surprised, Garrett laughed. "I can't imagine Stephanie singing karaoke, even as a kid."

"That's what I thought! But she's up there with me, and we're singing Lime in the Coconut and the whole place is laughing, booing, and cheering all at the same time. It was so lovely."

"I wish I could have been there."

"Me too." They watched the dogs romp around the park together, barking joyously. "This thing you do, this helping people. Are you careful?"

He nodded. "Do you remember the ghost I tried to tell you about, the one I saw named Murphy?" When she nodded, he continued. "He still travels with me. Been like a weird brother to me all these years. He watches my back. Hey, he's here, waiting for me at the car. Want to meet him?"

She smiled at him, gently and fondly. He remembered that smile from his childhood, when he'd try to help her cook dinner and he'd done something just right. "I'd like that," she said softly.

Garrett got up and jogged to the car. He hammered on the hood and Murphy popped up out of the top. "Gar—"

"Hey, man, I just talked things out with my mom—"

"I know, I watched, but—"

"She wants to meet you. She's… well, she's very sorry about everything, and—"

Frantic, Murphy said, "Garrett, you need to turn around, now. I'm sorry. I'm so sorry."

Knowing in the pit of his stomach what he was going to see even as he turned, it still hit him hard. Twirling in the air around a cloud of ever rising particles were a pair of ribbons, one violet, one pink. Garrett watched them until they disappeared into the sky. Finally, he whispered, "Goodbye, Mom. I love you."

* * *

224

Murphy left for California to see his son. When he watched Garrett say goodbye to his mother, his own need for his blood boiled over. He tried to beg Garrett's forgiveness for leaving him when he promised he would stay, but as far as Garrett was concerned, there was nothing to forgive. He bid his friend fast travels, and they promised to meet up in Montana.

Skulking like a rat around the fringes of the city, Garrett didn't see his family again until the funeral. He felt terrible dodging Auggie's phone calls, only responding to her when she'd text. He offered to pay for the services, but their parents had taken care of that inevitability years ago. He hadn't brought a suit, so he spent a long afternoon at a local tailor's. When he saw a violet pocket square that precisely matched his mother's fluttering life-ribbon, he bought it, too. He did not request a matching one in pink. He was sure his mom would have approved.

When the day came, he quietly took a seat in the back. Auggie, Stephanie, and her dad sat up front, the sisters on either side of Landry. He didn't think they spotted him. That was probably for the best. There was a moment of fear at the beginning when he was sure Yvette would officiate and cast him out of there, but instead, a kindly young man with steel gray-blue eyes delivered an earnest, short eulogy. He stuttered over himself a few times, obviously new at this, but Garrett liked him all the more for it. And when the young pastor brought out his even younger wife to sing Amazing Grace while he strummed on a battered old guitar, Garrett cried like a baby, head buried in his hands. He never saw Stephanie get up and walk to the back of the church. He only realized she was there when she took hold of his arm and pulled him to his feet, guiding him to the front of the church. His dad scooted to the aisle seat and Garrett sat between his sisters, holding their hands for the rest of the service.

After the service, at a coffee hour, he numbly shook hands and made small talk with extended family he hadn't seen in a lifetime. He politely ignored their whispers to each other about him, though he caught Auggie more than once cussing them out in private. Sweet, dear, prone-to-kicking-someone's-ass Auggie. At one point, one of his cousin's children, no more than four or five, his lips stained purple from the juice of a freezer pop, waddled over and gave him a close examination. When Garrett smiled at the kid, the boy said matter-of-factly, "Mommy says you're weird," and then tottered away. Garrett laughed so hard he bent over nearly double. At least the kid had the stones to say it straight to his face, he thought to himself.

When the coffee hour started to wrap up, he meandered outside with a bottle of iced tea. He wasn't sure who had pressed it into his hand but he was grateful to them nonetheless. A huge orange tree gave shade to a corner of the property. He shrugged out of his jacket and left it on a bench, then jumped for an orange off the limbs of the tree. He sprawled out on the ground, head resting on vibrant green grass. He tossed the orange up from hand to hand, thinking for the first time in over a decade of his mother's chicken and rice casserole. He missed her, but it was a good pain, free of the poison of the last decade and a half.

Light filtered through the tree's branches like a lazy kaleidoscope, drawing patterns across his face and the ground he couldn't interpret. There was hardly a breeze in the air, and it was getting hot. Birds, so many birds, sung and whistled and chirped at each other from the trees. He loved the not-quite-mad cacophony of it all.

A hand caught his orange in mid-air and dropped it on his crotch. He grunted more out of surprise than pain. Auggie leaned over him, looking down, an eyebrow cocked. "I saw a dog here earlier taking a shit."

He grinned at her lazily. "Is that what I'm smelling? Thought it was your perfume."

She dropped to the ground too, a little more artfully than his own backwards flop so as not to slosh around a half-filled Dixie cup. She sat with her hands on her knees. He was struck by how much she resembled neither their mom or dad but him—their narrow faces, angular bones and sharp features might have made people confuse them as twins were they closer in age. She held out the Dixie cup. "Want some bourbon?"

"Hell yes."

She passed him the cup and he drank it in one go, liking the mellow burn on the way down. "Another?" she asked and fumbled in her purse for a slim steel flask.

"You two want to get hammered, let's do it at a real bar." The voice was husky and hoarse from crying. It was the longest sentence he'd heard from her in fifteen years and it made the entire shitty day bearable to hear it.

He shoved himself off the ground, knocking over his bottle of iced tea and not caring. Stephanie and his dad had walked up on them without them noticing and stood there with their arms linked together. Stephanie's face was a mask at first, but she blinked a few times and smiled tentatively at him, He smiled back, just as uncertain as she was and then lost any and all control. He rushed forward and grabbed her in a fierce hug, unable to say anything. She didn't hug him back, just tapped him tentatively between the blades of his shoulders. He would take it. He'd take anything he could get with Stephanie.

"Oh shit," Auggie choked out. "Shit, you two. I just finished crying. You assholes."

Stephanie cleared her throat. "Uh, Garrett, you're, uh, kind of squeezing the life out—"

"Too bad," he said and squeezed her even harder before he let go. Maybe it was the bourbon, but he flashed back on what his mother said the other day. "So. A bar. Um, it's your town, Dad, but I kind of heard about this place, the Fat Parakeet?"

"The Fat Parrot," Stephanie said, bewildered. "That was Mom's favorite spot. How did you... August, did you-?"

"Yeah, I guess I must have mentioned something," Auggie said, glancing at him quizzically. "Anyways, yeah, that'd be the perfect place. Mom loved that stupid bar and she'd be happy as hell we all went there together."

Landry fumbled at his pockets and brought out a battered wallet. "Here, go have some fun. Have a drink on me and—"

"Dad," Garrett said, putting his hand on his father's wrist. He spoke quietly, but firmly. "Come with us. Please." His sisters echoed him. He squeezed his father's wrist and realized the older man was trembling.

"Is it okay?" There was fifteen years of guilt and sorrow packed into that question.

Garrett thought back on the flash of those fists, the vicious delight on his father's face at finally unloading on the son who had brought so much chaos into his life. If he wanted revenge on his father, this was his chance. One verbal push and the old man's spirit would break, probably forever.

Or he could let it go, he realized with complete certainty. There was no excusing what Landry had done to him—no father should ever hit their child without suffering—but he could make peace with it. He knew it even as his heart started to let it go. He was so tired of the bitterness. He clasped his father on the shoulder. "Of course it is. Never got a chance to have a drink with you as an adult. Time we changed that."

* * *

The Fat Parrot might not have had a lot of customers, but damned if it didn't seem lively. ZZ Top blared from a digital jukebox's speakers, and the patrons at the bar were a sharp contrast to the hunched-over eternally grim drinkers at Garrett's usual haunts. They laughed, they shouted over each other, and when the word got around that Megan Moranis had passed, none of the family had to pay for drinks. The bartender, dressed in a Hawaiian shirt and a pair of shorts, brought them by baskets of appetizers, on the house. In a way, it touched Garrett more than all the halfhearted well wishes at the coffee hour. Their dad, who didn't much care for alcohol anyways, collected their keys and agreed to be their DD, watching amused as his grown kids attacked alcohol with the same wild abandon of their childhood raids on their Halloween candy.

It wasn't easy for Garrett and Stephanie. That barrier still stood between them and he had a bad feeling there was maybe no way to bring it down completely. But after fifteen years of separation, there was at least a temporary friendliness, helped immensely by large quantities of rum and pineapple juice. They talked about the times before Garrett's accident, of what good shared memories they had of their mother and their childhood. But at one point, while Auggie punched up songs on the jukebox and their dad talked to a barfly friend of their mom's, Stephanie set her drink down a little too heavily and blurted, "You just... left."

There it was. They'd negotiated the minefield so well until that point. He settled his drink on the table and said quietly, "I did."

"Do you know how much that hurt?'

"Steph, I—"

She hunched over, her elbows resting on the table. She wasn't angry. If she'd been angry, he might have felt a little better. But her tone was that of the same hollow exhaustion he'd felt talking to his mom. That sense of long-ago defeat, of wounds that had never quite healed right. It was all there in her face, the way she spoke, the cringe in her expression. She was a beaten dog waiting to get kicked again and his heart broke for her. For them. Auggie started towards them but their dad pulled her away to her protestation. Sometimes fights needed to be had.

"It was bad enough. In high school. They damn near broke me, you know? Teasing me about you and your damn ghosts."

He tried to reach across the table for her hands but she recoiled. He settled instead for taking a napkin and shredding it into little piles, an old nervous habit. "I never meant to hurt you about that. I was... I didn't know how to deal with what I saw."

"It wasn't even that. I could deal with bullies eventually. So long as I had you and Auggie there at home." She hiccupped words out, as though she were fighting to talk through tears, but her eyes were dry and red. "And t-then you took that from muh-me too."

"I'm sorry I ran," he whispered almost so low she couldn't hear him. "I didn't know what else I could do. I was young and hurt and…" He shook his head and ripped another piece off the napkin. "That's no excuse."

"You could have stayed in the same town. It would have been hard, but we would have still been near each other."

"I could have, yeah," he said, not mentioning just how the fear had gripped his heart, how his first impulse had been to never stop running. "Should have."

"Las. Vegas," she snapped. "Of all the places I couldn't go. And at sixteen. You might as well have been on the fucking moon."

"You're not wrong."

"Stop that."

"What?"

"The platitudes. The hangdog bullshit. Fight with me, damn it. Tell me how bad it was for you. I know what Mom and that horrible woman did to you. Tell me it was them. Tell me anything and drop this let's-pity-Stephanie bullshit." She made a fist as though to bang the table, but stopped short. The last thing they wanted was more eyes on them.

"I hurt Mom as much as she hurt me," Garrett said. "Worse, even. I didn't mean to, I never did, but that doesn't make it any better. It doesn't fix what happened. I was to blame too. For all of it. She loved us all so much and she did what she thought was best. I was a coward and a little stupid. I don't pity you, Steph, but I am so very, horribly sorry." He reached across again and this time she did let him take her hands. "I don't want to lose you again. I don't know if things can ever be right between us but I want to try."

"How did you know?" she whispered.

"Know what?"

"You sent her in. When Mom died. How did you know?" Before he could speak, she went on. "And the Fat Parrot. You didn't get that from Aug or Dad, did you?"

Goodbye, Stephanie, he thought sadly to himself. And then a quick silent prayer to anyone upstairs who might be listening—thank you for these few hours with her. Thank you for that much, at least. Finally, out loud, he quietly said, "No."

Across the bar, Auggie finally broke from their father and stormed across the room, three fresh beers and shots in hand. She plunked them down on the table and said irritably, "We're not spoiling this shit." She jabbed a finger at him. "You are not spoiling this shit." Then at Steph. "You are not spoiling this shit." She raised her shot glass. Stephanie, her eyes still wide, raised hers with trembling hands and Garrett followed suit. Auggie said, "Here's to Mom."

Stephanie added to that quietly, "Here's to Garrett coming home."

He couldn't add anything to that, so they clinked their shots together and downed them as one.

At the end of the night, when Garrett told them he'd dial a cab and head back to his hotel, they looked as though he were crazy and, with Landry at the wheel, dragged him back to their parents' house. His sisters took the spare bedrooms and he crashed on the couch. Within minutes of setting his foot on the ground to stop the world from spinning around him, he was snoring peacefully. Landry dug out some spare sheets from the closet and wrapped them loosely around his son. He pushed his recliner at an angle to where he could watch Garrett sleep. He pulled a picture of his wife next to him on the end table, kicked out the legs of the chair, and marveled at just how incredible it was that one of the worst days of his life could also somehow be one of the best. He didn't mean to sleep, but watching the rise and fall of Garrett's chest, he did.

* * *

Rivulets of sweat dripped down his face as he turned back onto the street leading to his dad's house. Garrett couldn't believe the difference a change in elevation made on his time, but whereas the thicker oxygen made it functionally easier to run without tiring, the humidity made him sweat as though he were running a marathon. Still, it was a terrific cure for the hammering in his head when he woke up. He felt a little invasive ducking into his father's room for a pair of shorts and a tee shirt, but they were about the same size and he didn't think he'd mind. It beat sitting around that foreign house, staring at pictures of a life he hadn't been a part of. His bitterness was gone, but it didn't mean he wanted to be reminded of his time away from his family.

Stephanie's prodding questions from the night before were still fresh on his mind. She'd believed him, back in the day, and it had cost her so much. Had she ever really stopped? He didn't know. It wouldn't be the worst thing in the world for her to know, but it still troubled him that her mental state might be a little fragile. He would not stop her queries, if she continued poking at him. He knew that much. With Murphy gone, he couldn't provide her with the evidence he'd given Brianna, but that could come later.

He slowed as he reached the sidewalk to his father's house. It was nice, this place, but it was no match for their old home in Missouri. That place had a character and charm borne of its age. He had no doubt that if he set foot in there today, the same steps would squeak, the back porch door would still fit just a little oddly in the frame and catch sometimes in the winter, and the attic would whistle just a little bit whenever a hard wind blew. This place was too modern, too well designed for charm. It reminded him of his own place, in a funny way. He liked his condo, sure, but it was austere in a clinical, detached way and this house shared that.

He collapsed onto a wrought iron chair on the front porch. He rested for a while, enjoying the morning breeze rolling in over the ocean not all that far away. The front door opened and Auggie slipped outside. She set glasses of water on the table and fell into the chair beside him as though all the weight had drained from her all of a sudden. "I feel like crap. I haven't drank like that in… shit, at least three weeks. How're you holding up?"

He sipped at the water. "Good, now that I've got a run in me."

She eyed him grimly. "Running to solve a hangover is like pulling out a splinter with a chainsaw."

"That… how would you pull out a splinter with a chainsaw?" he asked.

"I don't know, look, it's early, I'm tired, shut your mouth hole."

He poured half the glass of water over his head. "I don't think I could ever get used to the humidity. It's like I'm always in a sauna." He snapped his fingers. "Oh, yeah, saw a gator, too, just hanging out in some guy's yard. About pissed myself."

The screen door creaked open again. "I hate those damn things," Stephanie muttered. "Always grinning at you like they're imagining you with your clothes off." She ruffled Auggie's hair. "How ya feeling? Been a while since I had to hold your hair like that."

"You're not hung over either?" As her sister shook her head, Auggie laid her forehead down on her folded arms. "I feel like Death just pooped me out."

Stephanie gestured at a chair beside Garrett. "Mind?" she asked, a little nervously. He kicked it out and she joined them. "Dad's still sleeping. Figure I'll make him waffles when he wakes up."

Garrett glanced at her, surprised. "You cook?"

"I do a lot of things now, Garrett, on my own." She winced at her own cattiness. "Sorry, I'm trying not to score points off you. It's just... you know."

"Hard to let go of it," Garrett grunted in agreement, thinking of his conversation with his mom. He rubbed her back, noting with some pleasure that she didn't flinch from him this time. "For what it's worth, I'm just glad we're talking again." He flashed her the peace sign, their childhood signal that all was well between them.

She smiled at that. "I almost forgot about that. And I'm glad we're talking too. It's weird. But it's good." Still, that hesitation, and she didn't make the gesture back. One step at a time, he reminded himself.

Her forehead still resting on her arms, Auggie flashed them a thumbs up.

"Are you two doing okay?" he asked. "I mean, apart from Mom. Auggie—"

"Stop calling me that," Auggie mumbled with no real conviction.

"-fills me in from time to time, but really, how are you?"

Stephanie shrugged. "Work's okay. Everyone wants a good electrician."

Auggie raised her head for just a moment. "So what happens when they hire you? Don't hit me. I swear I'll puke."

Stephanie stuck her tongue out at her sister. "Been keeping it light since Mom's stroke, but I had plenty saved so it's not so bad. Figure I'll take a little more time off, be with Dad for a bit, then get back on the horse."

"Same here," Auggie said. "I quit Doc Henson's."

Stephanie gaped at her sister. "You what?"

Auggie lifted her head and blew out a breath. "Yeah. I don't know. I was out of vacation days. He told me to take all the time I need, but I wasn't feeling it for a long time. Been thinking maybe about moving back and this just kind of seals it, you know?"

Garrett frowned. "What about your girlfriend?"

"Do you see her here?"

"I... oh. Sorry."

Auggie shrugged. "Okay. She'll spend the rest of her life hopping from person to person whenever she thinks she needs a spiritual enema.

232

People like her always do. Nothing left for me there."

"Stay with me," Steph said. She raised a hand to stop her sister from speaking. "Just for a while. I know we fight like cats and dogs, but whatever, we'll tough it out until you find work here."

"Did you finish the remodel of your basement?" Auggie asked.

"Yup. And yes, the pool table's on its way."

Auggie perked up. "Then we have a deal. I'll ride your coattails and you... I don't know, get someone who can make fried egg sandwiches."

"When things calm down here and back at my place," Garrett said measuredly, "you two could always come up to visit. Dad too. I'm living with someone now and I'd have to work out the details with her, but worst comes to worst, we get you guys a nice hotel room. I've even got a little cabin and some land up in the woods. Camping, hiking, sledding, beautiful mountains if you're willing to go a bit—"

"Skiing?" Stephanie asked.

He made a face. "Ugh, yeah, skiing."

"Holy shit, yeah, his place is awesome," Auggie said excitedly. "We should definitely go."

After a moment's hesitation, Stephanie nodded tentatively. "That would be... nice." She smiled at him and he grinned back. Maybe that wall between them wasn't so permanent after all. "Tell me about your girlfriend."

"She's got a smokin' body," Auggie said. "Like Keira Knightley, but with a bigger donk."

"Auggie!" Stephanie gasped, laughing.

Auggie shrugged. "I'd bang her."

So Garrett filled them in on Brianna. At one point, he texted her and told her they were talking about her, and she responded with a picture of her half covered in baking flour and gobs of something unidentifiable on her shirt. "Rose teaching me to cook," the text read. "Tell sisters I say COME UP TO MT AND SAVE ME FROM COOKIES AND MYSELF." Then a moment later, she wrote to Auggie and Garrett both—"So happy you all are together. Seriously. Tears."

"And that's why I love her," he said fondly.

* * *

He got some alone time that afternoon with his dad, so they drove to the beach, stopping along the way for shrimp tacos and citrus swirls. They ate leaning against Garrett's rental car, watching the ruffled waters sweep in and out rhythmically. A pair of children ran shrieking through the gentle waves. When they finished with their meal, they wandered down to the beach, mostly saying nothing until they hit the sands.

"Did you ever go to the beach?" his father asked.

Garrett nodded. "California. New Jersey. Texas." He kicked off his borrowed flip flops and let his toes make little divots in the sand. It felt good, being on that beach. It wasn't so hot as to be unbearable, but warm enough that the eternal chill of a Montana winter was finally leaching out of his bones.

"I missed so much," his father said quietly.

Garrett didn't know how to respond to that, so they just walked together.

"Garrett, I don't know how to ask this in any polite way, but… the scars."

Garrett still didn't say anything. He watched a young couple who reminded him vaguely of Wilfred and that excited young woman from the exercise class. He hoped they were getting on.

"Is it drugs?"

Garrett stopped then and glanced at his father. "Do you think it's drugs?"

Landry jammed his hands into his pockets. "No."

"If I told you I was doing a good thing, would you believe me?"

It was his father's turn to pause and think about that. "Yes," he finally said. And in a surreal moment, he echoed Garrett's mother Megan. "Are you careful?"

"Yes."

"And the ghosts?" his father asked casually, as though he were asking about the weather outside.

Some significant part of him wanted to scream that this was the sort of question that had led him to his father hitting him, laughing like one of the demons he saw in the mirror now. But that part of him was dying, and good riddance. All he wanted at that moment was peace and the sand beneath his toes. "Still there."

His father nodded. "I believe you."

* * *

Part of him wished he could stay longer. But his heart—and other parts—ached for Brianna. And the longer he stayed away, the more his fear of the blonde man at the gym settled in. He wouldn't feel comfortable until he saw Brianna and the rest of his friends again and knew they were safe.

He hugged each of them in turn, surprised that his eyes could remain dry. On some level though he realized this was most definitely not goodbye but a firm "see you later." One way or another he would find a way to bring them to him or take another, longer vacation to see them, hopefully with Bri.

His hands on Stephanie's shoulders, he said it again. "Promise me you're serious about coming to Montana sometime."

"I am," she said solemnly. "I promise. I think... I think it would be good for both of us. If that's what you want. And if it's okay with your better half."

"I do, And she said open invitation, any time," he said.

"I'm looking forward to meeting her," Steph said genuinely. "And I want you to know... I'm happy you came down. I wasn't sure I would be, but—"

"Me too, Steph." He hugged her tight and kissed her cheek. He moved on to Auggie, who tried to look all cool and bored. "Take care of Dad, all right?"

"Pft," Auggie said. "Dad and I are gonna take care of each other. Strip clubs, beer and corn flakes for brekkie, more strip clubs. We're gonna have a blast." She hit him hard and fast on his shoulder. "Next time we all get together we're gonna do some real drinking. None of this pussyfooting around bullshit."

He laughed and hugged her tight. Last was his father, looking lost and small and not a little miserable. "Dad—"

Landry's face went sheer white. "I'm sorry, Garrett. For everything." His father breaking down and sobbing was the worst moment of that trip. Worse than his mother's screams. Worse than her death. His father, once seemingly invincible, hunched over and cried into his now-hairy hands. "I hurt you, I made you run, I hurt you—"

Garrett helped him to a chair and sat beside him, wrapping his arm around him. "Dad. Look at me. Dad!"

"I can't."

"You can." His father's sobs died in his chest and he lifted his head just far enough to see Garrett's chest. "Dad, I love you. You want to make things right with me, you take care of Steph and Auggie now the way you always have, okay? And when you're ready, you come up. You meet my girlfriend. You go skiing with Stephanie because I'm sure as shit not going—"

"Hey!" Stephanie protested.

"-and you talk to me. Really talk to me. And I'll talk to you too. We'll work this out. Okay?"

"I can't watch you leave again."

"You have to," Auggie said gently. "And this time it's his choice. He's not running, Dad. He's going home. And he'll come back to us."

Garrett nodded at Auggie. "Better believe it."

His dad nodded then, and hugged Garrett to him. They parted and Garrett stood up. "I love all of you so much and I'll see you all soon."

He gave them one last hug each and made his way through security. On the other side, through a clear plastic window, he could see them standing together. His sisters stood on either side of his father, hugging him. Stephanie, sweet Stephanie, smiled tentatively at him and flashed him a V with her fingers.

Peace.

Chapter 18

He saw her. She saw him. And then they were together and whole and they kissed, one for the ages. When they finally pulled apart he stroked the scars on her face and said, "I love you."

She kissed his hand and said it right back.

* * *

The sheet over Ransom's frame was not just damp with sweat from night terrors, but soaked. Lost in feverish dreams his waking mind didn't dare comprehend, he scratched at his skin and moaned his wife's name over and over again. Jade knelt by his bedside, almost feeling sorry for this strange man. But she was also ready to be rid of him.

"Ransom."

His eyes fluttered and he muttered something like, "Wash it off. Get to the stream and wash it all off."

"Ransom!"

He sat bolt upright, eyes wide in terror, fists striking at nothing at all. He looked thinner, she thought. That was strange. It had only been a week. But there it was—his near double chin was noticeably smaller and he lacked some of the definition in his arms and chest, as though someone had deflated him just a little bit. She thought of his last words to her last week and had a crazy thought—what if he really had slept the entire week away? But she knew that wasn't true—he'd been busy in that time. There was an entire wall now in his study made into a rough mockery of Garrett Moranis's War Room. Along with three pictures of Brianna Reeve taken from her sparsely updated social media pages, he had managed to find a picture of a younger, less-scarred Garrett, standing beside several other poker players after a tournament in Vegas. That picture struck her as a little sad in a way—he stood just slightly apart, smiling abashedly and almost looking away from the camera. It was, she thought, the very definition of that man's particular contradictory nature. Here was someone who clearly craved violence and conflict but seemed on a personal level to be almost emotionally stunted, sweet and vulnerable but hard to get at. If she was alive, Moranis would have almost certainly been her type.

But she wasn't, and she had a job to do. She couldn't afford to feel guilty for the man and look out for her daughter at the same time. He seemed well enough prepared for any number of eventualities and his girlfriend certainly seemed ready to punch out anyone's lights if the need arose. That was what she told herself, anyways. And she felt less and less sure about it with every passing day.

"Ransom, it's me."

"What? I. What time is it?" He swung his legs over the edge of the bed. His thing glared up at her from the flap in his boxers and he covered himself quickly, but did not apologize. "What's happening?"

"They're home." In truth, Garrett had been home nearly twenty-four hours, but she felt an odd sort of affection for their blossoming relationship and gave them a day to enjoy together.

"Good," he said, blinking at her with those bulbous eyes. "Anything else?"

"They're ready to meet."

* * *

There were eyes on him. Finson knew it in his bones but he couldn't explain how. Bugs weren't entirely out of the question—maybe his cleaning crew had been flipped to the FBI, but he'd swept the office and his home himself and found no trace of them. Some vague remembrance of a night with Brennerman came to mind, before he'd gone to prison and ruined things between them. They'd lain in bed, smoking hash and staring up at the ceiling of her crappy studio apartment. Someday, they'd be among the most powerful, influential people within the city, but that night, they were just a couple of young, dumb Legion soldiers and deeply in lust.

She told him about Hamber, about all its mysteries—something forbidden, but their star was on the rise and they spoke with the brash frankness of youthful invincibility. She'd launched into a stoned, enthusiastic discourse on the unseen universes all around them, about how everything and anything was possible and all of it was just a matter of perception. The supernatural, the mythical, the afterlife, everything. He had asked her curiously if that meant that they shouldn't live better lives in avoidance of damnation, and she'd burst out laughing. The sound drew him in, and soon they were roaring with it. Finally, she calmed down enough to explain that there was a place for their kind too. That did little to comfort him, but he knew just enough to agree, to let

238

her excitement bubble over to a physical need for him again and again. What would she have said then about the eyes on him? Was it something extraordinary?

He thought about that then as Markham droned on about the possibilities for the exchange. Markham didn't feel any of it, of course. He was a good dog, a loyal soldier, but his mind was locked away in a bubble of disbelief and arrogance. So too had Finson's until recently. He wondered for the dozenth time if it was the cancer. Maybe it was, but it didn't stop him from believing more and more that Brennerman had been right—there were things out there, and they were keeping an eye on him.

Talking about the meet in his office was a bad idea. But location after location for the meet kept falling through, and even in the most secluded parking garages or abandoned buildings he'd felt the eyes on him. No more running from them, he thought.

"-so we can go with Billings, but frankly, that's going to be a bitch of a drive and there are any number of spots along the way they could ambush us. No way we're getting the tribute on board a plane either," Markham continued, either not noticing his boss's listlessness or not caring. "We've also got the Howell Designs building as a possibility, but logistically—"

That snapped Finson back to the moment in a flash. "The Howell building?"

Markham nodded. "It's still empty. No one's touched it in years. It's a mess on the inside, but there's a basement parking garage and—"

"I'm aware of the place," Finson snapped. What were the odds of Markham bringing up that particular building when he was thinking about Brennerman? The Howell Designs incident had been her doing, her pet project. It was a fascinating act of orchestrated violence. He still wasn't entirely sure he ever wanted to know how she'd pulled it off. "That will do."

"Sir, with all due respect, that's a security nightmare. The garage is open on three sides. There's any number of spots in the buildings around the area where people could hide out, and the building itself is... um, unstable."

"No," Finson said softly, flexing his fingers as he thought. He leaned forward, a hungry look in his eyes. "We keep this tight. You. Me. Have Dee run some surveillance cameras. We keep it as close to the vest as possible."

Markham reached for his cigarillos and pulled one out as he tried to figure out the best way to approach things. "Sir, with all due respect, how do we know she isn't the one leaking information?"

"How do I know you're not?" Finson asked levelly. The comment stung Markham, but he didn't care about the ex-cop's feelings. "But you have a point. Give her the right location, but tell her the day's changed. Let's see what shakes out. Get it set up."

* * *

Ordinarily, the Homefront Grill would have been hopping with couples at that hour. The owners recently enacted no-children policies and the dating crowd loved it. It was yet another one of those endless Western themed restaurants in the area—horseshoes from working ranches in the surrounding counties hung on nails from the walls, along with Charlie Russell-inspired artwork. Garrett had never eaten there and didn't know much about the clientele, but he guessed there should have been at least a few more patrons than just the blonde man, sitting alone at the head of a long table in the middle of the room. He rose to his feet, dressed to the nines in a blue suit, crisply pressed shirt, and slacks that looked as sleek as silk. Garrett and Brianna walked towards him slowly, eyeing the room for anyone who might take them by surprise. They took seats to his right, Garrett closer to the man. Brianna grasped his hand under the table and squeezed it gently.

The blonde man's smile widened as he sprawled back in his chair. "I should have told you they have a dress code here. Doesn't matter. Rented out the entire place for the night." He clapped his hands, and as if on cue, two of the staff members hurried out of the back. One took a place at the bar, the other hustled to them with glasses of water and menus. The blonde man ordered a slew of appetizers and a drink. Brianna and Garrett declined anything.

The blonde man leaned forward in his chair, his grin slipping just a crack. "Have a drink. I've been looking forward to this little meeting for weeks."

"Nah," Garrett said, leaning back in his chair with his hands folded behind his head.

Brianna shrugged. "Can't drink with a stranger now, can we?"

The blonde man folded his hands in front of him and thought about that. Finally, he said, "Ransom. Ransom Galbraith."

Glancing up at the waiter and smiling her most winning smile, Brianna said, "I'll just have water too."

240

Ransom opened his mouth as if to say something, then thought better of it and shrugged. The waiter hustled to the bar, brought over his drink, and they disappeared again. He drummed his fingers on the table and finally said, "Maybe we got off on the wrong foot here."

"You stalked us," Garrett said flatly. "With your... friend. There is no right foot to start off on here."

"I see," Ransom said. "Well, I couldn't be sure as to who you were, now, could I? Guys like us, we have—"

"There's no us, Galbraith," Garrett snapped. "You invaded my home."

"You made me feel threatened in my gym" Brianna added.

Galbraith glanced at her irritably then focused back on Garrett. His fingers stopped drumming on the table. "I made some bad decisions, that's true. I wasn't in a good place. Hell, I even got fired recently. Me! The best... well, the best at what I do!"

Garrett looked around the place and snorted. "You seem to be doing all right. Renting out a place for an entire night doesn't exactly paint you as poor."

Ransom's lips folded back from his pink gums even harder. "Yes, I do all right."

They studied their menus for a moment. Brianna's eyes nearly popped out of her head when she looked at the prices. Anyone who paid that much for a hamburger was stupid, plain and simple. When the waiter reappeared, she ordered the bourbon pecan chicken, Garrett the pesto shrimp, and Ransom the trout.

"Thank you for agreeing to meet without our mutual friends," Ransom said when the waiter was out of earshot. "Ms. Gibbons wouldn't be much of a conversationalist anyways and I do so love my privacy."

"What is it you want here, Galbraith?" Garrett asked.

Ransom considered that. "To get to know each other. Formally. I see you and I as equals. We're quite alike in some regards."

Brianna, who'd been drinking from her cup of water, nearly choked. "How?" she asked, dabbing at her lips with a napkin.

"Can you just..." Ransom took a deep breath and refocused that grin. It clashed wildly with his bulging eyes, which looked less happy than absolutely furious. "Besides the, ah, mutual friends, you and I both have money, Mr. Moranis. Mine is, of course, earned, and yours is... well, let's call it borrowed, but—"

241

"You really can't help but be an asshole, can you?" Brianna asked wonderingly.

Ransom banged the table with his fist. "Will you stop interrupting when the men are talking?" he demanded.

"Mm, no," she said, shrugging. "Sorry." To Garrett she stage whispered, "So not sorry." He grinned back at her.

Ransom knocked back the rest of his glass of scotch, got up, and retrieved the bottle from the bar. For a little moment, Garrett thought he heard the man mumble to himself. When he settled back at the table and refilled his glass almost to the top, he sipped it and asked casually, "Do you see the demons, Mr. Moranis?" That drained all the humor from Garrett's face. "You do. Tell me, and you don't have to get into details here, what started the whole thing with the ghosts for you?"

"I don't know," Garrett said honestly. He couldn't see any harm in answering the question and he had a feeling they were needling the bear of a man a little too hard. So he tried a different tact. Honesty. "It was before a car crash. Not after."

Ransom nodded thoughtfully. "Mine was before a certain, ah, tragedy took place in my life." The waiter brought out bowls of French onion soup, topped with a little cheese and some kind of crouton-like breading. Ransom tried his soup and nodded to the man. The waiter smiled and darted back to the kitchen. Ransom continued, "I don't recall a lot of what happened. It's... smoky." He smiled even wider and took a spoonful of soup. Some of it dripped down his chin, giving him an even more deranged look. He didn't seem to care about it spattering his shirt or his pants. "It was a strange time."

The rich scent of the onion soup made the gnawing in Garrett's stomach even worse. He dipped his spoon in, and under Ransom's watchful gaze, he lifted it to his lips. It didn't taste poisoned, he thought, but would he really know what poison tasted like? He waited a minute, then shrugged at Brianna. They dug in, and it was amazing. The cheese and breading made a nice little crust, and the soup underneath was rich, hot, and salty. They'd smell it in their pores for hours afterwards, but it was worth the stink.

Soon, the waiter came out to clear the bowls and replace them with a simple winter salad tossed with a huckleberry vinaigrette made somewhere locally. That too was good, though it couldn't compete with the soup, which was, she imagined why they brought it out first rather than the salad. Garrett had little interest in the greens, however, and said finally, "So where did you find me?"

"Mm," Ransom said as he finished chewing a bite of celery. "Saw you and your friend coming out of, oh, where was it? I don't recall."

"Uh huh," Garrett said, not believing it. "And you just decided, what, we're going to be besties? Maybe have sleepovers, do each other's hair?"

"I was thinking maybe we could exchange information. Tell war stories, so to speak. Hell, eventually, I even thought maybe I could help you out with your little side projects. I'm still hoping to. The city is so rife with a terrible element, don't you think?"

"So what exactly have you done to earn our trust?" Brianna asked.

Ransom's gaze could have boiled the sea. "I'll ask you one more time. Please. Stop talking."

Garrett slapped the table and leaned forward. "You talk to her one more time like that. Do it. I'll hold you for her."

Ransom hunched forward too. "Why are you even with her?" he said. A bubbling laugh rose in his throat, a guttural, ugly thing that she thought might be the first real glimpse at who or what he was. "Seriously? Why? She's got a face like a horse and an attitude like an ass. You're what, a nine, and she's a five? I'm only a seven and I could fuck someone hot—"

That was as far as he got before Garrett's fist crashed into his nose. Brianna had seen him fight and spar, but she'd never seen him punch anyone or anything like that. It was shockingly fast, less than a blink. Ransom flew backwards, crashing against the ground, the chair propping his legs up at awkward, crazy angles. Garrett leaped to his feet and clamped his foot down on Ransom's chest. "Apologize."

Ransom sneered at him. "I recognize that rage. The demons. You do see them."

Garrett ground his foot down harder. Any more pressure and he might start cracking the man's ribs. The waiter and bartender peeked out from the door and gasped. Garrett ignored them. "Apologize now."

"I'm sorry."

Garrett let off a little pressure and leaned down over the man. "Now listen up, you sociopathic shit stain. You're going to leave us be. You're going to never enter our lives again. Or I will hunt you down. If you know me, then you know what I'm capable of."

Garrett took Brianna's arm and they dashed to the door as she laughed madly with the rush of the moment. Before they left, she cast one glance back at the stunned waiters and shouted, "The soup was lovely, thanks!"

Chapter 19

Padraig paced the War Room impatiently while Garrett caught Brianna up on everything the ghost told him. Finally done, the Scotsman snapped, "Do we have to have her here? What use is she?"

Garrett and Murphy both gave him cold looks. "She stays," Garrett said. Brianna glanced up at him questioningly and he laid a hand on her shoulder. "She's a part of this now."

The air in the room couldn't have been any chillier, but there was still work to be done. Murphy studied the map of the city. "Gar, can you look up where this building is at?"

"Sure." He ran a quick search for it and blinked. "Huh."

"What?" Murphy asked.

All four crowded around the screen. The news article was old, maybe four or five years or so, and brief. It noted that a planned demolition of the Howell Designs building had been delayed by special interests groups. Very little about the article was of interest until the last paragraph, when it mentioned disturbingly offhanded that the building was the site of a mass shooting seventeen years before.

"That doesn't seem like the sort of thing a newspaper would just gloss over," Murphy remarked.

"I remember that," Brianna said, and shivered. "Everyone thought the guy was nice and normal, but one day he walks in with a duffel bag full of guns and… well." She shook her head. "Not one of the city's best moments."

"There's so little information on it," Garrett muttered out loud. The rest of the search results brought up a few more passing mentions in news articles and a memorial site created by friends and family of the dead, but very little else was out there about the shooting. It was as though it almost never happened.

They found an address and Brianna put in a colored pin on the city map. Garrett pulled up closer maps of the streets around the area and studied them closely. "We know the place, but we don't know the date or what they're selling yet." He shrugged. "It's a start, at least."

"I don't get this," Padraig muttered. "Why aren't we taking this son of a bitch out now? You know he's a monster. Why sit around and wait?"

Murphy settled against the wall and said, "Because we've got a chance to do this one the right way. If it's a hundred pounds of drugs, we call the cops. There's nothing we can do with that much dope that won't bring hell down on us."

Garrett nodded. "And I want those buyers. The way Finson's been talking, maybe these people are higher on the food chain than him."

"You are making a mistake," Padraig muttered. "And this Galbraith, what do you plan to do to him?"

"Nothing, for the moment," Garrett said. "He's crazy but he hasn't done anything to us that we haven't already retaliated for. My contact at the police department, Monica, will find his address tomorrow and we'll send another couple of your people there."

"My people are stretched thin enough, Moranis," Padraig spat. "Maybe you take this Galbraith up on his offer to help. Sounds like he's ready to fight." He sniffed as he stared contemptuously at Brianna. "And he can actually see me. It'd save us hours of this fumbling half-measured bullshit."

Murphy shoved off the wall. "Listen, asshole, you want to quit, there's the fuckin' wall. Me and Garrett got this, same as ever."

Padraig glared at him. "Careful, your gutter heritage is showing through."

"Man, fuck you—"

"Get out," Garrett snapped. "Get the fuck out of my condo right now." Brianna looked up sharply at his furious reaction. He shook off her hand on his arm and stepped forward. "You insult my girlfriend and my best friend? We're done."

Padraig folded his arms. "I don't see how you can—"

"Get out!" Garrett roared.

Without another word, Padraig spun on his heels and walked through the walls. Garrett stood there for a long moment, his fists clenching and unclenching, breathing hard. Murphy spoke up at the same time as Brianna. "We can't—"

"Are you okay?"

Garrett turned slowly. "We can," he said to Murphy. "And I am," he told Brianna. "But Padraig's out. This is going to take a lot more work than I thought."

Brianna got up and studied the maps, unaware that she was doing so side by side with Murphy. "We can't do much without more information," Murphy said. "I think we need eyes on the place."

Garrett nodded and repeated that. "Murphy's got a point. I don't think we can do much from here just with the Internet," she said. She held out her palm, face up. "Let's triple team these sumbitches. Whaddya say, Casper?"

"I still hate that nickname," he grumbled, but slapped through her skin anyways.

Brianna looked at Garrett expectantly. "Still not telling me when he's high fiving me, huh?"

"Nope," he replied cheerfully.

* * *

Ransom tore the pictures and sheets of paper off the walls and threw them into binders and file folders. Those he tossed carelessly into a cardboard box, the same one he'd used to haul home what little possessions he cared about from Agilumine Solutions. Next came the computer. The videos of the murders were still on his USB drive and not on the computer, but he still took the time to delete his browsing history, his personal document folder, and anything else Moranis might use against him. He hefted the camera, trying to think if any of the videos might have been stored on its internal memory instead of the drive. He couldn't be sure. He yanked the USB drive out just as Jade spoke up behind him.

"Galbraith."

He jumped a foot and shoved the USB drive instinctively at his coat pocket, never noticing it fall to the floor. He spun in his chair. "You have a bad habit of sneaking up on people," he snarled.

"Sorry."

He waited expectantly. "Well?" he finally asked.

She opened her mouth and shut it. There was a sorrow to her eyes, one he hadn't seen there before. "My daughter. She's dying."

That stopped him cold. The fog of his fear and growing fury cleared just enough for him to suddenly feel very old and very tired "Oh. How long does she have?"

"I overheard the doctor. Tonight. Maybe tomorrow." She looked down at her feet. "I want out. You can keep your money. I want to be with her now."

He stood up and scooted the chair in, knocking the USB drive under the desk. "Miss Gibbons... I... I'm sorry." She glanced up at him, her eyebrows raised. "You seem shocked."

"I thought you didn't care about her." Her mouth worked. "That you might try and hurt her to get me to do what you wanted."

He sighed and rubbed at his forehead. "No, Ms. Gibbons. I wouldn't hurt a child." He took out his cell phone and pulled up a website. After a few moments of typing, he held the phone up. "My bank. Tell me the name and address of who the check should be issued to."

"That's not—"

He held up his hand. "It's what we agreed to." He smiled at her a little painfully. For just a moment, she caught a glimpse of the man he maybe once was, without the madness stretching his face. She gave him the information. After tapping at a few more keys, he held up the phone again. "Sent. With a bonus. You went above and beyond, Ms. Gibbons."

She reached a hand out, as though to rest it on his shoulder. But her hand just swiped right through him and she looked down at her feet, embarrassed. "It's not too late to stop," she said quietly. "To do something good."

He tittered at that, a high, desperate sound. "Oh, I think it is. Much, much too late." He turned away. "Goodbye, Ms. Gibbons."

"Goodbye, Ransom," she said softly, and left.

* * *

"You're encouraging him," Garrett sighed.

"Well, he has a point. I think there's a real need out there for better cup holders. I mean, every time I go to put a go-mug in mine, the damn plastic ribbing pops out."

"See?" Murphy said enthusiastically. "That's what I mean!"

Garrett shook his head at the mirror. When Brianna looked at him questioningly, he shrugged. "He said something about me probably being right, and how I'm so smart and witty and handsome. I don't know, the usual."

"Asshole," Murphy muttered.

The city was just waking up, and on a relatively warm morning too. Brianna had to go to work soon, but they had enough morning light that she could get a few pictures of the building and they could do a little exploring. The Howell Designs building didn't seem very tactically advantageous for a meeting. Surrounded on all sides by taller residential and commercial buildings, the building would be easy to spy on from any number of angles. And with three entrances to the underground parking garage, the buyers could make a quick easy exit but just as handily be outflanked. It made no sense.

And then there was the building itself. The exterior was solid enough, but with plentiful clear glass windows, anyone on the outside could look inwards from a number of angles. A good chunk of the first floor windows were loosely boarded over, but gaps were plentiful. On every side, Garrett counted several points at which they could clearly look into the building itself if need be. Someone had shoveled the walks around the building recently, but no one had so much as touched the graffiti in years. It reminded him in no small way of the Holland Shelter where Padraig and his crew kept counsel. If what Padraig had said was correct, then the meet would happen in the garage, but still, none of it seemed right.

Garrett cruised around the building another time as Brianna snapped pictures with her window down. She took them of every possible angle, but by a certain point, they were mostly spinning their wheels. "I think we gotta go in there," she said as she pulled back into the car and rolled up her window.

At the next opportunity, Garrett pulled into the underground garage. Someone—the Legion, maybe?—had snapped off all the barrier gates and left them leaning up against a wall in the garage. A few abandoned husks of vehicles sat here and there, but other than that, the garage was devoid of any signs of life. It was dark down there, only barely illuminated by the light filtering in from the tops of the ramps. He thought he saw shadows moving in the corners and behind the cars. Nothing, he assured himself. Just a trick of the mind. That didn't stop him from shivering.

"Garrett," Murphy said lowly, "I don't like the feel of this place."

"Me either," Garrett muttered. When Brianna looked at him questioningly, he tried on a reassuring smile but it was too thin-lipped and grim to help. He could feel his own heart beat in his chest, but it felt like there was an echo there, like he could hear the blood pumping of someone else too. Someone just beyond his sight. And it was the damnedest thing, but he thought he heard the skritch skritch skritch of rats. They're in the walls, he thought to himself. Thousands of them. Millions.

"You okay?" Brianna asked.

Ice cold sweat beaded on his forehead. "You don't feel it?"

She spun slowly in a circle, taking in each car and the atmosphere.

"I mean, it's a little weird and sad, but… I don't think so?" She strode over to him and took his arm. "Hey, if you want to go, you said it yourself, this is one for the cops."

"I know, I'm fine. Really. I think we need to go in there." He stopped short as Murphy turned and started walking towards the ramp. "Hey, buddy, you okay?"

Murphy turned and walked backwards. His eyes glanced everywhere and everywhere. "That place is wrong, Garrett. Really wrong. I can't go in. I just… I can't."

Garrett jogged to catch up to him, not liking leaving Brianna behind. "Hey. Talk to me."

But Murphy wouldn't speak until they were at the edge of the ramp. "It's like when I meditate, Gar, and I can feel the edges what I can see. But that's peaceful and kind of amazing and this… this is just… there's something pressing in here. Something that wants in. I'm sorry, man, I can't do it. I can't."

"Hey. Hey. It's okay. Murphy." His friend refused to look him in the eyes. "Murphy!" Finally, Murphy glanced at him, eyes now wide with terror and shame. He tried to be gentle and not let his own fear show through. "Go. Find Monica, tail her if she hasn't left already. Okay? Find Galbraith."

Murphy nodded quickly and ran for the street.

When he turned back around, Garrett thought he saw a shadow swoop at him. He cried out and held up his arms defensively, but again, nothing was actually there. He lowered his arms just in time to see Brianna testing the big metal door leading to the building's staircase. "Hey, this thing's open," she called. He jogged over reluctantly, wishing for all the world that he could just get into the Santa Fe with her and take off. No way that door should have been unlocked.

It didn't surprise him in the slightest that when it was opened, the dark cavern within the door frame looked nothing so much like the gaping mouth of a man screaming.

* * *

The A-frame house wasn't so much ostentatious as it was contemptuous. The intricate retaining walls lined with wrought iron fencing and lanterns seemed to say, "This is mine, peasant, so stay the fuck out." The beams of the rounded cruck frame gleamed with laminate. Most A-frames in the state were angular, not rounded, but the design was striking and Monica found herself a little green with envy.

His landscaping must have been stunning in the late spring and early fall, she thought. Two pairs of elms and plum trees sat to either side of the house, and on the other side of the retaining wall and iron fence, lines of shrubs slumped under a heavy coat of snow. She didn't know elms could grow in the area—he must have spent a fortune on watering the place.

But even given the beauty of the place, she couldn't help but be bored with it after a few minutes. She managed to distract herself at first with a sack half full of greasy fast food breakfast items, but she didn't know how long she'd be and managed to keep her snacking at a minimum for fear of needing to make a mad sprint for the nearest public bathroom. She wiped her hands on her pants and switched instead to game after game of Bloons on her phone.

Just as she was thinking that he wasn't going to show, a BMW rolled down the street a little too fast and swerved into the driveway, parking erratically. She shoved her phone into her pocket and got out, hurrying across the street just as Galbraith was starting to get out. "Ransom Galbraith?" she called, brushing biscuit crumbs off her shirt.

He stopped with one foot out the door. "Yes?" he asked, glancing at her blankly. He was much as Garrett had described—big, somewhat well-built but leaning towards soft. His hair wasn't so much blonde as it was almost bleached. He was well dressed, in a gray suit and austere crisp white shirt that clashed mightily with his disheveled hair and haggard eyes that screamed of a lack of sleep. His gaze flicked between her and something behind her. Her car, she thought. She eyed his own appreciatively, thinking this would maybe be an in.

"Nice car. 228i, right?"

Appraising her from her head to her toes clinically, he said, "You know your cars."

"A bit, yeah. Not exactly the best winter daily driver, is it?"

He shrugged. "Does all right. Been thinking about the 320i when the lease is up."

Monica winked at him. "That is, if you're not in jail, right?"

He stiffened at that. "What makes you think I would be?" he asked as he finally got out of the car. He didn't seem all that threatening in the car, but now, looking down on her, she realized just how stupid it was that she hadn't called Garrett to tell him where the house was before she'd hatched this dumb plan.

"You've been harassing two of my friends," she said, ice entering

251

her voice. "Garrett Moranis and Brianna Reeve. You're aware, I'm sure, that stalking people is against the law?"

He started walking towards the house. "Am I on a game show right now? Do I get to phone a friend?"

She pulled out a pack of gum. It was her stress reliever whenever she was feeling particularly punch-happy. She popped a piece out and crushed it between her teeth. "I'm here," she said with forced calmness, "to tell you to fuck right off."

He stopped and smirked at her. She hated that smile. She wanted to rip his lips off and feed them to a tank full of piranhas. "And what will you do if I don't? Bring down the full might of the Rankin Flats police department? On what grounds?"

She chomped down on her gum harder. "We'll find something on you. And then we'll use it to ream out your asshole, make it nice and gaping for the boys down at Deer Lodge."

His smirk widened into a grin, full and toothy. "I should teach you some manners. You and your two little friends. Has he even told you who he is? What he sees?"

That was an odd question. Garrett was right. This guy wasn't playing with a full deck. "All I need to know, dickweed, is that he's a friend. And since I look out for me and mine, here I am. Back. Off."

He leaned in closer to her, so close they might have been getting ready to kiss. "Such vile language from a woman," he said. "It's unbecoming."

She spat the gum onto his impractical leather loafers. "I'll show you vile. Your face? It looks like a whole army of gangbangers came on it and you never bothered to wipe it off. You walk like someone yanked your pretty little princess panties all the way up the crack of your ass and never let go. You've got a crappy joke of a life so you spend your time stalking other people, good people. You're nothing but a little shitstain on the tighty whities of society." She looked him dead in the eyes, her teeth bared. "And if you come visit either of my friends again, I'll ram this gun right up into your stomach and pull the fucking trigger until your guts have painted this bullshit house fire hydrant red. Are we clear?"

His smile flickered for just a second, then turned megawatt bright. "And if you come around here without a warrant again, Detective Ames, you can kiss your little tin pot Nazi cop dreams goodbye. I'd tell you to suck my dick, but I'm guessing you've probably already had your quota of that for the day at the good old boys' club back at the precinct. Tell me, how many of them do you take at a time? Do you let them fuck you while you're stuffing your face with their cocks? I'll bet it looks like a blown-out roast beef sandwich down there." He beeped his car alarm, tipped an imaginary hat, and winked before he walked towards the door.

The fury had left her completely, replaced by shock. He knew her. Had known all along. "How the hell did you know my name?"

He punched his key into the lock without looking back. "Good day, Ms. Ames."

* * *

Inside, after slamming the locks in place, Ransom leaned back against the door, his hands clutched as though he were strangling the life out of that woman from the hospital again. God, how he wanted to break the neck of that cop bitch. He needed a kill. Needed it badly. All pretense of it being scientific had evaporated entirely from his mind. He recognized the black desire within himself and he no longer cared. The little sane part of his mind had receded into nothing more than a whisper.

The ghost who had arrived with the cop slipped through the doorway and passed through Ransom. He stopped inside the foyer and glanced around admiringly. "Beautiful home."

"You here to deliver another threat?" Ransom asked vehemently. "Maybe you'll, oh, I don't know, talk me to death?"

The ghost turned. "No," he said bemusedly. "I'm here to give you the chance you wanted with Garrett." The ghost had a funny accent he recognized from Ms. Gibbons reports. She'd thought he was British, but Galbraith knew enough of the world to recognize it as Scottish. It was faded, though, as a man's accent will do after being away from his homeland for decades.

"You're Padraig," he guessed.

The ghost folded his arms. "I am. And you want to impress Moranis, correct?"

"I do," Ransom said simply.

Padraig nodded slowly, as though he'd just made up his mind about something. "How willing are you to get your hands a little bloody?"

Chapter 20

Long-rotted papers and garbage littered the stairwell. The long dead corpse of a cat lay strewn in two halves beside the door. It was as though someone had simply snapped it in half and discarded the pieces. Brianna gagged when she saw it. It all reeked of mildew and rot. Their hands clasped, they worked their way slowly up the stairs.

"It's like the building is thrumming," Garrett muttered. He could feel the subtle vibration in his teeth.

"I don't feel anything." She glanced worriedly at him. "Maybe we should go."

"Yeah, maybe," he said, but took the next step anyways. He wanted to run, but he was helpless to see the rest of it. "Just… stay with me. I don't think this place likes me or Murphy."

"Was he okay?" she asked as they took the next couple of steps.

"No. Whatever I'm feeling, it was a hundred times worse for him. I sent him to find Monica."

She nodded but said nothing. At the first floor landing, Garrett was almost surprised that the door was locked. He fumbled out his picks and knelt next to the door. Brianna studied the graffiti around them. One crudely drawn picture showed a beast on two legs—a werewolf, she thought, but it was rough—dragging a body behind it with x's for eyes. Another one was nothing but a toothy, Cheshire cat grin with SMYLE written underneath. She shivered and laid her hand on Garrett's shoulder as he finished up.

A long hallway stretched to their left and right as they entered the first floor. Brianna took his hand again. "This was where the bulk of it happened," she whispered, as though they were in a library and breaking the silence was going to bring down someone's wrath upon them. "I remember that much. I was just a kid at the time, so it's all a bit hazy."

Dusty, faded pictures hung in the hallway of employees of the month. Police tape lay strewn on the floor. Here and there were brownish splatters. Garrett thought at first it might have been from rot or animals, then he realized what it was he was looking at. "Dried blood," he breathed. "Nobody ever cleaned it up."

She shivered and grasped his hand tighter. "Are you okay? Are there ghosts?"

He shook his head, not sure which part of that he was answering. Places weren't haunted. They weren't. He and Murphy surely would have seen their like by now. But this… "Let's keep going," he said.

Windows in the hallway looked in on the offices they passed. They stepped carefully over broken glass where either the shooter had fired into the window or someone had broken them by other means. Vandals, he guessed. There had certainly been some here. One office looked as though it had been used as a bathroom. In another, someone had gutted the desk and chairs. The graffiti lessened the deeper they made it in, but one entrepreneurial tagger seemed to have made it his duty to stick it out inside the building. His tags grew more and more bizarre and largely made no sense. On one wall, he'd drawn a man and a child, save that the child's eyes were scribbled out with thick, Frankenstein's monster-esque stitching. At other points, he had written gibberish. Brianna tried to take pictures of it, but the camera wouldn't cooperate. It would power on, beep, and then immediately shut off. "Weirder and weirder," she muttered.

The hallway opened to a large reception area at the front doors. Water from a broken pipe upstairs somewhere must have dripped down there. The floor was stained almost black from long dried liquid and rot. Garrett started towards it, but Brianna tugged at his hand and shook her head. "Floor might be rotten. And it's probably covered in spores," she said lowly. He nodded and they turned back, meaning to head for the stairwell.

Except that the light in the building was dimming into blackness, fast. Garrett stopped cold. Brianna stopped too, not seeing the encroaching darkness. "Gar?"

He tightened his grip on her hand. "I take it the room's not going pitch black for you?"

"No." Her voice sounded distant and fuzzy, like she was coming in over a distance on a walkie talkie.

He nodded. "Just keep my hand in yours, okay?"

The blackness rushed over and through him in a wave. A piercing keen nearly drove him to his knees, but he fought to keep moving. He could barely feel her touch. It was more like a weight pulling at him than a hand. Her voice was even more distant. "Sure… I… get… here?"

255

He shook his head in the pitch blackness. "Bri, I can't hear you." The air felt like spider's silk against his throat. He tried to cough it out but it wouldn't come up. Something tugged against his hand again. Brianna. That was her name, right? She pulled him forward, little by little. His head was pounding with the building's thrumming now and he could hear screams in the blackness. And something erratic. Maybe it was booming, once upon a time, but right then muffled by the blanket of darkness, it was nothing but a dull, sporadic thump. Gunshots, he realized. He leaned over and retched, bringing up nothing but strands of saliva. That weight tugging at his hand drew at him harder and he tried to bat it away. He wanted to let go.

Brianna pulled him forward inch by inch. The vomiting scared her, but not so much as the way he kept trying to pry his fingers loose from hers. At points she was doing little more than grazing his hand with her own, but she managed to keep him moving. It was all she could do. His eyes closed again and reopened, and this time, they blazed with a pale yellow light. "Garrett?" she asked timidly.

He could hear music now. A honky tonk tune, but played slow. He thought he recognized the song. Thought he'd heard it recently. Where had it been? His feet crunched on something. Snow, he thought at first, but that wasn't quite right, was it? It was ash and powdered bone, mixed together and pulsing under his feet. He took another step forward, felt wood underneath. Stairs. He was climbing up. He reached a hand out to steady himself—why was his arm so heavy, like it was being pulled?— and found a railing underneath his fingertips. He climbed, up and up. That music. The piano keys drilled into his skull. A door. Locked. He could hear hammering on the other side, and someone's voice he knew. Knew intimately. Didn't he know her? Wasn't that his...

What was she? His wife? That wasn't right. His family? No. Colder. A flash of an image of her in her favorite hip huggers, the tiny hard nubs of her nipples pressed against his chest as she kissed him. He could hear her in there, sobbing and screaming. He rammed his shoulder into the door. It wouldn't give way. Her screams alternated now with wet, sucking gasps, and he rammed into it again. The hinges creaked, and one more solid shove sent him sprawling through the door. The weight on his hand was gone.

From a radio deep in the bowels of that trailer, he heard the singer croon. His voice was jovial and jarring.

He stumbled through the laundry room, shouting a name as

unfamiliar to him now as his own, knowing he had to get to her as she sobbed in agony. Sickly orange moonlight shot in through the windows, giving the living room just enough illumination that he could see her laid out on a butcher's table, her wrists and ankles tied with steel cables. They'd tied her so tightly that her hands bloated, turning a dark, gangrenous purple. The ends of the cables stretched off into the darkness of the living room. Four figures came to the table, talking and laughing as though they were getting together for brunch.

A howl erupted from the radio, mocking and wild.

One of the figures threw back its hood. The elder Jamie Finson leaned in and licked her cheek, all the way up to her ear. "This one will do just fine for the tribute," he said lovingly. Where he licked, her skin hissed and burned and she strained against the cables, screaming wordlessly.

Another figure threw back her hood. Yvette. She stared right at Garrett, her eyes cold and dead. "This is the fate of all the world's sinners," she said, spreading her hands out over the table. She yanked up the woman's head by her hair, forcing her to look upon him as she traced the symbol for infinity on her forehead with a fingernail, digging deep into the flesh and stopping to force the tabled women to lick her own blood.

The other two remained hooded, but they approached the table too. Their fingers lengthened and the orange light of the moon glinted off the scales of their digits, now writhing and whipping towards each other. Their snake fingers entwined, nipping at each other and letting out sandpapery hisses. They spoke almost together, their words fading in and out with each other, creating an eerie staccato. "She'll be the main course." The snake hands dove at the woman's legs, biting and snapping at the flesh. Where they bit, purple boils erupted with pus and blood and the woman screamed again.

The four bowed their heads, turned, and dragged the cables outwards, stretching the scarred woman's limbs tight. She shrieked in pain and whipped her head up as bones and cartilage started to pop. "This is on you," she spat. "It's all on you." Her left arm ripped apart from her shoulder, leaving nothing but stringy bits of meat and tendon connecting the two. He could see the white of the bone underneath, like broken china. Then her other limbs were torn off too, and her screams turned into gurgles. Her eyes rolled back in her head, and with one final snarl of the name he'd forgotten he had, she slipped away.

He fell to his knees and crawled towards her, feeling the life sap out of him with every inch. He could smell a chemical tang now, a familiar one. Why had she thrown the chemical jugs in the fire? he wondered. He'd warned her not to, hadn't he? Another inch, and he loosed liquid sobs. His lungs burned now, worse than if by fire. It was as though millions of little lesions were opening up in his chest, all at once. But his focus was only on her, on the wreckage of her body. He reached out to touch her. Her flesh was cold and hard as marble.

"I'm sorry," he tried to choke out, but with the ever-growing napalm pain in his chest, it was growing hard to do anything at all. "I'm so sorry," he gasped with the last of his breath. He could move no further.

The radio faded out, its silence anticipatory.

His eyes burned, but he refused to close them. This was his fault. All of it, his fault. Her body twitched and her head rose. Her lips peeled back, revealing teeth as sharp as needles and nearly as long, distending her jaw to her chest. Yes, he thought. Yes, he would let her consume him, and all would be even, or as much as he could make it. He struggled forward so that his love could take his throat in her mouth and rip it out and end this nightmare.

Then fifty thousand volts of electricity shot through his body and he mercifully, blessedly blacked out.

* * *

She pulled him by his arms slowly but steadily towards the door. It was slow going and she was crying in fear for him. The way he'd looked, that impossible thousand-yard stare with those eyes like the sun through the smog, she didn't know what had happened and it terrified her. Not for herself—she could feel in her bones that this place was wrong, but it didn't seem to be affecting her as quickly as it did him. Still, she hurried as best as she could, sweat dripping off her forehead as she pulled him along. At one point, she tumbled and fell, and sat up screaming for someone to help her, anyone at all. She wept openly when only silence responded, her hand resting on Garrett's cheek as he trembled. Every shallow breath he took felt like a fight to her. A breath of air caressed her face, cutting the odor of the place just enough that she felt like she could breathe again. The tears stopped and she got back unsteadily to her feet, coming face to face with a bit of graffiti on the wall. OWN DO. Shaking her head in confusion, she muttered, "Own do yourself, asshole." She pulled him the rest of the way to the door.

On the stairwell, his breathing deepened and she gasped gratitude to God, Jesus, and all the saints she could remember. She sat him up with his back against the wall and knelt over him. "Garrett. Hey. Come back to me."

His eyes fluttered open. Though his eyes were no longer so bright, they were still tinged with yellow "Bri?" he croaked. "Did you zap me?"

She smiled apologetically. "Yes. I'm sorry."

"I think… I think my heart is beating about a million miles a minute," he muttered. Then his eyes fixed on her, and he raised his hands shakily to her face, her chest, and her stomach. "You're okay," he said wonderingly. "You're okay."

"Is that what you saw?" she asked. "Me getting hurt?"

Instead of answering, he kissed her, hard and powerfully long, his lips as dry and hot as the desert. Heat rolled off him in waves. He was sick, she realized. Whatever had been done to him in there had made him terribly, fiercely ill. When he was able, she helped him to his feet and they stumbled down the stairs together. Moments later they made it back out to the garage, and he sucked in the fresh air in great big gasps. "I'm going to get the car," she told him.

"No!" he bellowed, his eyes wild again. For a moment she thought he was slipping back into that dream world, but he only wanted to seek out her hand. "No. We go together. I can't lose you again," he said miserably. To the air beside her, he said quietly, "Thank you for coming back."

She started to look around, then remembered that cool breath of air inside the building and shivered. "Yes, Murphy," she said softly. "Thank you."

* * *

Jamie Finson could no longer feel the eyes on him. Whoever it was that had been watching him had moved on, but there was no guarantee they wouldn't be back. He drove halfway across town to meet her, the real love of his life, his deepest regret.

Even in her golden years, Anny Brennerman still burned bright. Her skin hung like drapes, her breasts now looked like nothing more than a couple of sacks in her dress, and liver spots dotted her arms and neck, but when she turned that smile on him, he felt like a teenager again, lost in the fervor of her belief, of her passion. He stumbled like a teenager too, only barely managing to keep his balance by pressing a hand on the bar. She laughed lightly at that as he righted himself. He was too old to be embarrassed by much these days and bowed good-naturedly at her applause.

He leaned in to kiss her in that old spot beneath her earlobe, and winced when she pulled back just a little, letting his lips brush her cheek but nothing more. She'd switched perfumes, he thought idly. "Anny. It's good to see you."

She folded her hands neatly in front of her and pretended not to notice him eyeing her up and down hungrily. "Jamie. I'm sorry about the cancer." She said it as though she were apologizing about some bad traffic he might have run into. That stung.

"Yes. Well."

"We'll want to know who you recommend for a replacement. I can't guarantee we'll pick him. Or her. But your recommendation will carry a lot of weight."

He ordered nothing but water from the bartender and grimaced at her when he left. "So... straight to business then?" he asked, his anger rising. "It's been, what, decades?"

"Shall we retire to the men's bathroom, then? Knock one out for old times' sake?" Her voice was light and curious, and he wasn't at all sure that she wasn't serious.

His water came and he used it as an excuse to look away from her. "I'm sorry. You know I am."

"It worked out well for the both of us, didn't it?" She smiled without any real humor. "I've enjoyed my life. By all reports, I hear you've enjoyed yours."

"Markham or Nolan."

"Excuse me?"

He crushed an ice cube between his teeth. "You asked. I answered. Markham's arrogant, his history will put him in sharp focus with the feds, and he's not a believer."

"Like you," she said. This time, it was fondness that tinged her voice, not bitterness. She too remembered their nights and nights of conversations on the mystical.

"Like me," he said, letting go of a hint of a smile. "Nolan won't get traction because he's fucking my granddaughter. He's a psychopath, but with a tight leash, he's learned to keep control. He's careful, he's meticulous, and he'd be able to provide one hell of a nice tribute every quarter. At the very least, he should be considered apart from any considerations of my family."

"What about your granddaughter?" she asked.

"Too green. She's already partaken," here his mouth bared over his gums in an animalistic grin, "but she hasn't gone through the rite yet. I'm remedying that when Hamber comes for the tribute. It's a surprise. She thinks it's a week later."

Brennerman raised her glass to him and they drank to her together. When she set her glass down, Brennerman touched his arm briefly. "We have other things we need to discuss."

"Oh?"

She dug in her purse and laid out a series of photographs. "Taken two days ago."

Finson leaned in and examined them closely. "Fuck. Here I thought Markham was wrong about the mole. I thought…" He laughed and shook his head a little self-consciously. "For a moment, I thought you were right."

She cocked an eyebrow. "About what?"

The water wasn't helping his guts settle. He pushed the glass away and dabbed at his sweating forehead with a napkin. "I've had the oddest feeling. That I'm being watched. I didn't think it was bugs or cameras, but if these are accurate—"

"They are," Brennerman said bluntly.

"-then I was just being old and foolish. Hoping that there was something greater waiting for me, I guess." He reached out and took her hand. "Sort of like what someone once taught me."

"Jamie," she sighed with exasperation. "That was half a century ago." She glanced down at the photos. "So what will you do?"

"She doesn't know about the meet. Not the specifics, anyways. Markham has her ready to put in some surveillance cameras. I'll send him over under the pretext of him getting her in there and ready to go to work. Then…" he shrugged. "Been a while since we've given Hamber a live tribute."

She drained the rest of her glass. "I liked that one."

"Me too."

She snorted. "Of course you did. She's exactly your type." Her cheeks flushing, she cleared her throat. "Anyways. I understand you're using the Howell Designs building. That should please the Hamber people."

"They do seem to love places with a certain kind of history, don't they?"

"Yes," she said, smiling a secretive little smile. "Yes, they do."

"I would still love to know what it was you did there."

"Come on now, Jamie," she said, a dreamy little look on her face. "You know I would have taught you everything. Your granddaughter has asked, by the way."

The churning in his guts got worse. Much, much worse. "And?"

"You won't try to talk her out of it?"

He shrugged. "If it's in the service of our friends, well... no." A timer on his cell phone started beeping. Time to go give his wife her pills. "I need to go," he said, his voice strained. "Anny, I'm sorry. About us. About—"

Her mood darkened in an instant. "How did you remain in power for so long with that kind of pissing and moaning attitude?" she snapped. "You're a man who gets his business done. So handle yourself with a degree of respect. Own what you did and move fucking forward. Die with some dignity, damn you."

He stiffened, nodded, and tried not to flee the bar too quickly. That had not gone at all like he had planned. There was nothing for it, though. He drove back to his lonely house, his lonely life, and his unloving wife and thought about how he was going to best offer up Dee as a sacrifice.

Back in the bar, Anny Brennerman snatched up a napkin and dug out a pen. Slowly, meticulously, she drew several symbols on the paper, making them nice and thick. She wet her tongue and placed it on one of the symbols, then did the same for the rest slowly and in turn. Her eyes rolled back up into her head and she muttered to herself indistinctly for a few minutes. The bartender, thinking she was having a stroke, rushed over, but as he reached out to snap his fingers in front of her face, her eyes fluttered back to normal and she breathed deeply. "Hey, you okay?" the guy asked her.

She pressed her lips together in a tight facsimile of a smile. "Never better."

Chapter 21

The blankets were too much. He kept trying to shove them away, but a pair of delicate hands kept insistently pushing them back onto him. With the sunlight glaring in and the heater cranked up, he felt like he was a bit of old dry wood in a stove, burning up merrily into nothing but ash. The hands pushed water at him, and he said through cracked lips, "S'okay, Mom, just lay off." That hand dribbled cool drops across his forehead. He didn't mind that so much and fell back down into darkness.

Two voices brought him back out of it. "...temperature's down, but I still don't think I should..." Brianna. Her voice was as nice as the ice chips running over his lips. He stumbled a little bit more towards consciousness.

"It's okay, Brianna." The voice was deeper, masculine. "Work's slow right now for us anyways. Go on."

"Thank you, Ed," she said quietly. Warm lips at his cheek. Garrett's eyes fluttered open. She smiled down at him. "Hey, baby."

Baby? When had she taken to calling him that? "Hey, Bri," he said, his voice cracked from thirst.

"I've gotta go to work. Just for a while. Ed's here to take care of you, okay?" She held his hand tightly under the blankets. He thought he felt her trembling.

"I'm fine," he tried to say. It came out as mm fahne, as though he were talking through cotton balls. "Get to work."

She hesitated then, as though she wanted to say something else, but just leaned in. "I love you," she whispered into his ear.

He swallowed hard to try to make sure the words came out right. "Love you too," he said with some difficulty. She smiled prettily at him, brushed his lips, and was out the door before she could change her mind.

Ed sat on one of the folding chairs beside him. "Hey, buddy," he said gently. "Water?"

Garrett nodded, almost imperceptibly. Ed brought up a glass to his lips. "Small sips, man." The little laps of water felt like heaven on his throat and swollen tongue. Little by little, Garrett finished half the glass and finally pulled away. "That's the most you've drank in a while. Holding it down okay?"

"Yeah," he said, still a little hoarse. "How long have I...?"

"A couple of days. I'm not going to ask you what happened, but it sure as heck isn't pneumonia like Brianna's been telling us, is it?"

Garrett thought back to that building and shuddered. "I lost her, Ed," he whispered. "They quartered her in the trailer and I didn't do anything..."

"You didn't lose anyone," Ed said carefully. "She was right here. You saw her. You told her you loved her, remember?"

Garrett tried to fight through the haze and realized he did remember. "Yes. I... yes." He drank more water when it was offered to him and slept fitfully. When he woke next, Ed was dabbing at his forehead with a cool wet cloth. "Welcome back, brother." That wasn't Ed speaking, but Murphy.

"Murph," Garrett croaked. "We can't go in there again."

"It's Ed, Garrett," the big man next to him said cheerfully.

Murphy ignored that. "You have to break out of this, man. The meet. They've set a date for it. We've got so much work to do."

"We don't have a plan," Garrett said feverishly. "Need a plan."

"Okay, a plan, we'll come up with one," Ed said agreeably.

"Not you," Garrett muttered. "Murphy. Talking to Murphy."

"Focus, Garrett," Murphy said cautiously. "You can't let him know about me. Stand up."

Garrett pushed down the covers. Even that much took an immense amount of effort. "Can't," he whimpered.

"Stand up!" Murphy roared.

"I can't!" Garrett said louder. He shoved the last of the blankets off.

Ed leaned back in his chair. "Garrett, I don't think you should—"

"The fever's breaking, Garrett," Murphy said. "You can feel it, can't you? The poison's leaving your system. You can do this. If you can't, that leaves her to do it for you, and if they get her, you'll never forgive yourself. That was who you saw in there, wasn't it? Well, she's alive, Gar, and she'll fight. With or without you."

"Can't lose her," Garrett said, and started to push himself up.

Ed put a hand on his chest. Garrett grabbed it instinctively and pushed it aside. Murphy leaned in next to him. "Get up, Garrett. I can't help you. You have to help yourself."

Garrett tried to push himself to his feet. He fell back to the chair, coughing up a viscous orange liquid, the same color as that of the moonlight in his vision. Ed paid it no mind as it splattered all over the floor. He couldn't see it. Garrett gasped in a clean lungful of air and tried again.

"C'mon brother. Time to get to work," Murphy said softly. "Time we figured out how to end this."

Garrett coughed up more of the orange crap, his lungs feeling better than they had in days, weeks, years. He drew in huge breaths, the sweaty, stale scent of the room roiling his stomach. Ed stood up. "Garrett, you need your rest—"

"I need... to move," Garrett grunted, and pushed himself to his feet. He looked down at his wobbly knees, laughed and took three steps forward. He would have fallen if Ed hadn't propped him up. "Thanks, man."

Then he blacked out again.

* * *

This time, when he woke up, there was no fever. He felt neither chilled nor particularly hot, just warm and comfortable. He tried out a little cough and was delighted to see there was no orange in it. Someone was frying something cheesy and wonderful in the kitchen. His stomach roared. "Hello?" he croaked. His throat was still parched, but this lacked the intensity of his feverish state. A big sun tea jar full of ice water rested on the coffee table. He peeled the blankets off and leaned forward to grab it. He felt weak as a kitten as he lifted it to his chest. He drank straight from the jar, taking cautious sips at first, and when there was no revolt in his stomach, great long gulps, draining nearly half the jar. Finally, sated, his stomach practically bursting with cold water, he tried the hello again. This time it almost sounded natural.

Bri rushed out of the kitchen to see him sitting on the edge of the chair with the jug in his hands. "Garrett!" she gasped, and ran to him. She set aside the jug and felt his forehead, his chest, his cheeks. "Are you..."

"I'm okay," he said. He sniffed at his armpits. "I reek, though."

She took his chin in her hand, kissing him. "I didn't know what to do or how to help you... Ed said you were talking to Murphy. He thought you were hallucinating, but he did something, didn't he?"

"Talked me up out of the soup, I think." He wrinkled his nose. "I think something's burning."

"Shit fuck damn!" she grunted, and sprinted for the kitchen. A minute later, he heard the hiss of a frying pan under water and more swearing. He got to his feet, a little unsteadily, and realized he was mostly naked save for a pair of boxers. At least someone had thought to cover the chair in a sheet, he thought ruefully. He padded towards the kitchen slowly, his stomach growling.

Brianna glanced up at him. "You shouldn't be up," she said reproachfully.

"I feel... well, not a hundred percent," he said honestly, "but maybe like eighty percent fine? Smelled good until, you know..."

"Grilled ham and cheese," she said, nodding towards the garbage can. "I'll fix us some more. Think you can manage one?"

"I feel like I could eat a dozen." Then he caught a whiff of himself again. "But maybe I ought to get a shower first."

She wrinkled her nose and laughed a little softly. "Yeah, sorry. I was trying to give you sponge baths, but you kept trying to fight me off." She grew serious. "You kept calling me Yvette."

"I'm sorry," he said softly. He kissed the side of her head as she buttered bread.

"Was it bad?"

He couldn't begin to tell her the truth. "I thought I lost you," he whispered into her ear.

Brianna swiveled on her heels and slapped his chest with the spatula. "Not gonna be that easy, you dope. You. Me. We're together for the long haul. We're gonna have like eighteen kids and—"

"Eighteen?" he asked weakly. "I was thinking like two."

"Eighteen," she nodded firmly. "You're just gonna wreck this vagina."

"Eighteen?"

"With your penis. Like a bulldozer. A bulldozing penis." She thought about that for a second and then nodded. "It's gonna look like the Grand Canyon down there by the time we're done poppin' 'em out." She kissed his nose. "Go get showered."

* * *

They went back to the Howell Building that night—or rather, that block. Brianna threatened violence if he stepped foot anywhere near the building. Still weak and a little dazed, he promised not to do anything of the sort. Instead, they were breaking and entering into the residential building across the street from the central entrance and exit to the underground garage. It was their best vantage point, offering a good view of not just that entrance but the side streets next to the other two entrances as well. Murphy scouted out the apartments, finding a suitable one on the second floor that gave them both easy access to the stairwell for a fast exit and the right angle for the best view. He swept through the floor, keeping an eye out for anyone who might see them coming. But the few residents in house were too engaged in their own lives to notice Garrett and Brianna's fast entrance into the apartment, where they set up shop quickly and silently.

Their pair of duffel bags were loaded with all the things they'd need both for an overnight stay—sleeping bags, a pair of pillows, assorted food and bottled water, unopened bathroom products, and fresh clothes, both fit for day to day life and some generic hoodies and ski masks for the meet, should they need them. The guns and equipment would come later. Garrett didn't want to leave anything there that couldn't be explained away by squatters. They left the duffel bags in an empty bedroom's closet, tucked far enough away that if someone came in and gave it a cursory glance, they wouldn't see anything out of the ordinary.

While they looked out the window together, Brianna told them her idea for a plan. It was absurd. It sounded like something right out of a cartoon. It was rough—very rough—and it would be almost impossible to pull off. But it was sort of genius and it captivated Murphy in its sheer ludicrousness.

As Brianna drove them to dinner with her dad, she chanted what they needed to prepare for the meet over and over again like a mantra. "Binoculars. Bullets. Guns. Camera."

Garrett wondered with amusement just what kind of a monster he'd created. At least she was a cute one, he supposed. His cell phone buzzed. "Monica, hey."

"Back from the dead, huh?"

"Yeah. The, ah, pneumonia cleared up this morning."

"Quickest case of that ever, I'd guess." Monica sounded amused and more than a little curious. "Someday, you might have to tell me what actually happened."

"Maybe someday. Putting you on speaker phone. Bri's here too. What's up?"

"While you were out, I dug up more about our friend Galbraith. Guess where he works?"

"Where?" Garrett asked. In the backseat, Murphy leaned forward hungrily.

"Agilumine Solutions."

"Is that name supposed to mean anything to me?"

"Nope, but the address will. Remember that murder you found? Foster? The one we could never get anywhere with? Well, turns out Agilumine Solutions has an office in the building right across the street."

"Son of a bitch," Garrett and Murphy both said.

"They're closed for the night. I'm headed there tomorrow morning. Figured you'd want to tag along."

"Absolutely. Oh, about that other thing."

"Yeah?"

"We've got a date. And some ideas." He filled her in.

She finally stopped laughing long enough to take a long, snorting breath. "If you can pull that off, it'll be one for the history books. That's genius."

"It was Brianna's idea," Garrett said.

Brianna grinned. "Oh, well, kind of, I guess. But it was just a dumb suggestion and..."

"Stop cutting yourself short," Monica said. "That's perfect."

Garrett jumped back in. "Can you round up a few cops to take care of the buyers? That's the only aspect we can't factor into this."

She thought about that for a minute. "Yeah. We've got a few people here I think I can trust. You don't have time to run their names through whoever your sources are, do you?"

"Not this time," he sighed. "We're on our own for this one."

"Okay, well, fingers crossed then." She hung up without another word.

Brianna glanced at him curiously. "Are we really going with my plan? I told you that as a joke. I didn't actually think—"

Garrett reached across and rubbed her leg. "Bri, I'm not kidding you, it's insane. It's going to be damn near impossible to make it work." His eyes were gleaming with good humor. "But we're going to try like hell to make it happen."

* * *

Monica leaned against the back of her car, hair whipping in the breeze. She eyeballed any vehicle that tried to park in the space behind hers, showing just a little bit of teeth and flashing the badge on her belt. At least it wasn't too damn cold, she thought to herself.

268

She spotted Garrett's Hyundai halfway down the block and waved him in. He got out and handed one of a pair of big cups of coffee to her after she pushed off the car. "You look like shit, Moranis."

"Thanks," he said dryly.

"You sure you're up for this?"

He nodded. "This the place?" he asked.

"Agilumine's a few floors up." She pointed up to a bank of windows then across the street. "Angle's right where someone could see over to the rooftop, but let's not assume anything until we get up there."

He nodded and they entered the building. It was surprisingly low-tech considering the shining glass-and-steel exterior. That wasn't to say it was an ugly building. Small rings of real plants and shrubbery adorned the lobby. A highly-polished slab of stone in the center bore a plaque with the names of all the businesses and their floors. A thickset guard scurried over to them. "Detective Ames, I went ahead and called down the elevator the second I saw you come in," he said amicably.

"Thank you," Monica said. "This is John Stephens. He's filling in for our regular photographer."

"I don't see any sort of camera," the guard said curiously.

Garrett dug out his cell phone. "Very high tech, what they can do with these nowadays."

Monica smiled blandly. "Besides, I'm just here to make a few inquiries. Fill in some gaps, that sort of thing."

"Oh. Of course." The man seemed more confused than ever, but walked them to the elevators anyways and wished them well.

As they rode up, Murphy snickered. "John Stephens? Sounds like a pharmacist's name." Garrett reached up as though he was going to scratch an itch and flipped Murphy off.

The elevator opened into a small vestibule gated by a pair of glass doors. Agilumine Solutions took up the entirety of the floor, and when Garrett entered, he was immediately taken aback. He'd expected tight-packed cubicles and typical office work stations, but was instead greeted with a few rows of open u-shaped desks, with workers who looked as though they were dressed more for Wall Street than Silicon Valley. The workers conversed with each other quietly and the whole place had an air of stuffiness and quality he hadn't expected. A young man rose and walked over to greet them. After they introduced themselves, he reached out to shake their hands. His handshake was firm, but Garrett noticed a hint of exhaustion in his eyes. "Detectives," he said.

"Oh, no, just her," Garrett said pleasantly. "I'm just helping out today."

Monica gave that same disinterested smile she'd shown the guard in the lobby. "You're the one I spoke to on the phone?"

"Yes," Benjamin said. "I'm not sure what all I can tell you that we haven't told the police already."

"Well, we'd just like to cross our t's on this and make sure Mr. Foster's death was what it really appeared to be," Monica said.

Benjamin stopped short. "The suicide?" he asked, confused. "I thought you were here to investigate Barb Kent's disappearance."

Monica and Garrett both fought to keep the surprise off their faces. As uninterested as possible, Monica said, "There's a possibility we think the two might be related, but today we're just rechecking stories on the Foster case, that sort of thing. Benjamin, would you mind showing Mr. Stephens here into the offices so he can get some pictures? I'll talk to a few people out here."

"Oh, sure," Benjamin said a little dejectedly. He beckoned for Garrett to follow him. "There are only two real offices here. Ms. Kent's and Mr. Galbraith's. Well, I guess the other one isn't Mr. Galbraith's anymore. He was let go. Which one would you like to start with?"

"Oh, I think the boys got plenty of pictures of Ms. Kent's," Garrett said, hoping he sounded reasonably like a real cop and not something out of a bad TV show. "Let's start with Mr. Galbraith's. Did you know him well?"

Benjamin nodded and shuffled towards one of the two offices. "He was my boss. I was his assistant. Very sharp guy, easily the best programmer in the place. That's why he had his own office. He was magic with code, just plain and simple." He unlocked the door and pushed it open for Garrett.

Galbraith's office was staggeringly refined and well decorated. His wall of windows definitely took center stage, with an eagle eyed view over the tops of several nearby buildings and the streets below. His enormous L-shaped desk took up a full quarter of the room. A small Zen garden had been fitted into the top of the desk at one corner, and at the other was his work station and office supplies. A well-stocked minibar in a corner of the room had seen a lot of love. Its bottles were half full at best. Good stuff, not cheap, but not overpriced, stuffy swill either.

"He has good taste," Garrett said appreciatively, eyeing a beautiful print of a dilapidated house near a gurgling stream.

"Remarkably so," Benjamin said a little sadly. "All of this is his. He still hasn't been by to pick any of it up. I... don't think he will be."

"Oh?" he asked. Garrett remembered he was supposed to be taking pictures, so he dug out his phone and started snapping some at random. "Parted on bad terms?"

"He stopped doing his work," Benjamin said. He sat on the edge of a leather chair, running his hand through his thinning hair. "It was his wife's passing, I think. He held on as long as he could, but..." Benjamin shrugged.

"What happened to his wife?" Garrett snapped pictures of the minibar and stepped towards the windows. He could clearly see the top of the building where Foster took a dive.

"She died in a fire. It was a bad deal. She'd been cheating on Mr. Galbraith. She and her boyfriend on the side were both killed. Lit cigarette, they called it. The place was old and went up like kindling."

Garrett half-turned. "You said they called it. What does that mean? Do you think something else might have happened?"

"Do you mean do I think Mr. Galbraith did it?" Benjamin asked. His eyes fell to the floor, then he glanced back up. "No. They investigated him, but he was having dinner downtown when the place went up. There was no way he did it."

Murphy sat in one of the chairs. "He's hiding something," he said unhelpfully.

"That must have been rough on him. Did he know about the affair?"

"No. Didn't have a clue. It broke him. I don't even think he's dated anyone since. He's been a little... edgy towards women since then." Benjamin looked down at his shoes. "I..."

"It's okay, Benjamin," Garrett coaxed. "You're not in any trouble here and I just want to listen."

"I think he had something to do with Ms. Kent being gone," Benjamin blurted. "He didn't like her. Called her a bitch and a c-c-c..."

"It's okay, I get the drift," Garrett said. "Did they fight a lot?"

"Never face to face. But he said a few things in private to me, things I didn't think much about. He was a good boss, and I didn't want him to get in trouble. But now..."

Garrett leaned against the desk, a little shaky. His strength still hadn't returned to him entirely and he felt like he'd just run a marathon.

271

"Can you remember him acting at all odd around the time when Mr. Foster was killed?"

"You say that like Mr. Galbraith might have had something to do with it," Benjamin observed. When Garrett didn't answer, he held his stomach like he was in pain. "Oh no. You think he—"

"I don't know anything for certain," Garrett said quietly. "I'm just trying to put some pieces together here."

Benjamin thought about it for a while. "He kinda did this glass clinking thing with his ring, looking out the window that whole week. I don't think he thought I could hear him, but my desk was right by his door."

"Ring clinking thing?"

Benjamin got up and grabbed a tumbler from the minibar. "Yeah. He'd stand at his window like this and clink his ring on his finger on the edge. Seemed like every minute or two, right around the same time of day every day late in the afternoon. Lost in thought, I guess."

"You're late," Murphy muttered, remembering what Foster had told them. "He was timing something."

Garrett reached a hand out and grasped Benjamin's shoulder. "Hey. Thanks for this."

Benjamin stared out the window. "I feel like I'm betraying him," he said sadly. "He was a good boss. Would you do me a favor? Try reasoning with him? He was a good guy. Maybe a bit standoffish and blunt, but I think he just sort of lost it, you know?"

"That all depends on him," Garrett said. "Do yourself a favor though. You got a girlfriend or something?" Benjamin nodded. "Go to her place for a while. Stay there until this whole thing blows over."

"Yeah. Yeah, that seems like a good idea." Benjamin turned and looked at him. Really looked at him. "Good luck, mister."

"Oh, it's up to the real police now," Garrett said lightly and he meant it.

On the elevator ride down, Monica glanced at him. "Well?"

"He murdered Foster," Garrett said grimly. "And I think he's murdered his boss, too."

* * *

Something audibly popped in Dee's kneecap. She would have fallen to the floor if she wasn't being held up by the manacles. She screamed. "Oh, I'm gonna kill you, Markham, you fucking son of a—" Finson Sr. punched her in the mouth, a straight right that mashed her lips against her teeth and snapped her head back. She spat blood and gurgled, "You hit pretty good for a grandmother, you know that, Finson?"

Jamie coughed out a chuckle and punched her again. Again. And again. Blood flowed from her broken nose and she spat a tooth out. "You'll never be pretty again," he said, almost apologetically.

"At least I'll never be as ugly as you assclowns," she said, spraying blood with every word.

Markham made as though he were going to punch her in the stomach, but Finson's hand caught his, lightning fast. "No internal injuries," Finson reminded him. "Fuck up her face and her extremities all you want, but touch the guts and you'll ruin her as a tribute."

Markham nodded, and Finson let go. Markham kicked her injured knee instead, sending another howl of pain from her. Finson watched him go to town, a pleasant little shiver running up and down his spine every time she grunted or screamed.

God, he loved his work.

Chapter 22

They went shopping.

It wasn't for the sorts of things you might pick up at a grocery store. After calling ahead the day before, they arrived at a medical supply store just after it opened. Garrett introduced Brianna to Kel Morgan, the man who had designed her Taser. He was angry at first that Garrett had brought someone new to his shop, but after a fat stack of cash and a fair bit of praise from Brianna about the Taser, he begrudgingly took them to the back of his warehouse, where he shoved aside boxes of oxygen tubing, cannulas, and other medical equipment. Underneath lay a perfectly flat cellar door, painted to look like the rest of the floor, immensely missable unless someone was actively looking for it.

The basement was full of odd weaponry. There were no guns as such, but lots of hand-to-hand weapons and what looked like grenade launchers lined the walls. They were ARWENs, Kel told her, anti-riot weaponry designed for non-lethal solutions to big problems. Kel, Garrett explained, was a friend of Froggy and Blake's, his old friends and mentors. He specialized in non-lethal weaponry, and had patents on several designs of weapons he hoped could be used to reduce the numbers of shootings around the nation by police. He fitted her with a Kevlar vest—Garrett had his own already. From there, he showed Garrett the boxes of ammo he'd requested.

"And they'll work?" Brianna asked.

That pissed Kel off, so he tossed her vest in a corner, grabbed a pistol from a lockbox, loaded it, and fired fifteen rounds while Garrett and Bri shoved their fingers in their ears. All three stood over the vest. "Satisfied?" Kel asked angrily.

Garrett grinned. "Very."

* * *

A few hours after the two unloaded the equipment at one of Garrett's storage units, they drove west in a caravan. Danny, Ed, Garrett, and Murphy rode in one car, and Brianna and Rose got in some time together in another. Highway 12 could be a gorgeous drive in the spring. It was a slow burn from the city's heart, through the suburbs and the plains and into the mountains some hundred miles west, but once they got into the Crazy Mountains and left the sprawl behind, it was absolutely stunning. Pine forests sprawled across the mountainsides, giving a hint as to what the landscape would have been like a century and a half ago before man had so affected the landscape. Snow still capped the tops of the mountains and would do so late into June or early July, feeding the countless streams and lakes in the region with cold, clear water. Ranchers held the land in a tight stranglehold, leaving little for the average person to buy this far west of the city, but it gave the land an almost empty feel to it. It was incredibly easy to forget the city within an hour of leaving it.

They rode all the way to White Sulphur Springs, nestled at the base of three mountain ranges. It was still too early to eat, so they went swimming in the area's hot spring-fed pools instead. Garrett was still immensely exhausted from his fight with the miasma of the Howell building, but managed to work up enough energy to let Brianna climb up on his shoulders and do battle in the gravest of water sport competitions—chicken fighting. They held their own valiantly, but Rose pulled out an old wrestling move and clotheslined Brianna off his shoulders in a fit of hilarious savagery that surprised them all.

Afterwards, they ate at a local bar and grill, mowing down Philly cheesesteaks and burgers. A rosy-cheeked, gray-haired waitress caught Danny's eye and soon he slipped away from the group to make bedroom eyes at her, promising he'd catch up to them in the morning if he was lucky. That came with a waggling of his bushy eyebrows and Brianna whooped him on.

The rest staggered back to relax in the hot pools, stopping at each bar on the way for a cocktail—and there were quite a few of those. They weren't long for the water, though, as soon Rose and Ed slipped away back to their hotel room. Garrett and Bri relaxed under the stars in the pool together. The heat of the water with the chill in the air made for a delicious combination. When they returned to their room, after a long shower together, they made love, slowly and tenderly.

In the morning, they went skiing at Showdown. Murphy planned on cutting it short and heading back to Rankin Flats early to keep an eye on things, but a pair of ghosts showed him that he could balance himself on the ends of the skis of people coming down the slopes. His whoops of joy almost made Garrett less miserable as he toppled over time and time again on the bunny slope, snarling curses at his equipment, the packed snow, other skiers, the sun glinting off the powder, anything and everything he could. Finally, his pride and his bruised ass could take no more, and when a long-haired yuppie instructor stopped to help him to his feet, he instead kicked off his boots—still attached to his skis somehow—and plodded down the hill in his thick wool socks to the lodge, where he dug out his Kindle and sat next to the fire, drinking nearly a half a gallon of hot cocoa and enjoying himself immeasurably more.

On the drive back to White Sulphur, they passed by a turnoff that drew Rose's attention. "We should come up to your cabin when the snow clears. Do some camping and hiking."

Brianna raised her eyebrows. "A cabin in the woods?"

Garrett grinned. "It's just a little place. I had a chance to buy a little bit of property up here and took it." That was a little lie, one he had to tell her because of the present company. He'd rectify it later, when they were sitting in the apartment overlooking the meet site. Even then he wouldn't tell her the whole truth. How do you tell the woman in your life you've bought a place simply because it has an incredibly useful murder hole?

When he came to Montana and camped in Glacier National Park, he and Murphy met a Chinese miner from the 1800s, a bad man who had once lived a more or less honest life as a miner in Butte and central Montana. He witnessed a lot of tragedy in Butte, including a friend getting hung simply because his neighbor thought the Chinese man's luck was better than his own. When a pair of brothers called for workers to join them in a mine in central Montana, he jumped at the chance to get out of there. It was a terrible mistake. The brothers were not cruel, but stupid. Their claim to their land was tenuous at best and they had no grasp on how to properly construct mine shafts. They dug straight into the earth with little care towards building up retaining walls. When one shaft didn't work out, they would simply build another on a whim, leaving the old shafts barely covered. Two men died on their watch, and after the bodies were brought up and given a burial, the brothers decided to try their luck as trappers in Canada. Their solution for the mine shafts was quick and dangerous—they simply tossed down sticks of dynamite until the earth collapsed in on itself. In their haste or their sloppiness, they forgot one shaft at the base of an enormous pair of pine trees.

Murphy and the miner grew into an easy friendship. Both had been criminals and were trying to atone for their sins. They poked around the mountains for a solid three weeks together, combing the hills for the mine shaft to see if it was still open. Time had changed the landscape quite a bit, but one day, nearly miraculously, they found the half-covered mouth of the shaft, still there after nearly a century and a half.

Garrett negotiated a price on the property, claiming he wanted it for a weekend home of sorts. He paid an exorbitant amount of money, and even more to have a cabin built near the edge of the property to keep up appearances. He spent his weekends there, beating down a trail in a long, circuitous loop that led near to the mine shaft, but not quite so near that anyone on the trail would find it without knowing where to look. The property was a precaution, an expensive one that also had the benefit of being close to nature. He'd never once had to use it for its grim, intended purpose. For that, he was grateful.

But he was also smart enough to know that at any point, that might need to change.

* * *

Back home in Rankin Flats, Garrett brushed the snow off the railing of his balcony with a sweatered arm and leaned out over it, lost in thought as he looked out over the city. The last embers of the sun would be sinking to the west, but he didn't pay any attention to them. All he could think about, all he could see, was those four hooded figures from his fever dreams. "She'll be the main course," he mumbled, not really sure why he was thinking it aloud.

Murphy slipped through the glass door quietly. "What's up, man?"

Garrett beckoned him towards the railing and Murphy slid in beside him. "We have to figure out who the Butcher is. Tonight or tomorrow. Without him and his guest of honor, the whole thing falls apart and we're back to square one."

Murphy blew out a breath. "Square one's not so bad. We still can play the cop card on them. See if they'll bust them." He glanced at his friend curiously. "You want them for yourself though, don't you?"

"I do," Garrett said honestly. "Since Richter Haas, Finson's been like a magnet pulling me towards him."

"The cancer will kill him, soon enough. And then he'll most assuredly get what's coming to him."

Garrett sighed and rubbed his hands together. "I know. That's maybe why I want to see this done before then. Of course he'll get his in the afterlife. But here, now, we can see a little bit of justice done for his lifetime of shit."

The door slid open and Brianna poked her head out. "You boys mind if I join you?"

Murphy turned his head at her and grinned a little. Garrett patted the rail to the other side of Murphy. "C'mon out." She handed him a steaming mug of coffee and he accepted it gratefully. "Not long now before we have to get to work on your plan."

Switching her own honey lemon tea to her other hand, she took his arm and leaned against his shoulder, looking out over the city with him. "There's a but to that, isn't there?" He nodded and explained what he'd told Murphy. "Hm. What would you do normally in this case?"

Garrett glanced at Murphy, who tapped through his chin. "Start from the beginning, I guess. Go back over everything we saw, everything we've heard." Garrett relayed that. "We don't have much time, though. And we might not get a chance to do it twice."

"We need to look at this with fresh eyes," Brianna mumbled. "Like we're seeing this for the first time."

Murphy lit up like a bulb. "She's right. She's absolutely right."

"Huh?" Garrett asked.

"We do need fresh eyes on this. Say someone trained to do a little detecting."

"Inviting Monica into the War Room's always been a strict no-no, Murph. I think that's a bad idea," Garrett warned. Brianna glanced at him questioningly, and he held up a finger. One second, he mouthed at her.

"Do you see much of a choice?" Murphy asked.

"No," Garrett said, sighing. "Nope, I do not."

* * *

Jade Gibbons wandered the streets, miserable, alone, and desperate for heaven or hell to take her. At least she wouldn't be alone anymore. She could feel something then. She couldn't even cry at her daughter's funeral. She laid on the grave afterward for a full day, watching the clouds above and feeling the thrum of traffic less than half a block away. Even after Ransom's generous check, her daughter's guardians hadn't even been able to afford a decent headstone. Instead, there was just a plaque barely jutting out of the earth with the name and the all-too-brief numbers of a child taken too early.

With the rains came the desire to move. She had no destination in mind, but worked in small concentric circles from the cemetery. She didn't want to go too far from her daughter's body. Why, she didn't know, save that it felt more like home to her than anywhere else in this godforsaken afterlife. She recognized little of this part of the city, but soon she was making large enough circles to encroach on some of the old territory she'd gone to when she had followed Garrett and his friends around. She'd liked them, despite the job. He was no saint—he took as much for himself as he did for the others around him. But he had heart and charisma. Murphy had been more standoffish, more cold towards her, but he was just looking out for his friend, after all. She couldn't blame him for that.

She wondered if Galbraith had hurt them. Wondered if it might not be too late to help them instead. That Padraig guy had seemed like an all right sort too. He and his friends lived somewhere nearby, she realized, and started walking towards the Holland Shelter for Hope with determination building in her heart. It might have been too late to save herself, but she could maybe start another chapter by helping someone else out. It would make for a nice change for once.

But her hopes were dashed when she arrived at the shelter and found it abandoned. Not a soul—she allowed herself a tiny little smile at that little joke—was left to point people in the right direction. Were they working with Garrett? she wondered. But there had been people left behind before. No. The place felt abandoned. She felt it in the fiber of where her bones used to be. No one had been there for days, living or dead.

This only fed her determination and her curiosity. Maybe something had happened. Something terrible. She started jogging towards the busy city streets, debating on where she should go. Garrett's condo seemed like as good a place to start as any. Be okay, people, she said silently to herself. Please be okay.

* * *

"Someday, you're going to explain all of this to me," Monica said testily. "And I mean all of it."

Garrett and Brianna sat in the War Room watching her flip through pages and pages of notes, pictures, transcribed conversations, and timelines. They remained largely silent, letting her work. "How did you get all these conversations?" she asked. "The FBI haven't been able to bug a Legion conversation above a recruiter in a decade."

"I can't tell you that," Garrett said. "I'm sorry."

Monica sighed and kept skimming. Every time she came across something regarding the Butcher or the special guest, she pinned it to the wall. Finally, she put aside the rest of the sheaf of papers. "Okay," she said, tapping her finger against the pages. "Let's start with the party. The guest must be going through one of their rites. We know they move their people up through the ranks in stages. Recruiters have candidates drug, rape, and brand recruits. That's stage one. After that, it gets a little more complicated. The second rank is given out when a Legion stands up for another member or makes their mark in some significant way. Usually murder or some kind of enterprise that brings in a ton of money. They used to give out tattoos for that back in the day, multi-headed animals, usually the person's choice."

Murphy said quietly, "Finson has a three-headed tiger across his ribs."

"Like a three-headed tiger," Garrett said, nodding at a picture of Finson on the wall.

"Exactly," Monica said. "After that, it gets even more fuzzy. If someone puts themselves in a public position that can help advance the Legion's cause, they're elevated again, but there hasn't been a bust of a rank that high in the last decade. They've changed up their tactics some. These are your high ranking cops, the public servants, bankers, that sort of thing. People of real worth. My guess is, that's your guest of honor. As to how they're initiated, your guess is as good as mine. But..." she hesitated. "And this is a big Slender Man of a ghost story, but the persistent rumor is that the few times they've managed to bust someone down from that high up, it's been because they went psycho and exhibited signs of a prion disease."

"A what now?" Garrett asked.

Brianna cocked her head. "Like mad cow?"

Monica grinned and gave her a nod. "Exactly right."

Brianna turned to Garrett and explained quickly. "I don't remember a lot of the specifics from the course I had to take in college, but basically, prions are these infectious agents that are introduced to the body. A protein, if I'm not mistaken, that's kind of gone bad."

"Like cancer?" he asked, feeling more than a little dumb.

"Mm. Not really. It's more like the proteins in your brain get changed on a fundamental level, except that the change can be transmitted to other animals. Or people."

This really wasn't helping to alleviate his feelings of stupidity. "How?"

"By eating meat tainted with the prions," she said. "Like how the world is concerned with eating tainted beef. Or like cannibalism."

It hit him hard. She'll make a fine tribute. A hundred pounds. She'll be the main course. He sucked in his breath. "Oh my God," he whispered. Brianna nodded grimly, and Monica just stared at them both, watching them figure it out. "The tribute. It's human meat. The disappearances around town. You said... you said what if it wasn't drugs."

Monica cut in. "It's just speculation. But it fits."

Murphy wished he could be sick. "We have to take these sons of bitches down," he said.

After they had a minute to process the what, they had to figure out the who. Garrett stood and paced the room. Monica returned to the notes. After a while, she put it aside and sighed. "This is all so... mechanical. There's no flavor here. It's all just reports and no inflection."

Brianna got up and looked through them. "Does that matter?" she asked.

Monica nodded. "There's a lack of humanity to all this. You want to get someone involved in a story, put them there in the room. Give them the sights and the sounds, sure, but give 'em scents, too, and the feel of things. Same goes for these transcriptions. I can't hear the voices in my head. It's all part of my process. Gotta relive the moments." She tapped Jamie Finson Sr.'s picture. "This guy. What's he sound like? Do you have the tapes?"

"No," Garrett said. "But it's a gravelly voice, rough and deep and sort of wheezy."

"OK. Good. Try to impersonate it. Give me a feel for it." She handed him a transcript of a conversation between Finson and the Butcher.

Garrett cleared his throat, and started reading as Finson. With Murphy's careful coaching, it took him a few minutes to get his voice to mimic Finson's. "That's not bad. Okay, the Butcher's voice is sort of reedy."

"Reedy?" Garrett asked, forgetting himself.

Monica shot an eyebrow up. "Sorry?"

"Reedy. High and sort of thin. That's how the Butcher sounded. Sorry," Garrett said. "Thinking out loud." That answer didn't seem to placate Monica, so instead he focused back on the pages. "Okay, thin and high." It took even longer for him to get it right this time. But finally,

Murphy gave a reluctant nod.

"It's missing something though. A cadence. Like… oh, you remember when Blake would get really angry and he'd have to focus on not stuttering? The strange carefulness to his voice. It's sort of like that."

"What's he doing?" Monica asked Brianna. "Is he listening to something?"

Brianna shushed her and watched Garrett work out the voice. Something was nibbling on her mind's hooks. Something they'd overlooked. Some forgotten voice from the past. Then Garrett tried again and it was gone. The pitch and timbre. Something about them…

"Not bad," Murphy said. "That's about as spot on as you've been. Try making it a little… I don't know what the word is. Um. A little more fancy, but a little less self-confident." He shrugged.

So Garrett read it again. And again. And as he spoke, Brianna closed her eyes. Flashed back through a litany of faces and names. Maybe the voice sounded like someone from the gym. Or from college. She'd heard a thousand voices like that in the past. A lack of confidence.

"She told me about the cancer," Garrett read aloud. Except he stumbled a little bit over cancer. Just a slip of the tongue, nothing more. But it came out as "cuh-cancer." Her eyes shot open and she gasped. Monica stared at her, wide-eyed as she jumped up and sat at the computer. Garrett raised an eyebrow. "Bri?"

"Try it again," she said. "But with a stutter."

"Huh?"

"On the harder letters. Stutter when you say it."

"There wasn't any stutter," Murphy said, confused. "What's she talking about?" Garrett echoed that.

She spun in her chair and starting navigating from page to page. "I know who it is. You do too," she said gleefully. "It was an act. And we bought right into it."

Behind her on the screen was a picture of Nate Nolan, his arm wrapped lazily around Jamie Finson, Jr.

Chapter 23

Brianna cruised down the street slowly, the headlights off. "Is it weird I'm kind of turned on right now?" she asked. "It's weird. I mean, we look like chomos creeping on a school right now, but I feel... intense."

"Maybe you have a ski mask fetish?"

"Ew. No." Then she pretended to reconsider. "Maybe if it was in blue. Oooh. We should get luchador masks for this."

"You're crazy. I love you for that."

She arched an eyebrow. "Just for that?"

"Well, that, and your butt."

"Damn straight," she said, and swatted his hip. "This is you."

Garrett popped the lock as she slowed even further. "Wish me luck," he said, and jumped out of the SUV when she eased to a stop. He closed the door gently so as to not make any noise and winced when an alarm started dinging inside the car to tell them the door wasn't all the way shut.

"Smooth," she whispered, grinning madly, and sped up slowly, turning the lights back on when she was half a block away.

Murphy met him outside the door. "Nobody inside," he said cheerfully. That night, he was sporting a checkered sport coat and matching slacks that looked as though they'd been pulled from the wardrobe of a car dealer in the 70's. "No idea where anything is at. Gonna go pop in on the neighbors, make sure no one's calling the cops. Be right back, man."

Garrett nodded and knelt next to the door, digging out his picks. When a car's headlights flashed down the street, he dove behind the cover of the porch, landing on his baton and driving the air right out of him. Everything was going great already, he thought. He knee-walked his way back to the door after the car passed, his penlight in his mouth, and he worked the locks open.

Murphy sauntered back out of the neighbor's walls as Garrett was just pushing open the door. "Holy shit, you're slow today. Get a move on, will you?" He walked on through to the other house, humming.

Garrett flipped him off and snuck into the house, swishing his light back and forth over the floor. He closed the door carefully behind him and glanced around. The house was much as he remembered it—meticulous, reeking of cleansers, and devoid of a speck of dust. Something electrical thrummed to life somewhere in the house. Heaters, maybe. He crept to the kitchen and started looking for proof they were right. There was no guarantee it was there, but he hoped they would at least find something. There was nothing in the freezer save for ice cream, frozen leftovers, vegetables, and very identifiable meats like chicken. He searched the fridge, but there was nothing suspicious there either. Then he rapidly checked the cupboards, the pantry, the garage, and the bedroom. There was simply no other place he could have stored the meats.

He was sure Brianna was right, but this wasn't the place. The meat wasn't the only reason they were there. There was his part in Brianna's plan to take care of. He found what he was looking for in the bedroom closet and replaced what he needed to. He searched the rest of the bedroom and the living room to make sure there were no more, but that was it. Done.

That electric humming stopped, but the hissing tick of the heaters continued. If the thrumming was the heaters, they should have died down. But if it wasn't the heat, what had kicked on and off then? He wandered back through the house. The computer was off. The fridge was running normally. This had been a deeper sound, almost enough to give the floor a little shake.

Murphy came in through the front door. "Hey, we're all clear. Find any of Butcher Pete's finest?" He cackled at the joke, one Garrett didn't understand. Garrett knelt with his ear pressed to the floor. "Bud? Whatcha doin'?"

"Sh," Garrett said. He knocked on the flooring loudly. "I can't be sure, but… mind taking a dive?"

"Don't like the dirt, Gar. You know that," Murphy said reproachfully.

"I think there's a basement," Garrett said. "Pretty sure of it."

Murphy sighed, rocked on his heels, and fell backwards through the floor. "Holy shit!" he shouted from down below. "You were right!"

"Are there lights down there? Can you see stairs?"

Murphy jumped up through the floor, keeping himself balanced on his hands half in and out of the basement. "No light. But judging from the way sound rolls around, I'm guessing there's a stairwell near the laundry room or the pantry."

Garrett stood up and opened the pantry doors again. It was too deep, he realized. Especially just for one wall of shelves. He felt at the wall, knocking on it. "Hollow." He traced the hidden door with his fingertips, feeling for a latch, a catch, something. At hip level was a hole just a little wider than his finger. Using it for leverage, he pulled on the door gently, and it swung open. All he'd need to do to close it again was push it shut.

He ran his penlight down the darkness. A stairwell. A delicate chain hung from a light bulb in front of his face. He ignored it and turned up the intensity of the flashlight to make his way down. He half expected the stairs to squeak or groan under his feet, but they had been expertly built recently and gave no sound of protest whatsoever.

At the base of the stairs, the room expanded out beyond the reach of his flashlight. He flashed it around to the walls, making doubly sure there were no windows down there. Preparing himself for what he might see, he took a deep breath and reached out to tug on the cords of one of the lights.

He needn't have worried. The room was sterile, clean, just as neat as the upstairs. No bodies were laid out on tables. Nothing unseemly swung from the meat hooks. It was remarkably clean. The large butcher's table in the center of the room was nicked and scarred all to hell, but it was completely devoid of body parts.

"This is cleaner than your place," Murphy said distastefully.

But lined up against one wall were three deep freezers. That was what had been powering on and off, he realized. He didn't want to look. Call the cops, his brain screamed at him. Call them now. Let them open it. But that would only take one piece of the Legion leadership off the board. He knew he had to open it himself and what he'd find inside.

Murphy stood side by side with him as he rested his hands on the lid of the freezer. As Garrett reached under the lip with gloved fingers, Murphy whispered, 'Aw, man…"

Garrett nodded and lifted the. A puff of cold air blasted him, obscuring his vision for just a moment. Inside were dozens of white wrapped packages, all clearly labeled with black marker. Garrett picked one of them up to read it. "F. 14-17 yrs., strip stk." He stood there for a long moment, his gorge rising. He gently put the package back in the freezer.

As he drew another one out, Murphy said quietly, "You don't have to—"

"M. Thirty to forty. Ground chuck," Garrett said out loud, his voice very hoarse. He drew another one. "F. Seventeen. Loin steak." Another. Another. Another.

Finally, he closed the lid gently and stumbled towards the next freezer. Checked it. Nodded numbly. The last one too. Nodded again. He turned off the light, made his way upstairs, and called Bri. She was parked on the next block and circled back around for him.

When he got in, she glanced at him searchingly. "Did you find the proof?"

He nodded mutely. A block away, he said quietly, "Pull over up here. Please."

She did, and he unbuckled his seat belt, practically falling out the door. He vomited noisily and repeatedly, tears rising unbidden as he replayed all the packages of meat in his mind. He pulled himself back in and wiped his mouth with the back of his hand. "One down," he said weakly.

* * *

Where Nate Nolan's house had been immaculate on the inside, Markham's place was a wreck of half empty beer cans and garbage strewn all over the place. The lone spot clear of detritus was an old brown recliner angled straight at an enormous TV. Since the place right across the street was in the middle of a raging party, parking nearby was a definite option. They were a bit too old to blend properly with the party-goers but either the kids didn't care or were too drunk to notice as they mock stumbled down the street, ducking into the cover of one of the cars across the way until no one was looking. Their mad dash to the back of Markham's house was too noisy by far, but he was passed out in his bedroom, one arm dangling off the bed. Padraig's people had observed his nightly ritual of half a bottle of whatever was cheap and plentiful, and Garrett wrote it down in their notes, but he hadn't actually thought it was going to be of any use. But here they were, sneaking through his house. They found what they needed in his bedroom in the last place they dared to look. Brianna stood on one side of the bed, ready with the Taser in case he moved. Garrett delicately lifted Markham's hand out of the way of the drawer and onto the bed. The man grunted and threatened to roll over, but then was still and snoring again. The nightstand held it. Garrett snuck it out of the bedroom and into the living room, where he slowly, quietly did what he needed to do and then replaced the item into the nightstand.

That was the last of their easy wins for the night.

* * *

They were very nearly caught at Jamie Finson Jr.'s apartment.

Brianna waited in the SUV, keeping tabs almost in the exact same spot as they'd parked during their first time together at the place, right across the street. She was air drumming along to the Heavy on her iPod when she saw the pair hand-in-hand right behind the Hyundai, walking hand in hand across the parking lot. She let out a bleat of fear and grasped not for the Taser, but for the holdout gun strapped to her ankle. That movement might have saved her life, as it hid her immensely recognizable face from Nate Nolan's view of her as they passed by.

Garrett was as quick as he could be, but he still didn't have enough time to find the right thing in the apartment. Sweat beaded on his forehead as he dug through absolutely everything and just as frantically putting it all back into place. His cell phone buzzed—SOS. two mins.

"Shit, shit, shit!" he growled. Murphy ran out to the hallway. Garrett hurriedly put everything back into the cupboard as fast he could, hoping like all hell he got the ordering right. He started for the door but Murphy popped his head in.

"No time," he hissed. "Hide!"

He thought through the house frantically. The couch was a futon. He could hide under there, but he was fucked if they sat down when they first came in. The shower? No guarantee they wouldn't see him behind the curtain. That left the bedroom. He sprinted for it and crawled under the bed just in time to hear someone rattle a key in the lock. As the door opened, his phone buzzed again and he shut it off without bothering to look at it. He held his breath, praying the sound hadn't been enough to draw their attention.

"-want to strangle that bitch. I can't believe she bit me." That was Finson, Jr., sounding as mad as a hornet. "The shit we have to go through for this meet, I swear." So she was involved. That much they hadn't been entirely certain on. It had seemed very likely, given her closeness with Nate Nolan, but still, confirmation was good.

"You'll live." Nate Nolan, sans stutter. Garrett heard the clatter of keys in a bowl next to the front door and the thump as someone unslung something out there and let it drop. "Ugh, you need to do dishes."

"What? Screw that."

"It smells like fruit gone bad."

Murphy rushed into the bedroom. "It's in her purse. By the door. She had it the whole time." Garrett nodded but there was nothing he could do about it. Not there, not then.

Something clanked, metal on metal. A pan on the stove, he realized. "Fine. I'll start the dishes, you get the burgers ready."

M. Thirty to forty. Ground chuck. He gagged, but Murphy said to him, "It's hamburger, not... you know." He had no idea if his friend was telling the truth or not, but he was grateful for it anyways. It helped settle his gorge.

He had to be patient. He needed to wait them out, find right moment to slip out unnoticed. Maybe he could get back there in the morning, or even later that night when they both went to bed and-

The building's fire alarm rang.

"Are you kidding me?" Finson Jr. growled. There was another click as they turned off the stove. "Let's just stay here. Probably Jenny burning incense again."

"Shit. I do smell smoke," Nolan said, sniffing the air.

"Shit, I do too. Well, hell." They shuffled towards the door, and Garrett waited with bated breath, daring not to breathe, not to hope. Then he heard the door opening and closing.

Murphy shouted, "Go, go now, the purse is there, then get to the rear stairwell."

Garrett rolled out under the bed and was to his feet in a flash. he sprinted for the door, stopping just long enough to replace what he needed to replace. "Stop," Murphy shouted outside in the hallway. "Give it five seconds, then get out. Ready? Go go go."

Garrett slipped out into the hallway and sprinted for the door leading to the rear stairwell. He could smell it now too, and on the stairs, greasy grayish-black smoke billowed out of the door to the second floor. He covered his mouth and took the steps two at a time. He hit the bottom landing, punched through the back door, and was gone into the night.

He circled way the hell around the building, sprinting to the other side of the street when he was sure he was out of sight. He came around the backside of the Hyundai. Brianna was already back inside and jumped when he knocked on the window. She unlocked the doors and he saw she had her pocket pistol on her lap. "Tell me we got it," she said excitedly.

He held it out for her and she breathed a big whoosh of air. "What'd you do in there?" he asked.

"Lit a fire in the second floor garbage can. Don't you check your texts?" She smiled innocently at him and he leaned across to kiss her. She pulled away just slightly. "Pukey breath. But you may kiss my hand ever so gently."

He did so, and with great relish.

* * *

Jamie Finson Sr. was their last stop for the night, but it had also been their first. With his cancer reaching its inevitable last stages, Finson was gobbling pills by the handful. His daily allotments were arranged ahead of time by a home health nurse. He hardly ever looked at what he was shoving down his throat. While Finson was out picking up a client, Garrett and Brianna snuck in to liberally mix a couple of extra sleeping pills into his medications for the night.

Garrett hadn't been entirely comfortable with the idea. They had no way of knowing if the pills wouldn't outright kill Finson Sr., but they could see no other choice. What they needed to get was always on Finson's person save for his showers or when he slept, and he didn't take long enough showers that they could gamble on getting in and out in time. So in they crept as Finson's wife sat in her recliner, mouth agape at the blaring TV. Garrett added the pills to Finson's nightly dosage and got the hell out.

Several hours later, they returned. Murphy did a pass through the house. Both Finsons were sound asleep, he said. Brianna kept a close eye on both the front door and the rest of the house as Garrett crept into the bedroom, past the snoring couple, and to the walk-in closet where Finson kept his day to day accoutrements. He grabbed what they needed and replaced it, grinding his teeth at the sound of the noise in the darkness. Jamie slept on unperturbed, but Mrs. Finson stirred. Murphy said loudly, "Gar, get Brianna out. The wife's moving."

Garrett turned off his flashlight and slipped out of the closet as silently and quickly as he could. Brianna glanced at him and he pointed at the door. Run, he mouthed. She shook her head firmly. He rolled his eyes.

"Are you here for him?" asked Finson's wife in the darkness. The question lacked any emotion save curiosity.

Garrett glanced at her. She was still lovely in a haunted, gaunt way, her skin still smooth and largely unwrinkled, save for the lines around her eyes and mouth. How beautiful she must have been back in the day, he thought. But her eyes were sorrowful and vacant, just as Padraig's people had described, and her hair hung in greasy clumps. This was a woman who had stopped caring.

"Are you here for him?" she asked again. Tears started rolling out of the corners of her eyes, fat, slow drops that fell untouched to the sheets she clutched up past her breasts.

"Not today," Garrett said softly.

"He killed our child," Mrs. Finson said, almost dreamily. "Our boy. His wife. It's okay if you are. The devil's coming for him sooner or later."

Was that what he was? Garrett wondered. This man's personal devil? In a way, he guessed he was. If all went to plan, Finson's life would be a smoldering crater by the time he was finished. "I promise he'll pay soon," Garrett said.

She nodded slowly at that. "I'm glad. Goodbye."

"Goodbye," Garrett said, blinking at the strange conversation.

In the living room, he cast one terrified glance back over his shoulder. Mrs. Finson sat on the edge of her bed, staring after him and rocking ever so slowly.

* * *

They stumbled through the door just hours before dawn. Garrett wanted nothing more than to get a shower and pass out in bed with Brianna, but the ghost standing in his living room brought him up short.

"Oh, not fucking again," Murphy growled. "Can't you leave us in peace?"

Jade Gibbons held up her hands in protest. "Wait."

"You've got nothing to say to me that I want to hear," Garrett snapped. "C'mon, Bri. I need to brush and—"

"My daughter. He paid for her medical care. I thought he would hurt her if I didn't work for him." Garrett relayed that and Brianna shook her head. Jade hurried on as fast as her clipped speech would let her. "I came to ask for your forgiveness. And to help you out. I want to make amends."

"How do we know that whatever we do, wherever we go, it won't just be some story you feed Galbraith?" Garrett asked.

"Because my daughter's dead," she said hollowly. "I spent the last day or so wondering if I shouldn't just give up. Sink into the earth and let whatever's there take me. It was my fault she's dead and I deserve worse."

290

"Nobody deserves what's down there," Murphy muttered.

Taken aback, Garrett said softly, "Crap. I'm sorry." He told Bri about her daughter, and Brianna offered her condolences too.

"I'm free of him. And I'm sorry. I want to help you. If I can." Her voice was genuine, her face earnest.

Murphy glanced at Garrett. "With her help, we can track the buyers and I can focus on Finson."

Rubbing at his grainy eyes, Garrett gave up. "Fine. Brief her, show her the building. Whatever you two do, don't go in there, okay? We'll all meet up there tomorrow night. Showtime's in two days... well, a day and a half now, I guess."

"Mr. Moranis," Jade called after him as he zombie-walked towards the bedroom, talking to Brianna. He turned back. "I'm sorry. For what it's worth."

"Yeah. Well. If you're serious about helping us—"

"I am."

"-then welcome to Team... uh... something clever."

Brianna yawned so hard the base of her chin hurt. "We'll come up with something awesome when we've got some sleep. Go team ghost."

Chapter 24

A door slammed down the hallway, making Brianna jump. Her gaze darted to the door, as though the owner of the echoing footsteps was going to burst through it at any moment. She shivered when she was sure they weren't headed for the little apartment. "Next time, we rent," she muttered.

Garrett glanced up from her 3DS then at Murphy. He nodded and grinned sheepishly. "We, uh, we didn't even think about that."

She rolled her eyes. "That's why you've got me here now, dope. I'm the brains, Murphy's the brawn, Jade's the ninja."

"What am I?" Garrett asked.

She thought about that for a minute. "You order Chinese really well?"

Garrett held up two fingers and sighed after Murphy finished speaking. "She does have a good point," he agreed. His stomach rumbled. "Ugh, speaking of Chinese, I wouldn't commit murder for some General Tso's, but maybe a felony of some sort."

"Mail fraud," Brianna said.

"Bingo." He dug out a bag of jerky and offered some to her. She took a few pieces, and he grabbed a handful for himself. He tilted his head to the side, listening to Murphy and nodded. "He's going to go see how Jade's holding up."

"Is she okay next to the garage?" Brianna asked, real concern in her voice. She didn't like what the woman had done to them, but that place was a pure little piece of hell and she didn't wish its like on anyone.

Garrett nodded. "There's this little invisible perimeter around the building. I could feel it. Murph and Jade can too. It's like a bubble, I guess, except all the bad juju is really inside the building."

She finished chewing and pointed the end of the remaining jerky at him. "You're not going back in there."

"If this goes well, we won't have to." He stood and gazed out the window. The snow was falling softly now, thick fat flakes that melted as they hit the street. Somewhere in the building, someone was watching a movie so loud it made the floors rumble. They could have shouted at each other in there and no one would have noticed. He glanced back at her, at the way she tried to hide her pensiveness with that half-lipped smile of hers, the one that never quite tugged up the scarred half of her face. He loved that smile. "Bri, if something goes wrong... remember the safe in my room, okay?"

She glanced up. "Nothing's going to happen."

"I can't guarantee—"

"Nothing. Is. Going. To. Happen." She said this as matter-of-factly as if she were discussing the verity of her jeans being blue. He nodded and turned back to the window. She let the smile fade away. Nothing was going to happen because she wasn't going to let it, she vowed.

He sat back down beside her and she rested her head on his shoulder. Together, they waited.

* * *

"Do you think they've seen us?" Ransom asked, grinning like a child whose hand has been caught in the cookie jar when he's already had a half dozen.

Padraig closed his eyes and forced himself to be calm. "No."

"How do you know?"

"Because Moranis loves his plans. If he thought something was out of place, he'd just wait for another day." He opened one eye and glared at the madman. "And we're assuredly something out of place."

For the dozenth time, Ransom checked the pump-action shotgun he'd taken from one of Garrett's storage units under Padraig's watchful eye. He wore a fisherman's vest over his button-down, the many pockets stuffed full of shells and road flares. His father's hunting knife sat on the old, musty mattress next to him. Unlike that idiot Moranis, he'd rented the apartment he sat in now. Dirt cheap, too. The landlord had practically begged him to take it.

Some queasy part of his mind wondered why he hadn't thrown away the knife. It was the same one that he'd used to slit the throat of that college woman and he knew better than to hang onto it. But that very careful, very safe part of him was waving bye-bye very quickly now. He'd seen the cops at his place, talked to them with eager fervor. Had he seen his former boss? Oh yes, he wanted to titter, yes, yes, he had in fact seen her that very morning. Instead, he shook his head and very politely, in not quite the exact words, to fuck right off, please and thank you. Ransom found he didn't much care if they bought his story or not.

The whole charade was getting exhausting. The drugs took the edge off, but the need for them disgusted him, so he'd quit them cold turkey days before. He was growing restless for an end of things, or at the very least, a change.

But he couldn't quite give up the life yet. There was still Garrett Moranis to consider, and that bitch girlfriend of his. He needed to show Garrett what he was capable of. Maybe he could pull him back from the brink. If only he could get him to see how well they'd work together without that nag holding him back from his real potential. Maybe it was time to deal with her after this was done. Her and the cop.

Soon, he promised himself. After they finished with the day's work.

* * *

"So they're robots that look like people and they want to destroy mankind?"

Brianna nodded excitedly. "Yeah. Except you never know who's a robot and who isn't. It's so good. You're gonna love Gaius Baltar. He… well, I don't want to spoil anything. But he's great." She cocked her head at the window. "Garrett. Look."

At first, he didn't see it. It looked like just another cloud of smoke in the sky, born from a chimney fire or someone burning garbage. But it wasn't smoke. It was moving with purpose. And "it" wasn't really an it, he realized, but they—hundreds of birds, maybe thousands. They settled on the rooftops and cars below.

"That can't be good," Brianna breathed, standing at the window next to him. Silently, he agreed.

He did a double take down to the street. "Bri. Game's on."

She could see nothing. He aimed her chin with his hand gently. "That's Murph right down there, on the corner. He's waving us on."

She started throwing all their things into their duffel bags. All they had out was the food and her game system, so they were good to go. The Kevlar vests were on the floor next to the duffel bags along with their weapons. They geared up and she patted herself down. He held her shoulders, leaned in, and kissed her forehead. She hugged him, her heart beating so hard she was sure he could feel it even through the bulletproof armor. "It's such a dumb plan," she whispered.

"It's a great plan. But if this is too much, we can stay right here until they're gone." He held her out at arm's length. "Monica and her people are ready to take them down. And if anything has changed, anything at all, we're waiting here. We see one unfamiliar gun in that place, we don't move an inch."

She shook her head. "No, I'm okay. I really, really want to punch out one of those evil fucking bastards."

"You're sure as hell going to get your chance," he said grimly. "All right, stay away from the windows from here on out. Jade will run interference from the garage to here when the buyers come. The minute she says go, we're out the door. Have your key in your hand ready to go. Seconds will count for everything."

She nodded. They'd rehearsed this a dozen times before, but she knew he was saying it more for his benefit than hers. "And if the buyers come back, then we get out. We got this."

"I love you,"

"I love you too."

A half a minute later, Jade jumped up through the floor. "Mr. Moranis," she gasped. "We've got a problem."

"What?" he asked. "What is it?"

"They've got someone down there with them. She's hurt bad. Very bad. They said something about making her a live tribute. Murphy said her name was Dee."

"Shit," Garrett said, then the severity of it hit him even harder. "Shit shit shit." He turned to Brianna. "We've got to hit them now. Before the buyers come. Something happened with their tech person, Dee. They're going to trade her off to the buyers along with the meat."

"Can't Monica... oh my God, that would give them a live hostage," she said, despair tinging her voice. "How much time?"

"We go now."

Chapter 25

Minutes after they arrived, Markham dragged her out of the back of the SUV, his arm up under her armpit, not bothering to try and keep her steady. When she threatened to fall, he just yanked her along behind him and she screamed as her bad leg scraped across the ground. Finson Sr. got out too, trying hard not to lean on the vehicle for support. The old man looked terrible, Markham thought, as though a hangover were compounding his already fragile state. He let Dee fall to the ground as a vehicle bumped up over the top of the incline and started down.

The CR-V rolled to a stop a few feet away from the Lincoln. Jamie Finson Jr. hopped out and practically ran to her grandfather, flashing a new ring on her finger as she bubbled with excitement. "He proposed and I said yes!"

Jamie Finson Sr.'s face broke in a sunny smile. His granddaughter hadn't made the same mistakes he'd had. Thank whatever deity it was that looked over the Legion for that one, he thought. Married, only her or the Butcher would be allowed to run half the city. The other would have to serve by his or her side. Still a highly regarded position, but a glass ceiling nonetheless. He clasped his granddaughter to his chest, kissing her cheek. Nate Nolan stepped over, proud and puffed up as a dog after a shit, and Finson ignored his hand and brought him in for a hug too. After all, he'd be family soon enough.

"We don't have much time to celebrate," Finson Sr. said after Markham had shook their hands too. "Did you bring the amount I asked for?"

"And then some," the Butcher said, grinning. "We've got the usual tribute, and a hundred ten besides. Been a good month for catching them off the street."

Finson slapped his shoulder. "Good man. And you, my love," he said, turning his attention back to his granddaughter. "No doubt you've figured it out by now, but today's meet serves a dual purpose. Are you ready for the formal induction of consumption?"

Inwardly, Markham snorted at that. The younger Finson had been partaking of long pork as long as he had, if not longer. But he allowed a tight-lipped smile as Jamie Jr. grabbed her grandfather again in a bear hug, never noticing the old man's grimace of pain. Nate Nolan slapped him on the shoulder. "Help me set everything up, won't you?"

Apart from the other three, Markham said quietly, "Nice pull. You keep her out of power and get yourself a little action on the side."

The Butcher pulled out a cardboard box loaded with paper plates and plastic silverware and handed it off to him. He dipped his head in towards Markham and said, "Why so bitter? More room for the both of us to take over someday, don't you think?"

Markham snorted, but inwardly he wondered if that was possible. Surely they wouldn't let him any further, would they? Still, the acid bitterness in his stomach of the Butcher's good fortune did abate somewhat. They set everything up in the back end of the Lincoln. Whatever he'd cooked up and kept warm in the chafing dish smelled amazing. "Since we're tailgating of sorts," the Butcher said, rubbing his hands together, "I figured we'd have an old favorite. Pulled people sandwiches." He chortled at that, and removed the lid. Markham took a deep whiff of the tangy, almost fruity sauce and the sweet meats underneath.

"You people are fucking sick," Dee muttered.

"Just for that," Finson Sr. said, "you'll get to try the first bite." His grin showed off his slightly crooked teeth, stained with age. "How about that, Dee? You get to go through another initiation rite. Funny. It took me years to get where you're at now."

The Butcher loaded up a plate with a forkful of the tender meat. He brought it over and ran it under her nose. "Smell that?" he asked. "Slow roasted for nearly a day. The meat was perfectly fatty and juicy, see. Just perfect for a long, slow cook. And I made the sauce myself. Used some of the drippings. You'll love it."

She bit at the plate and yanked it from his hands, sending the meat spilling all over the ground. "I'll die before I eat that," she spat.

The Butcher knelt down. "Hey boss," he said. "You aren't particular if she eats off a plate, are you?"

Jamie Finson Sr. snickered. "If she can't be civilized, let her eat like a fucking pig."

Finson Jr. stepped behind her and grabbed her nose. "When she opens her mouth, baby, shove it in there."

The Butcher grabbed up a bite of the meat and slathered it across

Dee's lips. She visibly gagged. "This one was a straight B student. Not terribly great at anything else besides sucking off old fat guys on a corner." She squirmed away from hi, holding her breath in desperately. "See," he whispered to her, "I like to get to know where my food comes from, don't you?"

He grasped her cheeks, forcing her mouth open for just a moment, and there it was, salty, smoky, and sickeningly sweet. He forced her lips shut with his fingers and Dee screamed wordlessly against the meat in her mouth.

Car engines. Finson Sr. checked his watch. "Huh. They're early for a change. Sorry, love, we're going to have to do this after—"

The pair of SUVs came up and over the ramps too fast to react. The Bronco even got a little air, bouncing the driver hard when the tires hit the ground. It rammed into the CR-V, not terribly fast, but hitting it just hard enough that it came up off the ground for a second or two before slamming back down. The Explorer hit the Lincoln a moment later with a hollow, plastic kathump. "For fuck's sakes, it's them!" Finson Sr. yelled. On her knees still, Dee spat out the meat and vomited out a thin stream of brownish drool.

One of the driver's got out of the car slowly, rolling his head and shoulders. "Shit, that hurt," he complained. "Stupid airbag didn't go off."

"Did they even have them in that year?" the female asked as she slammed her door shut. Their faces were obscured by ski masks and their hands gloved. In hoodies and jeans, they would be almost unrecognizable in a city where that was the winter norm.

"Are you two for real? Do you even have guns?" Markham asked. "Seriously, boss, you okay with us just shooting them?"

Finson Sr. shrugged. "Light 'em up like it's fucking Christmas."

Markham and both Finsons drew their pistols as the two advanced on them. The Butcher had no gun and watched the proceedings cautiously. The woman yawned. "Oh no, stop, don't shoot," she muttered disinterestedly.

"Guess we didn't really think this through, did we, baby?" the man asked.

"Guess not. Oh!" She slapped her forehead. "Code names. We should have code names."

"Would you please shoot these idiots?" Nolan screamed.

They fired. And fired. And fired.

The two just stood there, looking down at their chests. The woman glanced up, grinning slyly. "Ninja Sloth. That's my code name."

"I like it," the man said as he flicked his baton out to its full length. "I think I'll be Doctor Boo. You know, because of the ghosts." He advanced on Markham. The ex-cop came at him in a fury, his gun clattering uselessly to the ground. The blanks inside weren't exactly going to help him much.

"You haven't seen Lord of the Rings, but you've seen Doctor Who?" she asked as Finson Sr. stormed at her, his gun reversed in his hand like a club. She dodged his swing easily and punched him in the gut, nearly doubling him over in pain.

The masked man jumped back twice at Markham's measured swings and caught him across the back with the baton. "Well, of course I have. I love British TV."

She hammered Finson Sr. with a left on the bridge of the nose and Finson Jr. ran at her screaming, the Butcher close at her heels. "You are full of surprises, Doctor Boo."

He shoved Markham face first into the Lincoln, grabbed him by the hair, and again bashed him against the window. It didn't break, but it sent Markham reeling away. The masked man took him down with two massive blows to the back of the head with the baton. "Let's wrap this up quick. The buyers will be here fast."

Folded over and gasping for air, Finson Sr. wondered what the hell they were talking about. There were no buyers. The tribute was given freely. The less they knew would serve the Legion though. He hoped the others knew enough to keep their mouths shut. He pulled himself upright, tasting copper from the stream coming from his nose.

"Little help here?" The masked woman dealt with his granddaughter's wild, untrained swings handily. She brought up a Taser into the base of Jamie Junior's neck and soon her face was bouncing off the pavement. The light in her eyes winked out just like that. But the Butcher didn't go down so easily. He caught her with a running tackle, hitting her hard and low and knocking her to the ground. He loomed up over her, leering down, his eyes bulging. But he left her arms free, and that was all she needed. She clapped his ears, which only served to stun him, but it gave her a split second to jam her knuckles into his eyes, sending him falling backwards on his ass. She Tasered him, once, twice, a third time just for good measure and he was still. "Oops. Never mind. Handled it myself." The masked man clapped.

"Who the hell are you people?" Finson Sr. screamed. He pointed behind the masked man. "And who are you?"

The masked man shifted the baton to his other hand. "You're really going to try the who's that routine with me? Maybe you want to try telling me my shoelaces are untied."

Surging forward, Dee shouted, "No, he's got a gun—"

"Howdy, friend," Ransom Galbraith said cheerfully behind him. He put his boot on Markham's back and leveled the shotgun at the base of his skull. The gun licked thunder, and the back of his head was gone in a splatter of blood and gore.

* * *

"No," Brianna gasped. Murphy sprinted down the ramp at Garrett, wordlessly roaring. Jade watched it all from the top of her ramp, her hand raised to her lips in horror.

Garrett stepped in front of Brianna, arms spread wide. "Ransom, don't—"

Ransom pumped the shotgun, raised it, and it boomed again. This shot struck the Butcher's hip. Finson Jr. crawled towards him, making a keening little sound in the back of her throat. Behind Garrett, Brianna knelt and drew the little holdout pistol. At any range further than five or six feet, she might as well as throw bullets at him, but it was all they had. She yanked Garrett with her behind the cover of the CR-V, but Ransom was ignoring them.

Murphy screamed, "What the everloving hell is going on?"

"I swear, this wasn't me!" Jade shouted.

"Not my granddaughter," Finson Sr. begged. "Please, not her."

"Okay," Ransom said agreeably, and shot the young woman point blank in the stomach, blowing out her guts all across the concrete floor. "Hey, Moranis, you ever see anything like this? I think I can see what she had—"

Brianna fired at him twice. Both bullets missed, but he shrieked like he'd been hit anyways. "Hey, what the hell are you doing, you psycho bitch? I'm helping you here!"

"We never wanted your help!" Garrett shouted. He jerked his head to the side of the SUV. "Go around," he mouthed to Brianna. She nodded and started circling away from Galbraith.

Ransom was still standing over the wreckage of Finson Jr. "Ugh, this is disgusting. I dissected a pig once in high school, but this? This is nothing like that."

Finson Sr. fell to his knees, wheezing. "You monster."

"You. Eat. People," Ransom said, advancing on him. "And I'm the monster? Actually. Wait. Now I'm curious." He sauntered over to the CR-V and pulled the lid off the chafing dish. "That doesn't smell half bad." He dug out a fork from the box. There was a moment when it looked like some clarity entered his eyes, Garrett thought, and he might have gagged just a little bit, but then Galbraith speared a glob of meat and brought it up to his nose to sniff it. He examined it and then popped it into his mouth, chewing thoughtfully. "Huh. Different. Kind of gamier than you'd expect." Brianna fired at him. The shot grazed his ribs and he accidentally fired the shotgun into the ground. "Oh, hell!" he snapped

Garrett hurtled at him from the other side before he could jack another shell into the chamber. As Galbraith started to aim, he hit him hard across the knee with the baton. To his dismay, it didn't topple the big man. Instead Ransom spun with him, bringing the gun up and leveling it at Garrett's face. Time did not slow and it certainly did not stop, but for Garrett, the world outside of that gun ceased to exist.

Murphy roared and raced for them both. Brianna sucked in her breath and shouted his name. Garrett held up his hand behind him, a reverse stop motion, and she held perfectly still, afraid to even breathe. Jade watched it all in blank, abject horror, her mouth agape.

"Can you feel it, Moranis?" Ransom asked, his face shining bright. "How beautiful this place is?"

"Ransom," he said very carefully. He'd read a few books where the authors described the barrel of a gun as an all-consuming black hole, but the business end of the shotgun looked nothing more to him than what it was—a thumb's width of a hole that would end him when it fired. We'll be together soon, Murph, he thought silently. I'm sorry, Bri. "This place is poison. Some part of you can feel that, right?"

Ransom shook his head, his shark-like mouth of teeth bared. "You can feel them pressing at the walls," he whispered gleefully. "They're here, all the things we see in the mirrors." Turning his attention away from Garrett for just a second, he nodded at the bodies of Jamie Junior and Markham. "Look, Garrett, they're rising already."

So they were. Markham looked down at his nearly headless body and shook his head. "Well, that's pretty fucked," he said, examining the backs of his hands.

"What the hell?" Finson Jr. said as she rose to her knees, hands buried in her former innards. "What's going on?"

They looked each other over, but before they could speak again, black smoke rose up from under Markham's feet. He glanced down. Fingers of steam curled up around his legs, and his eyes bulged. His colors flitted around him desperately trying to stay out of reach of the tendrils, but they had no chance as he was pulled down in the earth, screaming until smoke poured from his lips and he was consumed entirely by it.

Something whipped around Finson Jr.'s stomach like a big tongue. She scrabbled at it with fingers that couldn't do anything but sink right through it. It flexed and her frame elongated like a balloon being squeezed by a fist. She opened her mouth and sprayed out a gasp of orange, that same sickly color Garrett had exhaled after his own visit inside the building. Something gurgled deep within the ground and then she was yanked into the earth too.

Off to the side, Finson Sr. staggered towards the door to the stairwell. Garrett watched him move, grimacing. Galbraith spun and fired the shotgun again, nearly deafening Garrett. "I'm going to show you, Garrett," he said as he pumped another shell into the chamber. He stormed towards the stairwell, turning only to pump one more shell into the moaning Butcher, imploding his ribcage with a mushroom-sized hole. The Butcher gargled on blood and was still.

Garrett started after him, but Brianna darted out from behind cover and grabbed him. "Are you crazy?" she asked. "That place nearly killed you the first time."

"We can't let them get away," he said.

She shook her head firmly. "Murphy and Jade can watch the streets. Right?" She glanced all around.

Murphy stood right beside Garrett. "She's right. The minute they're free, we chase them down. Jade," he said to the other ghost. "You had nothing do with him?"

"I swear," she said, that look of pure wide-eyed horror never leaving her face.

Murphy nodded. "Then take this door. I'll take the front of the building. The minute we see either one of them, we meet at the rendezvous with Garrett." She nodded and leaned against the wall.

Dee coughed hard behind them, a wet, whooping sound. Brianna raced to her side. "Garrett, help me. We need to get her out of here before the buyers come."

He gave the stairwell entrance one last look, then turned and jogged to his girlfriend's side.

"Okay, help me lift her. Dee, this is going to be painful—"

"Shannon," the woman muttered, her eyes rolling back in pain. "Shannon Oliver. FBI."

They got her to a standing position and helped her balance on her one good leg. They were able to help her hop up into the Bronco, which had suffered the least in the pair of collisions and held all their gear. Brianna sat in the back with her, tending to her wounds as best she could. "She needs a hospital, now," she said, ripping off her ski mask.

Garrett sucked in a breath at that, but nodded and pulled off his own. Their game was up, he knew. "We need to get rid of the car," he said. "Cops are gonna be looking for stolen vehicles. We'll get her to the Hyundai and take it from there."

Dee—Shannon, Garrett corrected himself—mumbled, "Finson. Can't let that cocksucker run."

"It's okay," Garrett said. "We've got people who'll keep an eye on him."

Shannon nodded and seemed to relax. Garrett pulled onto the street. Somewhere in the distance, he could hear sirens. "What the hell happened back there?" he muttered.

"Do you think it was Jade that told him?"

"No. Not one bit. The look on her face when he showed up, it wasn't her. That leaves Murphy. Or..." He hammered the steering wheel with his gloved fist. "Damn it. Padraig."

"You don't think..."

"Unless Ransom has me bugged, it's the only thing that makes sense."

"You knew him?" Shannon asked quietly. Her voice was faint, but she looked like she was hanging in there.

"In for a penny," Garrett said to himself. Over his shoulder, he said, "Yeah. He's been stalking us. I think he got ahold of our information on the meet somehow."

"Who are you?"

Garrett glanced back in the mirror. Brianna nodded gently. It was over. Best to come clean with it. "Whatever I tell you, she's left out of it. Everything I've done, I'm guilty for. Not her."

"Don't be such a martyr," Brianna growled. "We're in this together, remember that."

"You're the ones that hit Haas's shop," Dee guessed. "And you were at the airport, the meth lab, and the barbershop again, right?" She seemed to seize upon something. "Wait. You're the one that's been hitting criminals all over town, haven't you?" She coughed up a laugh. "We thought you were a they, as in a new gang. How many of you are there?"

"The two of us work the cases. We have two others who do some, ah, inside work for us," Garrett said vaguely.

"What'll happen to us?" Brianna asked nervously.

Shannon leaned her head against the window and closed her eyes, sighing. "I don't know."

"Whatever happens," Garrett said, "you need to keep your people out of the building."

"Leave some evidence behind?" she asked, almost angrily.

"You're not going to believe me, but that place isn't right. It'll poison your people's minds. It's haunted, in a way."

Shannon glared at him. "That's crazy."

Garrett flexed his hands around the steering wheel, frustrated. "I can't show you without showing you. That's maybe the dumbest sentence I've ever said, but your people... they'll suffer if they go in there. Somehow, some way."

They switched cars in the parking lot of a busy big-box store that did brisk business even at night. Someone had left a note on Garrett's window asking him to please move his car or have it towed. He balled it up, laughing at the absurdity of it.

As they neared the hospital, Shannon asked for a pen and paper. Brianna dug around in the back and came up with a book of crosswords with a pen clipped to the cover. She handed it over, and Shannon wrote down a phone number. "Here's what's going to happen. You're going to drop me off halfway down the block, then you're going to go live your lives. If the cops show up at your door, you're going to call this number and ask for me or Annalise Fox. Do not say a fucking word to them until we get back to you. Do I make myself clear?" By the end of that speech, her voice went raspy. Something hurt deep inside her chest. Broken ribs, she thought, not for the first time. Not the worst they'd done to her, not by a long shot, but inconvenient. "For what it's worth... thank you both."

They had nothing to say to that. When they spotted an empty bus stop, she nodded. "This'll do. Pull over here. Call ahead, tell the hospital you saw me sitting here, looked like I could use help bad." Garrett nodded and stopped the car. Brianna came around to the other side and Shannon grasped her shoulder. "We'll be talking again soon," she said. Whether that was a threat or something else, she had no idea. Neither of them did.

Chapter 26

Finson stumbled up the stairs, past the first landing and on to the second floor. His guts writhed like a thousand snakes, but the discomfort was almost lost on his careening mind. His granddaughter was dead. Markham was dead. Given the gunfire out there, it wasn't but a matter of time before the Butcher was finished too. He tested the door, found it unlocked, and stumbled through. Rows and rows of old office furniture greeted him and he limped towards the desks, stopping only long enough to fire off one text message—run. He had to hope the Hamber reps would get it in time before they walked into an army of cops or those mad nutjobs. He couldn't stop to worry about it. He rounded a corner and a shadow flickered across the floor. He stumbled over his own feet and crashed hard to the ground. Nothing was there. Behind him in the darkness of the stairwell, the door to the garage banged open and closed. He crawled into an abandoned, half-rotted cubicle, closing his eyes and trying to calm his breathing. Long minutes passed.

When he opened his eyes again, his granddaughter sat right beside him, holding the intestines spilling out of a gaping hole in her stomach. "Hey, grampa, want a bite?" she asked cheerfully, and reached for him with bloodied, clawed talons for fingers.

*　*　*

Ransom stopped at the first landing, breathing hard and slinging the shotgun across his shoulder. Where was the old bastard? he thought to himself. He tried to listen, but all he could hear was the thudding of his own heart. And somewhere, the sound of running water.

A scream. A shriek, really. He sprinted up the stairs. That sound of running water was louder now. Like a stream, he thought to himself. He knew that gurgle, didn't he? No, that was impossible. It was just water. Probably a broken pipe.

He pushed open the door to where he'd heard the shriek. All he could spy were rows and rows of cubicles and office furniture, all torn up, shredded, and falling apart. He turned sideways, strafing the cubicles with his gun unslung and ready to fire. "I'm looking for the geriatric ward. Can anybody help me out?"

A shadow lurched out from under one of the desks. He fired instinctively, the blast shredding nothing but the partition. Nothing was there. He dug out more shells and reloaded, humming tunelessly.

That skritch-skritch-skritching again. He held his ear to the wall. "I can feel you in there," he said softly. "Just tell me how I can let you out, and I will." There was no response, so he shrugged and kept moving.

The flowing water sounded even closer. He expected to step onto a wet, rotting patch of ground at any moment, or see a soaked wall, or something. But no, there was nothing, not even in the bathrooms, where the fixtures had long been yanked out. "I know you're here somewhere," he said uncertainly, not sure if he was talking to Finson Sr. or the source of the water. And was there laughter? There was. A woman's. Delicate, slightly drunk, the sort of laugh a woman might give a lover tickling at her thighs. He knew that laugh. It had been months since he heard it.

Upstairs? He thought so. He shouldered the gun again and bounded up there. Had she lived somehow? Or was this her ghost, taunting him come to haunt him at last? He'd never seen her go, save in dreams. Maybe she'd finally decided to take revenge on him. Let her try, he decided cheerfully. This was his place, his moment.

He stormed through the third floor door and his feet crunched on leaves. He blinked against the sudden sunshine, the crisp bite of a late fall day, the smell of wood smoke hanging lazily in the air. This was... this was his home in Checkerboard. Before it had burned. Before he'd found out about her infidelity.

The stream crossed right in front of him. A little wooden pedestrian bridge stretched across it. He stepped on it tentatively, knowing the way it would just ever so slightly bend under his weight. A meadowlark sang somewhere off to his right. The only thing wrong with the vision was the solar-powered lamp hanging from the eaves of the house. It shone with a dim, orange light instead of its usual faint white glow.

A steady thumping brought his head whipping up towards the house. He knew that sound too. The headboard in the place thumped the wall when they made love there. Not that it happened often. Galbraith hadn't had sex with his wife for two months before her death. Shocker that she'd been such a cold, frigid bitch to him and so willing to open her legs to anyone else with a dick, he sneered. Were they fucking right then? He knew it to be true. Knew what he'd see even as he crept to the window. Her legs up over his shoulders, her butt raised up off the bed, him plowing into her with abandon, her eyes on his, saying a name that wasn't Ransom. And the man, wasn't he familiar to him too? Yes, he thought, seeing the sparse peppering of gray throughout his hair. It was Garrett fucking his wife, wasn't it? That confused him for a moment. It hadn't been Garrett, had it? It had been a coworker of hers. Or a friend. Or… but that was him, unmistakably pounding his wife like a beast. Galbraith's hands twisted into knots.

He hadn't been there when the house burned. No sir. But the scene played out exactly as he'd imagined it a hundred times. She caught him looking through the window and leered at him, taunting him with her wantonness with another man. But there were no cigarettes beside the bed this time.

Instead at his feet was an old oil can and a book of matches that said Carson's Guzzlin' Garage, Hamber, MT. He'd never heard of the city before, but the smiling face on the matchbook looked familiar to him. It was the grin, he realized. It matched his own so well. "Well, hello, new friend," Ransom said as he leaned over and picked up the matches. Then he glanced up. His wife was at the window, bare breasts pressed against the glass as she bared her teeth at him, her eyes bright and wild with rage. He jumped back a foot, dropping the shotgun. Somewhere, somehow, he thought he heard it clatter away, as though it had hit an office floor rather than the soft leaves and grass around the house. But that couldn't be right, could it? No, he was imagining things. He was there in Checkerboard. This was how things were supposed to be.

Her tongue forked out at him like a snake's, hands pounding at the glass. He grabbed the gas can and doused the walls with it, grinning at her the whole while. She watched him approvingly, her rage subsiding. "Is that what you want?" he said to her through the glass. "Did you want to burn

He lit a match, and she watched it with glee. He tossed it towards the gas soaked walls, and the whole building went up, great orange licks of flame that consumed the whole side of the house, just as the pictures and the cops had described to him later.

Shift.

He glanced around, confused. This was the building after it had burned so hot that the fireman had to sit back and watch it go, unable to do anything at all. The front door's frame stood at a crazy angle and jagged corners of the walls rose up largely intact, but other than that , the house was nothing more than rubble and ash. Out of one pile of debris, a skeletal hand emerged, covered in black soot. "No," he muttered to himself, tasting the ash in the air. "No, this is wrong, I didn't kill her, I didn't want her to die."

You did, something inside him said out loud. Maybe it was after the fact, but you wanted her to burn for what she did to you. And worse. You wanted her in pain. You wanted her in hell.

The hand crooked a finger at him, begging him to come closer.

"No," he said, shaking his head. "Not her. I never wanted that for her."

Admit it, that voice teased. You've known exactly what you've been doing ever since the fire. You've been in complete control. It's not some disease. Not a mental illness. You've been doing to them what you wished you could do to her.

He shoved his way through the door frame, trying desperately to get to her.

You can lie to yourself all you want to after this, the voice said. Because it won't matter anymore. You've been careless. You're in the end game now. You want it all to turn to ash. You want them to kill you. The wraith man. The scarred woman. The cops. You won't go to prison. You'll die bloody.

He took her bony hand in his. The tendons and cartilage burned his fingers where he touched. It was an impossibility, but all of this was.

Not so, the voice said smugly. Maybe this is then. Maybe you caused the fire. Maybe it never happened until you came here and went back. And does it matter anyways?

"Wash it off," Ransom muttered. "Gotta wash it all off."

The stream, then, the voice reasoned. You can wash it all away in the cool water.

Ransom stumbled through the carnage. He fell to his knees feet from the water's edge and crawled to it. The water was clear enough that he could see the moss, lichen, and stones at the bottom. He dipped his hands in, crying as the soot wouldn't wash away. The sun reflected off the water's surface, orange and grinning. And another face, too. An old man. Where his eyes should have been, two slimy strings of fiber hung out across the tops of his cheeks. Bloody, dried tears streaked his face and his raised hands were stained with gore.

Ransom fell sideways, back in the office, back in reality. The shotgun was out of reach. The old man swiped at the spot where he'd been, cocking his head as though listening to something not quite there. "It's an illusion," Ransom gasped. "All of it. Whatever you're seeing, it's not real."

The old man spun and dove at him, teeth gnashing at the air. Ransom scrabbled at his pockets. The knife. He almost lost hold, his fingers still shaky and burned (how was that possible? his mind screamed). But as the old man hovered over him on his knees, reaching for his own eyes, he plunged the knife up and into the man's sternum, scraping along a rib and burying it deep. Finson Sr. fell on his side and screamed wordless fury. But that fury turned to a garbled moan when Ransom grasped the blade with his hands and twisted, carving into the man's flesh like he was cutting up a Thanksgiving turkey.

Ransom pulled himself to his feet and stumbled away. He took the stairs two at a time, trying to get out the garage door before the shadows flitting at the corners of the stairwell could take shape again and suck him back in. With every breath, he gasped out a thick orange gas. He burst out the bottom door, hand on his chest. He could hear the wail of sirens in the distance. He had to get out of there, fast.

Jade Gibbons stood twenty feet from him, her mouth open, staring at something he couldn't see. The building, he realized, had her in its grip. He stumbled towards her, feeling one last bit of pity stabbing through his heart for the poor woman. "Ms. Gibbons," he croaked. "It's not real. None of it is real."

She turned towards him, her eyes yellow and unseeing. He shook his head and ran. He had no more time to waste.

* * *

Murphy sprinted down the ramp. "Jade," he called. "Have you seen him?"

The cops buzzed around them, though there was a certain lethargy to their actions. Distracted and annoyed, they made slow, fumbling progress. Upon later review, it would be found that they made a staggering number of forensic errors and rookie mistakes. Almost all of them would get written up, but anyone at the scene knew with a vague unease that their inability to do their job wasn't their fault.

She stood in their midst, arms wrapped around herself, trembling. Her eyes were that same shade of yellow as Garrett's had been. He knew in his gut that Ransom and Finson were gone, that they'd missed their opportunity to track them down. Later, he would find out that Finson Sr.'s body had been found in the building, but in that instant, he felt the weight of all their inability to act on his shoulders.

Gently, he tried to get her attention. "Jade."

"Murphy?" she asked, unseeing.

"It's me. Can you see me? We need to get you out of here."

"She was here, Murphy. She wanted me to sink into the earth. She was down there in the dark. That we could be together. I wanted to. But I've felt the things under there and I was scared. I couldn't... I was a coward."

"No," he said softly. "That wasn't her."

"It was," she wailed.

"Jade. Were you with her when she died?"

"Y-yes."

"What happened to her? Think. Try to fight past the fog."

"She... she... had colors."

"Did the one you see by the door have the ribbons?"

Jade shook her head. "No."

"Follow me. You'll think clearer in the daylight. The sunshine will feel good. Trust me." he coaxed her forward, up the ramp slowly, leading her like they were playing a game of Marco Polo. It was slow going, and took minutes of talking her away from that place, but once they were in the sunshine, he was right. Orange mist seeped from her pores and evaporated into the ground.

She raised her hands to her face, marveling at their realness—or at least their ghostly realness, anyways. "Why didn't you just leave me there?" she asked. "I've screwed you over so many times."

He smiled thinly. She had, but so had they all, he guessed. "Team Casper, right?"

A small smile broke through her veil of misery. "What now, then? Meet back up with Garrett?"

He glanced at the sky, gauging the position of the sun. "Soon. First, though, we're going to go see an old backstabbing friend."

* * *

Padraig sat atop the Holland Shelter, feet dangling over the side of the building. The snow let up to a fine misting of rain. When the temperatures dropped that night, it would make for seriously dangerous driving, but he didn't care. At that moment, the misty air above the near untouched snowy ground brought a sense of calm to his soul.

Two ghosts approached from a distance. His eyes were as sharp as those of a hawk's, unfettered by human degradation. In life, by the time he was forty, he'd been almost blind, so terrible had the optics of his time been. But ghostliness healed all wounds, save those of the corrupt mind.

He watched them idly. He'd expected Garrett and Brianna too but wasn't surprised by their absence. Probably picked up by the cops by now, he supposed. There was nothing for it. If the idiot had listened to him, he wouldn't have had to go through with that stupid plan of his. And Padraig wouldn't have been forced to listen in from the next apartment, half expecting Murphy to pop through at any moment and realize he was there. The woman had made them both sloppy. Now they were reaping the consequences.

Now he was stuck dealing with Murphy, his least favorite of the three. He was glad he'd sent his people away, so that he wouldn't have to reason with them about his actions. They were greedy, sometimes unreliable, and always assholes, but at heart, most of them wanted to be decent people. His agreement with Ransom Galbraith would have seemed like a deal with the devil to them. Maybe they weren't far off. "Hello, Murphy," he shouted down.

"Padraig," the man said.

Padraig gestured to the landscape around them. "Beautiful and appropriate for the day, don't you think?"

"Are you even going to try to deny what you did?" Murphy asked. He was furious. Good, Padraig thought.

"Did Ransom hurt Garrett or his woman?" Padraig asked curiously. Those had been his conditions, much as Ransom had wanted to kill the woman.

"No. But it was a close thing."

"And did he deal with the Legion threat?"

Murphy sighed heavily. "The local chapter? More or less. We don't know who the meat buyers were. We've still got half the Legion management in town to deal with. Jamie Finson Sr. got away—"

"Shit," Padraig spat.

The woman—Jade—broke in. "Ransom Galbraith is still out there. Do you know where he is?"

Padraig was silent.

"He will try to come after them," she said with calm certainty. There was a curious faintness to her, as though she were ill. That was impossible. "You can stop this."

Padraig looked away. "I'm leaving," he finally said. "Traveling again, for the first time in a long while."

"The world's smallest violin and all that," Murphy said, rubbing a finger over two others like a bow. "Where will you go?"

"Back to Scotland, for starters. Then… I don't know. Somewhere peaceful. Where the corruption won't stain my soul even more."

"Running won't help," Jade said firmly.

Padraig jumped off the side of the building. "What do you know?" he asked as he landed on his feet. "You're a child compared to me. A baby. I've been around for over two centuries. Who are you to judge me?"

She was silent for a while. "I'll make this place mine," she said finally. "I'll take over for you. And we'll be better than you ever were."

Padraig snorted and started walking. "Good luck with that, dear. Haven't you heard by now?" He turned and held his arms out to the sides, a gesture of equanimity. "We're assholes. Every last one of us."

Chapter 27

The cops did not come for them.

Whether it was by Shannon Oliver's hand or not, they never knew. They spent that afternoon huddled together, unable to eat, sleep, make love, nothing. They just simply held each other, refreshing the local news every few minutes, waiting to hear their names be mentioned or find out word on any survivors.

When it was finally released that both Jamie Finson Jr. and Sr. had been killed, they breathed a little easier. Police were on the lookout for Ransom Galbraith, who had been seen near the Howell building and whose knife killed Finson Sr. He was believed to be the shooter at large, but his motivations were unclear.

Then came the double whammy. It was revealed by police that they were also looking into Ransom Galbraith as the possible murderer of a college student, a CNA from a local hospital, and several other potentially related cases. Then came the other half—his former employer, Barb Kent, was found in the garage of a rental he'd been living in under an assumed name, paying cash to the owner who came forward with the information once he saw Galbraith's face on TV. Though still alive, she was listed in critical condition.

Galbraith's whereabouts were still unknown.

* * *

They slept fitfully.

He kept dreaming of that table bathed in the orange light, of Brianna being pulled apart by the revenants of that place. And when he wasn't dreaming of losing Brianna, he kept running nightmare scenarios through his mind. Of Galbraith training that shotgun on her instead of him. Of him pulling that trigger and splattering her innards all over the black of that Lincoln. Of her face disappearing in a spray like Markham's.

Her dreams weren't all that dissimilar. She kept seeing that shotgun coming up at Garrett, again and again and again. Of the red pool spreading from the younger Jamie Finson's body. She saw Galbraith above her in the darkness, his hands coming for her throat. She woke up gasping.

There was nothing in the darkness but them. She rolled over, grabbed her phone, and texted her dad. It was going on one in the morning, but she needed to hear from him. He responded back in minutes. She breathed a sigh of relief, rolled back over, and watched Garrett breathe for a few minutes before she decided she was being creepy and closed her eyes. Sleep came to her a little easier that time.

* * *

Monica brought by breakfast in the morning, though none of them felt much like eating. She updated them on the search for Galbraith, but it didn't sound hopeful. In true Rankin Flats fashion, some people were heralding him as a hero for taking down so many criminals, inventing conspiracy theories or what-ifs about his other victims, including the worst, that they were criminals themselves or deserved it for other reasons. The world was fucking sick, Monica said tonelessly, and they agreed with her wholeheartedly.

Murphy and Jade alternated reports. Jade watched his old haunts, since she was most familiar with Galbraith, but confessed she hadn't taken a great deal of interest in his life. Murphy spent most his time watching over Shannon Oliver, trying to find out what their situation was, but he spent a few hours at the police station when she slipped into a deep, pill-induced sleep. Their names were never brought up. The Bronco was found, but apart from Shannon's blood, there wasn't anything to link them to it.

Early in the afternoon, Brianna and Garrett traveled to the Hammerdown. It was furiously busy in there, with two trainers running classes. Brianna helped her dad keep an eye on things while Garrett worked out. Soon Brianna joined him on the treadmill, and for a moment, they breathed easy again.

Night fell, and still, Garrett felt like they were waiting for the other shoe to drop. Murphy and Jade sat with them, catching up on each other's stories as well as trying to figure out the next move. The plan was that they had no plan. They were in a holding pattern of waiting and watching. It was frustrating, but it was all they could do. In the meantime, Brianna said, she wanted to return to work the next day. It would give her something to do.

His cell phone rang as he and Brianna started talking dinner, something along the lines of ramen and a sandwich. That something, anything, sounded good to eat amazed Garrett. He picked up his cell phone, his stomach rumbling. Danny, no doubt checking on Brianna. "Hey, Danny, what's up?"

"Hello, Garrett." That voice was definitely not Danny's. It was currently the most wanted man in Rankin Flats. Maybe the whole United States.

"Hello, Ransom." Brianna dropped a pan in the kitchen and rushed out, her hand over her mouth. Garrett leaned forward as Murphy and Jade both swept in and through him to listen in. "Ransom, where's Danny? What did you do with him?"

"Sitting right here. Want to say hello, Danny?" There was a muffled garble, then Ransom came back on. "He says hi. Closed early though. I think he's feeling a bit under the weather."

Garrett stood up and nodded towards the door. Brianna grabbed her shoes, not even bothering to put them on. He got his gun from the nightstand and tucked it into his waistband under a jacket. Murphy and Jade both jumped out through the walls and the building to the parking lot. Brianna and Garrett ran for the stairs while he talked. "This is between us, you son of a bitch."

"You know, it is. It really, really is." Ransom's laugh seemed quieter, more subdued this time. "The demons left me. Or I left them. Did you go into that place, Garrett?"

"Yes," Garrett said hollowly.

"I can tell by the sound of your voice that you saw something too. Tell me, what was it?"

They hit the second floor. "Guilt. Loss."

"It showed you her death, didn't it? That's what would disturb you the most."

"Yes." At the door, punching through it. "What about you?"

There was a pause. "Clarity. An end to the madness."

"And yet you're still playing games with me."

"This isn't a game, Garrett. Well. Maybe an endgame, I think. For one of us, anyways. Either you kill me, or I destroy everything in your life, piece by piece." Ransom held the phone closer to Danny, who screamed against a gag of some sort. "I've got a knife to his cheek right now. Not my dad's good knife. I left that in Finson Sr. He went down hard, by the way. Whatever he saw, it was bad enough he ripped out his own eyes."

Garrett flinched at that thought as he took the corner too fast, the rear of the Hyundai swinging out. "What were you trying to do there?"

"Prove a point, I think. I wanted us to work together. I wanted you to recognize me as your equal, your superior. I don't know. Thinking back on everything before that building hurts so much." He paused. "I'm going to hang up now. Get here soon."

Down through the residential district, hitting the Interstate, pounding the pedal to the floor. Skyscrapers loomed in the darkness like modern lighthouses. The wind screamed against the side of the SUV, threatening to send it careening. Past cars that seemed to be standing still. He barely slowed down off the exit. Murphy had to remind him the cops would be out in full force before he eased off the gas, but even then, he went a full fifteen miles over the speed limit as he raced down the back roads.

His phone rang again. He tossed it to Brianna as he focused on driving. "Put me on with my dad," she snarled. "He'd better be alive, you asshole, or—"

"You really, really need to curb that mouth of yours. I realize with the filth you put in it every night, you must think it's okay, but really, it's so unladylike. Tell Moranis I'll be seeing him later. I'm getting bored." He hung up again.

"Shit!" she screamed. "I think he left the gym."

Garrett rubbed his jaw. "Jade, he wants to make this about me. Apart from Brianna, who in my life did he know the most about?"

She thought about that. "We never talked about your friends Rose and Ed. He didn't have much interest in your accounts. I'd say Monica Ames."

He nodded. "Can you get there ahead of him?"

"I can try." Without another word, she jumped out of the car and into an oncoming vehicle. In the rear view, he could see her leapfrogging into faster moving cars.

"Where do you want me?" Murphy asked.

"Here." He glanced up into the rear view mirror and saw Murphy staring right back.

"And by here, you mean with her, don't you? Don't say anything if that's what you mean."

Garrett was dead silent.

The gym's lights were almost all dimmed. He could see a few on inside as he came to a fast stop. A shaggy, caramel colored mutt of a dog barked at them from across the street. It sniffed the air as though looking for something and barked again. Garrett paid it no mind. He was looking at something else. Someone else.

Brianna ran to the door, fumbling at her keys. "Brianna," Garrett said. "Don't—"

She jammed the key home and twisted, yanking open the door. Garrett grabbed her and said quietly, "Don't look. Please, Bri, just don't."

"I have to," she whispered and pulled away from him.

The only lights on illuminated the ring and the body lying in the middle of it. She sucked in her breath and ran, jumping up the steps and slipping in through the ropes. Garrett followed her a little more slowly.

He lay with his eyes open, staring up at the ceiling. His gag was still tied around his mouth and blood clotted his goatee from a cut on his cheek. His leg was bent awkwardly underneath him. Galbraith had shot his knee Three neat little bullet holes peppered his chest too. "Daddy, no," Brianna cried as she knelt over him, tears dropping onto his face. She lifted his hand to her lips and said it again, crying even harder.

Garrett climbed into the ring too and knelt beside her. "Bri," he said very gently. "He's still here." She glanced up at him, eyes huge, tears streaming down her face. He took her arm and guided her to her feet. "I'm going to guide your body and your head so you're looking right at him, okay?" He turned her gently towards the corner of the ring and tipped her chin just slightly up. "He's right there." He smiled apologetically over her shoulder. "I wish we had more time to explain."

"Dad?" she asked, and reached her hands out.

"He's resting his hands on yours. He's young now, like that picture of him in Germany. He's standing straight, and he's so alive. Younger than we are right now. He still has that scruffy goatee though."

She laughed at that, a little helplessly, and snuffled, "I'm sorry, Dad, I'm so sorry."

"Me too, Danny. I brought you—" he listened for a moment and sighed. "He says for me to shut up and for you to listen. He was so glad he had this time with you. That the last few weeks have been the best of his life. He says nothing is your fault, that everything, no matter how little or big, is forgiven." She trembled under his hands as he listened some more. "He says the moment you chased him down at your mom's house, to tell him you wanted to come back, that's what he'll hold on to.

He wants you to…" Garrett cleared his throat, growing hoarse. "He wants you to have something, he says. It's in a VHS case in his apartment. He says you'll know the right one."

"Planes, Trains, and Automobiles." She smiled through the tears. "It was our favorite."

Garrett listened again. "He wants you to know he's sorry he ever hurt you. With the divorce, with everything. He wishes he could have been a better father."

"Dad, you w-were the best," she sobbed. "Don't think that."

"He wants you to…" Garrett blushed furiously. "Crap, Danny, I can't say that."

"Say what?" she asked.

"He, uh, wants us to have kids. Apparently you told him about the eighteen children? Well, he wants us to have twice as many as that. And he wants us to be happy." He leaned in close and kissed her cheek. "He wants me to fight for you every day. And he wants you to kick my ass every day. Just for his amusement."

She laughed.

"Bri," Garrett said quietly, "he's starting to go now. He's got a minute, maybe less."

"Dad!" she cried, "Daddy, I love you so much."

"He loves you, he will always be up there looking out for you, he's tweaking your nose and he's telling you how proud of you he is." He lifted her chin with his fingers, his hands as gentle as he could will them. He took her hands in his and slowly brought them down to her sides, kissing her cheek and tasting her tears. He whispered to her, "He's gone. Bri, I'm so sorry."

She turned and grabbed him in a fierce hug, crying into his chest with loud, gasping sobs. He stroked her hair and said nothing, letting her cry. After a minute, she pushed him away and wiped at her eyes. "Did he tell you where Galbraith is going?"

He nodded. "Monica's." He jerked his head towards the door. "He talked to Murphy outside before he… well…"

She nodded and kissed him hard. She rasped, "I'm staying here with my dad. I can't leave him alone. Find Ransom."

"I will."

* * *

319

In the SUV, he called Monica frantically. When she picked up, he started talking immediately. "Monica. Get out. He's coming for you."

"Galbraith?"

"Yes. Where are you?"

"My living room. Well, now I'm headed to the bedroom. Getting my gun. And ammo. Lots of fucking ammo." She paused. "Garrett, what's happening? What is it this time?"

"He killed Danny Reeve."

There was a pause and she blew out a breath. "Fuck. How do you know he's headed my way? Never mind, you won't tell me anyways. I'm putting you on speakerphone and I'm going to the kitchen. He can't see me if I'm in there. And he won't have a shot at me but I'll sure as shit hear him coming."

"Good." He paused. "This feels weird."

"How so?"

He tapped the steering wheel. "I don't know. He disappeared for a whole, what two days, and now he slips up and tells us right where he's going?"

"Huh." She thought about it for a minute. "Who else would he go after?"

"My accountant, maybe. Doubtful though. He and his wife are about my only friends."

"And security's too tight at the hospital to go back after that Barb Kent."

"My family's across the country. Doesn't really make sense for him to go for them. It's like he's manipulating me." It hit him like a splash of cold water. "Shit. Shit shit shit." He spun a U-turn, hoping he wasn't too late. "Stay geared up. Maybe I'm wrong."

But in his gut, he knew he wasn't.

* * *

She hummed and cried as she sat beside her father's cooling body, stroking his hair and waiting for the moment for the horror to die down in her mind so she could call the cops and make a cohesive statement. She didn't know what she was going to say. What she could do. She and Garrett had never planned for this.

That dog was outside again, barking spuriously. She wished she could bring it in out of the cold. It looked like a sweetheart. Surely it had to be someone's pet. She hadn't seen a wild dog around the city in ages. It scratched at the windows and barked again, its focus on something in the room. She hoped its owners came for it soon. Snow was accumulating on its brown coat quickly. Brown dog, her mind murmured gently.

What was it Garrett had said? That he wasn't sure if old dogs could sense ghosts? Maybe that was what had attracted the dog to the door. Her father's ghost. She smiled at that. Brown dog. Or maybe Murphy was there, she thought. It would be like Garrett to tell him to wait there with her, even if they couldn't do anything. Brown dog. Funny. Why did that seem important?

A Schnauzer mix, maybe. It was taller than most she'd ever seen, though. Almost Labrador sized. But it had that funny little tuft of fur at its chin. Brown dog. It kind of reminded her of her dad, really. The mutt barked louder, scratched harder.

What was it barking so much for? It was almost as if something in there was making noise. Trying to attract its attention. "Is that you, Murphy?" Are you calling for that dog? Why? To get her attention?

OWN DO.

The graffiti flashed in front of her eyes and she gasped.

BROWN DOG.

She shoved herself to her feet and bounded through the ropes, jumping down to the mats below. She could hear the squelching now, coming from the men's locker room on the mat they used in the showers. She had precious few seconds, she knew. She sprinted for the office, leaping up and over a workout bench, passed the desk, and was in the office.

He padded out of the locker room, no longer grinning.

Brianna scrambled through the desk and grabbed the gun. She loaded it very carefully and slowly, trying not to drop the bullets. Ransom rounded the corner. His tallow cheeks had lost the redness of mirth. Black bags hung from his eyes and vomit stained the front of his shirt. He took in her gun, her steady hands, and the look of icy cold determination in her eyes. "Do it, you bitch," he muttered. He started to raise his own gun, his hand trembling terribly.

She fired.

* * *

Garrett slammed on the brakes as Galbraith stumbled out of the door, holding his stomach and wincing in pain. He fell to his knees and crawled towards a car in the parking lot, one Garrett didn't recognize from Padraig's reports. He ignored the man and raced inside. "Brianna?" he shouted. "Are you-?"

She stormed out of the office, her gun still in her hand, shaking like a leaf. "Is he dead? Tell me that son of a bitch is dead."

"Not yet," Garrett said grimly. "Soon."

"It was Murphy," she said crazily. "He saved me. Him and that dog."

They walked out and stood over him together, her hand in his, the gun still hanging loosely by her side. Ransom stared up at them, mouth working. A little dribble of blood ran from his mouth down the side of his cheek. Snowflakes landed on his face. It was strange, but to Garrett, they seemed more like ash.

There was no moment of recognition. No last words. He convulsed, gagged on his own blood, and died.

His ghost rose a minute later. This was a younger, thinner version of Galbraith. He examined himself cursorily, then glanced up at Garrett. "Moranis," he said, grinning. "Looks like maybe I get to spend the afterlife here. When you and your bitch are going at it, I'll be right there, leering at her terrible little tits. We'll have so much fun together, you and me, because I understand us now. We're killers. Monsters. We're going to make history. We'll—"

A black spike shot up from the earth, impaling itself through Galbraith's throat. He gurgled on it silently, his eyes wide and horrified. He fought it, tried to pull himself away, but it pulled him down slowly, sucking him into the earth. His hands flailed, trying to reach out to Garrett or Murphy or anyone out there. But before the end, his horrified look slipped away and he caught Garrett's gaze. Then he grinned, one final time, his lips peeled back wider than they'd ever been, and in his mouth black maggot-like things gnawed at his teeth, his gums, his tongue. See you soon, that smile seemed to promise. See you real soon.

Then he was gone. The brown dog sniffed at his corpse, raised a leg gamely, and pissed on his knee.

* * *

When the cop handed him back his ID and he put it back in his wallet, the glint of white cards in there surprised him. He didn't remember putting the business cards in the wallet. He pulled them out and flipped through them. They had been the Butcher's, he realized. Something else tingled in the back of his brain. Something forgotten. Some unimportant little piece of the puzzle. He flipped through them after the cops finished questioning him. Dr. Schmidt. Dr. Bond. Dr. A. Brennerman.

A professor, picked up for protesting. Monica had told him that. He hadn't thought anything more about it. Had thought A. Brennerman was going to get away.

He slapped the card against his palm, thinking very, very hard.

* * *

Annalise Fox cut through the throng of cops and sent them skittering away. She had Brianna in tow. Garrett stood up to meet her. "What's going on here? Who are you? Why is she-?"

She pulled them both away from prying ears and showed them her ID. Garrett's heart sank and Brianna took his arm. She thought this was it. She thought they'd soon be separated, him to a black box site somewhere, being dissected on a table, her to prison. She pressed against his shoulder, tears threatening to take over again.

"We're going to talk in hypotheticals here," the older woman said brusquely, brushing her long gray hair back out of her face. "Hypothetically, let's say a vigilante type was working the streets in Rankin Flats. Hypothetically, maybe the government is very worried that this individual will cause more collateral damage than he'll do good. Now, in that very hypothetical situation, the government would probably be inclined to stop that man. But..." Her eyes gleamed and she smirked. "Let's say in another for-instance that said vigilante did the government a big service, several times over. Let's also say that the government isn't necessarily in the habit of stopping anything less than terrorist level attacks, because that's what the hot button political issues are these days. Now maybe the government is willing to say, as a thank you, that this vigilante is theoretically off the hook for now, assuming he doesn't cause more trouble than he's worth. Let's finally say that the government would still like to keep an open line with said vigilante, with the understanding that if they say jump, he asks how high." Before he could speak, she added, "But the holder of that leash will be very, very discriminate."

"I'd say, in that situation, that so long as that individual—"

"That remarkably handsome, charming individual," Brianna added, letting hope make her giddy.

He kissed her cheek. "-that individual would be obliged to say thank you. So long as said individual's loved ones were never once threatened by that government." His gaze was very, very serious. "Because that's the only way this would ever work. And believe me, my—I mean, this hypothetical person's—resources and natural talents are not something the government would ever want to screw with."

Annalise's smile grew hard and cold. "Then I think we have an understanding." She reached her hand out. Garrett and Brianna shook it in turn. "We'll be in touch," she said quietly, and then they were free to go.

* * *

He had one more piece of business that night. He hated to leave Brianna in her night of the most need, but one last loose end remained and he couldn't afford to waste time. He dropped her off with Ed and Rose. Ed's gaze spoke volumes about how shitty he thought Garrett was being by not being with her, but he couldn't help it.

Monica called him on a burner phone a few minutes later. She gave him an address. That was the end of their conversation.

* * *

She saw him coming. Or the birds did, anyways, just as they had seen him at the meet, taking down their people with such ease. She could have fought. Could have called a whole army. But he'd figure out a way through them, wouldn't he? And she was so tired. She didn't want to spend her life running. Jamie waited for her on the other side. She knew it. Had seen him in the mirrors.

So when he came, she glided out her front door in her favorite dress. He eyed her up and down and said only, "You're going to want a coat."

He bound her hands and feet and they drove. She'd been to those mountains before, many, many times, but not the very specific area he drove to. It must have been gorgeous in the day, she thought to herself. In the night, it was deliciously oppressing being so close to the mountains and forests.

He spoke to someone she didn't see along the way, but that didn't surprise her. He had so much information on their organization that he couldn't have been a normal man. Insane, maybe. Probably. But he was a do-gooder, a man of principle and he'd twisted his insanity into a knife he could use to keep himself sleeping at night. Someday, she thought, he would pay for all his sins, but it would not be that moment. She would not fight.

They turned off onto a snow-packed dirt road and he had to resort

324

to four-wheel drive to navigate the drifts of snow. Even then, it still took them a goodish amount of time to reach the cabin. He pulled her out of the SUV, still not speaking to her. She was forced to sit in a corner while he added fuel to a snowmobile's tank. It would not start at first, and for a moment, he contemplated snowshoes. But then he tried it again after letting it sit for a while, and it buzzed right to life. He forced her to ride behind him, saddle style, tying a short rope from her bonds to his waist so that if she should fall off or try to flee, he'd feel it.

Together, they rode through the hills and into the forest. He was careful and slow and took all the time in the world to reach what she thought was just a stand of trees. Her birds sat among their branches, watching them silently. She could have called them down to her and didn't. Her legs were numb by this point. Utterly, completely numb. She had no doubt she was long beyond frostbite and well into hypothermia. She could feel warmth spreading from her belly, radiating outwards like a pleasant little furnace. He didn't bother trying to make her walk. He just lifted her up over his shoulders like a fireman and punched through the snow slowly. It was exhausting to fight both the drifts and carry her weight, and he had to stop frequently. His headlamp illuminated little but trees until they reached the base of a great boulder and a pair of felled trees. Then she saw it, the black gaping maw of a cavern cut into the ground.

"Do you have any last words?" he asked her.

"Yes," she said as he eased her off his shoulders and sat her in the snow. "Next time you look in a mirror, it'll be me you're seeing. Or maybe Jamie. Or his granddaughter. Because you're one of us," she said softly. She really was getting nice and warm. "Nothing but another monster."

Her words had stunned him, but he was so very tired. He wanted to go home to Brianna. No. She was his home. Brennerman would die and that would be the end of it. "Maybe," he said hollowly. So very, very tired. With a hand on each shoulder, he shoved her in, and she fell and fell until she cracked her neck upon the cold, hard ground deep below the earth. And even with her life ended, she fell further still.

* * *

They stumbled into the condo well after dawn and he collapsed before he could even make the couch. His exposed skin was blotchy and beet red. Frostbite. Brianna got him undressed and into a warm shower, careful not to make it too hot. He could barely muster the energy to move from the shower to the bed, but slowly she got him there and under the blankets. Before he could drift off, he muttered, "It's over."

She had the horrible, dead certain feeling it wasn't. Not even close.

* * *

They were mostly silent with each other for the better part of a week. Garrett couldn't look her in the eyes, and she couldn't stop the nightmares. She ate next to nothing, he only a little more. They tried to make awkward, slow love one night, but their hearts weren't in it and they soon fumbled apart, him apologizing and her trying not to scream.

Danny's funeral came and went. Her mother flew up for it, and they wept together and reminisced. The gym fell to his ex-wife—he hadn't taken the time to sign it over to Brianna—but she told Bri it and everything else of his was hers, save for a few photos and mementos she took with her home. Brianna couldn't comprehend what she was going to do with the place or his things. All she wanted at that moment was a hint of normalcy.

One night she rolled on top of Garrett, kissing him fiercely, her eyes blazing with tears and her heart hammering hard. She took him in her without speaking, rolling her hips and leaning down to kiss his cheeks, his shoulders his mouth. Her hips bucked harder and harder and she soon shook to an orgasm, powerful and fast. He lay with her afterwards, fearing what was to come and knowing it was inevitable.

In the morning, she woke ahead of him and stole out to the living room. She grabbed a piece of paper. The note was brief. She folded and kissed it before setting it down on the coffee table. Then she grabbed up her car keys and left.

Garrett rolled out of bed moments later. He'd heard her wake up before him, felt her slip out of bed, knew she was gone. He walked out to the living room and there was the note, the goodbye he'd known was coming. Murphy came out of the now-empty War Room, blinking at his friend as Garrett collapsed onto the couch, rolling up into a ball and hating himself more than he'd ever done before, even more than when he'd hurt his mother so damn badly. He just laid there for hours. Murphy sat beside him, wishing there were words. But there weren't.

Then a key clicked in the lock and the door swung open. Brianna stood there, holding four or five plastic bags of groceries and a VHS tape. She glanced at him on the couch. "What are you doing? You haven't even showered yet?" she asked.

"What are you doing?" he echoed in response, sitting back up.

"I went to go get groceries and find that damn VHS tape Dad talked about. Like the note says." She paused. "Wait. Did you think I... you didn't even read it?"

He was on his feet in a flash. Within a heartbeat, he was yanking the bags from her hands and dropping them on the floor. He lifted her up, her legs wrapping around his back instinctively, and carried her to the couch. "Leave," he shouted at Murphy gleefully.

"With pleasure, brother."

Brianna giggled as he kissed her neck. "Garrett, there's ice cream and I should put the meat in the fridge and... oh, screw it."

And then he was taking her, laughing deliriously, and she was laughing too, and for a while at least, things were okay.

* * *

Murphy sat down on the coffee table, rubbing through his knuckles. "Shannon's hurt bad, but she's recovering. They're flying her out when she can travel. Her handler or her boss or whatever she is flew out this afternoon. Gotta say this for Shannon. She refused much more than a mild painkiller."

"And this Barb Kent?" Garrett asked.

"Worse off. I don't know what he did to her face, but... it's bad. She had little puncture wounds on her lips. I... this is sick, but I think he sewed her mouth shut. Literally."

"Shit."

"Yeah."

Garrett sat back and rubbed at the stubble on his face. He still hadn't shaved and they were hosting dinner with Ed and Rose soon. Brianna came back out from the kitchen, fresh bottles of beer in hand. "Do I want to know?" she asked weakly.

"Murphy says they're hurt, but they'll live." It wasn't a lie, not really. "More than that, no."

Murphy glanced at the VHS box on the table. "So what's in there?"

"She won't say," Garrett said, a little smile playing at his lips.

"And you didn't peek?"

"Nope. More fun this way."

She grinned, knowing what they were talking about, knowing when and where she'd pull the old family ring out of there. Maybe it wasn't traditional, but tradition be damned. She unscrewed the cap off a beer, and toasted the air where she thought Murphy was sitting. "I don't know what would have happened without you getting that dog's attention, Murph. Sometimes I think you're the real MVP here, Casper. Cheers."

Garrett watched her expectantly as she drained half her bottle of beer and belched. It would have indeed rattled the silverware if they had any out. "What?" she asked him.

"Well, this time, you left him hanging for a high five."

She gave them both that little half smirk. "Oh hell. One of these days we'll get it right."

ACKNOWLEDGEMENTS

First and foremost, I need to thank Robin Zehntner. Without your support, this book simply wouldn't exist. For all the times I woke you up in the middle of the night and wouldn't shut up about it, thank you. Robin is also responsible for the terrific cover. Get to writing, Robin. The world is made lovelier by your voice.

To Suzie O'Connell, thanks for helping me figure this big mess of words out. If this is at all readable on your device or in your hands, it is due to her hard work and experience. Suzie is a terrific novelist and you should probably be reading her work instead of mine. And thanks to Ella Medler for helping prepare the paperback version of this book.

Big thanks to my brother Ryan, who also had to endure non-stop complaints from me about my progress or lack thereof. You're the best brother in the world. And to my absurdly cool and supportive parents Matt and Kay, thank you for always being there. You are the antithesis of the bad parenting in this novel and I hope you know how much you are loved.

To the Retreat—thanks for the years of tips, experience, and the laughs. You folks are the best.

And to you, each and every one of you, thank you for reading. Garrett, Brianna, and Murphy will be back to bust some more skulls in Shifting Furies.

I do not condone vigilantism nor do I encourage anyone to take the law into their own hands. This has been a work of fiction. Don't let a wicked few discourage you from thanking a police officer or a serviceman for doing their job. When we sleep well at night, it's because of them. So thank you to all those who serve others selflessly and make this world a safer, calmer place.

* * * * *

i

About the Author

Cameron Lowe lives with his snoring, grunting, fussy, immensely spoiled pug Yoda in White Sulphur Springs, Montana. He has been voted the world's most eligible bachelor at least twelve years in a row in his own mind and is an absolutely phenomenal lover. Just ask... um... well... someone. In his spare time, he reads, writes, games, and spends way too much time bullshitting on GiantBomb.com. He encourages everyone to have at least one squirt-gun fight per day and has no idea what the hell he is supposed to write in these things. Good talk.

Also by Cameron Lowe

Short Fiction
Sir Jensen and the Snowy, Cozy Cottage of Doom (Flights of Fantasy)

Novels
The Ghost At His Back
Shifting Furies
For All the Sins of Man (coming November, 2016)

Made in the USA
Lexington, KY
06 June 2017